BACKWOODS JUSTICE

Ruiz charged again, and Cooper Willoughby grabbed his arm, spun him around and brought a hard knee up into his belly. The *mestizo* was injured but he was tough. Even as he fell to his knees his hands closed on the knife he had dropped. With a final surge of rage he came off the ground, the knife flashing straight toward Cooper's mid-section.

There was a roar of thunder. Ruiz stopped in mid-strike, his eyes widening, then swayed and fell.

Through a red mist Cooper saw little Felipe Ramos over by the wagon, a shotgun in his hands, a double cloud of white smoke spreading around him.

BEST OF THE WEST
from Zebra Books

THOMPSON'S MOUNTAIN (2042, $3.95)
by G. Clifton Wisler

Jeff Thompson was a boy of fifteen when his pa refused to sell out his mountain to the Union Pacific and got gunned down in return, along with the boy's mother. Jeff fled to Colorado, but he knew he'd even the score with the railroad man who had his parents killed . . . and either death or glory was at the end of the vengeance trail he'd blaze!

BROTHER WOLF (1728, $2.95)
by Dan Parkinson

Only two men could help Lattimer run down the sheriff's killers—a stranger named Stillwell and an Apache who was as deadly with a Colt as he was with a knife. One of them would see justice done—from the muzzle of a six-gun.

BLOOD ARROW (1549, $2.50)
by Dan Parkinson

Randall Kerry returned to his camp to find his companion slaughtered and scalped. With a war cry as wild as the savages,' the young scout raced forward with his pistol held high to meet them in battle.

THUNDERLAND (1991, $3.50)
by Dan Parkinson

Men were suddenly dying all around Jonathan, and he needed to know why—before he became the next bloody victim of the ancient sword that would shape the future of the Texas frontier.

Available wherever paperbacks are sold, or order direct from the Publisher. Send cover price plus 50¢ per copy for mailing and handling to Zebra Books, Dept. 2456, 475 Park Avenue South, New York, N.Y. 10016. Residents of New York, New Jersey and Pennsylvania must include sales tax. DO NOT SEND CASH.

GUNPOWDER WIND

**DAN PARKINSON
AND DAVID HICKS**

ZEBRA BOOKS
KENSINGTON PUBLISHING CORP.

ZEBRA BOOKS

are published by

Kensington Publishing Corp.
475 Park Avenue South
New York, NY 10016

First printing: September, 1988

Printed in the United States of America

To Ty

PART ONE

THE BRIGHT LADY

CHAPTER I

*"The hardest thing for folks to handle is peace.
Most of us have no stomach for it."*
—Alexander Horton

Bright morning lay summer-soft across the wooded hills above Little Pace Crossing as Coop Willoughby stepped from the door of Bed To Let, knuckled his eyes into wakefulness, and stretched lavishly, getting the kinks out of his spare frame. Bed To Let was no bargain even at ten cents a night. Coop Willoughby had slept in tack sheds more noted for their amenities.

On the other hand, nobody paid much mind at Bed To Let. Nobody asked a man's business. Situated two miles west of bustling Natchitoches, the jumping-off place to the shadow lands bordering East Texas, Little Pace Crossing was off the main road and was a haven for those whose enterprises would stand little scrutiny. Coop Willoughby had stopped there off and on in the course of his occasional trips overland from the warehouses of Alexandria to Mexican Texas.

Willoughby considered himself a freighter and, in modest fashion, a businessman. His contacts in Alexandria knew him as a reliable customer for various goods desired in Texas, and those in Texas knew him as a smuggler.

He had no qualms about his line of business. He worked at tending to the needs of his customers. And if the manner of his enterprise was not always—as some in Texas would point out—just exactly legal, still it was a basically honorable profession. There were drawbacks, but he generally could show a decent profit for each trip through the shadow lands—a profit not undeserved considering that it was always precarious and sometimes downright hazardous to venture into that no-man's-land between the Arroyo Hondo and the Rio Sabine. For a man carrying valuables of any kind, in any manner, the border zone between American Louisiana and Mexican Texas was in no way a healthy place to be.

There had been no profit, though, on his latest trip. It had been a disaster all the way. The loss of two mules, some fine linen, and a keg of expensive brandy to a roaming band of hell-raising Kickapoo Indians had set him back a good bit. Worse, it had set back all his plans for a new life, and his dreams of Mistletoe.

The Indians fortunately had not managed to get his horse, his rifle, or his money. They had settled for the mules, the yard goods, and the brandy, and for putting a good scare into him. The world of Coop Willoughby was full of ups and downs, but a man made out as best he could. His greatest regret was the linens . . . fine, expensive material all the way from Connecticut. That material was no ordinary merchandise. He had saved and scrimped for it. It was to have been a gift to Nanitsa, the mother of Udali—little Mistletoe. Utsada had told him it wasn't necessary to make gifts. It wasn't Cherokee custom. But Willoughby had decided it was the thing to do . . . and then had let it be known what he planned. Now he was stuck with it, custom or not. The keeping of one's word *was* Cherokee custom. Besides, he suspected that old Cutter, Udali's father, did not think much of him as a prospective son-in-law.

Some of the brandy had been intended for Cutter. Ditastaye-sgi was a more reasonable man with a good belt under his belt.

The rest of the brandy was to have been for Padre de Leon, the moody little priest in Nacogdoches. Willoughby

10

was a sensibly thorough man. If he could, somehow, get past the Cutter and get Nanitsa's blessing, then after the Cherokee ceremony he intended to pack Udali off to Nacogdoches and get the priest to make her his legal wife. She would adore it, and Willoughby would feel better about a Christian wedding—even if it was Roman Catholic.

Padre de Leon would have appreciated that brandy. The priest was not a happy man, and church wine just wasn't as soothing to the nerves as good brandy.

Now Nanitsa's linen was gone, Dita-staye-sgi's and the Padre's gifts were gone, Willoughby's mules were gone, and the profits from at least two good hauls were gone. He hoped those Kickapoos were soothed by the brandy. He hoped they were so soothed they would all fall into a bog.

From Natchitoches to Alexandria would be another day and a half by horseback. Once there, he had money enough to buy another load of hardware, spices, and coffee, and credit enough to pick up a couple of mules. Then he would start over again.

Willoughby was almost at the privy door when he noticed the tall man standing there, long rifle slung casually across his arm. He blinked and stopped, mouth open, eyes wide. Alexander Horton was a long way from home.

"Mornin', Coop," the tall young man told him.

Willoughby regained some of his composure. "Mornin', Sheriff. What you doin' all the way over here?"

"Lookin' for you, Coop. The *Alcalde* wants to talk to you. You're under arrest."

Willoughby was dumbfounded. For lack of anything else to say, he said, "I got to go to the privy, Sheriff."

"That's fine. You go ahead on. I'll wait here and hold your rifle for you."

Willoughby's visit to the high-smelling little outhouse brought him thoroughly awake and gave him a chance to marshal his thoughts. He came back out in a few minutes, buckling his belt and prepared to reason with the Sheriff of Ayish Bayou.

"Right nice seein' you here, Sheriff," he said, "but I don't

11

see how you can arrest me over here in the States like we are. I mean, where you're Sheriff is back there in Texas, not over here."

"That's all right," Horton told him. "I arrested you two days ago when you were still in my jurisdiction. I just now found you to tell you about it. The *Alcalde* wants to see you about some liquored-up Kickapoos that raised a ruckus out on the Camino Real."

Willoughby paled. "They didn't hurt anybody, did they?"

"No, but they could have. You ready to ride?"

"Look, Sheriff." Willoughby spread his hands. "You don't have any evidence that I've done anything wrong, and even if you did, you don't have any authority to arrest me in Louisiana. Now I got to go on down to Alexandria and tend to some business, but I'll be coming back to Texas in a week or so and we can talk about it then. That'll be all right, won't it?" He put on his most winning smile and held out a tentative hand for his rifle.

Horton's amiable expression didn't alter. "I saddled your horse for you, Coop. Let's get going."

The grin withered on Willoughby's face. "Now look, Sheriff. You know my word is good, and I give you my word I never sold any liquor to any Indians. Now, how about that?"

"Let's go, Coop. We got a long way to ride."

As they mounted their horses outside the tack shed Willoughby grumbled, "Some people got no sense of justice whatsomever."

It was nearly noon when they crossed Arroyo Hondo and headed down into the dense lowlands that were the border zone of Texas, leaving the relative civilization of the American frontier behind them while the relative civilization of the Mexican frontier was still thirty wild miles ahead. Without a word Alexander Horton handed Coop Willoughby's rifle back to him, and without a word Willoughby accepted it. Nobody went unarmed through the Neutral Strip. And they both knew Willoughby had better sense than to try to escape from Alexander Horton.

There was a principal trace through the Strip. Armed trains used it with regularity. Ill-prepared greeners used it, and sometimes did not come out at the other end. Many avoided it, for it was there the outlaws and predators were sure to be.

Willoughby knew the back ways through the lawless zone, and recognized the one Horton chose—a rambling track often no more than a deer trail. Both men were trail-wise and wary. They moved silently through the dense greenery of the thicket woods, alert for unaccounted sounds and movements. At a point more than two hours into the zone they both reined up when a mockingbird, yammering in a tree behind them, went silent and then took flight. As one of the men turned their mounts to the right, through an opening between laden sweet-gum trees, then around a berry-vine thicket, where they pulled up. A moment later a group of horsemen passed on the trail, moving at a canter. From the sound there were four or five of them.

When they were gone Horton listened for a minute or more, then said, "Come along," and edged his horse back onto the trail.

Coop remarked conversationally, "Crowded out today, ain't it?"

They had ridden for another half hour, then had stopped to rest their mounts where the track crossed a stream, when they heard the sound of a gunshot, ahead and to the left. There were shouting voices, then another shot, then silence.

Horton had frozen into position at the first sound. Now he seemed to make up his mind about something. He looked Willoughby up and down, shook his head sadly, and said, "Well, you're all there is so you'll have to do. Raise your right hand."

Willoughby, baffled, did as he was told.

"By authority of the *Alcalde* of Ayish Bayou, Ayzes District, I hereby deputize you, Cooper . . . what's your middle name?"

"Uh . . . Ezekiel."

13

"I deputize you, Cooper Ezekiel Willoughby, to help me carry out whatever duties I see fit for as long as I see fit. Pay is a dollar a day. Do you swear to uphold the laws and ordinances of the Ayzes District? Say, 'I do.' "

"Hell I will," Willoughby sputtered, his hand still in the air. "Am I under arrest or ain't I?"

"You are."

"And now you going to make me a deputy? Come on, Sandy, you can't do both. Why, you haven't got the authority out here to do either one."

Horton was impatient. "I'm deputizing you retroactively back to when we were in Texas. Say, 'I do.' "

Willoughby stood his ground. "Retroactive to before or after I was retroactively arrested?"

"The same identical time. Now say, 'I do,' before I have to brain you."

Coop shrugged. "I do. Now what am I, a prisoner or a deputy?"

"Both," Horton said. "Follow me and be quiet."

Afoot, they moved silently down the creek bed for a hundred yards, then hearing muted voices just ahead, they eased up the bank and over a brush-choked knoll. Ahead of them in a small clearing were seven white men and four blacks, several saddled horses, and a lead of pack mules. Two of the white men stood stiffly to one side, their hands empty. The other five men were armed. Four held guns trained on the first two while the fifth walked toward the mules. One of the unarmed men was Samuel Looney, from the Neches settlements beyond Nacogdoches.

Horton didn't hesitate. In a strong voice that carried the impression of a troop of seasoned cavalry at his back he shouted, "You men, lay down those rifles and stand aside. Now!"

The shock froze them all for a moment, and then they complied—all but one, who started to turn, bringing his old musket up. Horton said quickly, "If you come to point, mister, you're a dead man."

The man hesitated, then sagged. He put his gun on the

14

ground and stepped back. Leaving Willoughby in the brush, Horton stepped out and looked them over.

"Howdy, Sam. These men molesting you all?"

Sam Looney looked surprised and, oddly, embarrassed. "Evening, Sheriff. What you doing out this way?"

"Passing by," Horton responded. At the word "sheriff" the five border ruffians—for such they appeared to be—began to back away. At a glare from Horton they stopped. Likely they had heard of Alexander Horton. Few in these parts had not.

Horton looked back to Looney. "Well?"

"Ah, nothing serious, Sheriff. We were just having a little disagreement here, but I think it's all resolved now."

"That's all?" Horton looked from one to another. "Just a disagreement?"

Looney nodded. "That's all. These gentlemen were just on their way to somewhere else."

After a long moment Horton said, "Well, if that's how it is." He gestured with his gun barrel. "If you fellows are leaving, you'd best be on your way. No, not all at once. One at a time, as I tell you, you can pick up your guns and go."

One at a time, as he told them, they did. When the last of them was gone and the hoofbeats had faded, Horton lowered his rifle and Willoughby came out of the brush.

After a moment of silence Horton said, "I suppose everything is all right here then?"

Looney nodded, again looking strangely embarrassed. "Just fine."

Horton looked at the man with Looney. The stranger was a well-dressed, distinguished-looking man of early middle years. At Horton's scrutiny Sam Looney stepped forward. "Ah, Sheriff Sandy Horton, this is a friend of mine from the States. John Smith."

The man said, "How do you do, Sheriff."

"Howdy, Mr. Smith. Are you going into Texas?"

"Why, yes. I have traveled a way with Mr. Looney. Why do you ask?"

"I was just curious. Yours is a famous name in Texas,

15

you know. About half the people coming in nowadays are named John Smith. I guess those are your mules there?"

He started toward them and Sam Looney stepped in front of him, smiling apologetically. "No, they're mine. Just some supplies, Sandy. Nice seeing you, but I believe we have to be on our way now."

Horton strugged. It was really none of his business. "Nice seeing you, too, Sam. Guess I'll see you around again soon. Nice to meet you, Mr. Smith. Come see us at Ayish Bayou some time."

"I'll do that," Smith said, an easy smile creasing his face.

Back on the track Horton rode in silence until Willoughby finally asked, "What was that all about?"

Horton shrugged. "Sam's probably runnin' guns again."

They camped that night well off the trail on a slough that Willoughby thought of as Plum Creek but Horton called Esperanza. There was no shortage of places that had various names, especially in the Neutral Strip.

Mid-morning of the following day found them descending into the willow-brushed Sabine Valley on a slanting course that would bring them to the river near Gaines' Ferry on the Camino Real. All of Willoughby's grumbling had availed him nothing with the stolid young sheriff. Now he rode along deep in gloom, sometimes ahead of and sometimes behind Horton, never once thinking of trying to escape.

The early morning had brought on a new attempt at a plea when Willoughby asked Horton what he was charged with.

"Nothing right now," Horton answered amiably. "I can't charge you with anything outside of Texas, Coop, you know that."

"Then what did you charge me with three days ago when you arrested me yesterday retroactive to? Dammit, Sandy, you're not being fair!"

In the pause while Horton relished these well-chosen words, Willoughby thought he saw a spark of devilish humor in the sheriff's hooded eyes.

"Why, Coop, I charged you with being somebody the *Alcalde* wants to talk to."

Now as they approached the river — and Texas soil — Willoughby pulled up alongside his captor. "I 'spect you want to carry my rifle now," he said sourly.

Horton eyed him casually. "How much does that rifle of yours weigh, do you reckon?"

"Ten pounds by the scale!" Willoughby snorted.

"Then you hang onto it. I'm carryin' load enough."

They waited a quarter hour on the east bank of the Sabine while Gaines's helpers shuttled two mule trains across, then boarded the barge and went across the narrow river into Texas. It was the first time Willoughby had used the ferry. He had always found it less obtrusive — and cheaper — to cross a mile upstream where there were shallows with a little island in midstream.

James Gaines greeted them as they led their mounts off the ferry on the Texas side. A short, wide-shouldered man in high boots and leather galluses, Gaines chewed on a battered pipe and took their hands in turn.

"Howdy, Sandy. Howdy, Coop. How's the huntin'?"

"Just fine," Horton said, cutting off Willoughby's muttered comments. "What's the news the past few days?"

"Quite a bit," Gaines said. "You hear about the ruckus down to Anahuac?"

"Just that there was one. What happened?"

"Well, seems like the Trinity settlers got up in arms and ran Colonel Bradburn and his troops into that brick fort down there and set up a siege. After his hide, they are. John Austin and some of the Brazoria bunch rode over to help 'em out. There was some shootin', and the settlers drafted up a set of resolutions against Bradburn, then some of them went on back to Brazoria for cannon."

Horton's mouth dropped open. "They're going to fire on the fort with cannon? Against federal troops?"

"Well, accordin' to the resolutions, they ain't shootin' at anybody but Bradburn, though how they can aim that fine with field pieces is beyond me. While they were at it they

17

took up sides for Santa Anna against Bustamente too."

Horton whistled. "Piedras isn't gonna like that."

"Not a bit," Gaines allowed. "He's already left with some of his troops. Our little colonel's gone south to sort things out at Anahuac." His face darkened. "Hear he taken some Shawnee bucks with him too."

"Bad to worse," Horton muttered, shaking his head. "Bad to worse for sure. Nothin' more so far?"

"Well, we're gettin' the story a little at a time from folks coming through. Likely there'll be more to tell before long. One fella this morning said there was doin's down at Brazoria too. Colonel Ugartechea at Velasco has orders not to let those cannons get through. He didn't know no more about it, though."

"Well, I guess we better be moving then. Coop and me have to get on down the road and talk to the *Alcalde*."

Gaines squinted at Willoughby curiously, wondering why the high sheriff of Ayish Bayou and a known smuggler would be traveling together in search of an *alcalde*, but he was too polite a man to ask. He simply said, "I doubt if Ben Lindsay is to home, Sandy. Some of 'em went on over to Nacogdoches to find out more about what's goin' on."

"If he isn't home, then we'll go on to Nacogdoches. Thank you, James, and a fine day to you. Come on, Coop, let's ride."

A few miles of heavy forest, and they came into settled areas. It was mid-afternoon when they reached the crossing at Ayish Bayou. Almazon Huston's inn, some tackle sheds, a set of barns, and a smithy marked what might someday be a town. As Gaines had said, the *Alcalde*, Benjamin Lindsay, was not at home.

Horton ordered Willoughby to dismount in front of the smithy, then looked down at him from his saddle.

"Now I tell you what, Coop. You go sit in the shade over there and keep yourself under arrest 'til I get back. I'm gonna ride down the bayou and let my sisters know I'm alive, then I'll be back to get you."

"Which am I now, Sheriff, a prisoner or a deputy?"

18

Willoughby bristled.

"Why, both, Coop. As a prisoner I'm ordering you to sit in the shade there until I get back. And as a deputy I'm ordering you to make dang sure you don't get away."

Willoughby thrust out a belligerent jaw. "And supposin' when I ain't payin' attention I just up and ride off and I don't even notice I'm gone until it's too late to catch me. Supposin' that, Sandy Horton, then what?"

Horton didn't bat an eye. "In a case like that, I expect you to track yourself down and bring yourself back, dead or alive. We can't have escaped prisoners runnin' loose, can we?"

CHAPTER II

*"The problem in Texas isn't too many people,
it's too many different people."*
—William Goyens

Late afternoon's reddening sun was edging into the banked clouds to the west when the lean man on the blooded bay rode out of woodlands on the Camino Real and saw ahead of him, on a cleared rise, a farmstead. New pole barns and a low-roofed shed flanked a solid two-story house so new it glistened in the lowering light. The song of hammers and the staccato drone of a saw reached him, and he could see figures working at the front of the place—black slaves constructing what appeared to be a porch.

The place was well-planned and had the appearance of permanence. The new house was one of the largest he had seen in Texas. Stakes and twine marked where there would be spacious lawns. Several tall pines and a cluster of dogwood had been left standing, selected with an eye to graceful symmetry. Even as the porch was going up, flowers had been planted in the dooryard. A neat place, he thought. A gracious home.

Drawing near, he saw more blacks at work, dark faces and arms shiny with sweat. Under the shed roof a tall, sweating mulatto tended a forge and wielded a maul, perfecting an iron tire for a carriage wheel. The carriage itself, tongue-down in the wagon yard, was a trim vehicle of the surrey design with brass ornamentation on its buckwall and rails. A row of newly made copper pots hung on the shed's back wall. A youth, tow-headed and gawky in recently

20

outgrown britches, stood near the workmen at the porch, watching him approach. Somewhere in back, food was cooking.

Timothy Ralls's eyes took in the scene and he nodded his approval. He appreciated a well-appointed place. This was the home of a successful man.

Entering through the wagon yard, Ralls dismounted as the sweating mulatto in the shed turned, wiped a sleeve across his brow, and said, "Evening, sir."

Ralls nodded at him, handed him the bay's reins, and said, "Tend him for me, if you please. He can use some water." Then he turned toward the house. At the dooryard fence he met the boy, an alert youth in early to middle teens. Ralls nodded and smiled.

"Good evening, young sir. I wonder if you could direct me to the master of this place."

The boy's eyes sparkled as he suppressed a grin. "Yes, sir. I sure can. That was him you just handed your horse to."

The tall mulatto had given his horse to a black servant and was approaching across the wagon yard. He held out a hand. "My name is Goyens, sir. May I help you?"

Startled, off guard, Ralls saw Goyens's dark hand before him and took it without thinking. The grip was firm and businesslike, not at all the tentative, embarrassed grip of a slave. Discovering what he was doing, Ralls withdrew his hand quickly.

"I'm just passing by." He glanced quizzically back and forth at the mulatto and the white youth. "How . . . uh, how far is it to Nacogdoches?"

"Just keep going east," the mulatto said easily. "It's about four miles from here. You come far?"

"Far."

"Leaving Texas, are you?" The dark eyes were mild, but the man caught a spark of quick interest there.

"For a time. My business is done here. Ah, the boy said this is . . . your place?"

"That's right. Building it for my new wife." Goyens indicated the boy. "This is my stepson, Henry Sibley. His

21

mother and I were married just recently."

The man looked at him in astonishment. "A white woman?"

Goyens's gaze was slow and reserved. "That's right. My wife is a white woman. So was my mother. And I am a free man, sir. So was my father."

Under Goyens's challenging scrutiny, Ralls looked away. "Well." He shrugged. "None of my business."

"No." The word closed the subject. "Now if you'd like to sit over here in the shade and rest a bit, we have coffee. What is the news from the Brazos?"

Despite his unease, Ralls found himself sitting on a bench under a shade tree, a mug of steaming coffee in his hand, telling the news to a Negro.

"Hell is breaking loose down there, for sure. I don't know what you've heard up here, but a militia unit out of Brazoria went downriver and attacked the fort at Velasco. They fought for eleven hours, someone said. Then the Brazorians captured the fort and sent all the troops packing."

"Who led the militia?"

"Fellow by the name of John Austin. They lost some men, I hear, but the soldiers lost a lot more. What it was about was, those Brazorians had some cannon loaded on a ship and were bound for Anahuac. The Velasco garrison tried to stop them."

"Were you there?"

"Where? Velasco? No, I was just passing through Brazoria when riders came in with the news. I got on out of there. It isn't my fight."

"I take it you are not a Texian."

"Texian?" The man cocked a brow at Goyens. "I thought the word was Texican."

Goyens shook his head. "It used to be."

"I guess"—the man peered at him over his coffee cup—"the 'Texians' have declared for Santa Anna now?"

"Sounds like some of them have." Goyens sat for a moment, deep in worried thought. The stranger was gazing around him at the lush bottoms overlooked from the home-

22

site.

"Nice land here," said Ralls. "Grow a crop, I'd wager. Whose is all that?"

"It's mine," Goyens said distractedly. "That colonel down there, the one at Velasco, what happened to him? Colonel Ugartechea?"

"I guess they sent him home. Listen, are you fooling me? I mean this place . . . the land, the house, is it really yours?"

Goyens looked at him levelly. "It really is mine. This isn't the United States of America, sir, this is Mexico."

"But those nig . . . those workers over there . . ."

"They're mine too. Would you care to stay for supper, Mr., ah . . ."

Ralls shook his head quickly. The idea of sitting down to supper in a fine house with a white woman and her black husband was a little too much for him. "No, thank you. I'll be going. Four miles to Nacogdoches, you say? Can you tell me if there is an inn there where I could put up for the night?"

"There's a fine inn, just across the way from the Stone House. Tell them Will Goyens sent you and they'll find room. I own it."

When the man was gone Goyens walked up to the house. A wash bench was set up at the side, with rainwater in a pail, yellow soap hanging on a string, a clean basin, and toweling. As he stripped off his shirt and washed himself Mary came around from the back. She looked flushed and radiant from working with her servants over the cook fire.

"Will, who was that?"

Goyens considered. "Well, my lady, by his speech I'd say he was a tidelander, probably a Virginian. And a man of some schooling, by his manner. His clothing and his horse indicate affluence, and the way he looked over our land here was 'old family.' Also, he recovered quickly from confusion, indicating either some legal experience or . . . possibly . . . some illegal experience, and he had a way about him — a furtiveness, I suppose — like that of a man in the

23

pay of someone and afraid he'll be asked about it. Therefore, I expect he was one of those Jackson agents out here to scout Texas and report back on how soon we might be fair game."

"Will Goyens!" She stamped a foot. "You stop that. What was the gentleman's name?"

"I don't know, Mary. He didn't tell me. How's supper coming?"

"Be ready in a bit. Scrub good, Will. Working that forge leaves you absolutely black."

She giggled, dodged aside as he snapped a towel at her, and hurried away around the house. A moment later a Negro man came out and handed him a fresh shirt. Goyens slipped into it and ran fingers through his glistening black hair.

"Thank you, Jupiter. Now bring whiskey and cool water out to the front porch, please. And after supper, Mrs. Goyens and I will want brandy."

Jupiter nodded, said, "Yassuh, Mr. Goyens," and went back into the house.

In skin color, Jupiter was no darker than Will Goyens. The similarity ended there. Goyens was a free man. Jupiter was not. Goyens had bought him from a man in Louisiana some years before. Jupiter and the other Negroes on his place belonged to him just as surely as did the land on which he stood, the cattle in his field, the inn and freight company he owned in town, the smithy and gunsmith shop he maintained and operated as time permitted, the horses, grain, and hides he bought from the Indians for export, and the profits that derived from all of these.

Right now, Goyens was worried. As he sat in his rocking chair on the partially completed front porch and watched the last rays of evening sun strike fire from the thunderheads in the west, he reviewed again the news the stranger had brought him. Fighting at Velasco. Militia against federal troops. Settlers declaring for Santa Anna. Declaring for what? Freedom from oppression? Or, more subtly, freedom from Mexico? Texican, they had called themselves.

24

Now the word in common use was Texian. The difference was slight. The implications, considered, were profound. "Texican" was simply a contraction — Texas-Mexican. Texian? That was something else.

He thought back to another American he had heard recently, expounding at Sim's Tavern in Nacogdoches. The man had been full of rum and importance as he held forth before the travelers sharing the common room with him. He spoke of high cotton prices in the States, good for some and bad for others, and of the famine that plagued the northern states. One sentence hung in Goyens's mind, verbatim:

"Mr. Jackson presses for westward expansion as the solution to many problems, though the Mexican immigration law has badly stunted our . . . ah, that is, blunted the hopes of many who would emigrate here."

A slip of the tongue? Possibly. But the words were vivid in Goyens's mind because he had been near the door at the time, and had seen who overheard the remark. Colonel Piedras had entered as the man was talking.

Goyens remembered the colonel's face when he heard the words. Rage had been there, he thought, and possibly a trace of fear. The colonel had left quickly, unnoticed.

Will Goyens did not like Piedras. He could think of few who did. The colonel was arrogant, imperious, and abrupt with the citizens whose interests he was supposed to protect. He had long ago made it clear that he saw himself as commander of *all* elements of his region, not just the military. And when the citizens of the region reacted by turning more and more to their civil structures of government, Piedras in turn reacted by — it seemed — spending his days finding new ways to harass and insult them.

For a time Goyens, in his easygoing, judicious way, had considered the interplay to be just a game that would pass. He knew now it would not. He saw in the complex actions of the commandant a true disdain for the Spanish-derived civilians that he wielded like a slap in the face to proud people who did not consider themselves peons. He saw

25

there a vicious hatred for the industrious Anglo settlers who were constitutionally unable to recognize the trappings of "authority" in anyone. And he saw there a deep fear of almost everything. He suspected that Piedras was, in some subtle way, a sick man.

To top off the hostility that Piedras had built about him, the colonel was a royalist. He seemed to go out of his way to express his support for the type of tyranny that had developed under President Bustamente's regime. It was as though, Goyens thought, the colonel were trying to taunt his populace, to goad them into rash statements—possibly even into rash actions—to somehow justify to himself that he was right all along.

The last rays of the summer sun faded into a faint glow above the cloud banks to the west, where distant lightning etched the skyscape in grand design. The light was about gone as several of his slaves approached from the tack shed carrying fresh-cut lumber for the porch trim and bannisters. Goyens looked around him at the work they had done today. It was good. He took care of his workers, and they in turn took care of him. Skilled hands had framed in the long, open gallery so cunningly that in the dim light of evening he could see no seams. He noted that the handrails were set on their uprights with mitered joints. He hadn't told them to do that, but it was far better craft than he would have called for.

As they set down their loads of cut lengths Goyens said, "Fine job y'all have done today. You go on now and let your women feed you, and get some rest. You can do the rest of it tomorrow." As they nodded and turned away he added, "You, Samson, stay a minute."

Samson was a powerfully built man whose age—nearly sixty years—showed only in the grizzled hair on his head and the lines in his face.

"Samson, who did the joints on these rails?"

"It was that boy Ambrose done it, Mistah Goyens. He say he do good work so I let him." Concern crept into the man's eyes. "My fault if it ain' right, Mistah Goyens."

26

"No, Samson, it's fine. It is very good work. You did just right. What tools did Ambrose use?"

"Why, he cut the boa'ds wit' a saw set in a box he built, an' he work 'em wit' a rasp an' chisel 'til dey fit right."

"What do you have him doing now?"

"Mos'ly totin', Mistah Goyens. He ain' as strong as some. He mos'ly tote an' fetch."

"Thank you, Samson. I believe I'll take Ambrose into town tomorrow and see what he can do in the shop. You tell him be ready, will you?"

"Yassuh."

"You go eat and rest now, Samson. Good night."

"Good night, suh."

Henry Sibley had come around the house in time to hear most of the conversation. Watching Samson walk away he said, "Ma says tell you supper's almost ready, Mr. Goyens." He was still watching Samson's receding form in the gloom, outlined now against the lights from the little compound of servants' cabins. He turned back to Goyens. "You don't have as much trouble with slaves as most . . . uh, men do. Tom Roland's pa, he has two and he has to beat 'em to get a lick of work out of 'em."

Goyens studied his new stepson. The boy would be a man soon enough. "You suspect it's because I'm black, Henry? You started to say I don't have as much trouble as most *white* men, didn't you?"

The boy shuffled his feet, embarrassed, and Goyens grinned. "Come sit with me for a bit, then we'll go have supper."

For long minutes they sat and watched the evening. The clouds in the west were putting on a show. There was a real storm going on out there somewhere. But overhead the east Texas sky was breaking out in brilliant stars.

"The reason my slaves look after me, Henry, is because I realize that they are people. And that isn't because I have Negro blood. Anyone with a mind to think with knows that people are people, no matter what their color or their station. And people need some things . . . like understanding

27

of each other, and loyalty they can count on, and pride in what they do well. I know that, and they know that, and that's why they do good work for me."

The boy made a noncommittal sound, but Goyens knew he was thinking it over.

"There's something I need to talk to you about, Henry. That black wench, Bess."

The boy's eyes came around to him, quickly, and Goyens suspected his young face reddened. It was a delicate subject, and the man had been considering how to approach it. Head-on, he had decided, was best.

"You know what I'm talking about, son. Don't let that gal keep getting you out in the hay barn. It's no good. Just no good."

Henry's voice was strained. "Hell, everybody does that, Mr. Goyens. She's just a . . ." He stopped, then tried a new tack. "You mean she's black and I'm white? Shoot, you and Ma . . ."

"Are man and wife now, Henry. I know that isn't an easy thing for you, but don't misunderstand it. I am a rich man, son, no matter what blood I carry. And I'm rich because I've earned it. We can have a good life here, because I'm rich and because this is Mexico, not the United States. The standards are different."

"Tom Roland's pa says—" The tone was diffident, challenging, and Goyens cut him off before the words were said.

"Tom Roland's pa is a lazy man, Henry. He envies me. I recognize that. If I were white he would envy me quietly. Since I am black, he envies me openly. I just ignore it. There aren't too many like him. The subject, though, is you and Bess. What if you should make her with child? That would be your child then, Henry, and it would be a little mulatto, with not a chance in a thousand of being as lucky as I have been. You wouldn't want that. And Henry, that girl is a slave. She isn't free, and that makes a world of difference.

"Look, son, I know how it is, when you're young and the

sap is running. But that's when you have to grow up. Any capability is a responsibility, including that one. You nor I, neither one, is ever going to do anything to bring your mother grief, not if I can help it."

Henry was quiet for a long time. When he spoke the diffidence of youth was still there, but it was softened. "Since you put it that way . . ."

"That's the way it is, son. You think about it. Now, what do you say we go find our supper?"

That night he told Mary that he must go into town the next morning, and wasn't sure when he would be back.

"Is there trouble, Will?"

"My love, there is always trouble. But no, I just need to visit with Frost Thorn and some others. And I'm taking one of the boys in to work in the shops."

She wasn't to be diverted. "You seem distracted, Will. I want to know what's wrong."

Will Goyens's instincts were true to the manhood of his time. It was generally understood that a woman was happiest when kept in blissful ignorance—barefoot, pregnant, and in the kitchen. It was a code. And like most codes, it was impossible to keep. True to the womanhood of any time, Mary flatly refused to abide by it. Reluctantly, he told her.

"I see storms coming, Mary. This revolution of Santa Anna's, it's having an effect up here and I don't like it. Some of the colonies are declaring for Santa Anna. They're taking sides, and some have taken up arms. There has been fighting on the Trinity, and now over on the Brazos.

"You know how some of the settlers here feel about me, Mary . . . about us. I'm a black man and these are mostly Southern people. A lot of them wouldn't hesitate to impress me into slavery if they could, and take everything I have."

She put a soft hand on his arm. "You don't have to worry, Will. Not in Mexico. The government will never let that happen here."

"No, not if the government *is* here. But those settlers

29

down there in Austin's colonies, they're driving the soldiers out. Sending them home to join Santa Anna. And these here are thinking along the same lines. It spreads, Mary. It's like a disease. At this minute, the only military left in Texas might be just those at Nacogdoches and maybe some at Bexar or Gonzales. I don't know.

"Piedras is a hated man. If enough of the wild ones up here find an excuse to chase him out, then we'll have a howling mob here with no army to control it."

Her eyes were wide. "I don't think any of the people we know want to break off from Mexico or anything like that."

"The ones we know are the best of them, Mary. There are others. And beyond that border out there"—he pointed to the east—"are thousands more who have no allegiance to Mexico, no friendships in Texas, and no loyalty to anyone. If the army goes, there won't be much to stop them."

She was quiet for a time. Then she said, "It will be all right, Will. It will all work out." She turned a smile on him that was only slightly forced. "There will be no trouble for us, Will Goyens. I just won't stand for it."

In spite of himself, he laughed aloud. "You're quite a woman, Mary Pate Sibley."

"Mary Pate Sibley *Goyens*, Mr. Goyens."

Far away to the west thunder rolled along the Brazos River valley. But here, in the wooded redlands, stars hung in a clear night sky.

In Nacogdoches Timothy Ralls, Captain, United States Army Surveyors (Detached), completed a leisurely evening meal at a little *hacienda* where a Spanish woman served travelers in her courtyard.

Before returning to Goyens' Inn, where he had a bed for the night, he walked across to the stables to see to the tending of his horse. The regal bay was a gift from his uncle in Virginia, one of a matched string of racers old Colonel Ralls was breeding, and he was very pleased with it. He had hesitated to bring it into Texas, and then on second thought had hesitated not to. In a wild and foreign land there was danger of such a horse being coveted. But there was greater danger for a man whose mission was—at best—questionable. A man's liberty—even his life—could depend upon his horse. He had no desire to have to explain himself under duress to some backwoods Mexican officer with a dagger at his belt and a gang of tough *presidarios* grinning brutally over his shoulder.

Timothy Ralls was more than ready to get out of Texas. The province was a powder keg.

At the stable a hunched, aged *mestizo* bid him *"Buenas tardes"* and led him to where the bay was stalled. Carefully he inspected the animal, dug a hand into the stall's short grain bin, looked around at the straw underfoot, and nodded. The animal was in good hands.

Walking back toward the inn, he reviewed what he had learned. He had gone as far west as Bexar, as far south as Brazoria. He had been a drifter. He had listened and looked. He had talked with the people. He had been there when the Brazorian riders came in from Velasco. He had not gone to Anahuac—Ramage would get the story from there—but instead had circled Tenoxtitlan and visited briefly at Harrisburg. He had a great deal to confide to Mr. Whitmire. He had surveyed the forces at work in Texas . . .

He stopped. All but one. With a mental snap of the fingers he cursed himself and his haste. No, the picture was not complete. There was another thing he needed to do.

In the darkness he turned and stood, looking out to the north. No, there was one more fiber in the tapestry, and Mr. Whitmire would require it all. Tomorrow then. Tomorrow he would ride north. A few more days at most, then he could leave Texas and go home. First he would survey the Indians.

The rest he would leave to Ramage and to John Sanford Smith.

CHAPTER III

*"The promised land is a fearsome place
for those who don't belong there."*
— John Sanford Smith

In earliest light of morning Timothy Ralls packed his gear, walked softly through the inn, now quiet except for the easy snores wafting from some of the strewn mats, and eased his way out through the open front door.

Outside he sat on the stoop to pull on his boots, then stood and stretched. Leaving his duffel at the porch rail, he went around to the side of the building where there was night-cool water in a bucket, and carefully bathed his face and hands, letting the water bring him fully awake.

From there he walked to the outhouse, scolding himself as full recollection of the evening before came back to him. He had talked too much. Possibly it was relief that the journey through Texas was near an end. Whatever the reason, though, he had been improvident.

Timothy Ralls was no fool. He knew his weaknesses. So far, from the day he had entered Texas all those weeks — was it months? — ago, he had not touched spirits. He had been sorely tempted. There had been times when he would have given his horse for a jug of that liquid lightning these Texians consumed so freely. But he was a man on guard, and he had kept up his guard, his mind cold sober and his mouth closed as tight as a naturally gregarious man might manage.

Until last night.

Ralls had entered the inn just behind two pack-laden

men coming from the stables. He had had much on his mind and had stumbled right up on the heels of the taller of the two, then backed off, mumbling an apology.

The man had turned, eyed him briefly. The voice was soft and disinterested, "No harm." Then he had turned away. But Ralls had a distinct impression in that gaze of a large hawk just waiting to swoop on prey.

The man with him, a slim, loose-jointed young man of medium height with two days' growth of whiskers on his chin, gave Ralls an easy grin. "Best to watch your step," he said. "They tell a story 'bout a man walked up on ol' Sandy one time when he was asleep, an' . . ."

The taller of the two turned and glowered at his companion. The whiskered one just grinned wider, all angelic innocence, and the tall one walked away into the common room.

In an exaggerated whisper the whiskered one said, "Don't fool with the sheriff, mister. He'll arrest you or deputize you, or maybe both."

Ralls nodded and started to turn away, but the lanky man wasn't through. "That your bay horse over in the stalls? I guess I never saw a finer. By the way, my name's Willoughby."

"How did you know he was mine?"

"Oh, I asked the stabler. He described you. Wouldn't care to trade, I suppose?"

"No, I wouldn't care to trade him."

"Wouldn't if he was mine either." Willoughby shrugged. "Nice meeting you, Mister . . ." But Ralls had already turned away.

There were a dozen or more men in the common room, relaxing on benches and stretch-hide chairs. Conversation was lively. An inn like this, in the cool of evening, was where news was commonly traded. A favorite topic was the recent ruckus at Anahuac. Colonel Piedras had taken troops and headed down there to resolve the conflict.

"Troops ain't all he took," a local added. "The bastid's got Injuns with him too."

Several of the travelers looked around in surprise. "Indians?"

"You bet," the local said. "Took him some young bucks to scout trail."

An older man in the crowd shook his head. "Damn fool could get a redskin war goin' quicker'n you can shake a spider off yer hand."

"Amen."

"Didn't nobody talk to him about that?" a traveler asked.

"Mister"—one of the locals looked at him pityingly—"there ain't nobody can talk to Piedras about nothin'."

Ralls had started through toward the sleeping quarters, but he hung back to listen. He hadn't been to Anahuac, and he knew little of Piedras. He stood for a while, then looked around for a place to sit. There was an open spot on a wide bench. When he reached it he found the man with the friendly grin sitting next to him. Willoughby.

"Interesting talk," Ralls muttered.

"Ain't it, though."

"Won't be no war," a man in the far corner asserted thickly. "Wasn't Cherokee ol' Piedras took along, just a passel o' young Shawnee out on a lark. Shawnee cain't git organized enough for no war anyhow."

The way the man slurred his words sounded comfortable to Ralls, and he realized he was tired. He had been taut as a wound spring for too long.

"Hesh up and think a minute, Pete," another man said seriously. "Injuns is all the same color. If Piedras springs a batch of redskins on white folks an' there's shootin', the white folks is goin' lookin' for redskins. An' if they go lookin' for Injuns north of here, you know who it is they'll find."

There was silence for a moment. Then someone said, "Diwali."

"Yeah," the serious one said. "The Cherokees."

Again there was a tense silence in the room. Ralls decided his intent to visit the Cherokees before he left Texas was a wise choice.

34

"Diwali?" One of the travelers broke the silence. "But he's friendly, isn't he? I heard there was no Indian trouble in East Texas."

The serious one shrugged. "You ever see a old curly wolf, mister? Like out in the wild, travelin' alone an' mindin' his business? If he ain't hungry he can be friendly too. One time I walked right up to a big old lobo . . . didn't see him 'til I's right on him . . . an' he just looked me over, grinned, and went on his way. Wagged his tail damn near like a puppy dog, he did.

"But I guarantee you, mister, had I stepped on him it would of been a different story."

Some of them chuckled at this. Others nodded seriously. Doors at both ends of the sprawling room stood open, and there was a cool breeze coming through, jiggling the lantern flames to make dancing shadows on the walls. For the first time in a long time, Ralls felt comfortable and easy. He hardly noticed when Willoughby handed him a cup and said, "Here, you look tired. Wet your whistle."

The talk drifted on. A few men left, a few more came in, and someone built a little fire on the hearth.

They talked of tariffs, of border patrols, of *presidarios*— convict-soldiers who made up a large part of the 12th Battalion.

"Piedras just lets 'em run loose, do as they please . . . cain't talk to the man at all no more, seems like."

"Lot of stealin' goin' on around here past couple years."

"Damn taxes so high a man cain't afford to eat no more . . . hardly feed a family 'cept what he grows hisself . . ."

"Why buy taxed goods? Plenty comin' over the border that ain't."

"Some don't hold with smugglers."

"Who don't? Name one." Laughter. Understanding grins.

At Ralls's shoulder Willoughby looked around in amusement. Quietly, to Ralls, he said, "Nobody in here that doesn't trade with smugglers."

"Santa Anna," someone was saying, "now there's our

35

man for sure. Bustamente's gone plumb rotten, is my thinkin' on it."

"Bustamente's a royalist."

"Mexico ain't got a royalist constitution, though."

"Hell, Mexico ain't got any constitution. That royalist Bustamente rescinded it. Where you been?"

"Santa Anna'll whip his tail for him, you wait and see."

Ralls noticed his cup was full again, and nodded his thanks to no one in particular. At the back of his mind a voice of caution was nagging at him but he shut it out. He was tired, he was relaxing, and he was almost through in Texas. A few more days, then . . .

". . . from Brazoria, I heard. John Austin led 'em. They went back to get cannons. Gonna blow that Anahuac fort down around Bradburn's ears if they have to."

". . . never get through with cannons. Ugartechea's down at Velasco. He'll stop 'em."

"He tried." The voice was too loud, and Ralls realized it was his own. Faces around the room turned toward him, politely, interested in the news he implied.

"You been there, mister?"

"I just came from there," Ralls said. ("Quiet," the inner voice said, and he hushed it again. He was enjoying the friendly conversation.)

"Well," someone asked, "what happened?"

"They fought at Velasco. Militia against troops. Militia attacked the fort and took it. That's about all I heard."

The man beside him—Willoughby—was eyeing him. "You were at Velasco?"

"I was at Brazoria when the word came. They wiped out more than half of Ugartechea's command. They took the fort, and they're holding it."

Wide eyes around him. Someone whistled, low and solemnly. Willoughby filled his cup again.

"Man!" a grizzled woodsman on the far bench allowed. "That ought too bust things wide open, surer'n hell."

Several of them turned to the tall young man standing across the room. "You know about that, Sheriff?"

"Some of it. I hadn't heard for sure."

"Hell, no," Willoughby murmured sourly. "He's been to busy importin' deputies."

It gave new muscle to the conversation, and Ralls leaned back and let it flow around him. The nagging voice had gone away. He was, after all, just another nameless traveler in their midst, adding a bit of news.

". . . get my wife an' kids out of here before it swings up thisaway."

". . . if it's comin' it's comin'. Piedras ain't agonna stand for it."

"He ain't here. He went to Anahuac."

"Yeah, an' he'll be back."

"No cause for fightin' up here. Not way up here."

"Damn Piedras is cause enough, strikes me . . ."

Ralls was thinking of his family now, and moisture pooled in his eyes. He missed Molly. Molly, he thought, be safe for me. I'm on my way. One more trip, and I'll be home. Be safe for me. He shook his head, trying to clear his mind, but it didn't work. He set down the empty cup, murmured "Good night" to no one in particular, and had to catch himself when he tripped over a man's outstretched leg. " 'Scuse me."

" 'Sall right. Better watch it, though, this floor tilts mighty high some nights."

With extravagant poise Ralls had wended his way through the common room to the sleeping rooms, found his pallet, and collapsed.

Now he stood in the thin gray light of predawn and judged himself. No harm done, apparently, but he was a fool to let his guard down while still in Texas. The accursed place was like a covered snake. It could sting a man without warning.

There was just too much of it — too much in too many ways. Mr. Whitmire would be welcome to it. For Timothy Ralls, the goal in life now was to get home to Virginia.

The great bay was skittish, but Ralls calmed him, saddled him carefully, and led him out into the street. He slung

37

his pack on the saddle, unwrapped his two coat pistols, and placed them in his tail pockets, primed and ready, then swung up into the saddle.

"Leavin' mighty early, huh?"

In the dim light he saw a familiar form on the inn porch stoop. The man from last night. Willoughby.

"Need to get an early start." As an afterthought he added, lamely, "I'm going east."

Willoughby waved a languid hand. "Have a nice trip."

He heeled the bay and rode out of town, going east. Some distance away he turned and headed north, swinging around to intersect Nacogdoches's north road a mile or two above town. It was barely full light, and the pink rays of sun touched the tops of pine trees and set the birds to calling. Here now, in this part of Texas, if a man didn't look too close, it could remind him of Virginia. He rode on.

The sun was high when he passed a crossroad and came up to a little stream. He was sore from riding, still fuzzy from the night's drinking. With a sigh he stepped down, let the bay drink from the clear water, then tied its reins to a pine stub and took off his coat.

On his knees he drank from the stream, then bathed his face and drank again. Last night's thought still hung in his mind. Be safe for me, Molly. I'm coming home. Finally he stood, replaced his coat, and turned. And stopped.

A man stood before him, not ten feet away, a large-shouldered, glum-faced man in homespun shirt and buckskin trousers, dark hair flying wild from his slouch hat, dark eyes flat and unreadable. He held a large rifle, rested across his arm.

Startled, Ralls said, "Hello, I didn't hear you."

The man looked at him without comment. Ralls found no expression in those lifeless eyes, and his hands crept closer to the tail pockets of his coat. The man's eyes flickered at the movement, and Ralls stopped. "My name's Ralls," he said. "Can I do something for you?"

"Yeah," the man said, a slight accent to his words, "I need that horse."

"My horse? Sorry, sir, he's not for sale."

"Didn't say for sell," the man said. "I need him. Official business."

Ralls suddenly was afraid and angry. "And I said he is not for sale. I don't intend to part with him. Maybe you . . ."

With a shrug the man raised his rifle, the movement cat-quick. "That's too bad. I need him."

Ralls's hand dived for the tail pocket of his coat, but never reached it. Suddenly he was lying on his back, half in the creek, with thunder ringing in his ears. Now isn't that odd, he thought. I have fallen. I . . . the thought faded. In the gathering darkness there was someone standing over him. He couldn't think who it was. He felt very weak, and it was dark. Be safe for me, Molly . . .

As Timothy Ralls's lifeless head rolled to the side, staring eyes glazing, the man poured powder into his long rifle and proceeded to reload, methodically. "Ralls, huh?" he murmured. "Glad to meet you, *señor*. My name is Anton Moro."

CHAPTER IV

"Our government makes a mistake when it confuses soldiers with policemen. The two are not the same.
— *Don* Francisco Encarnacion Chireno

Varied rooftops caught the first warm rays of the morning sun and shared their color with the streets below. The Bright Lady of East Texas began to come awake. The Cenis of antiquity had called her Ne-ghi-dos. It meant a brightness. Later tongues adopted the word. Those of the Hasinai who homed here became the people of the Nacogdoche, those of the brightness.

Others came. In the place of Ne-ghi-dos, in 1716 Padre Margill raised the Mission of Nuestra Señora de Guadalupe de los Nacogdoches. Its builders brought war with them. Much was destroyed. By 1773 all the newcomers were gone, but only for a time. Six years later they returned, survivors now of yet another war, and among the structures they raised was a stone fortress, a house of two floors with stone walls three feet thick. Antonio Gil Y'Barbo's people had seen the Comanche. They would never again feel secure without stone walls.

Nolan passed through Nacogdoches, and Musquiz, and left no mark. Not so *Don* Jose Bernardo Maximilliano Gutierrez de Lara and Augustus W. Magee. In 1813 they marched out against General Joaquin de Arredondo y Miono, and the town's young men went with them. None came back. But Arredondo came, and when he left there was no one to watch him depart.

Dr. James Long passed through in 1819, and found few

people. Arredondo's rape of the Bright Lady was still fresh.

In 1821 the Republic of Mexico was born, and Erasmus Sequin was sent to lead the old refugees back to their home. Others had come as well: the Tsalagi and Shawani fleeing before the plague of Anglos to the east. Anglos came too: Haden and Benjamin Edwards, Frost Thorn and others received *empressario* grants.

Still another drama occurred in 1826-27. The Edwards brothers brought it on. Benjamin Edwards raised the flag of the Republic of Fredonia. Stephen Prather, with seven white men and seventy Cherokee braves, brought it down.

And in that year Colonel Piedras arrived in Nacogdoches, empowered as military commander in East Texas and acutely aware of the forces at bay in his regime. The bloody Bright Lady, he knew, was only resting.

She rested, slowly awakening this June morning, and her varied rooftops caught the morning sun. The first touched was the largest, the home of Frost Thorn. A block from the Stone House, across the Plaza Principal from the Red House of Colonel Piedras, Thorn's house was grand in a style not yet common in Texas. Three stories high, solid and gracious, it was the home of a man not just using his wealth, but increasing it.

Next door to Thorn's house, smaller but only slightly less elegant, was the home of the *Alcalde* of Nacogdoches, *Don* Francisco Encarnacion Chireno. Directly across the little square from it was Goyens' Inn, its long front gallery cool and hushed in the dawn radiance. Cooper Willoughby sat there, full of ham and cornbread and wishing he were two hundred miles away. Alexander Horton came out, picking his teeth with a splinter, and stood on the edge of the porch to stretch and yawn. His head barely cleared the rafter beam.

"Mornin', Coop. And a fine mornin' at that."

"It'll turn hot in an hour," Willoughby grunted.

"Time to get crackin' then, before the hour is up." Horton's serenity was unmarred. "Did you happen to get the name of that man that brought in the news last night?"

"About the fight at Velasco? No. I didn't ask."

"Coop, if you're going to make a go of deputying, you're going to have to be more inquisitive."

"I don't give a damn about deputying," Willoughby blurted out. "If you wanted to know who he was, why didn't you ask him?"

"Had my mind on other matters. Has he gone?"

"Yeah. He rode out before sunup. Had him a fine-looking bay horse, I'll say that. He went east."

"Well." Horton shrugged and surveyed the town from the porch. "It doesn't matter. But there's going to be hell to pay when Piedras hears about Velasco. You seen Ben Lindsay?"

"No."

"All right. I'm going to walk around a bit. You wait here and keep an eye on Chireno's house over there. That's where Ben put up last night. When he comes out you tell him you and me have you in custody."

Willoughby's temper flared. "I ain't gonna tell him any such fool thing as that. He'll think I'm as crazy as you are."

"Then just tell him I need to see him. How's that?" Horton picked up his rifle, stepped down into the red dirt street, and strolled away, leaving a fuming Willoughby behind him. He turned at the corner and walked along the Plaza Principal, enjoying the fresh morning air.

Down the way he saw two horsemen approaching — Will Goyens and a skinny young Negro. They turned off in the direction of the gunshop and smithy that Goyens owned and maintained.

Across the way at the Old Stone House, two young officers stood outside the door, watching the morning happen. Horton cut across and waved to them. He recognized Jose Torres and Mariano Lopez, sub-lieutenants with the 12th Battalion. As he approached he called, *"¡Buena mañana, excelentes! ¿Como estan ustedes?"* and saw their teeth flash in tanned faces as they grinned at him.

"¡Mañana, Señor Horton!" Torres called. As he neared them the officer added, *"Me gusta encontrarse."*

"¿Donde esta el comandante hoy, amigos?" The way they grinned at him reminded Horton again that he was no great linguist.

"Amigo," Torres said gently, "it is my hope to be kinder to your language than you are to mine. The colonel is gone to Anahuac. There has been a disturbance. He will return soon." His eyes narrowed slightly. "Don't tell me the *Alguazil* of Ayzes District has not already heard this?"

"Yeah," Horton admitted. "I knew he was gone. I just couldn't remember how to ask in Spanish when he'll be back. Take some men with him, did he?"

"Sí," Torres shrugged. "You could say he took some men. Two full companies of the battalion, and the Company of Monclova. It has been more than a week. They should be back soon. I think things may not be pleasant then, *Señor* Horton."

"Are things ever pleasant when the colonel is around? Ah, forgive me, *amigos*. I know you can't respond to that. Never mind. How have things been here? I just got in last night."

"Quiet enough," Torres said, adding something aside to Lopez in Spanish too rapid for Horton to catch. Lopez responded, and Torres looked troubled. "Quiet, but not . . . ah . . . serene," he told Horton. "There is a strain . . . a tension . . . since news of the trouble at Anahuac. There is worry, among the people and among our soldiers as well."

"Well"—Horton could not restrain himself—"things should be a little brighter as long as Piedras stays gone." A thought struck him and he scowled. "I don't suppose Moro is around?"

The two soldiers glanced at each other. The enmity between the tall young sheriff and the colonel's "agent" was well known. Torres shook his head.

"No, *Señor* Moro is not here either. He left on a mission the day *El Comandante* departed, and has not returned."

"A mission?"

Lopez looked around him and said, in a hushed voice,

"A los Indios."

Torres jerked his head around. *"¡Silencio, Teniente! ¿Quieres a encarase con El Comandante?"* He glanced at Horton, who looked as blank as he knew how. Apparently Torres was satisfied Horton had not understood the other officer's careless remark. "We do not know where he is."

They talked of trivia for a few more minutes, then Horton gave them a tongue-tortured *"Hasta luega,"* and continued his stroll. A young soldier came out of the Red House, Piedras's quarters, and waved a greeting to him. In the distance he could see others around the old church, which was now used as a barracks for the *presidarios*.

The Red House, built almost five years before at Piedras's order, was one of the sore points among the Anglo settlers in and around Nacogdoches. It was a fine house, combining in structure the upright sturdiness of the *jacale*, common among the Mexican settlers, and the permanence of the frame building preferred by the Anglos. It had a large, overhanging gabled roof and the walls were plastered with red clay. It was a commanding, somewhat pretentious structure, and had required a great deal of precious milled lumber to build. This lumber Piedras had ordered from Peter Ellis Bean's sawmill. Much of the construction had been contracted from various other settlers in the area, and some of the refinements had been furnished by men who could supply master craftsmen . . . Frost Thorn and Will Goyens among them.

For all their goods and services, the contributors to Piedras's house received *boletas*—due bills on the Mexican government—in lieu of cash payment. Then Piedras refused to validate the *boletas*. It was his right, he decided, as military commander, to have a house provided for him by the people of his jurisdiction.

Horton had heard that Thorn kept all his "red house bills" in a glassed frame in his study, a sort of memento "in honor of the honor of honoring the honorable Piedras." The story was that Colonel Bean, being of a different turn of mind, had solemnly consigned his *boletas* to the pit

44

beneath his outhouse, where they could be "in good company."

He was heading back toward the inn when he saw Coop Willoughby coming toward him with a sleepy-looking Benjamin Lindsay in tow.

Lindsay was more than a little ruffled. "What's this all about, Alex? This man came pounding on the door at Chireno's and said you needed to see me right away."

Horton turned a ferocious scowl on the untroubled Willoughby. "I told you to wait for him to come out," he rasped.

Willoughby shrugged. "Time flies."

Lindsay said, "Well?"

"This is Cooper Willoughby, Ben." Horton was acutely embarrassed. "You said you wanted to talk to him."

Lindsay looked at Willoughby and then at Horton. "I did? About what?"

"Why, about those Kickapoos that . . ." He saw a devilish grin forming on Willoughby's face and pointed imperiously across the square. "Coop, you see that tree over there? You go lean on it and don't move until I tell you to."

As Willoughby slouched away, rifle across his arm and his cheeks spread wide around his grin, Lindsay said again, "Well?"

When his prisoner was out of earshot Horton said, "Ben, I need your help. The *Ayuntamiento* authorized me to hire a deputy when I need one, and I need one now. I need *him.*"

"So hire him, dammit! That's your concern, not mine."

"Well, it's a little tricky. You see, he's my prisoner. I had to arrest him to get him back here. That's the only way he'd come."

"You arrested your deputy?"

"No. It was more like I deputized my prisoner."

Lindsay, still rubbing sleep from his eyes, looked lost. He waited in silence for an explanation he could understand.

Horton tried again. "You know those borderers who have been stealing us blind around Ayish? Well, I figure to put a stop to that. All I need is the right man—somebody

45

who can get in among them and help me set them up. Willoughby is that man. So when you said you wanted to talk to him, I went and got him. Ben, I know he doesn't look like much, but Coop Willoughby knows everything there is to know about that border. He knows the people on both sides of the Neutral Strip and those in the middle. He can track, he can think when he feels like it, and he can take care of himself. And he speaks Spanish like a Mexican, Cherokee like a Cherokee, Shawnee like Tecumseh himself, and some other languages too. Everybody knows him, nobody pays much attention to him, and he's the best man I know to do a job of work."

Lindsay looked around. Willoughby was propped against the trunk of a large pine tree, grinning at them and stoking his pipe. "Him?"

"Him. For what I need, he's the best there is."

Lindsay shrugged. "Then use him."

"That's my problem. He doesn't want to be a deputy. I need a string to keep him on."

Lindsay considered that. "I see," he said finally.

"Besides, Ben, we have a bigger problem now. I just found out something that Piedras did before he left here. He sent Moro up to talk to the Cherokee."

As it soaked in, Lindsay's eyes widened. He was aware of the doings of recent days at Anahuac and Velasco, and of the likelihood of Piedras reacting violently to what he would see as a threat. But to bring the Indians into it . . . he shuddered. Ben Lindsay had seen firsthand the results of the red people being involved in white men's disputes.

"When did you learn that?"

"Just a few minutes ago."

"Have you told anyone else?"

"Of course not. But you see, now we need Willoughby more than ever."

Lindsay nodded distractedly. "With a string on him."

Will Goyens had rounded the corner and was walking toward them, leading two horses. The young black man was no longer with him. Lindsay considered for a moment, then hailed him. To Horton he said, "Take your prisoner . . . or deputy or whatever in hell he is . . . over to Chireno's and wait there for me." He hurried toward the street where Goyens waited.

Horton stalked past Willoughby with a curt "Come with me."

From the dooryard of Encarnacion Chireno's house they watched Lindsay and Will Goyens. Lindsay's gestures were animated. Goyens listened, a deepening concern on his dark face. Then they came along the street, walking rapidly. Goyens stopped in front of Frost Thorn's house, tied his horses, and rapped at the door. Lindsay continued to where Horton and Willoughby were waiting. He wasted no time on formalities, but stuck a finger under Willoughby's startled nose and said, "As *Alcalde* of Ayish Bayou I hereby sustain such sundry charges as may have been lodged against you and remand you to the custody of the sheriff, here present, until such time as I see fit to conduct a proper hearing into those charges. Both of you wait here."

With that he turned, walked up to Chireno's door, rapped on the frame, and went in. Willoughby stared after him. "What was all that?"

"Coop, you just got strung," Horton told him.

When Lindsay came out again Encarnacion Chireno, the *Alcalde* of Nacogdoches, was with him. Both men looked troubled. They crossed the dooryard and turned toward Thorn's house, and Horton and Willoughby fell in behind them.

At the door of the big house Susan Thorn met them, a hospitable smile on her pretty face. "Good morning, gentlemen," she said to Chireno and Lindsay. "Frost is around back having his breakfast. Would you care for breakfast?"

Before they could answer, Willoughby's voice came from down on the walk. "Yes, ma'am, please." The other three men turned and glared at him.

"I'll have the servants set places on the patio," Susan said, undisturbed. "Would you like to come through?"

"No, *señora,*" Chireno said with a slight bow. "We will go

around, Is *Señor* Goyens here?"

"He's here. He and Frost are talking."

As Chireno and Lindsay started around the house, Horton snapped at Willoughby, "You already had breakfast, you damn beggar."

"Well, I'm hungry again."

At thirty-nine years of age Frost Thorn was without question the wealthiest man in East Texas, and possibly in all of Texas. Those who had the idle time to make such comparisons suspected that he was wealthier even than Jared Groce, over on the Brazos, or Jim Bowie, who had married the wealth of a great family because it came with the girl he loved.

Those who knew Frost Thorn well knew him as an open, outgoing man who loved his wife, enjoyed living well, was honest in his dealings, was a shrewd judge of both people — whom he liked — and politics — which he didn't, and could afford to live as he enjoyed.

He was the very picture of the successful man, robust and portly, usually jovial in nature. But this morning he was less than jovial. He was a worried man. Will Goyens had told him of the news from Velasco, and he had read a copy of the Turtle Bayou Resolutions drafted by the combined militia companies of John Austin and Frank Johnson, declaring for Santa Anna. Since the first word of trouble at Anahuac, when Piedras had ridden south with his infantry and the proud Company of Monclova, Thorn had kept up to date, day by day, on the happenings along the coast and those further into Mexico. It was a powder keg, and now he feared John Austin's militia had just lit the fuse at Velasco.

As his four new guests came around the house Thorn greeted them, and pointed to the copy of the Turtle Bayou document beside his empty plate. "We were discussing this. I'll admit the Brazoria and Trinity men covered themselves very well. It is hard to find fault with what they have done, in this light. But some are not going to see it in this light."

"Meaning Piedras," Lindsay said. At Thorn's nod, Horton sat down to read it. Willoughby poured himself a cup of expensive coffee and waited for the food to arrive.

"It won't matter," Chireno said. "The colonel has gone further than we thought."

Goyens raised worried brows. "What does that mean?"

Chireno turned to Lindsay, who said, "Tell them, Alex."

Horton looked up from his reading. "It means Piedras is already taking action, Will. I just learned this morning that he sent Anton Moro to see the Cherokee."

Thorn was awestruck. "When?"

"Before he left for Anahuac. More than a week ago. Moro hasn't come back."

"My God in Heaven," Thorn muttered. "He thinks it's Fredonia all over again. The madman will get us all killed."

Goyens's dark face had paled slightly. "The man is crazy. He must be crazy."

"You know what this means," Thorn said. "It means he has tried us all for what those settlers on the coast may or may not have done, found us guilty, and sentenced us . . . even before he left to find out what they had done."

Chireno nodded. "My thoughts. That is, assuming he sent his man up there to enlist the *Indios*. There may have been some other reason."

Horton snorted. "Then he would have sent a lackey, not Anton Moro."

Goyens was deep in thought. "It seems to me," he said finally, "that we had better go up there and talk to Diwali ourselves. Frost, we both know him and he respects us. I think we had better go there."

"I wonder if Bean would go with us?"

"I'd think so. He *is* the Indian agent. He also has no love for Piedras—nor for Bustamente, for that matter. *Señor* Chireno, could you have a message sent to *Señor* Bean to join us on the road?"

"Of course. Do you want men to go along?"

"No, I think not," Thorn said. "All the armed men we

49

could muster wouldn't be worth a hang if Diwali has decided for war. But Will and I, and Bean—we know them and they know us. We'll go and talk." He stood. "Also, *mi alcalde,* I think we should find Adolphus Sterne and some of the others and advise them."

Goyens also had risen. "I'll see to horses for us," he said. "Frost, I'd appreciate if one of your people could go out to my place and tell Mary I'll be gone for a while, and not to worry."

Lindsay told Chireno, "I think I'd best get home and meet with my own people. My regards to *Doña* Candida, and thank you both for your hospitality. I'll pick up my horse at the stable and be on my way."

Goyens was the first to leave, then Lindsay and Chireno. Willoughby was halfway through his breakfast. Horton said, "Come on, Coop. We have work to do."

"But I haven't finished," Willoughby protested.

"You've finished. Come along."

Half dragged by the sheriff, Willoughby managed a quick bow to Susan Thorn, who had just come out the back door, and held out a hand to Frost. "Sorry I can't stay, Mr. Thorn. Mighty good food. And that is especially good coffee."

Thorn took his hand and grinned at him. They both knew where Thorn's coffee came from. Willoughby had smuggled it into Texas with his last load.

Thorn said, "Horton, if you want to go with us, we'd be glad to have you."

"No thanks, Mr. Thorn. The first thing Ben Lindsay will do when he gets back to Ayish is call a meeting. Then he'll tell them all about what's going on, and only about half of them will understand it. I got to be there to break a few heads among the other half if necessary."

Back on the street, they headed for the Inn and Willoughby said, "Well, it looks like you won't be needing me anymore, so why don't I just head on east from here and tend to my business. I'll look you up when I get back."

Horton didn't even look at him. "You know those Cher-

50

okees up there, don't you?"

"Some, but just the regular folk. I don't have any dealin's with the Bowl or Big Mush or any of the other high-ups."

"Who do you know?"

"Well, I've hobnobbed some with Edahi and Ganososa-sdi. And Utsada, I guess he's my best friend up there. And I've trailed with Atasi and some of them. Few others, I guess."

Horton was translating the names, slowly. "Edahi, that's the Traveler. Ganososa-sdi, I know of him. Call him the Broom. I've heard old man Prather talk about Utsada. He calls him Going Back. Says he's a *u-ne-ga-di-hi*." He had a hard time with the word.

"Yeah. White-man-killer. That's what he calls himself too. Nice enough fella, he and me get along pretty good. Atasi . . . that means War Club . . . I haven't seen him in a time, but I sure know him. He's got a sister, name of Udali, that's just . . . just . . . mmm."

At the enraptured note in his deputy's voice Horton turned. "Udali?"

"Yeah," Willoughby breathed. "It means Mistletoe."

"How long's it been since you've seen Mistletoe?"

"Way too long," Coop exclaimed, carried away with his own line of thought. "And that's a fact. Although her old man would have my eyeballs on his necklace if he knew what I was thinking about half the time."

"Who's her old man?"

"His name's Dita-staye-sgi. Means the Cutter. He's a clan elder under Diwali. Also he claims he's some kin of Egg. Have you heard of Egg?"

"Who hasn't?" Horton frowned.

"Well, that's my problem with Mistletoe. The Cutter is so eat up with his own importance, he doesn't want me around his daughter."

"Coop, are you afraid of Egg?"

"Hell, isn't everybody?"

"But you still go see Mistletoe sometimes?"

"What I had in mind," Willoughby said, his eyes slitted.

"That's where I was going, before I got tangled up with some damn Kickapoos . . . and a damn sheriff."

"Then I think it's time you saw her again," Horton told him. "If you leave right now and head cross-country, you can be there before Mr. Goyens and Mr. Thorn get there with Colonel Bean. And when you get there, I want you to nose around and find out what Moro has been up to, then come straight back to Ayish and tell me."

Willoughby tried to say about six things at once and nearly strangled. He had helped the sheriff trap him into another long ride in the wrong direction.

"Dammit, Sandy, I got to be going to Alexandria before I can go up there!"

"Later, Coop. Later. Right now let's get you saddled up and on your way to see Mistletoe. Pretty little thing, is she?"

"Pretty as a warm fire on a cold night, but that doesn't have anything to do with—"

"Coop, don't forget, you're in custody and under orders. Now I reckon you can get there in a day and a half easy, spend a day maybe, and a day and a half back to Ayish. I'll be looking for you."

Willoughby was still cursing valiantly in at least three languages when he spurred his horse north from Nacogdoches, traveling alone.

CHAPTER V

"Nobody in his right mind wants war. But any man worth his salt might enjoy a good fight."
— Haden Edwards

Frost Thorn left Will Goyens to make hasty arrangements for a trip to the Indian lands, and headed for the mercantile. The town's leaders, the *Ayuntamiento,* needed to be notified. If Piedras were to succeed in winning the Indians over to whatever side he thought he was on, no one—not the settlers, the townspeople, not even the army of Mexico—would save Nacogdoches. Frost thought it unlikely that Diwali would be persuaded to violence. Diwali was a wise man. But there were plenty of young bucks in the tribes up there who would welcome a fight. The *Ayuntamiento* needed to know. There were contingency measures that could be taken to protect the women and children.

Piedras had sent Moro. That was significant. Anton Moro was not a man to stop at anything. Only Piedras's protection had prevented a lot of people from hunting him down like a mad dog.

Didn't Piedras know the danger of provoking the Cherokee? Everyone else knew. But who knew what was in the mind of Piedras?

Far down the street a wide-bed wagon rumbled, Luis Ramos and his son bringing milk in from their dairy.

At the mercantile, Thorn entered a side door and went to his private office. Most of his business he conducted at home, in the large library of his house, but not this morning. This was business to be conducted outside the home.

He wondered, idly, if some might one day consider him a traitor for what he was about to do. He did not feel treasonous — quite the opposite. He had sworn allegiance to the Republic of Mexico and he aimed to keep his word. He had pledged himself to Mexico, had sworn to uphold the Constitution of 1824. But he had never pledged himself to Bustamente, or to Piedras.

His father-in-law, Haden Edwards, was waiting for him. "Frost, I've been hearing talk . . . very disturbing talk. I want to know what is going on."

Word travels with amazing speed, Thorn thought. "Sit down, Papa. Some others will be here soon and we'll talk about it."

At age sixty-one Haden Edwards was not the firebrand he had been just five years before. The bitter disappointments arising from the Fredonian incident had nearly broken him, in more ways than one. He was still a distinguished man, with hair of midnight black and sideburns cut full, but much of the fire was gone now from those deep, intelligent eyes. His great adventure, his *empressario* grant from Mexico in 1825, had resulted in a series of disasters, culminating in that tragic, comic rebellion in which he had been caught up, thanks to forces of his own making which had gone beyond his control.

Fifty thousand dollars it had cost him, and more. It had broken the great spirit that Thorn had always admired in the older man. Thorn loved Haden Edwards, as a natural adjunct to his love for the old man's daughter. His precious Susan was Haden's flesh, and loving her, he loved all that was hers.

There were still some subjects that could bring the fire back to Edwards's eyes. Confrontation with the Mexican military was one of them, especially if it involved confrontation with Jose de las Piedras, whom Edwards held in angry contempt.

"In the south, they have fought the army," Edwards said.

Thorn nodded.

"What caused it?"

Thorn shrugged. "They fought Bradburn at Anahuac, over the prisoners he had taken. They fought at Velasco because of Bradburn. They fought because they were frustrated, I suppose. I don't know what caused it."

Edwards's eyes narrowed. He knew his son-in-law was withholding a fear from him, and he went straight to it with unerring logic. "Then what do they say caused it?"

Thorn leaned against a door frame. "They say it was in support of General Santa Anna against Bustamente."

"I see. And Piedras will see that as the reason, of course. He will be a raving ass when he comes back." His eyes sparkling with anger, he spread his feet and clasped his hands behind him in the Napoleonic stance favored by the colonel. In a fair imitation of Piedras's voice and manner he mockingly said, "This now is proof. The Anglos are trying to take Texas away from Mexico and give it to President Jackson. They are all part of a criminal conspiracy."

In spite of himself, Thorn chuckled. It was indeed a good likeness. But he was serious when he said, "There may be a grain of truth in it, you know."

"Bah! Grain of truth is it? Then let us sift it out. A great conspiracy? Ridiculous. Who has time to conspire these days? For two years now it has been all a man can do in Mexico to survive. Take Texas away from Mexico then? What Texian would want that? Mexico is not the problem. Bustamente is the problem . . . and asses like Piedras and Bradburn. Better to take Mexico away from the royalists. It was a good land, it can be again. Give Texas to the States? That is what the riffraff beyond the border want, but why should we? Do you know what they are doing now in the States? Taxing a man's land, that's what. Mexico may dream up a lot of ridiculous ways to steal the bread from a man's mouth, but never a tax on land."

"We do want to separate Texas from Coahuila," Thorn pointed out mildly.

"Well, of course we do. It's ridiculous. Would your kin in New York want their legislature sitting in Virginia? Texas statehood is not the issue here, as we both know."

"The issue here is whatever Colonel Piedras thinks the issue is."

"We are at the mercy of a lunatic."

"Precisely. That's why I have asked—"

A knock at the door cut him off. Thorn opened it to admit Encarnacion Chireno, and then Adolphus Sterne, who was arriving just behind him.

Chireno greeted Edwards, and Sterne turned directly to Thorn. He was slightly breathless. "Your man said this was a matter of 'God and Liberty,' Frost."

"It is, Dolph. It is. Come in."

He had been sure to instruct Jaren to use those words. It was the old rallying cry of this country. He knew it would bring Sterne. It had been the cry at Fredonia . . . on both sides.

Sterne was a survivor of that affair. Following the rebellion he had been the only one convicted and sentenced for collaboration with the Fredonians, led by Edwards's brother Benjamin. He had been sentenced to death. Only his membership in the Masonic Lodge had saved him. It was a bond the German-Jew shared with most of the Catholic officers of Mexico's military establishment, as well as with the leading elements of Anglo and Mexican national settlers in the region. He had been pardoned.

Edwards turned from Chireno to the newcomer. His voice was deep with excitement. "Dolpg, they have fought the soldiers down on the coast. They have won."

Before Sterne could respond Chireno said, "They have won nothing. But there is trouble for us."

"Nothing!" Edwards rounded on him. "Driving the troops from Velasco is nothing? And at Anahuac—"

"Papa!" Thorn cut him off, raising his hands in a plea. "Later, please. Our time is short. Come, let's sit here around the table. Help yourselves to the brandy, gentlemen."

Sterne took a seat, and looked around at the others. "I guess I miss something. Tell me about it."

"*En la noche un hombre Americano dizó. . .*" Chireno

56

began in Spanish, then noticed Edwards's frown. "Pardon, *Don* Haden. This morning, *Don* Adolphus, an American coming through from the west brought word of fighting at Velasco. The Brazoria militia has taken the fort there, and evicted Colonel Ugartechea's command."

"Velasco?" Sterne's eyes widened. "I thought the trouble was at Anahuac. Bradburn—"

"It is all the same trouble. The militia from Liberty began it. The militia at Brazoria continued it."

"And what of Anahuac?"

Chireno looked to Thorn. He spread his hands on the oak table. "We don't know all of it yet, Dolph. The settlers there laid siege to the fort, and Colonel Piedras went south from here with fifty men. I have a copy of resolutions drawn at Turtle Bayou. They say they are fighting Bradburn, not Mexico. And they declare themselves for Santa Anna and against Bustamente."

"Ah. *Santanistas* are flowering in Texas."

"Liberals have always had strength in Texas," Edwards declared. "Though some of us have been a little cautious about declaring ourselves." He cast a pointed glare at his son-in-law.

"Why invite trouble, Papa? You know Piedras's feelings on the subject."

"What more can he do?" Edwards wasn't finished. "Turn his *presidarios* loose to roam the streets and steal us blind? He's already done that. Hire civilian agents to harass us? Like Pinada . . . and Anton Moro? What more?"

"Patience, Papa, please. There's more to tell. Dolph, we learned also this morning that before he left here Piedras sent Anton Moro north to the Cherokee."

The color drained from Sterne's face, and Edwards's too. The old man hadn't heard that part of it. "Why, he *is* crazy!"

"How do you know this?" Sterne asked.

Chireno answered him. "*El Alguazil* . . . the sheriff from Ayes Bayou, he learned it. He told us."

"Horton? He is a *yonker,* though. Is he sure?"

57

Thorn smiled gently. "When you were twenty-two years old, Dolph, were you sure?"

Sterne paused. *"Ja.* I would be sure. And correct."

"Very well. We know Moro has gone to the Cherokee." Chireno accepted the brandy urn from Thorn. *"Gracias, amigo.* And knowing the mind of our colonel, we can deduce why he has gone there. Do we agree?" He looked at Sterne.

"Of course. The colonel has convinced himself we are all traitors. *Santanistas* or worse. Maybe he thinks we are all conspiring with *Herr* Jackson to add Texas to the United States. For whatever reason, he is enlisting the Indians."

"I agree," Thorn said.

Edwards nodded. "And I. And if he gets those savages started, there won't be a civilized person left alive in East Texas by the end of a month."

"Diwali's people aren't savages, Papa."

"Maybe not, but they are not like us. In my own family, we have lost people to the Shawnee."

"That was the Shawnee, Papa, not the Cherokee."

Edwards glared at him. "And who was it the Shawnee always feared? It was the Cherokee. Don't forget that."

"Besides," Chireno said, supporting Edwards now, "in Texas they are becoming one. They would ally if necessary."

"The point is, we have a serious problem," Thorn said, interrupting them. "Will Goyens and I are going north, to see Diwali. I have sent word, asking that Colonel Bean join us. I think Diwali will listen to us, if Moro has not yet forced a decision."

"And if he has?" Chireno frowned.

"Then we had better prepare to defend ourselves, because they will come. Piedras may incite them, but he will never control them. Think of Egg leading warriors down upon us."

Chireno made the sign of the cross.

"We must convene the *Ayuntamiento,*" he told Sterne. "Send word to all our people, they must look to their guns, keep their families close, be prepared to flee if necessary."

58

"The militia?"

"*Sí,* we should have the militia at the ready."

"At the ready, hell," Edwards said. "Call them to arms."

"Papa," Thorn said, "if Piedras comes back from Anahuac and finds militia assembled here, we will have a war on our hands. He won't ask questions."

Edwards dipped his head. "At the ready then."

"I suggest one other thing," Thorn said, standing. "When Piedras returns he will see us all as *Santanistas,* whether we have declared or not. I think we have no choice. I believe Santa Anna will win in Mexico, and if we have Piedras to contend with, I'd prefer to have Santa Anna on my side. I am ready to declare for the general. I suggest you all consider it."

"Good!" Edwards snorted.

Chireno frowned. "The *Ayuntamiento* has agreed to remain neutral."

"The revolution had not reached Texas then, *Don* Encarnaction. Now it has."

Adolphus Sterne pursed his lips. "I have been once on the wrong side in Mexico . . . as have others." He glanced at Edwards, who looked away. "Maybe next time we would not be so fortunate."

"It is a suggestion," Thorn said. He crossed to the door. "You may want to discuss it further."

When he was gone, the *Alcalde* spread his hands on the table. "Sometimes I feel very lonely, *señores.* We tell ourselves that our families are secure, that we live in a civilized place. Yet men like Piedras and Bradburn . . . and Moro . . . are among us while our government is so very far away."

"Farther the better," Edwards stated.

Sterne chuckled. "There is another of our problems. The Anglo can't live with government and the Spaniard can't live without it. Yet in Texas we are both."

"Some of us, *señor,*" Chireno said, challenging him.

"Of course." Sterne chuckled again. "But you see, I am more of both than the rest of you, because I am neither."

"Jewish wit before lunch, Dolph?" Edwards chided.

"I believe that was Prussian wit, *Herr* Edwards."

Edwards snorted. "There is no such thing."

"History will prove it," Frost Thorn told Susan as he packed provisions into a saddlebag. "The wisest of all tribes will have been the Scotch-Irish. They place their greatest distrust in their own governments, and are never wrong."

Susan scowled at him, not liking the irony that rang in his words. Frost was not a cynic by nature. Therefore, something was troubling him. She tapped a toe and folded her arms. "Do you realize that you're sounding just like Papa?"

"At times your father is right. I've even heard Chireno admit it."

"Oh, pooh! It isn't the government, it's only that strutting little Colonel Piedras. Frost, I do think you are making far too much of this. Piedras isn't the law here. The *Ayuntamiento* is the law. It's in our—"

"In our Constitution?" He turned from his packing and saw the quick realization in her. *"Querida mia,* there is no Constitution. That's what this is all about. President Bustamente has rescinded the Constitution. Piedras is Bustamente's man. And Piedras is in command in East Texas."

At the flicker of fear in her soft eyes, Thorn cursed himself. There was little he could keep from Susan Edwards Thorn. Whatever was news, she learned almost as quickly as he did. Through Papa Edwards, Chireno's wife, and others, she kept well abreast of what was going on in the world around her. She had a quick mind, and she was a practiced listener. But she was, still in all, a woman, and he did his best to protect her from the cold realities of life. A very few times in their life together he had seen tears in her eyes. He wanted never to see them there again.

He had told her nothing at all about Piedras sending Anton Moro to see the Cherokee, and he hoped no one else would either. Papa Edwards, he thought, for once in your

60

life, keep your mouth shut.

Jaren's voice came through the open door. "Mistah Thorn, Mistah Goyens is here waitin' for you. You 'bout ready?"

"Coming," he called, then turned back to his wife. "Please don't worry, Susan. I should be back in just a few days. Do as I said, stay close to home. If anything should occur that might be uncomfortable, you might want to go to Ayish. If so, I'll come for you there as soon as I return." He gave her a quick kiss, turned to reach for his pack, then turned back and caught her up in his arms and kissed her again, fervently. "Ah," he whispered. "It gets lonely out there on those trails."

She blushed, then held tightly to him for a moment. When they parted, he smiled cheerfully at her. "And you be a good girl while I'm gone. If there's lechery in my house, I aim to be the culprit."

Then he was gone, and she watched from the shadows beside a window as he mounted his horse, spoke to Will Goyens, and rode away, Jaren following behind on his favorite mule.

She was glad he hadn't seen the moisture that sprang to her eyes as he left. A man with much on his mind didn't need to be burdened by a weeping woman too. A little later, she decided, she must go and visit with Candida Chireno. Susan Thorn knew her husband well enough to know he had not told her all of what concerned him. She also knew that in order to prepare for trouble, she must know what kind of trouble it might be.

CHAPTER VI

"I think it is foolish to fight the yonegs. *What use is a warrior's death if no one remains to mourn him?"*
— Chief Diwali (the Bowl)

Three villages, spaced along two miles of creekfront, made up the Texas homesite of the people called Ani-Tsalagi, who thought of themselves as the Aniyunwiya — the principal people. To their Anglo and Mexican neighbors to the south, they were the Cherokee. To their copper-skinned neighbors in all directions, they were the respected — and sometimes feared — *encenches,* the leaders of the Indian confederation in East Texas.

Because he was principal chief of the principal people, Diwali — the Bowl — lived in the central and largest of the villages where his son, John Bowles, was leader. Diwali and the peace chief Gatunwali, known as Big Mush, and their families were among more than three hundred people in the central village. On their flanks, a mile or so away, were the upper village where Osoota was chief, and the lower village commanded by Nicolet. Most of the families of the tribe lived in these three villages. A few, and many of the unmarried young men, resided much of the time in more isolated small villages and camps scattered throughout the tribe's extensive landholdings. The outermost ring of these camps — long days from the three villages — formed a defense perimeter around the little nation, and many of the young men wishing to establish themselves as warriors gravitated to these, for it was there that enemies could sometimes be encountered. It was as near to a time of peace as any of the people could remember, but there were always enemies. Osages raided into Texas from the north. Untamed Kickapoos and Choctaws sometimes dared a raid on a Cherokee outpost. And to the east, beyond the river called Sabine, were savages. They were white-skinned and ruthless, and would as soon kill a man as kill a deer.

There was a reason why Diwali, now seventy-six years old, was war chief and principal chief of the Texas Cherokee, and why the Mexican government had put him in nominal charge of all the Indians in East Texas. He was wise in the ways of people. In the fourteen years since he had led his people into the Spanish lands there had been incidents of bloodshed, but never once had the Cherokee been found guilty of starting it.

Of all the forces in East Texas in 1832, the strongest by far was the Cherokee nation. Small in number, they were yet the most feared among their red cousins. And Diwali knew that, while he could count on only four hundred Cherokee warriors, should the time ever come that he had to confront the Mexicans or the Anglos—or both—he would win the early battles, for those four hundred Cherokee warriors might each lead a company of Shawnees, Caddos, Koasatis, Alabamas, and others, and the assembled army would number nearly five thousand strong.

Were the Cherokees to take up arms against their brown and white neighbors, there would soon be none but Indians left in Texas. And Diwali knew that would be the beginning of the end for his people. They would win the battles, but they would lose the war. The Mexicans might be defeated, for a time. The Anglos would not be. Without Mexico in Texas, those white border savages would stream in by the thousands. Diwali knew. It was he who had led the Aniyunwiya from their home in Tennessee in 1794, to escape annihilation by just such savages. And after Texas, there was nowhere else to go.

On a hot summer afternoon Diwali stood tall and solemn

before his lodge and watched the activity of his village around him. Long gray hair hung loose across shoulders which still swelled with the power of a much younger man. Nor had age dimmed at all those piercing blue eyes which many white men found so disconcerting. In his youth, in the old lands to the east, some had called him Dah-tsi. It meant Dutch.

He had been told that white men were coming in from the south, through the forest, and had estimated from the report when they would arrive. Now he glanced occasionally at the clearing across the stream, where trails converged. Near the bank of the stream, a group of women washed clothing in heated tubs. Children played tag around and among them. Two tall men, full warriors in rank, trudged up from the stream carrying a kettle suspended from a stout pole. A tiny, wizened woman walked with them, chattering in irritation at their slowness. The men's faces were impassive masks, but at one particularly vitriolic outburst by the crone, Diwali saw their eyes turn toward each other. A faint smile touched the old chief's face. Were Nanyehi not such a revered old mother among the people, she would long since have been tossed into the creek to cool her temper.

He glanced again at the clearing across the way, and saw a white man on a tired horse, coming out of the wood there. Diwali shrugged. It was only Willoughby. At the stream the white man dismounted, waded across leading his mount, and stopped to talk for a moment with some of the women there. One of them gestured, and Willoughby looked up the hill and saw Diwali. Rifle across his arm, leading his head-down horse, he started up the hill.

At the chief's lodge he stopped and raised a hand. *"Osiyo,* Diwali," he said respectfully. *"Tsi-ta yage'i Aniyun-wiya."*

Diwali noted that there was barely a trace of alien accent to Willoughby's speech. Though he himself, as a matter of principle, had refused ever to learn any language except his own, he admired others who handled tongues well.

" 'Siyo, Willoughby. You know you are always welcome among the Tsalagi. Do you come to trade?" He noticed that the man's usual string of laden mules was missing.

"This time I have nothing to trade. I have had a misfortune, and my wares now belong to six Kickapoos."

Diwali looked solemnly at the man's belt. "I see no Kickapoo scalps hanging at your side, Willoughby."

"I am fortunate, *Ani-ghtahi,* to still have my own. If any of your warriors should come across six Kickapoos with mules, please tell them I would consider buying them again—the mules, I mean. Not the Kickapoos. You can keep the Kickapoos."

The white man's expression was so gloomy that Diwali could not help smiling. "I will tell them, Willoughby. But since you are not here to trade, then you must be here just to renew acquaintances among your friends. I believe"— he pointed to his left, up the hill—"that you might find the maiden Udali among those grinding corn yonder by the longhouse."

Willoughby flushed. The old man obviously didn't miss a thing.

"My house is yours, Willoughby," Diwali said formally, ending the conversation before his guest's embarrassment became severe. "There is food in the pot whenever you wish it."

"My thanks, Diwali. *Dona'dagohui.*"

"Yes, we will see each other again."

As he turned away, Willoughby circled Diwali's lodge and went on up the hill in a direction diagonally away from the longhouse where Udali was grinding corn. Diwali noticed this and smiled, the fleeting twitch of cheeks that was his nearest approach to mirth. He liked Willoughby, and suspected that the young man was not nearly so harmless nor predictable as he always seemed. Another white man, heading for the longhouse, would have set his course in that direction. Not Willoughby. He would go the long way around. But when he arrived there, he would know the lay of the land. It was a thing an Indian would do.

Some distance away Diwali's son, John Bowles, squatted with several other men around a stretched hide that they were using as a table. They were cleaning and repairing a case of flintlock rifles John Bowles had got in trade from one of the *presidarios* at the Nacogdoches fort. The *presidario,* he knew, had stolen them from someone. Diwali well understood the resentment Anglo and Mexican settlers felt for the convict-soldiers who made up a part of Colonel Piedras's garrison. They would steal anything that wasn't nailed down, even from their own people. And he suspected they would be worthless in battle.

He knew what he would do should he ever have such men in his own command. He would single them out, form them into a company with one of themselves as leader, and send them north to raid the Ani-wasasi—the Osages. He would not expect any of them to come back.

John Bowles approached him now, carrying one of the rifles.

"Three of the lot have broken springs. We will need parts to fix them. What did Willoughby bring?"

"Nothing but a dreaming heart and a curious eye. He has looked upon the Cutter's daughter, Udali."

John Bowles nodded. "That, then, explains the dreaming heart. What of the curious eye?"

"I believe he is scouting us. There is something he wants to know but does not ask."

John Bowles pondered this. A younger, stockier version of his tall father, he was a man of note among the Aniyunwiya. It was said that when Diwali laid down the fan of seven eagle feathers, John Bowles would be chosen to pick it up.

"When men scout new grounds," Diwali said, "it is because they expect to find game or enemies there. Willoughby would not scout the Aniyunwiya for game. He knows what we have to trade. Therefore he seeks sign of enemies."

"Moro," John Bowles grunted. "Moro has been here seeking our help for the soldier, Piedras."

"Dohiyu'i. Piedras would turn the Tsalagi against the Anglos."

"It would be a very bad thing for the Anglos."

"When Moro left, where did he go?"

"South." John Bowles pointed. "Off the trails, into the forest."

Diwali lifted his head and looked around him, scanning the blue skies beyond the treetops. "White man trouble," he said absently. "There is a smell of it in the winds."

"The Aniyunwiya can avoid it or use it, as we choose."

"Hohwah. Provided the Aniyunwiya remain very wise."

"Some are, as always," John Bowles said respectfully. "Some others are young and seek glory. I can well remember."

"And I. Let us begin a count of our young men, my son. It is well to know where the young warriors are when white men are in conflict."

"Where is Gu'nasoquo? Where he goes, young ones follow."

"He is here, or in the upper village. No, I think there are no war parties now. But let us begin to keep a count."

Across the brow of the hill Coop Willoughby made his way to the area of houses that was the Wolf-people clan center, unsaddled his tired mount, and led it into a community corral with the clan's stock. Several people were around, and one man came over to him and raised a hand. " *'Siyo,* Willoughby."

" *'Siyo,* Utsada," he responded, and then in English, "How's the hunting?"

"Been good. Lotta deer now, turkey sometimes. You tradin'?" Utsada was a muscular man of thirty-five or forty. They had become acquainted two years before, soon after Willoughby came into Texas from Arkansas. They had been hunting, separately, and had both picked the same deer for supper. Utsada had been stalking it, and it browsed into a clearing where Willoughby lay in wait. He had shot it, Utsada had claimed it, and for a time it had looked like war. Then Willoughby had spoken in Cherokee, Utsada had answered in broken English, and they had wound up sharing fresh backstrap and biscuits over an evening fire and getting acquainted. It was Utsada who had introduced Willoughby into the Cherokee town the first time he visited there. Utsada took great pride in calling himself an *unega-dihi,* but Willoughby didn't know just when or where the friendly warrior had become a white-man-killer.

"Just visiting," Willoughby told him. "I got a little eastern tea here. You want some?"

Utsada's eyes lit up. "My fire." He pointed.

Willoughby's "little tea" was barely enough for the crowd that gathered around Utsada's fire. Tea, one of the items heavily taxed by the Mexican government, was a real treat among those of the Cherokee who had a taste for it. They had less access to casual smugglers like Willoughby than did the Anglos.

Ganososa-sdi, the Broom, an older man, wandered over from his own house. Edahi showed up from somewhere, and prankish Tenuto appeared. By the time the tea was brewed more than a dozen cups were waiting. As the sun crept downward in its arc Cooper Willoughby sat on the ground with a ring of half-naked savages and drank tea, smoked cigars, and traded gossip. In less than an hour he learned everything Alexander Horton had sent him for, and he made a mental note that Horton owed him a supply of tea and cigars.

The hulking Basque, Moro, had been around for several days, arguing, talking, sometimes threatening, making promises, drifting around with various groups of young, unblooded warriors. He'd told them that the government was in grave danger from Anglo outlaws along the border and in Nacogdoches. He'd said the army would need the help of its Cherokee friends. To the chiefs and elders he'd promised that the little colonel, Piedras, would get them title to their lands from the government. To the warriors among them he'd talked of strengthening the Cherokee nation. And to the young braves he'd promised glory in battle.

Utsada was frank in his appraisal: "I think Moro promises too many things too easy." Some of the others nodded, and one or two expressed contempt for the man, clouded by uneasiness. They considered Moro "touched by the shadow." Some, Willoughby noticed, withheld their opinions.

No deals had been made. The chiefs had remained aloof. Most of the clan leaders and ranking warriors were little interested in getting involved in white men's disputes, and most had little regard for Piedras—or Moro either, for that matter. Some of the young, though, might take up the war club if a chance for glory were offered. Who could say?

Moro had left, traveling south.

Through it all, Willoughby kept his eyes open for Atasi, Mistletoe's brother. Finally he inquired about him.

"Atasi is in his hut." Utsada gestured casually. "Damnfool Injun sat on a copperhead. Got a sore butt on him you bet." He said it again in Cherokee and the others rocked with laughter.

When the tea was gone the party broke up. Willoughby went across to Atasi's house and peered inside. His friend lay face down on a bearskin mat, propped up with straw so that his naked rear end was elevated. Willoughby whistled. That was as sore a posterior as he had ever seen.

An old woman mixing poultice in the shadows—a healer named Groundhog's Mother—waved an imperious hand at him. "Atasi sleeps," she said. "Go away."

"Will Atasi heal, Mother?"

"Yes," she scowled. "If no more curious people come to look at his great misfortune, he will heal in time. You go away."

He went away, disappointed. He had planned to get Atasi to walk with him over to the longhouse, where he could just happen to run across Udali. Then Atasi could go on his way, and maybe Udali would walk with him out through the evening forest to hear the night-birds sing. It was the way of Indians to go to great pains to make such encounters casual, particularly when no family arrangements had been made. Willoughby had lost his arrangement wherewithal to the Kickapoos.

Time was limited, however, so he shrugged and headed straight across to the town house. This was a busy part of the village. The house itself measured more than sixty feet in length and served as a combination community hall, dance house, place for sacred relics, guest house, and council room. The area around it was cleared except for one huge oak tree thirty paces beyond, which was known as Diwali's tree because the chief favored it over others in the village.

In the shade of the tree, a number of women were preparing corn and meat for storage. Mistletoe saw him as he rounded the corner of the town house, and dropped what she was doing.

"Willow-bee!" Her greeting rang across the clearing like tones from a silver bell, and those within earshot looked up. Braves grinned and women giggled, and Udali, little Mistletoe, flew to him and locked her arms around his neck. Willoughby was stunned.

In a glance he could see a dozen coppery faces grinning in his direction, and as many more turned away, pretending not to notice his welcome. He heard laughter behind him, and turned to find most of his tea-drinking friends from Utsada's fire looking on. They had followed him. Through it all Udali was straining on tiptoe to croon endearments into his ear.

With the determination of surprise Willoughby managed to unlock her from his neck and hold her off at arm's length.

"Udali," he began, *"idigoti'a,* ah, *nia wadali a—"*

"No, Willow-bee." She put a small, firm finger to his lips. "We speak you and I in *yonega,* white-man-speak, now. You see, I learn. You come too soon, is good. Day is good for you come . . . I make most robe from *a'wi-anida* to you one time . . ."

70

With great patience he let the chatter run on until she stopped for a breath and then said, in Cherokee, "Mistletoe, I don't understand what you're saying. Tell me in Tsalagi."

An instant of disappointment clouded her bright eyes, then was washed aside by a greater enthusiasm.

"I must learn the white speech more," she declared. "A woman should speak her husband's tongue."

For a moment all Willoughby could do was stare into those great dark eyes and think disjointed thoughts. He felt like a man walking into the third act of a play. Somewhere along the line he had missed something.

From behind him a deep voice rumbled, " 'Siyo, Willoughby. *Dho hitsu?*"

In a fog he said, *"Dho, higawo,* I am fine." He turned and was brought back to quick awareness by the sight of a massive bare chest before his eyes. Many of the Cherokee men were tall but none as tall as Egg. Most of the warriors were muscular, but none were as broadly corded as the warrior who stood here now, beaming hugely down upon the astonished white man. Directly behind Egg was Dita-staye-sgi, the Cutter, Mistletoe's father, looking extremely sour.

"Oh, God," Willoughby breathed, though none who might have heard him understood him. A hand the size of a small ham came forward and he tensed, then realized that Egg was waiting for him to shake hands. His good right hand was swallowed by the large red one and Willoughby felt his bones grind as the Indian squeezed playfully. Determination knotting his jaw he squeezed back, and saw Egg's eyes widen.

"Ai, Willoughby, you are a good man. One day we will wrestle, you and I. But not now. Diwali has called council. There are visitors here." The great hand withdrew, then descended upon his shoulder blades in a friendly slap that staggered him. Egg strode away toward the longhouse. Dita-staye-sgi stepped up and stuck out a hand. He looked as though he had eaten spoiled meat.

71

"Welcome to the Cutter's fireside, Willoughby," he said, reluctantly. He shook hands solemnly, then trailed off after Egg. Others around also were heading for the longhouse, and Willoughby saw Diwali and some others walking up the hill accompanied by Frost Thorn, Will Goyens, and the dark, uniformed figure of Peter Ellis Bean, green tunic replete with the insignia of a full colonel of Mexico and the beaded badge of Indian agent swinging at his breast. Diwali, he noted, was also wearing his "colonel coat," and carried his turtle-shell staff. It was a formal occasion.

For a moment Willoughby and Mistletoe were left alone, standing there in the shade of Diwali's tree. Udali had not once taken her eyes from Willoughby, and they shone with a happy glow.

"Udali, please tell me what this is all about."

She glanced toward the longhouse. "Diwali has called council for the people, to speak with Bean and the other *asgaya'unega.*"

"I don't mean that! What is this about, this welcome?"

Her eyes lit again, as she realized he didn't know what everyone else knew, and she stepped forward and locked her arms around his chest.

"Oh, Willow-bee, A's-gayaga-lulati, Man Above, has smiled upon you and me. Nanitsa my mother has said she will accept your gift. At first my father Dita-staye-sgi would not agree, but my mother sent me away and talked with him." She giggled, white teeth flashing in her wide, elfin face. "I think everyone in the village heard her talk with him. Nanitsa talks better and louder than my father Dita-staye-sgi. After a while she called me back and my father said he would allow my mother to receive your gift for me. Oh, Willow-bee, I am so happy."

Willoughby was shaking his head, slowly. "What gift?" he asked. "How did they know of a gift?"

"Utsada," she told him, pointing. "Utsada is a great friend of you, Willow-bee. He told Nanitsa my mother that you were coming with a gift, and that since you are *asgaya yonega,* that meant that you would marry me."

72

"But . . ." he stammered, his heart sinking within him. "How did Utsada know I brought a gift?"

"Oh, Willow-bee," she scolded gently, "don't you know Utsada keeps his ears and his eyes to you? He has since first you came to the Aniyunwiya. Utsada says now that you are his friend he is both *unegadihi* and *unega-dohviatsi*. He thinks it is very good to be both a white-man-killer and a white-man-protector.

"Utsada told Nanitsa my mother that you told Ben Burch you were bringing a gift and Ben Burch told John Tree and John Tree told the Shawani Tetsuma and Tetsuma told him. That's what Utsada told Nanitsa."

With his heart thudding in his breast Coop Willoughby let the words flow across him. He stood with his hands liked with those of Udali and let himself be dazzled by the beauty of her, the bubbling enthusiasm of her, the sureness of her that now he was here all things were right.

But in her lodge across the way, near Atasi's house, he knew Nanitsa sat waiting for a gift — the formal gift that, as she understood his ways, was the token for which she would bequeath to him her daughter.

And he had no gift to bring.

The Kickapoo had taken Nanitsa's fine linen.

From the front of the longhouse to the copse of dogwood and peppervine jutting from heavy forest beyond the creek was a distance of nearly three hundred yards. But the man crouched there was expert with the long rifle and knew what he could do.

With the patience of a hunter he crouched motionless through the long hours of afternoon, waiting. Indian women and children passed within yards of him and saw nothing. A party of braves stood in the clearing fifty feet from him for long minutes, while he breathed slowly through his mouth to make no sound. In his rifle was a measured ninety-five grains' weight of powder behind a carefully patched 50-caliber ball. The frizzen was down over a charge of fine powder in the pan, and the hammer was on half cock.

He tensed as old Diwali stepped from his house on the face of the hill across the way and folded his arms in the sun. The rifle had come up. But then two braves and an old woman wandered across his line, coming toward the creek, directly toward him.

The man in the brush waited.

CHAPTER VII

"Fredonia was nothing . . . a comedy of fools.
But look at the mess it left behind it."
— Peter Ellis Bean

Peter Ellis Bean was only seventeen years old when he came to Texas with Philip Nolan in the year 1800, and only eighteen when he went to prison with the survivors of the Nolan expedition. He was twenty-one when his case came to trial in Chihuahua. He was twenty-eight at the time the rebellion of Jose Maria Morelos threatened Spanish Acapulco. The Spanish freed him with the understanding that he would fight.

He did. He escaped from the Spanish and fought for Morelos. He was there when Acapulco fell, and was made a colonel in the rebel army. Now, at age forty-nine, he was twice a veteran of Spanish Mexican revolutions, had fought with Jackson at the Battle of New Orleans, had wives and families in both Jalapa and Texas, was a full colonel of Mexico and official Indian agent for East Texas.

No one in Texas was indifferent toward Peter Ellis Bean. Some hated him, some loved him, many feared him, and most respected him. He was stocky and tough, and wore his black hair cut in the manner of a Spanish gentleman. When he put on his uniform he appeared far more Mexican than Anglo.

He and two of his sons were waiting at the Neches Trace crossing when Goyens and Thorn arrived there from Nacogdoches, followed by Jaren on a heavily packed mule. Samuel Bean was already taller than his father. Eleven-year-old Isaac would be, one day. When the party came around the base of a bluff and into the cleared crossing, all three Beans had their rifles at the ready. They had heard them coming.

The elder Bean lowered his rifle and favored them with a scowl. "Anybody else sent me a message and said 'God and Liberty,' I'd have ignored it. I got corn a-tasselin' and hogs to butcher, and I'm shorthanded at the mill."

Thorn smiled faintly. "But I see you're wearing your uniform, so I guess you know where we need to go."

"To the Cherokee, I reckon. What I don't know is why."

"Do you know Anton Moro, Ellis?"

Bean's nose lifted in distaste. "I know of him. He's a thief and a murderer."

"And I guess you know about the incident at Anahuac, and that Piedras went down there."

"Heard he took some Shawnee with him. I'm of a mind to roast his butt for that."

"Well, that isn't the worst of it. You heard about Velasco?"

Bean nodded. It wasn't a thing he would have missed. "Piedras will be spittin' nails when he comes back. He thinks most everybody in Texas is traitors as it is."

"Well, he couldn't have heard about Velasco before he left Nacogdoches. The word just came in. But he sent Anton Moro up to see the Cherokee."

Bean stared at him, not wanting to understand. Yet he did. Like his president, Bustamente—like so many of the powerful in Mexico—Colonel Piedras believed in the principle of rule or ruin . . . control at any cost. And like so many of the powers in Mexico, he failed to understand his subjects. To provoke the Indians as an instrument against the Anglos would be like turning a tiger loose in one's house to control mice.

"Are you sure?"

Thorn nodded. "As sure as we can be. Are you with us, Ellis?"

Bean turned to his sons. "Samuel, get the horses. Isaac,

pack up our possibles."

They camped that night on Morales Creek, and reach⌐ ⌐
the Cherokee villages the following afternoon. As they
crossed the stream to dismount and leave their horses with
Jaren, Goyens pointed toward the longhouse in the distance. "Willoughby is here," he said.

Bean stepped down from his horse and looked around,
frowning. "Damned if I don't have a itchy feeling! Like
somebody was lookin' at me down a gun barrel."

In the copse beyond the stream, the man named Moro
waited. He had one thing in mind now, and it wasn't just
for Piedras that he would act. His time had been wasted.
Piedras had wasted it with his instructions that Moro was
to go among the savages and talk. It did no good to talk to
Indians. It was a waste of time. Diwali had wasted his time,
letting him spend days among the red men when he knew
all along that he was not going to agree to support Piedras.
They had all wasted his time.

Now he would do things his way. The irritation that had
grown in him was a cold fire and he used its energies to fuel
the massive patience of the forest hunter. For hours he had
been here, and several times had held the old chief in his
sights, but always there were others in the way, or other
Indians too near to his own hiding place for him to escape
after the shot was fired. But the opportunity would come.
He waited.

He saw Cooper Willoughby emerge from the forest off
to his left and walk up the hill toward Diwali. Behind him
two warriors emerged and stood, watching the conversation. They were too close. He waited.

He watched as John Bowles and his father talked, and
brought his sights to bear again, tensing. But the warriors
south of the stream were still lurking about somewhere,
near at hand. He waited.

Then Diwali had gone off with John Bowles, out of
sight. The man in the copse cursed under his breath, but

made no move. After a while there was commotion off to the left, and riders emerged on the main trail. He recognized Frost Thorn and Ellis Bean, then the *hombre negro,* Will Goyens, followed by two youngsters on saddle horses — Bean's sons. After them came a black slave on a laden mule. They crossed the creek, dismounted and walked up the hill, all but the Negro slave, who stayed with his mule by the creek and held the others' horses. Diwali reappeared above them, coming from his bread-loaf house with Big Mush at his heels. But now the Negro was in the line of fire.

There was conversation up there. Moro saw Diwali signal to some of his young warriors, who set off in various directions. A council was being called. A crowd began to gather near the longhouse. The man in the copse shifted slightly and laid his rifle across a low dogwood limb. The light would fail soon. He held his sights on the longhouse door.

A knot of people was gathering there, but it parted slightly as the chief approached, and then he saw Diwali step ahead, separate for a moment from those with him.

He took a deep breath, held it, steadied his rifle, eased the blade sight down into the rear buckeye notch, and found Diwali's back as another Indian stepped forward to say something to the chief. Hammer on full cock, he sighted on Diwali and touched the trigger. The rifle bucked and roared and white smoke blocked his view. Anton Moro scurried backward out of the thicket. Then without looking back, he turned and ran.

Diwali and old Gatunwali, the peace chief, known as Big Mush, met their guests on the hillside in front of Diwali's house. The greetings were cordial. All three of the white men were valued friends among the Tsalagi, and two of them were regular customers for trade. They considered Will Goyens white, for he surely was not red.

"It must be a great occasion when three such as you come

together to visit the *Aniyunwiya*." Gatunwali peered at them, one by one. His aged, hunched figure was a shadow of the tall old war chief beside him, but his dark eyes shone with intuition. *"Ghal'tsodeh.* Welcome to you."

"It is an occasion," Bean told him, "but not a pleasant one. We wish to speak with the Ani-Tsalagi in council."

Diwali nodded, raised his hand, and several young warriors hurried to him. "Call a council of the people," he told them. "We will have talk in the longhouse."

Called by Diwali's runners, people already were gathering in front of the community house—men and women alike. The chiefs and their *aniyonega* visitors trudged up the hill, pacing their steps to the labored progress of Gatunwali. The old peace chief was well past eighty years, and crippled by illness.

Ellis Bean walked beside Diwali, in the lead. Each of them wore the tunic of a Mexican colonel.

"It is said that Colonel Piedras sent his agent to speak to the Tsalagi of war," Bean said.

"Anton Moro has been here. He spoke of many things. He is not here now."

"Did the Ani-Tsalagi meet with him in council?"

Diwali looked down at him, his blue eyes piercing. Still, Bean thought, there was a trace of humor there. "Moro requested a council of the people," the chief said. "He requested it in the name of Colonel Piedras. I said to Moro that I will call a council for Piedras when Piedras is here, not when he is not."

Thorn and Goyens glanced at each other, exchanging sighs of relief. Whatever damage Moro might have done, he had not fooled the principal chief of the Cherokee. Diwali had held the upper hand.

At the longhouse door a cluster of people drew back to let them pass, several addressing the chiefs as they went by. A stocky warrior of middle years stepped in behind Diwali, started to say something, then straightened suddenly, a look of agony on his face. From somewhere near the creek or beyond came the crack of a rifle. Utsada, the *yonega-*

dihi, gasped an incoherent word and toppled to the ground.

Shocked faces turned toward the stream, where a drift of white smoke hung in the summer air. Abruptly the giant Egg was among them, towering over the rest. In one swift motion he wrenched Ellis Bean's rifle from his hand, raised it, and fired toward the smoke. Then a double file of armed warriors was streaming down the hill, toward the creek.

An old woman pushed through the crowd and knelt beside Utsada. She looked up and spoke, then rapped her stick sharply across the shins of several men within reach. "You," she commanded. "And you. Help Utsada. Bring a litter and carry him to his house."

Utsada lay still, bleeding from a hole in his back. Nanyehi grabbed the breechclout of a warrior hurrying past and ripped it from him, leaving him naked and pained as he raced away down the hill. She sniffed at the garment, wrinkled her nose, then wadded a corner of it and thrust it into the bullet hole.

Willoughby and Udali pushed through the crowd and Nanyehi frowned. "Udali, go and fetch Groundhog's Mother. And you, *yoneg,* stay out of the way."

Willoughby stared in shock at the still form on the ground. Utsada. A friend. He turned to stare after the line of Indians disappearing into the brush beyond the creek, anger welling as he reviewed—coldly—the lay of the land beyond. A moment, then he ran after them, angling to the left. When he entered the brush he was fifty yards east of where the warriors had entered.

Gatunwali had been hustled into the shelter of the long house. Diwali herded his guests in, then turned to watch his warriors streaming down the hill, his eyes bleak with the knowledge that he was too old to go with them. When the litter came for Utsada, Nanyehi and Agana-unitsi— Groundhog's Mother—supervised the loading. The old chief still stood there, his eyes on the distant forest.

They returned by twos and threes as evening settled over the piney woods, and eventually Diwali's council began. The longhouse was packed and hot. Men and women of all ages were there, for among the *Aniyunwiya* all had a voice and a vote in council. And except for certain emergency situations, a decision made in council was binding only upon those present in council when it was made. Nothing in Tsalagi law gave anyone the right to decide for anyone else. Such a thing was unthinkable.

Egg was missing, and some other warriors. Some were still out looking for the one who had shot Utsada. Some, apparently, simply chose not to attend.

When those who would come were assembled, with Bean, Thorn, and Goyens in the place of honor, Diwali stood and invoked A's-gayaga-lulati to hear what would be said. When people speak, gods should listen.

Some who were present were late arrivals, from the neighboring villages, and there was much to tell among them. Utsada was gravely hurt, Nanyehi said. He was in his house, surrounded by his wife and children, with clansmen smoking pipes at each end of the house to ward off *tsgilis* and other bad things. The young shaman Kanuga was there as well, but most of the tending of Utsada was by Ground-hog's Mother, who knew the remedies for most things.

Would he live?

Nanyehi lowered her eyes. Who could say?

Some of those who had gone into the forest and returned verified now that it was a white man—a *yoneg*—who had fired the shot. They had found the place where he had waited. He had been there for a long time. They had found where he had left his horse, and some who were expert at such things had examined its tracks, its graze patterns, and its excrement. It was not a horse that they could identify, though it was an unusually fine horse, shod in the manner of a racer. It had gone south. Also, it was a bay.

"Your people may not find him then," Will Goyens said, speaking softly to Diwali. "With a good horse under him, he can get past the Camino Real. After that he might go anywhere."

"Some greener, probably," Bean decided. "Some murderous skunk havin' a little sport." He said it in English and

81

Diwali did not understand, but that didn't matter. The chief was looking at Goyens, thoughtfully, something like intuition in his strange blue eyes, and Goyens felt the hackles rise on his neck. Someone had told him once that Diwali was called Dah-tsi because of those eyes. But seeing him now, no one would call him Dutch. Those eyes were Indian.

"If I were the man who shot Utsada," the old chief said thinly, "I would worry most about Cooper Willoughby. He was here. He saw. He went and studied the forest, then came for his horse and left."

"Willoughby?"

"Sometimes a man is more than he seems," Diwali said. "Utsada is Willoughby's friend." The blue eyes looked past Goyens, seeing things far away. "If I were that man, I would also think of Egg."

Goyens shuddered, suddenly remembering that the giant Cherokee also had blue eyes.

When the general talk was done, Diwali raised his fan for silence. "We have visitors among us," he told his people. "Bean has asked for council."

Peter Ellis Bean looked around him at the seventy or more dark faces in the hot room. "There may be trouble again among the white men," he said. "The high chief in Mexico, Bustamente, has been challenged by General Santa Anna. Many soldiers are leaving Texas for the interior, to fight. Many of the white people in Texas support Santa Anna, and there has been trouble on the Brazos and at Anahuac. Many are afraid now that Colonel Piedras will punish the whites in East Texas because of this. The Ani-Tsalagi know Piedras. He carries his honor in his hat, not in his heart. We have heard that Piedras already has sent one among the Ani-Tsalagi to seek their help against their white neighbors. This would be a very bad thing. Brave men would die and women would weep, and only to gain glory for Piedras, nothing more. This is why we came here."

Dita-staye-sgi spoke then, from his place near the door. "We know of Bustamente. We do not know this Santa

Anna."

"Do you *know* Bustamente?" Bean asked. "Has anyone here smoked with him? Has he given the Tsalagi — or any of the Aniyunwiya — title to their lands?"

"He has promised."

"The Tsalagi are *anigtah'i*. Wise people. They know the differences between different promises."

Tenuto of the *aniwaya* clan raised a hand. "Bean has made promises to us. So too have Goyens and Thorn. Should we believe these?"

Will Goyens cast him a friendly glare. "I remember a time, Tenuto, when you promised fifty baskets of peas for a mule and a plow. When I received the peas, each basket was a hand-width less than full."

"I should have used smaller baskets." Tenuto shrugged.

Big Mush had been listening. Now he spoke and all strained to hear his words.

"We know of the trouble in the south. There is war. I have seen war many times. Each time the white men make war it seems they ask the Indian to take sides in it. Then when it is done, it is the Indian who has lost. I think the Tsalagi should ignore the white people and let them kill one another as long as they stay away from us."

He paused and Dita-staye-sgi interrupted, angrily. "When do they stay away from us? It was a white man's bullet that struck Utsada today, not two paces from the door of this house."

"Then we should do war upon that man," Gatunwali nodded. "But not upon all the whites."

"The white man knows that if the Tsalagi fight him the Tsalagi will win," Nanyehi said.

Bean turned to her. "And in winning, Mother, the Tsalagi would lose. We would all lose."

"Will our neighbors fight the soldiers?" Dita-staye-sgi asked.

Frost Thorn nodded, bleakly. "We may have to. It is not our wish, but Piedras may force it."

"And if the soldiers are driven away — as they were to the

south—what is to keep the Americans on the border from coming in?"

There was no answer to that, and Dita-staye-sgi grunted. He had made his point. There was more talk for a time, then Diwali raised his fan again. "Colonel Piedras has sent Moro among us to ask for help against the white settlers. Moro received no promises from the Tsalagi. But many of the young men seek a warrior's name. Some would fight for the high chief Bustamente. Some would fight for the general Santa Anna. Some just wish to fight . . . anybody. If the Tsalagi were to join the white men's fights, each man might face his clan brother's war club. For this reason I say, the people will take no side in this. It is not our affair.

"I tell you, though"—he nodded at the visitors—"if the white men fight in East Texas, expect to see young warriors there. They will decide, each for himself, what each will do. But the Ani-Tsalagi will have no part in it."

Dita-staye-sgi rose to his feet, angrily. "Does Diwali think it can be avoided?"

"I have said my words. Let the council decide."

There was muttering throughout the longhouse, and Dita-staye-sgi wrapped his cloak around him and strode out the door. Several others followed, but most remained. Diwali looked around. "So it is," he said.

Bean leaned close to Thorn to whisper, "Just so long as nothing else happens to change it."

CHAPTER VIII

"The worst kind of war is when both sides stand for 'God and Liberty.' "
— Vicente Cordova

Captain Francisco Medina, commander of the 12th Battalion, paused at his work when a knock came at his door. Brushing moist hair back from his brow he buttoned the collar of his tunic, arose from his chair, and stood behind the desk, his hands behind his back. "Enter," he called, and the door opened to admit a sergeant, Marcos Sanchez.

Sanchez saluted. "The men you asked for are here, *mi capitán*. But"—he lowered his voice—"they are not in very good condition. Somewhere they found tequila."

Medina frowned. "In the stockade?"

"Si, Capitán." The sergeant's shrug was eloquent. Both he and Medina knew the difficulties of maintaining order in a command that was half true soldiers and half *presidarios*—convict soldiers, the dregs of Mexico's prisons.

Medina shook his head. "Very well, Sergeant. Bring them in."

Sanchez stepped to the door, gestured, and then stood aside as two armed privates escorted a trio of slouching, averted-eyed prisoners into the room. Medina wrinkled his nose. The men stank. They were slovenly, unwashed, and smelled of alcohol.

"Attention!" Sanchez ordered, and they drew themselves up in a travesty of military discipline. Bareheaded, they did not salute.

"Mi capitán," Sanchez intoned formally, *"aqui estan Ruiz, Santos y Garcia, a sus ordenes."*

The captain stood for a long moment, looking from one to another of them. As always, faced with this element of the army of Mexico, he was shamed. The three men were not as drunk as they were trying to appear, and he let the silence build until each had raised his eyes to look at him. Two were sullen, obviously resentful of his authority. The third, a husky, hard-eyed man, gazed at him shrewdly with the look of a cornered wolf. Medina singled out this one.

"You, Ruiz," he said. "You and these others are charged with entering a private residence and stealing household goods. Do you have anything to say?"

"Si capitán." The man's tone was insinuating, his manner subtly mocking. "We have done nothing wrong. We have done nothing except what we were told."

"What you were told? Who told you to go into *Señor* Arredondo's house?"

"Why, *Capitán,* is it not understood that there is much contraband hidden in the houses in Nacogdoches? Are we of the army not charged with keeping the laws?" There was such scorn in the fellow's voice that Captain Medina's hackles rose and he heard Sergeant Sanchez growl something, which the prisoner ignored. The other two prisoners had averted their eyes again, but one of them grinned.

"Do you know the penalty for insubordination?" Medina asked.

The man shrugged, but the defiance was still there.

86

"Ah, no, *Capitán,* I am only a poor *soldado,* as you can see. I do not know of such things." Both of the other prisoners were grinning now, and both had raised their heads to return Medina's stare when he looked at them.

"The penalty can be—" he started, and one of the other prisoners, Garcia, interrupted him.

"It seems to me such things would be in the hands of *El Commandante,*" he said, a direct challenge.

Ruiz nodded. "Of course, *Capitán,* you could always put us back in the stockade to await *El Commandante*'s return. The stockade!" He raised his hands in mock horror. "Such a terrible place! Ai!"

Sergeant Sanchez was bristling. *"¡Silencio,* dog! *Basta."*

Captain Medina saw that it was hopeless. He had not the means to discipline these rabble The stockade, to them, was a welcome place where they could loaf and drink tequila smuggled to them by others of their kind, and from which Colonel Piedras would free them. The colonel had, indeed, by his attitude, given these criminals license to prey upon the civilians in their jurisdiction.

"Enough," he said. "No, you shall not go back into the stockade. There is work to do here, and I believe you will be just the right ones to do it. Sergeant."

"¿Si, Capitán?"

"There may be a leak in the roof. See to it that these three men go up there, and stay there until it is fixed."

"Si, Capitán. But how are we to know when it is fixed?"

"We will know when it rains." He turned back to the prisoners. "You are dismissed."

Sergeant Sanchez wasted no time obeying. Within a half hour the three felons were on the unshaded roof of the Quartel, sweltering in the hot morning sun and hating Captain Medina.

Sanchez left them there until after noon before taking pity on them. He called them down. He pointed out a shade tree by the Quartel's back gate. "You will rest there for an hour," he said. "There is water. In an hour you go back up on the roof. Were I not tender-hearted you would not come down at all." He left them there with one young guard. Ruiz leaned against the bole of the tree, and Garcia and Santos collapsed at his feet. For a time they rested there. The guard—a uniformed youth of barely seventeen—hovered near, nervous and observant. After a while Ruiz fixed him with a malevolent stare, held his eyes for a moment, then crouched suddenly and said, "Boo!" The guard back-pedaled and nearly fell in his haste. Santos and Garcia laughed. Ruiz leaned back against the tree.

"I am tired of this," he said.

"Of what, *compadre?*"

"I am tired of this whole business. I got out of a stinking *presidio* in Guadalajara so I could be *soldado*. Well, I think being a soldier is no more good than being in jail, and I am tired of both."

"Ah," Garcia breathed, "aren't we all."

"Then why don't we go away?"

"And how can we do that, *compadre?* The army will not let us go. We would just go back to jail."

Ruiz gazed at him with contempt. "They would have to catch us first. Do you know what lies east of here? It is a place where there is no army, and no laws. It is called the Neutral Strip. It is neither Mexico nor the Estados Unidos del Norte. A man with a fast horse could go there in a day. And there are trade roads there where fat merchants travel back and forth with wagon loads of whiskey ... *si,* and money. And pretty women. A man with a gun there could take what he wants, no?"

He had their rapt attention now. "But we have no horses," Garcia pointed out. "And no guns."

"Both are easy to get, *amigo*. That little boy playing guard, there. He has a gun."

"Bah," Santos spat. "That old musket is trash. A man would need a rifle where you talk about, Ruiz."

Ruiz didn't answer. His eyes were on a man approaching on foot from the direction of Frost Thorn's big house. The man was well dressed, a slim, graying *hidalgo* of early middle years, and the tails of his loose coat sagged with the weight of a brace of pistols.

With sudden inspiration Ruiz outlined a whispered plan to his comrades, and they nodded. As the man neared them Ruiz signaled the guard, who came toward them, musket at the ready. Santos and Garcia squatted, tensed, watching the approaching man out of the corners of their eyes.

It was over in seconds. As Ruiz lept at the young guard and battered him to the ground, the other two were on the *hidalgo,* pummeling him. When he fell Santos pulled a knife from his boot and raised it.

"No, idiot!" Ruiz's voice stopped him. "If we kill anyone they will hunt us down. Just tie them, and gag them."

Susan Thorn returned through her house to the backyard, where her guests were seated around a table, in the shade. Candida Chireno looked up as she came out.

"Was it news, Susan?"

"No, no news, just *Señor* Sepulveda asking about Frost. They do business sometimes."

"A nice man," Elena Ybarbo pronounced. "But he spoils his children. I always think children should not have more than a family can afford, so they do not become disappointed when they are grown."

Feliciana Menchaca, one of the two youngest women present, lowered her eyes but said nothing. She had her husband Antonio, a tailor, were doing everything in their power to spoil their four little daughters in exactly the fashion *Señora* Ybarbo declaimed against. She noticed that Eva Sterne didn't comment either.

Jane Norris, the fifth lady present this noontime, poured tea in the cups that needed it. "Well, I wish it had been someone with news of Mr. Thorn. I'll tell you, I am plain worried about what might happen here. I've seen heathen in warpaint, when I was just a child, and I never want to see that again."

"You will not." *Señora* Ybarbo was firm. "Isn't that what we have soldiers for, to protect us against such things?"

"But that's just it," Feliciana interjected. "The men think it was Colonel Piedras who—"

Señora Ybarbo, using her seniority among the group to full advantage, cut the young woman off: "Colonel Piedras. Yes. Well, when Colonel Piedras returns I'm sure the men will tell him that we must have protection against the Indians, and that will be that."

Susan Thorn looked away to hide the smile she couldn't suppress. It must be wonderful, she thought, to never have a doubt and never understand a situation. It would do no good to remind *Señora* Ybarbo that the colonel was the cause of the problem. She caught Eva Sterne's eyes on her and flushed. Eva was also trying not to laugh.

Susan turned to Feliciana. "Do you have a plan in case there is trouble?"

"Just to get the children away as quickly as possible," Feliciana said seriously. "Antonio has a cousin at Liberty. I would take the children and go there."

"Just you, alone?" *Señora* Ybarbo asked. "Child, if you go out there with those babies, your husband must

90

go with you."

"Si, *señora*, but my Antonio has his duty. He feels that if there is fighting in Nacogdoches he must stay and fight. They have said, 'God and Liberty,' and he says when a man is told that he must do his duty."

Señora Ybarbo snorted, "Ridiculous! What kind of man would let his family travel alone out there?" She waved an arm in eloquent horror at the wilderness she couldn't see but knew to be there. "I say if there must be fighting, let the soldiers tend to it. It is their job."

Susan decided she had better step in before Feliciana got to the hair-pulling stage with Mrs. Ybarbo. Feliciana had not yet learned to ignore her, and was quick to take offense at any slight against her beloved Antonio. "My," she exclaimed. "But hasn't it been hot lately!"

The brief exchange had given her a serious idea. Later she would get Candida to help and they would organize a contingency plan for the women and children around Nacogdoches to evacuate should the trouble Frost expected come to pass. Mrs. Ybarbo was right about one thing. Feliciana and her babies should not go into the forest alone. None of them should. She glanced around the table and knew intuitively that Candida Chireno, Jane Norris, and Eva Sterne were thinking the same thing.

She picked up her bell to call for more tea, then stopped. Loud in the heavy air came the sound of a gunshot. She saw the color drain from Candida's face.

"Por Dios," her friend whispered. "Has it begun?"

Encarnacion Chireno presided over the meeting of the *Ayuntamiento,* the town council of Nacogdoches, at the home of *Don* Adolphus Sterne. With him were Jose Mora, Juan Mora, Antonio Menchaca, and Sterne. The

91

German-Jew immigrant was at present the only member of the *Ayuntamiento* not of Mexican origin.

Vicente Cordova would join them soon. He had gone first to Goyens's gunshop to see about some of the militia's muskets that were being repaired.

In this hour past noon the heat of the day was intense, and Sterne had all the windows and doors open to allow for any vagrant breeze that might occur. There was very little traffic on the street outside.

Jose Mora squinted at the written report Chireno had handed him, rubbed his eyes, and passed it to his son. "I cannot make this out, Juan, the writing is so dim. Tell me what it says."

"It confirms the earlier report from Brazoria," Chireno told him as Juan Mora looked it over. "John Austin's militia has attacked and captured the fort at Velasco. Colonel Ugartechea's command has been sent to Matamoros. The colonists on the Brazos have declared for Santa Ana, as did those at Anahuac and Liberty. Also, Captain Rosto has withdrawn his company from Harrisburg, to go fight for Santa Anna."

"Ai!" the elder Mora exclaimed. "And with Colonel Bradburn defeated at Anahuac, who is left in East Texas?"

"Piedras," Menchaca said. "Piedras is left."

"And when he returns here," Sterne said, "he is going to be a very angry colonel."

Jose Mora nodded. "We must be prepared for any actions he may take."

"That is why I have asked Vicente Cordova to join us today," Chireno told them. "I have given thought to what Piedras might do, and I think the militia should be ready."

"But what can the colonel do," Menchaca asked, "other than curse and rave? We have done nothing here to warrant any military action against us."

92

Chireno nodded. "A very sensible assessment, if we were dealing with a sensible man. Unfortunately, we are dealing with Piedras."

"You make him sound like a lunatic."

Sterne turned from the open window. "He *is* a lunatic, Antonio. That is our problem."

"A despot!" Juan Mora corrected. "How many times have we complained to him about his *presidarios* stealing from people? And what has he done about them? Encouraged them."

"He can't move without his officers," Menchaca argued. "And most of them are decent men. Musquiz and Medina are both thirty-second-degree Masons."

Chireno shook his head. "If Piedras decides to move against the settlers here, they will be with him. Piedras is no Mason, and his officers are career soldiers. They will obey their commander. You know the law of Masonry. No man shall practice treason against his country, nor induce another to do so. Treason is easier to define for a soldier than for the rest of us."

"We may be concerned over nothing," Menchaca pointed out. "Piedras may do nothing at all. I would like to think that."

Chireno nodded. "And I. Had he not sent a man to the Cherokee I might think that. But look at it. Piedras is afraid of the Americans on the east border, and with some reason. They would come in if they could. Piedras is afraid of the Anglo settlers right here among us, and maybe he has reason to fear some of them, I don't know. Piedras now finds himself all alone, far from home, surrounded by what he considers enemies, and if he decides to move he will make no distinctions. Americans, Anglos, Mexicans, we will all be the same to him.

"No, I think there will be trouble when he returns. One little incident, one trivial thing, can set it off."

"There have been no incidents . . ." Menchaca began,

then stopped at the sound of footsteps coming up the walk. Cooper Willoughby, looking tired and unshaven, came to the open door, peered in and removed his hat. *"Perdoname, señores, por favor. ¿Esta aquí Señor* Sterne?"

"I am here, *Herr* Willoughby. Come in. You look very tired."

"No, gracias," Willoughby said. "I need to borrow a horse, Mister Sterne. Mine's gone lame and I'm in a hurry."

"Of course," Sterne said. "Take any one of mine that you wish. What is wrong? Has something happened?"

"You could say so," Willoughby nodded. "One of Diwali's people has been shot. By a white man."

His words hung in the air, and in the silence came the sound of a gunshot, somewhere nearby.

CHAPTER IX

*"You take a step, and then you take another
step, and pretty soon
you notice that you ain't standing still."*
— Cooper Willoughby

Ambrose had not seen Will Goyens since the morning
Goyens left him at the gunshop in Nacogdoches, but he
knew where his master had gone. He had ridden off to
talk to some Indians. So Ambrose was somewhat at
loose ends. He had the shop to himself, since the white
man who kept the place for Goyens had gone off somewhere as soon as Goyens was gone and had not come
back.

But there was a bunk in the back room where he
could sleep, and Goyens had instructed the woman who
served food next door to keep him fed. Ambrose had
never in his life run a shop, but he knew how to cipher,
and some people didn't mind him asking them things.
So, having nothing better to do, Ambrose kept shop.

There was plenty of work. The man who was supposed to keep the place up had not done much, and
the jobs were piled up. Ambrose had never used a gun,
but he was good with tools and he knew basically what
was supposed to happen when a man touched a trigger.
If it didn't happen, then there was something wrong.

And if a thing is wrong, it can be fixed. He didn't know a frizzen from a sear, a mainspring from a hammer bolt. But once a lock was off a gun, and he could trace the visible parts with his eyes, he could usually figure out what went where.

His first day on the job, his first hour alone there, a man had come in with a rifle and said, "Where's Ruben?"

"Gone, suh," Ambrose told him. "He didn' say."

The man had eyed him skeptically. "You work here, boy?"

"Yessuh. Mistah Goyens put me here."

That seemed to satisfy the man. He laid his rifle on the bench and said, "Hammer-fall is soft. Sometimes she don't pop a cap. I need her fixed by this evening."

"Yessuh."

As the man went out the door he turned back. "This evening for sure. You hear?"

"Yessuh."

When he was gone, Ambrose stared at the gun. Mister Goyens hadn't had time to show him anything about guns, and Mister Ruben hadn't said anything to him at all. So, carefully, he took the gun apart, finding the screws and pins as he went, drawing himself a picture of the parts in order so he wouldn't forget where they all belonged. Within a half hour he had a barrel, a stock, a lock mechanism, a trigger assembly, a trigger guard, a hammer, a side plate, two long bolts, a long screw, and three iron pins laid out on the bench. he deciphered the purpose of the double triggers by holding them against the lock. Then he went to work on the lock. It had nearly thirty parts on it, and he drew another picture as he worked. He found the problem—a cracked mainspring, held in place only by its mounts and giving almost no strength to the hammer it was supposed to drive.

96

There was a box of odd parts on a shelf, and he rummaged through it. The first two springs he found were too short, the third one too long. None fit. So he set the long spring in a vise, found a small file, and began reshaping it, using the broken spring as a model. Another man came in, a Spanish gentleman, and pointed out his gun on a shelf. Ambrose got it for him. It had a tag on it saying what was owed, and Ambrose took the money and put it in a cup under the counter. Then he went back to work on the lock spring.

It was mid-afternoon when he finished reassembling the lock and tested the hammer. It fell with authority. Satisfied, he reassembled the gun. He had barely finished when he saw its owner crossing toward the shop.

Ambrose had found some primer caps in a box, and as the man came in he cocked the hammer, placed a cap on the nipple, squeezed the set-trigger, held the gun out barrel-up, grinned, and touched the trigger.

The roar was deafening. The room was hazed instantly with powder smoke. The butt of the gun thudded against the bench top and a ray of sunlight pierced the roiling smoke from a hole in the roof.

Ambrose stood with his mouth open and the man, frozen in position at the door, gaped at him. For a long moment there was only silence. Then the man found his tongue. "Good God, boy! Didn't you check to see there was a load in that piece?"

Ambrose was stunned. "Nossuh. I didn' know to do that." He hesitated, then forced a placating grin onto his dark face. "But she do pop a cap now, don' she?"

Some of those who gathered in the shop then, drawn by the sound of the shot, stifled their mirth long enough to advise him about prices for gun repair, and the man paid his bill and went away, shaking his head.

In the three days since then, Ambrose and the gun shop had done fairly well. There was a lot of money in the cup under the counter, he had caught up on most of the backlog of work, and patched the hole in the roof. He had tended customers, done several minor repairs on guns that people brought in, and had nearly figured out how to use the bore-pull assembly to rerifle barrels, though he hadn't actually tried it yet.

On this hot afternoon he was cleaning and oiling a batch of muskets that Mister Cordova had brought by. The guns belonged to the local civil militia, and were seldom used. As a result, they were in sad shape, and Ambrose was making them right.

It was quiet out on the street, hardly a soul in sight. The heat was oppressive, and the townspeople were at siesta. He looked up from his work at the sound of the door opening, and smiled at the three soldiers who entered. The smile froze on his face. The three were not regular soldiers. Their uniforms were sloppy and ill-kept. They looked dirty, and all three had been drinking. Ambrose knew about *presidarios*. He had heard the talk.

One of the three remained at the door, watching the street outside. The other two came forward to the counter. One said something in Spanish and the other laughed.

Ambrose squared his shoulders. "Can I he'p you, suhs?"

This seemed to strike them as outrageously funny. They laughed, and the one at the door said something in Spanish and they laughed again. The one to Ambrose's right, a short, muscular man with hard eyes, gazed casually around the room. His eyes lit on a brace of Kentucky rifles behind the counter, and he pointed toward them and said something to his partner, who nodded. Then the first one said, haltingly, "You help us, yes. We need good guns . . . good rifles. We need those there." He pointed. "And that one. Ah, *negrito,* maybe we jus' take them all."

"These here guns, they all belong to Mistah Goyens an' his folks. I can't sell 'em to you, suh."

At this the man laughed again and repeated it in Spanish to his friends. But when he looked back at Ambrose his eyes were hard and cold. "We don' buy nothing, *negrito*. We jus' take. Now you han' us those. *¡Ahora!*"

His partner said, *"Y dinero, amigo. Todo el dinero."*

At Ambrose's blank stare the first one said, "You got money here, *si?* We take that too."

For an instant Ambrose stood, tensed, and a hot rage crept upward from his shoulders. Mister Goyens was a good man. Mister Goyens trusted him with his shop. Nobody was going to take Mister Goyens's things. Keeping his face blank, he turned casually and lifted down one of the Kentucky rifles the man had indicated. It was five feet long and weighed ten pounds. Holding it carefully with both hands on the buttstock he turned, and as he came around he leveled the long barrel outward and swung with all his might. It took the grinning man on the side of his head and dropped him like a rag doll. Without stopping, Ambrose reversed his swing and tried for the second man, but this one dodged aside and shouted. The one at the door turned, pulled a pistol from his belt, and fired it. Ambrose felt a pain in his side like a hot iron. Dropping the rifle he ducked behind the bench and came up with a double-barreled shotgun that had been left there for sale. He had no idea whether it was loaded.

The hard-eyed man was struggling to pull a pistol from his coat, and Ambrose cocked the hammers and brought the gun to his shoulder as he had seen men do.

"¡Alto, hombre!" The voice was a command, and it hung in the air as both Ambrose and the soldiers froze

where they were. Vicente Cordova stood in the doorway, a pistol in each hand, his feet braced wide apart. Slowly the soldier lowered the pistol he had pulled, then dropped it on the floor. Ambrose raised the shotgun with shaking hands and let the hammers down gently. He felt very weak, and the room seemed hazy. He noticed that the shotgun had no caps on it. It was not loaded. It slipped from his grasp and he leaned heavily on the counter, then went to one knee. He heard voices. Mister Cordova was giving orders, and there were others there. He closed his eyes for a moment.

When he opened them, he was lying on his bunk in the back of the shop and there was a Mexican woman fussing over him. He felt very weak. His side hurt terribly. He could still hear voices, but they were further away now, quieter. He wanted to sleep. He just wanted to sleep.

That night Frost Thorn, Will Goyens, and Jaren reached Nacogdoches. They went along the dark streets to Thorn's house, where there was light in the windows. Jaren took their tired animals around to the stable yard to be unpacked, curried, and fed. Susan met Thorn at the front door, hugged him and kissed him soundly, then noticed Will Goyens standing behind him, hugged him too, and brought them both into the house. Haden Edwards came from the study with brandy and glasses and waited impatiently while the tired men got their bodies into easy chairs, their feet up and an ounce of brandy under their belts.

"Well," he said finally, "tell us."

Briefly, Thorn described their meeting with Diwali and the Cherokee council. "The nation will not go to war," he said. "We have their word on that. But a lot of the young braves could decide to join in. Especially since—"

"Since one of them was shot by a white man," Edward interrupted. "Yes, we heard of that."

"You heard?"

"That man Willoughby—the smuggler—he came through earlier today. He told Sterne and the *Ayuntamiento*. Is the Indian dead?"

"Don't know," Goyens told him. "He was still alive when we left, but hard hit. It was Utsada."

"Going Back? Wasn't he with Prather at Fredonia?"

"I think so. I know he is a friend of Egg."

"That is bad." Edwards shook his head. "Very bad."

"Oh, Will," Susan said. "There's something else. The boy you had at the gunshop . . . Ambrose? He's hurt. *Presidarios* tried to rob him and he fought them."

Goyens stood. "Where is he?"

"He's at the shop. Captain Cordova thought it better not to move him. Victoria Saco is tending him there."

Goyens turned to the door. "I'm going over there, Frost. I may need to borrow a buggy, if Ambrose can be moved."

"Of course. Do you want me to go along, or send someone?"

"No. I'll send word if I need help. Thank you. Thank you, Mrs. Thorn. Mr. Edwards."

When he was gone Thorn asked Edwards, "What else did Willoughby have to say?"

"That was all, I guess. He borrowed a horse from Sterne and lit out again. Chireno thinks he knows who shot that Indian—or at least where to find him."

Far to the south of Nacogdoches, on a road that was only a trail through heavy woods, Cooper Willoughby built himself a small fire and unrolled a blanket, impa-

101

tience clear in his every move. It was full dark, and further travel was impossible until there was light enough to see. But he wasn't ready to stop. Out ahead of him somewhere, he knew, another man also was making night camp. That man had shot—possibly killed—a friend.

Fixed in his mind were the cleated tracks of a horse, tracks Willoughby had sought, found, and followed doggedly for seventy miles. Cleated tracks—shoes with a bit of wear but carefully tended, shoes of a variety one might find back East but seldom in Texas, racing shoes. And the long, sure stride of a racing horse. Again and again, through this long chase, he recalled the great blooded bay he had seen in Nacogdoches and the slim, quiet man who rode him. A man who held himself silent and wary, but who could not hold his liquor. A man with something to hide.

Far to the north Utsada lay dying or dead. Willoughby knew wounds. He had seen them. And the man who did it was out there, with a racing horse. Maybe a blooded bay.

Willoughby wasn't thinking now of his lost mules, the Padre's brandy, his grievance with Sheriff Sandy Horton, or his need to go to Alexandria. He even reserved his thoughts of Udali—Mistletoe of the pretty face. He would think of those things later. Right now there was something he had to do.

Further south that night, on a road that intersected the trail, Colonel Piedras was camped with a unit of the 12th Battalion and the Company of Monclova. The colonel was returning from Anahuac.

Fifty miles north of Nacogdoches, only hours before,

a band of somber warriors had gathered their weapons, packed trail provisions, and mounted their best horses.

Chief Nicolet of the lower village watched them depart, heading south.

They were only a handful, but at the lead rode Gu'nasoquo of the scarred face, One Arrow to the white men, and the silent Nunnehidihi, the Path Killer, who had donned his war shirt.

They had no part of the pledge the council had made to Bean, Thorn, and Goyens. There were acting on their own.

Utsada, Going Back of the Tsalagi, the cheerful *unegadihi,* had died.

PART TWO

THE REDLANDERS

CHAPTER X

"How many reasons does a body need? It just don't feel right to pray in a foreign language."
—Samuel Looney

A hundred yards from the new house of Will Goyens, a row of servants' quarters was going up. There would be eight of these cabins in all, and each would house either a family or four single slaves. On this day only two had been completed, and the first one had but one bed in it. Around the bed were three chairs and a table holding ointments, towels, clean muslin, a lantern, and a pitcher of fresh water.

Ambrose lay on his side in the bed, his left arm propped up by makeshift splints fashioned into a triangle and lashed to him with a bandage that covered his upper arm and the upper part of his chest.

Will Goyens had listened to the accounts of Ambrose's battle with the *presidarios,* and to the reports on Ambrose's handling of the gunshop and its business. Will Goyens had talked at length with Vicente Cordova, and then with Captain Medina. Then Will Goyens had gently loaded Ambrose into a wagon and brought him home.

Ambrose's wound was a deep scar along his side, just

below the armpit. It would heal, and in time he would be as good as new. But it would take time.

He was in better condition than the *presidario* he had hit. That one now lay half-dead in a bunk in the Quartel stockade, and the garrison's doctor questioned whether he would recover.

Henry Sibley had listened in awe to his stepfather's account of Ambrose's encounter in the gunshop, then went and sat with the sleeping young Negro for a time. Matilde was there, assigned to look after him, but she had her own man and a handful of little ones to look after, and kept leaving and coming back. Once when she was gone Ambrose cried out in his sleep, rolled over onto his back, and cried out again in pain. Henry Sibley straightened him on the bed, re-propped his arm, and then bathed his head with a cool cloth until Matilde returned. After that he went and found his stepfather.

"Ambrose needs someone with him all the time until he's better," he said.

Goyens thought it over. "I don't know how we can spare any of the women except Matilde. They have their work to do. Who do you suggest?"

Henry bit his lip, stared at the ground, then shrugged his shoulder. "Put Bess in there then. She ain't old enough to be much good to Ma yet, but she can tend a sick man."

Goyens nodded soberly and sent for Bess. He wouldn't say so, but he was very proud of his stepson at that moment.

When he went around to see Ambrose later, Bess was there, and she hovered over her charge like a dark little angel of mercy. Ambrose was awake and feeling terrible.

"Anything you need, boy?" Goyens asked him.

"No, suh. Doin' all right, I guess."

"I want to tell you, Ambrose, you did a good job handling that shop while I was gone. We made money, and the customers are happy."

"Yes, suh. I know. Can I go back there when I'm fix, Mistah Goyens?"

"You like gunsmithing, do you?"

"Yes, suh. I like it fine. Need to learn some more things, but I can. I do you a good job there if you let me, suh."

Bess couldn't restrain herself. "This Ambrose, he awful hurt, Mistah Goyens. Even when he walkin' aroun' he gon' need somebody look after him."

Goyens nodded. He would think about it.

The new porch was completed, its whitewashed latticework glistening against the green of the dooryard. Jupiter set out crafted rocking chairs, and Will and Mary inaugurated the porch by having afternoon coffee there. Henry had taken his shotgun and his two dogs and gone hunting. Goyens sent Samson along to look after him.

Mary had been so relieved to see him return from the Cherokee land that she had not inquired further about what was happening. She did now.

"It doesn't look good," he told her. "Piedras will be back soon, and there is going to be trouble between the settlers and the soldiers. It's in the air, everyone expects it, and that alone, if nothing else, will make it happen.

"Piedras did send a man to the Cherokee, just as we heard. But Diwali and the tribe leaders will stay out of it if they can. Some of their young men might not, though."

"Antonia Cordova drove out yesterday morning," she said. "She brought the cake we're having for supper. She said her husband and Mr. Chireno have sent word to all the settlements around to have their militia ready. But I don't understand, Will. Ready for what? What

109

do they expect Colonel Piedras is going to do?"

"They really don't know. He might do anything if he thinks he's being threatened. He might go house to house and drag the men out to face a firing squad, he might—"

"Oh, Will, he wouldn't do that. He wouldn't do anything like that, would he?"

"He might. He could. But no, I don't think it would be that dramatic. What he is likely to do, I think, is to try to . . . as the Spanish say . . . 'reduce' the population. Maybe set curfews, close the roads, close down all the businesses, maybe confiscate all the settlers' guns, who knows? He *will* do something."

"But why?"

"Because there is a war going on, Mary, and Piedras thinks the war is here. We knew that before he left."

She looked around at the broad, peaceful green fields, the cattle grazing in their new-fenced pasture, field hands going about their chores. Field larks were singing in the bright sunshine, and a brace of does with their fawns grazed at the forest's edge beyond. The breeze smelled of pine boughs and new lumber. "That is ridiculous," she said.

"Yes, that's because we don't see through Piedras's eyes. We look off across there and we see pine trees. He would see enemies there. Most people see enemies where they are, Mary. Piedras sees them were they are not."

She shivered. "He must be a very lonely little man." After a time she asked, "What will we do?"

He shrugged. "Nothing. If I can stay out of it, I will. I have no love for Piedras, and I believe most of his enemies are imaginary. But he does have some . . . back there"—he gestured toward the east—"and those are my enemies too. Diwali doesn't want the Americans coming into Texas. Neither do I. For just about the same reasons."

"We would support Piedras then, if we had to?"

"No. Heaven help me, Mary, I've everything to lose and nothing to gain if the army withdraws. Nobody will gain but the Anglos. But deep down I'm on their side."

He grinned. "I guess I'm about the only black Anglo in East Texas."

"They ain't much to stop us now," Sam Looney said as he stepped down from his horse and handed the reins to a gangly, streaked-faced youth with a black eye and a missing front tooth. "Put this animal up good, boy. He done earned his oats. You been fightin' ag'in. You win?"

"Sure, Pa." The boy grinned at him.

"That's good. Now git." Looney turned to his companion, who remained mounted. "Sure you can't set an' jaw a spell? I got me some New Orleans likker over in the shed."

"Sorry," Smith said. "Another time, maybe. There's still two hours of daylight and I want to get to San Felipe as soon as possible."

"Yeah. But like I said, you gonna find they ain't much can stop us now. You heard the news same as me. They run all the soldiers out of Velasco, and they be gone from Anahuac 'fore long. An' all them places we stopped at, ain't they gettin' their militias primed for war? You reckon we gonna stop now 'til all the Meskins is run clean outta Texas?"

"Some of those militia units are mostly Mexican," Smith pointed out.

"Makes no nevermind." Looney grinned. "Once we get started we ain't gonna stop easy."

As he waved his farewell, Smith took one more look

111

around the ramshackle homestead of Sam Looney and wondered again at the strange, random mixture that was Texas. It was his first visit to the Mexican province, and the more he saw, the more confusing he found it.

Since the day he entered Texas with Sam Looney, whom he had met at Natchitoches, he had covered a great deal of ground. He suspected there would be a great deal more to cover before he could draft any sort of sensible treatise on the situation here. How do you report on chaos? Where do you start?

He had talked to a great many people since he and Looney had deposited Looney's mule-train load of powder and ball for the Neches militia units. Looney had been his willing guide around this interior section of East Texas, anxious that he get the full report he needed as quickly as possible. Smith was aware that Looney and some of his associates saw him as a direct contact with the White House and were trying to use him to further their own aims, but to this point he didn't know just what the aims of these Texians might be.

Some said their goal was to get Texas separated from Coahuila, as a distinct state. Others said their goal was to see a return to the constitutional government which had preceded the Law of 1830 and Bustamente's royalist movement. Still others said the goal was to unseat Bustamente and put Santa Anna in power.

The recent upheaval at Anahuac was a mixture of *Santanista* support, impatience with the laws and tariffs that now existed, and just plain exasperation with Colonel Juan Davis Bradburn.

He was withholding judgment for the moment on the nature of the battle at Velasco. The Brazoria militia, it was reported, had taken the fort there and was holding it. But for what? Or against whom?

Some he had talked with said the point of all the

hostilities in Texas boiled down simply to Mexico's selecting a poor class of colonels to put in charge of frontier outposts.

Others—and these were few and spoke softly—said the aim was to kick Mexico out of Texas so the United States could take it over. These latter, though, seemed to be in the minority. He had the impression most Texians didn't like American government any better than they liked Mexican government. He wondered—do they want their own?

With the sun in his face he headed westward. Maybe he could get some answers at San Felipe de Austin on the Brazos. If not, he would go down to Brazoria.

Despite the skepticism of Alexander Horton, the real name of this well-dressed, distinguished man of middle years was in fact John Smith. He was not an employe of the United States Government but was, rather, an employee of a very private service established by President Thomas Jefferson and now reporting to President Andrew Jackson.

President Jefferson had felt a president should know what was occurring in the world around him. President Jackson wanted specifically to know what was going on in Texas.

Smith did not know President Jackson. But he knew a man who did. He knew also that some of the "greeners" filtering into East Texas these days had been encouraged to come. The going price was forty dollars and a horse.

Luck was not running with Cooper Willoughby on this day. In the deep woods south of Nacogdoches he knelt in the clearing where the old Indian trail crossed El Camino Sud. The tired black gelding he had borrowed from Adolphus Sterne stood head-down beside him, its coat moist and glistening in the sprinkle of sunlight filtering down through tall lodge-pole pines and sweet-gum boughs.

The sod where Willoughby knelt was cut and trampled by the passing of a large group of horsemen. The droppings of their mounts were fresh. He had missed them by less than an hour. But the man he sought, the man he had pursued for nearly a hundred miles, had not missed them. He could see where the tracks of his quarry entered the crossroads from the old Indian trail and veered northward, then were overprinted by the marks of other horses in the group that had passed.

He judged at least fifty riders had passed here within the hour. And among the horse tracks were smaller, sharper prints of a string of mules, trailing along behind. A large party with provisions. Piedras, he decided. The colonel was on his way home. And the man Willoughby sought had joined him.

"Hell!" he told the black horse. "I could've just waited in Nacogdoches."

Nearly a hundred miles. From Diwali's village to El Camino Real, then a detour into Nacogdoches to find a horse, then south on the Indian trail to El Camino Sud. Willoughby straightened himself with a sigh, walked stiffly to the middle of the crossroads clearing, and stood facing north. He sighed again. He hurt all over, and he felt crusty and beat from too much hard riding.

On protesting legs he walked back to where the horse stood and picked up its reins.

"Well, sport, there's a creek down there a ways where we can get a drink of water. I hope you still got some go left in you, because as soon as we finish we're moving again." As he led the beast downslope to the west he added, "And this time we gotta chase the whole dam' Mexican army."

114

Four hours later, in full darkness, Willoughby led his faltering mount to the crest of a ridge on the Camino Sud and saw firelights in the distance, a large encampment. He judged it a mile.

"Closer'n we were, at any rate," he advised the tired horse. "You know, I been goin' about this the hard way." Back at the Indian village, after Utsada had been struck down, the Cherokee in true Indian fashion had gone looking for a trail to follow, and had looked where the trail should not be. Willoughby, following a hunch, had decided the man who fired the shot probably knew Indians and would have foreseen that, so Willoughby looked where the Indians did not. He looked where the trail should be, and found it. Then he got his horse and followed it.

"Been a hell of a lot easier," he told the horse for the dozenth time, "if I'd just showed Egg where the feller started out. Egg, or Gu'nasoquo. They'd have had the bastard by now." He shuddered at his own words. The man he was trailing, after all, might be an Anglo. And bastard or not, he would not have sent Egg to find him.

Most of another hour had passed before Willoughby, working in darkness, got Sterne's tired horse picketed in a grassy clearing well off the road and made his way silently to the outskirts of the army camp. Then he scouted the layout.

There were six fires, spread out across the road and into the woods on both sides. He spotted Colonel Piedras's bivouac easily, for there was a tent erected there for the colonel. There were no other tents. Around and eastward from the colonel's enclave were the fires of men of the 12th Battalion, in two groups. Those nearest Piedras's fire were mostly *presidarios,* with a couple of tough old sergeants to keep them in line. Further on, straddling the cleared road itself, were the regulars of the 12th, about a dozen of them. Most of them Willoughby knew by name. At the east end of the camp were two fires close together where the men of the Company of Monclova were bedding down. There were no Indians with them now. The fun over, they wouldn't have waited on a slow army unit.

Willoughby noted with quick insight that Captain Musquiz's proud cavalry troops were as far removed as was seemly from the colonel's tent—and from the *presidarios*.

Token guards patrolled the perimeter. Willoughby passed them with ease, and walked to the fireside where Musquiz sat on a stump, boots beside him, massaging a sore foot. Without preamble Willoughby crouched by the fire, picked up a battered cup, and filled it with coffee from Musquiz's pot. The captain glanced up, nodded at him, and remarked in Spanish, "You keep strange hours in your business, *Señor* Willoughby. Please help yourself to my coffee."

"*Gracias, Capitán.*" He was already sipping the strong brew. "I'll see you get a fresh supply. I looked over the camp, and I don't see anyone here but soldiers."

Musquiz glanced at him again, puzzled. "Who else would you expect on a military expedition?"

"Oh, I don't know. I thought there might be at least one civilian with you. Maybe an Anglo civilian?"

"Since we left Nacogdoches," Musquiz said, sighing, "we have gone all the way to Anahuac and back. We have seen many Anglo civilians . . . far more than are good for *El Coronel*'s disposition." He glanced around. They were alone at the fireside. Several of the captain's men were asleep nearby, and a few others sat around a second fire fifty feet away, but they were all out of earshot. "Our commander's disposition is not happy at the moment, *amigo*. It would be best if you were somewhere else."

"Bad trip?"

"*Si*, a bad trip. Much is happening in Mexico that the colonel does not like, and much is happening here in Texas. Who is it you seek?"

Willoughby finished the coffee and set the cup down. "A little after midday today a rider joined your party. He met you at the Indian road crossing."

"Ah. That was only Moro. He joined us and came this far with us."

"The man had a racing horse."

"Ah, yes. A fine bay. I had not seen it before."

"Is he here?"

"I don't think so. Maybe an hour ago there was a scene at the colonel's tent. We could hear the colonel's voice clear over here. He called Moro some things few men would have stood for, then sent him away. Moro took a horse and rode out, east into the woods. I think he was very angry. I know the colonel was." Dark eyes under graying brows fixed Willoughby, curious and alert. "Why do you ask about him?"

Willoughby ignored it. "I wonder, do you remember any of the particular things that were said?"

"No, I couldn't hear very much. Just a lot of cursing. As I said, *El Comandante* was very angry."

"I can imagine," Willoughby said, and the face that seemed made for humor held none at all.

Musquiz asked again, "Why do you ask about Moro?"

The smuggler shook his head. "Believe me, Captain, you don't want to know."

Musquiz looked again around the camp, and turned back, questions on his tongue, but Willoughby was gone. It was as though he had never been there. Musquiz poured himself a cup of coffee and sat staring into the fire for a long time. It was very puzzling. Why would a harmless smuggler be out in the woods this

117

time of night, asking questions about Piedras's civilian agent? Why did Willoughby, with his habitual, ingratiating smile, not smile now?

And why, come to think of it, would Colonel Piedras, with all the epithets at his command, choose to call Moro an assassin?

CHAPTER XI

"We've all come to Texas for the same reason. It's better here than where we were before."
— Frost Thorn

"I honestly don't believe the greeners are our problem," Frost Thorn said. "Certainly they aren't the immediate problem. Sure, there are a lot of them coming into Texas. But you'll notice they pass us right on by. They're going west."

The *Ayuntamiento* of Nacogdoches was in session again, for the third time in the past week. *Don* Encarnacion Chireno, presiding as *Alcalde,* was determined to get to the bottom of his district's current troubles. A "patchwork quilt" he called it. Conflict piled upon conflict, and he meant to sort it out. In this session he was holding the discussion to the questions of Anglo intent and the concerns of the Hispanic settlers of the region.

Mostly, he looked to Thorn to analyze the former.

The Moras, father and son, were present, as were Adolphus Sterne and Vicente Cordova. Thorn had been called, and had come.

"Please understand, *amigo*," Chireno said, "we are not questioning you, our good friend, nor the other

119

Anglo settlers among us. But some of the people see the trouble coming again and many have heard Colonel Piedras's view that the American Anglos are the root of our problem here. We do not believe it." He looked around him. "None of us believe it. But we must know how to reassure those who question us. As the *Ayuntamiento,* we represent them."

"Please, my friends." Thorn held up a hand. "I understand perfectly. A lot of our neighbors are concerned, and not just the Hispanics. Mexico is in trouble, and we are vulnerable out here on the frontier.

"You ask, what are the chances that Americans will come in and wrest Texas away from Mexico during her difficulties?"

"Yes," Chireno said solemnly. "This is what we must ask today."

"I don't think we have to worry on that score," Thorn told them, looking around from face to face. "To move in here, the Americans would have to have support from the Anglo settlers. They don't. There are very few . . . if any . . . of the established settlers here, Anglo or otherwise, who want to see Texas become a part of the United States of the North. Oh, there are some who would like to see Texas become independent. I suspect a lot of those down on the coast, and maybe some up here, would seek that. But independent from everyone, not just Mexico.

"No matter how much we may complain about Mexican rule, *señores,* and no matter how much we seek statehood for Texas — "

"Verdad," Juan Mora interjected.

"Yes, that is a real issue. But no matter our feelings on that, we are loyal citizens of Mexico and most of us intend to remain so. A lot of the complaint, as you well know, is just the griping of people adjusting to a system they're not used to. But keep in mind, as we

120

Anglos need to, we are all here by choice. There is better opportunity here than in the United States of the North. That's why most of us came here. The truth of the matter is, we paid higher taxes in the States than we normally do here, and we had a lot more control by government."

"Higher taxes, *señor?*" Chireno asked. "When is the last time you bought a sack of legal coffee?" Sterne chuckled at this. Many here had bought very little legally imported produce since the exorbitant tariffs of the past two years went into effect. It was a heyday for smugglers.

Thorn smiled, but went on seriously, "I said, *normally* the taxes there are more. We have to do something about this present law. But that is an internal matter, not something to breed treason.

"In the States, as I've told you before, they are always having economic disasters. One after another. It is the nature of the place, I think. The government of the United States since its inception has been hell-bent on punishing its enemies by constraining its own citizens. Here in Mexico, though, no matter what kind of chaos our government is in, the citizens can always keep an economy going. We can always produce trade goods to sell to buyers in other countries. The United States cuts off trade with the countries it doesn't like. It always punishes its own citizens far more than it punishes its enemies."

Chireno and the Moras shook their heads in wonder at such unreasonable policy. Sterne pursed his lips and nodded. He too had seen it.

"The present outward pressure in the United States—what is causing our border pressure here in Texas—is an example. It was an economic disaster that started people moving here, the great depression of '98. There was no reason for it, except political tomfoolery. But it

121

has caused havoc now for nearly thirty-five years."

Cordova had been holding his tongue, just listening. Now he asked, "How does such a country survive?"

"It's huge," Thorn told him. "The Estados Unidos del Norte is a huge country. That's how."

"At least there is not so much military intervention in private affairs there as we have here," Chireno said.

"No. And that, like separation from Coahuila, is a problem we need to resolve here. But we will do so as citizens of Mexico. We don't want to be a part of the States."

"You speak for the Anglo settlers, our neighbors," Chireno noted. "Can you say as much for those drifting in across the border?"

Thorn's eyes clouded. "I wish I could. No telling what the greeners want. Maybe they don't know themselves. But, as I said, most of them aren't stopping here. Most are drifting on west."

"And some of them," Cordova said, "come with money and a horse they didn't have before they reached the frontier."

Footsteps on the porch brought their heads around. Cooper Willoughby stepped up and rapped at the sill of Sterne's open door, peering into the room. He looked gaunt and drawn. His clothing was dirty, his shirt brush-torn, and he hadn't shaved in a day or two.

"Mr. Sterne," he said, spotting the German, "I brought your horse back and put him in your corral. He's wore down a mite, but he's a sturdy animal and he'll rest out of it. I got my own horse back." As his eyes accommodated to the dark interior he added, "Howdy, Mr. Thorn . . . *buenos dias, Señor Chireno . . . señores. Mis felicidades al Ayuntamiento, y perdoneme.*"

Thorn cocked his head at him. "You've been afar, Mr. Willoughby."

"Some," he admitted. "But I got a ways to go yet. Thank you for the loan of the horse, Mr. Sterne. I got to find something to eat now, then get on my way."

"But what about the man . . ." Thorn started, but he was talking to an empty doorway. From the window they watched Willoughby, sore and tired, amble across toward the inn.

Sterne shrugged. "We will learn from him something only when he wishes to tell us."

They had barely returned to their seats, Cordova still at the window, when there was a sound of running hooves out in the street.

"Los Indios," someone shouted in a voice pitched to panic.

"*Los Indios!*" The *ayuntamiento* of Nacogdoches hurried back to the open window and door, then crowded out onto the porch. In the street a rider was clinging to a frightened, lathered horse. He spotted them and pointed back the way he had come, out the old north road. "*¡Señores, los Indios! ¡Aqui!*" His horse almost pitched him, dancing around as it was, and he struggled to control it, then let it have its head and continued south at a run through the plaza, calling, "*¡Los Indios! Los Indios . . . Aqui!*"

The men on the porch looked to one another in puzzlement. Vicente Cordova ran down the steps and into the plaza. They heard shouting and hurried, high-pitched orders from the military compound. Around the square and along the streets a few people had come out to see what was going on.

At first they could see nothing along the north road. From where they stood the road ran wide past a few buildings, some houses, and beyond them a scattering of barns and sheds, where it crossed a brushy draw, then narrowed as it entered thin forest and disappeared in a curve. At first there was nothing there, then a mounted form appeared—and another, and another. As they watched, a file of mounted Cherokee warriors came around the curve, horses at the walk, and approached the bridged draw. At the far side they reined in and spread out, a silent line of copper-skinned fighting men across the road.

"*¡Por Dios!*" Chireno gaped. "*Mira ustedes. Alla es* Egg."

Tall in the center of the line of Indians, nearly dwarfing the tough little horse he rode, was a warrior who seemed in comparison to be half again the size of those flanking him. Few in Nacogdoches had ever seen the man called Egg, but they knew of him. And the stories, Chireno thought now, were not exaggerated. The warrior was awesome.

There was a pause, and they heard a bugle sounding from the Quartel. A handful of soldiers ran from the Red House and stopped in dismay as they saw the display across the draw. Thorn turned at the sound of men approaching from the Quartel and held up a hand to Captain Francisco Medina. "Hold your men there, Captain," he shouted, then turned back. From the rank of Indians, one rode forward, across the wooden bridge.

Vicente Cordova stood firm in the middle of the street, hand on the butt of his pistol. "*Señor* Frost, do you know that one?"

Thorn squinted. Then in the bright sunlight he made out the scarred face of the approaching warrior. "Yes. His name is Gu'nasoquo, One Arrow. I know him. He speaks some English."

"Will you speak with him?"

"Of course." As the Indian neared, he stepped forward and raised his hand. "*Osiyo, Gu'nasoquo.*"

One Arrow reined in his pony three paces from Thorn and Cordova. Ignoring the greeting for a mo-

124

ment, he let expressionless eyes sweep slowly across the growing crowd in the mouth of North Road. Behind Thorn and Cordova were Adolphus Sterne, the Ruizes, and Chireno. People were crowding the long porch of the inn to one side, and the gaping doorways of the houses across from it. Several men had come into the street, and others were hurrying toward them. In the background, at the plaza, Captain Medina, a lieutenant, and two sergeants were grouping the various soldiers who had come running from the Quartel, the Old Church, and the commandant's quarters.

There was nothing uncommon in seeing Cherokees in Nacogdoches. The Tsalagi people came often to this town. But they came bearing baskets of produce or stacks of hides, not carrying their war clubs in anger.

One Arrow of the Tsalagi looked around him and let them look at him. Naked except for breechclout and high moccasins, he wore his bow of honeyed bois d'arc wood and a sheaf of arrows on his back. His topknot was loose and, although he wore no paint, the little pots were in evidence at his waist. The lance he carried was a steel-tipped shaft nearly eight feet long, with owl feathers fluttering at its head. It was the same Pawnee lance that had scarred him years ago. He let them look long before speaking. He wanted their full attention. Behind him, a hundred yards away, lined across the road beyond the bridge, were more than thirty of his kind, and in their center was the great, solemn figure of Egg.

Finally, slowly, Gu'nasoquo raised a hand. *"Osiyo,* Frost Thorn." Then in halting English: "A warrior of the Tsalagi has died. Utsada has gone from us. His spirit has gone to Black Man in the west. He was clan brother, protector, and food-bringer. A white man killed him."

Thorn nodded. "I was there, Gu'nasoquo."

"We come for that man. Give him to us."

Thorn shook his head. "The man who killed Utsada is not among us. We do not know him."

The scarred face studied him. "If you do not know him, Frost Thorn, how do you know he is not here?"

"He is not here, Gu'nasoquo."

"Then where is he?"

Thorn shrugged. "We do not—" There was a bustling in the crowd toward the inn, and Cooper Willoughby pushed through, a slab of cornbread in one hand. He raised the other. *"Osiyo, Gu'nasoquo,"* he said, *"ona'a dhesta yunwiadihi neghidos."*

One Arrow frowned. "Speak the *ani'unega* tongue, so all hear, Willoughby. How you know the killer of Utsada is not in Na'ghdoche?"

"I know because I know where he has gone."

"Then tell us, Willoughby."

Willoughby shrugged. "No. I will find him."

The tip of the tall lance dipped slightly. "You know him?"

Willoughby stood his ground. "I will find him, Gu'nasoquo."

The lance tip dropped and its needle point touched Willoughby's chest. "You want to fight the Tsalagi, Willoughby? You want to fight Gu'nasoquo? You want to fight Nunnehidihi? You want to fight Egg?"

There was cold sweat now on the smuggler's brow, but he held the Indian's eyes and with elaborate calm took a bite from the slab of cornbread he held. In the background some of the soldiers had raised their muskets and Medina called them down.

"I do not fight my friends," Willoughby said.

Gu'nasoquo's stare was flat and hard. "You are no friend of mine, Willoughby. I have not taken your arm."

"Utsada was my friend."

126

One Arrow of the Cherokee was silent for a moment, then nodded and withdrew the lance. With no further glance at Willoughby he turned to Frost Thorn. In rapid Cherokee he said, "You have dealt fairly with the Tsalagi. Do you say this man will find the one who killed Utsada?"

Thorn looked from Willoughby back to the warrior. "He says he will, Gu'nasoquo. I believe him."

"Do you say he will?"

Thorn was irritated at this. He knew what the Indian was asking. He wanted a guarantee. But Thorn's puritan background had no place in it for unreasonableness, even from an Indian. "Can a man say what another man might do? Can a man say where birds will fly? Can a man say that the sun will rise tomorrow? I believe Willoughby."

Gu'nasoquo said, "The chief of soldiers has asked the Tsalagi to help him keep order. Utsada's blood cries for blood."

"I was in Diwali's council, Gu'nasoquo. The council said the Tsalagi will remain aside."

Gu'nasoquo spat. "Then the council will not fight. We were not in that council, Thorn. We did not say we would not fight." Raising his head, the Indian looked around him at the crowd in the street. In English he said, so all could hear, "A warrior of the Tsalagi has died. *Yoneg* blood must answer. This one says he will find the killer of Utsada, and this one has friends among the Tsalagi. So we will wait. Willoughby will have his chance.

"But"—he paused and the square was silent—"we will not wait long."

Without further word he turned his mount and rode away, his long lance catching the sunlight on its honed tip. A burst of talk swept through the crowd that had watched the drama. Some among them spoke no En-

127

glish. Most spoke no Cherokee. But within moments they all knew what had transpired.

Thorn turned to Willoughby. "For the love of God, man, why didn't you tell them what they wanted to know?"

Willoughby was abashed, but he stood his ground. He looked very tired. "I ain't much around here, Mr. Thorn, but I've got some good friends in Texas. Don't you know what will happen if those braves go on the trail of a white man down through the Redlands? Do you think all these folk are going to stand around and watch a pack of Indians hunt down a white man? Hell, Mr. Thorn, do you want an Indian war?"

Thorn's anger subsided. The man was right. "Well, then, let's get up a group and go after the man ourselves."

"Looks to me," Willoughby said, "like you all have your hands full right here. Colonel Piedras will be back sometime today. Hell, I don't want to go all by myself, Mr. Thorn. I don't want to get killed. But I just don't know anything else to do. Besides, like I told One Arrow, old Utsada was a friend of mine."

Thorn thought about it, and nodded. "Then at least tell me who the man is, so we can deal with him later if you . . . ah, if you don't find him."

Willoughby looked around. The crowd was dispersing. Only Chireno and Cordova stood near enough now to hear what was said. "I'll tell Sandy Horton if I see him. But I got to do this."

Thorn frowned. "No disrespect, Mr. Willoughby, but I don't see what you're going to do with the man, even if you can find him. Obviously he is an accomplished woodsman, and an expert marksman."

"Yeah." Willoughby shrugged. "I know that." He turned away, his shoulders sagging, and headed back toward the inn. He hoped no one else had eaten the meal

128

he had left there.

Frost Thorn watched him go, then turned to Cordova. "He's going to get himself killed," he said, a simple statement of fact. Cordova nodded. "I wonder if he has everything he needs."

Thorn pulled a purse from his waistcoat and counted out some coin. "Would you mind, Vicente? See to it there is food and powder in the packs of Mr. Willoughby's horse, and pay his bill at the inn."

Cordova waved the money away. "It is my pleasure, *señor*. I too have things in my house that no taxes were paid on."

The excitement past, Captain Francisco Medina dispersed his men and returned to his office in the Quartel. He had been there only a few minutes when Sergeant Marcos Sanchez came pounding at the door.

There had been a desertion. Two *presidarios* imprisoned in the stockade had gotten loose during the time the troops had been out watching the visit of the Indians. Privates Ruiz and Santos had stolen muskets, horses, blankets, and food, and were headed east.

CHAPTER XII

"There are Anglo spies and sympathizers everywhere, waiting for the chance to incite a rebellion."
—Colonel Jose de las Piedras

Colonel Jose de las Piedras returned from Anahuac as a conquering hero. He rode at the head of his mounted troops with Captain Renaldo Musquiz, commander of the Company of Monclova, to his left, and the unit colors immediately behind them. Blue cavalry jackets of the Company of Monclova and the green and white uniforms of mounted infantry were flashes of bright color in the high sunlight. Boots and trappings were polished, fine horses well groomed, and although many of the unit—indeed more than half of those in green—were criminals, still they had the appearance of military elegance and awesome bearing.

Piedras's stop the night before, south of Nacogdoches, had been for that purpose. The morning hours had been spent cleaning, shining, currying, and dressing ranks so the colonel's civilian subjects could witness this display. Only a few might have noticed the sour expressions of Captain Musquiz and one or two of the older sergeants, or the tight-lipped, contained anger of Piedras himself.

The colonel led his troops into the Plaza Principal and across to the Red House, where Captain Medina and an escort saluted in greeting. Piedras, Musquiz, and their lieutenants returned the salute while the sergeants arrayed the troops in parade-ground formation. This done, Piedras hauled tight rein and turned his mount slowly, full around, his gaze taking in the town around him. A few civilians were in view, but not many. It was the first hour of siesta, and most of Nacogdoches apparently did not choose to interrupt its quiet time to watch the soldiers perform. Piedras's lips tightened until white showed at their corners. With a snort of disgust he dismounted, flipped the reins to an orderly, and strode toward the Red House door.

Medina bowed slightly. "Welcome back, my colonel. Was your mission a success?"

Piedras glared at him. "Is everything in order here, Captain?"

"Yes, Colonel. Everything is in order."

"There have been no incidents then?"

"A band of Cherokee came this morning." Medina shrugged. "But they left peacefully. I have had two desertions. But, altogether, nothing out of the ordinary."

Piedras bristled. "I warn you, Captain, do not play games with me. You know what I am asking. Have the Anglo settlers—or some of these Mexicans who seem to think they are Anglos—been meeting? Are there spies? Is there rebellion here?"

Medina's face was a mask. How to answer such questions? What did the colonel think had been happening in his absence? "No, my colonel," he answered. "Nothing such as that. I have kept a journal day by day. You will find it on your desk."

"A journal!" The colonel pursed his lips in a parody of approval. "What a fine idea! I am sure it will tell me everything my commanding captain has observed

131

since I left here . . . absolutely nothing."

With a final, contemptuous glare at Medina, Piedras squared his shoulders and marched past him to enter the Red House.

Musquiz snapped orders to disperse the returning troops, then dismounted and let his face relax into a tired smile as he greeted Medina. The two stood together to watch the last of the soldiers breaking up into groups. Some wandered away toward the Quartel, some toward the Stone House, most toward the now-dilapidated old church that the colonel had commandeered to quarter them.

"Were you not my friend," Musquiz said, "I would wish a thing upon you."

"And what is that?"

"I would wish you would have been on the trail with our good colonel instead of me. That man is crazy, Francisco. He sees a spy behind every tree and a conspiracy in every group. I swear, I am almost ready to believe that everyone in Texas is in league with Andrew Jackson and those who aren't plotting revolution are plotting to murder our colonel."

"Por Dios." Medina shook his head wearily. "Does it never end?"

Musquiz glanced toward the Red House. "At this very moment, I imagine, the good colonel is observing us and determining that because we talk together we are plotting the overthrow of Mexico."

"In that case, we had better go talk somewhere else. I think some good Anglo beer would suit you after the long trail, would it not?"

"Si, it would. But be careful, *amigo.* Don't let our commander hear you refer to anything Anglo as 'good.' "

As they walked away toward Sim's Tavern they passed Antonio Menchaca hurrying toward the Red House.

132

The tailor had been occupied through the morning with sittings and fittings, among them the traditional, annual new suits the Rueg brothers bought themselves each July to celebrate the anniversary of their arrival in Texas. Menchaca had missed the meeting of the *Ayuntamiento,* but would talk with Chireno later to learn what had transpired.

From his shop door Menchaca had watched the return of Colonel Piedras and his troops, and he was anxious to talk with the colonel as soon as possible.

At the Red House Menchaca knocked at the door and entered the small, neat office of the commander of forces of East Texas. Piedras was seated at a table, reading through a journal of reports, and glanced up with irritation at the arrival. Menchaca, determined, bowed and said, "Welcome back, Colonel. I hope your trip was not too tiring."

Piedras closed the journal. "I am very busy, *Señor* Menchaca. What do you want?" There were to be no pleasantries, no small talk.

"I have waited for your return, Colonel. I must talk with you. May I be seated?"

Cool, arrogant eyes focused on him. "I told you I am very busy, *señor.* Just say what you want to say."

The young tailor gritted his teeth and pushed back the anger that threatened to dissolve his good intentions. "Very well. I am concerned, Colonel. We are all concerned, with the reports we hear from the south. There is great concern among our people here that trouble may come upon us in East Texas because of what other people have done in other places . . ." His voice trailed off, and his eyes sought approval or agreement from the colonel seated before him. There was none. The fine, aristocratic face of Piedras was a mask of chiseled stone.

Piedras let the silence prolong itself, then he asked

quietly, "And just what is it you believe those 'other people in other places' have done?"

"Why, they have . . . that is, the reports are that they . . . ah . . . that they stood and fought for their principles."

The mask cracked and sheer malevolence spread across Piedras's features. "For their principles? Tailor, are you a simple fool? Can't you recognize plain rebellion when you see it? That is what is occurring, *señor*. Plain rebellion, by Anglo aliens and sympathizers, against the authority of the Republic of Mexico. And it does not just happen, it is planned . . . carefully planned, by agents of the Estados Unidos del Norte. High treason is what is happening in Texas, *señor*. It is all around us. Now, what do you want?"

Menchaca was speechless for a moment. He had not been prepared for the vehemence of Piedras's response, nor for the man's single-minded certainty of a situation no one else could see.

"Colonel Piedras," he started, "I really don't think there is evidence of treason anywhere. With due respect, sir, it seems to me that the people at Anahuac and Velasco were simply standing up against what they considered—right or wrong—as tyranny. There may have been some merit—"

Piedras was on his feet, and a manicured finger wavered before Menchaca's face. "That kind of talk comes from traitors! You are apologizing for rebellion! Tell me, *Señor* Tailor, are you also a *Santanista?* Are you too conspiring against your country?"

Menchaca had about reached his limit. A young man with a young wife and young children becomes concerned when their peace is threatened. It had cost him a good deal of courage to come here, to try and talk reasonably with this little despot before him, and he could see he was getting nowhere. Piedras's mind was a closed world all its own, and whatever was going on in that world could not be affected by the rationale of this one.

Squaring his shoulders, the tailor made one more attempt, going straight to the subject of his greatest concern. "Colonel, whatever differences we may have among ourselves in East Texas, we can resolve them peacefully. There is no need of hostility . . . and now even the Indians are upset. Certainly no one wants that, sir."

Piedras's expression changed abruptly to bland indifference. "Indians are unpredictable, tailor. No one can say what they will do, particularly now that someone—an Anglo, I believe—has killed their chief. I am certain, though, that the Cherokee mean no harm to the law-abiding citizens of Mexico. It was no Mexican who shot Diwali . . . so I have heard."

Menchaca was stunned. "Shot . . . Diwali? But Colonel . . ."

"I have no more time to talk," Piedras said. "I have work to do. You go cut patterns or something. Or maybe you can get the *Ayuntamiento* together and discuss how the streets could be cleaned better. Leave important affairs to your supreme government and its assigned officers. And by the way, *Señor* Menchaca, you did not answer my question. Are you also a *Santanista?*"

Menchaca's temper finally got the best of him. Unable to speak, he turned on his heel and walked out, slamming the door behind him. If he had not been a *Santanista* before, by the Blessed Holy Mother, he was now.

He was almost back to his shop before the enormity of Piedras's remarks dawned on him. An Indian had been shot, but it was not Diwali. Who, then, might have thought that it was Diwali? Only the man who

135

fired the shot and then ran—or the one he reported to. Menchaca stopped in confusion, then turned left. He needed to talk to someone. Chireno perhaps, or Vicente Cordova, or maybe Frost Thorn. And then he wanted to go home and spend time with Feliciana and the children. The young tailor had a hunch that the colonel would not long tolerate whatever specters inhabited that closed little world of his. He would strike out. And when he did, it would be those of this world who would be hurt.

In his office Colonel Piedras finished reading the accumulated journals and reports that had piled up in his absence. There was no mention, anywhere, of the rebellion he knew to be building up at his very doorstep. By his own calculations, he estimated the Anglo American settlers in Texas could field more than two thousand fighting men, once organized, and he had no doubt the organization was under way. And now, with Anahuac and Velasco out of the picture, only he at Nacogdoches and the garrison at Tenoxtitlan on the Brazos stood between the Anglo threat and Texas. He was fairly sure, also, that he could trust no one at Tenoxtitlan. Many of the soldiers in Texas already had turned *Santanista,* and more would follow.

Damn Santa Anna, he thought. Damn his soul to hell, why couldn't he have died in battle four years ago. Piedras had met General Santa Anna only once—they were both lieutenant colonels then—and had disliked the strutting, ambitious young officer instantly. His star rose too fast. And it was *his* star, not Mexico's. The word was that Santa Anna was now calling himself the "Napoleon of the West." The thought of it was gall in Piedras's throat. Why in God's name, he asked himself, must there be men like that? Why couldn't the world

136

settle into the orderly, properly aligned place it so desperately needed to be, without some ambitious, self-centered young traitor coming along and overthrowing the very foundations of it for his own personal satisfaction?

Squaring the papers neatly on his desk, Piedras turned to gaze at the flag on the wall behind him. The flag of the Republic of Mexico. Bars of flame-red, white, and green offset the emblem of the eagle rampant with the serpent in its beak.

Jose de las Piedras did not love the flag. Somewhere in his carefully ordered life he had missed the learning of love. But he worshipped what, to him, the flag stood for . . . stability. Precise, regimented, ordered stability. Without such assurance his world was a vague, haunted place.

When he was a youth, the priests had made him read Plato. He had learned to hate the priests, but he had come to worship Plato. That ancient sage had spelled it all out, just how the world should be. Through the mouth of Socrates he had displayed for the world to behold a perfect order, the purest form of royalty in which all men behaved perfectly because they had no other choice—each man to his assigned place, each satisfied to be subservient, with the military power of Guardians to assure there would never be dissension.

It was perfect. It was beautiful. And it was slipping away, because Mexico had allowed barbarians into the perfect society. The Anglos had nothing but contempt for an orderly society. They would kill it if they could, just as—he knew—they were plotting to do at this very moment.

Turning back to his desk, Piedras looked around him furtively. Then, reassured that he was alone, he buried his face in his hands and sobbed, epauletted shoulders rocking gently. He was lonely and afraid, and he didn't know where to turn.

Gradually, by an act of will, he forced the jumbled thoughts in his aching head back into proper order. There was, of course, a proper thing to do. He had done it before, each time the burdens of his command seemed too much. He would turn to higher authority. That, after all, was as Plato had dictated it. Higher authority would resolve his problem, if he could only wait.

The simple resolution made him feel better. Straightening his tunic he strode to the inner door, opened it, and asked of the sergeant on duty there, "*¿Que dia es?*"

"*El doce de julio, mi colonel.*"

Piedras nodded, ordered paper, pen, and ink placed on his desk, then dismissed the sergeant and closed the door firmly. With both doors and the window closed, the heat in the colonel's office was stifling. But this way, he knew, there were no spies watching what he did.

In the final hour of siesta, the 12th of July, 1832, Colonel Jose de las Piedras sat at his desk writing communiques. The principal one was a dispatch to the military commander of Texas and Coahuila. In it he reiterated his fears of rebellion by American settlers. Revolution was in the air, and he stated flatly what he knew was about to happen. There would be war in Texas. Mexico would lose Texas. He must be sent reinforcements and money.

Next, he urged, the authorities must severely punish those Anglos who had instigated the disturbance at Anahuac. He reminded them again, as he had repeatedly over the past three years, of his urgent warning that "the introduction of foreigners, their insolence and the scorn they display toward the Republic of Mexico, leaves room for no doubt that they will soon be the masters of Texas."

138

How many men could the Anglos field in pitched battle? he asked himself, pausing, and the answer was clear. When the rebellion started, adventurers and deserters by the thousands would stream across the Sabine to swell the ranks of the interlopers. Dipping his pen again, he stated that the American settlers in Texas could field 2500 armed military-aged men.

And against that horde, he thought, only himself and a pitiful handful of troops. Of course, there were the Indians . . . but no, there was no counting on the Indians. He didn't know whether what Moro had done would prove to be good or bad. Nothing was resolved there, although the armed visit by a band of Cherokee earlier today, which Medina had reported in his journal, argued that he might be able to count on Indian support against the Anglos.

Much better, though, to be cautious on the subject of the Indians. In his letter he said, simply, that the Indians would "go with whoever pays them the most."

The final part of his letter was to absolve himself of responsibility should he fail to hold the frontier in this time of troubles. He had warned Mexico repeatedly of the price it might pay should these Anglo rebels get out of hand. Now it was happening. He would do what he could, but he could do nothing more.

Captains Renaldo Musquiz of the Company of Monclova and Francisco Medina of the 12th Battalion were professional soldiers, sharing all of the qualities the term had come to denote. Fiercely loyal to their commands, each was prepared to lay down his life at a moment's notice in the proper defense of his country. But neither had any reservation about saying exactly what he thought, to anyone willing to listen, as long as he was on his own time.

For the moment, they were both on their own time, relaxing at Sim's Tavern across the square from Frost Thorn's Mercantile, and they had plenty of willing listeners. Time and again Colonel Piedras had demanded—had all but ordered—that his men not associate with Anglos. But for a small garrison stationed in a town of fewer than four hundred people, a third of whom were Anglos owning most of the establishments, such a thing was next to impossible. Besides, there were only twelve officers assigned to Nacogdoches, and a man needs association with others who smell of things other than gun oil and boot polish.

On his hot afternoon, with all the portals open, it was dim and cool in the shadowed interior of Sim's Tavern. Captain Musquiz was holding forth. For the purpose of protocol, he spoke directly to Medina, but he made no effort to keep his words from the others there, and Sim was doing a right brisk business. The word had gone out that there were interesting things to be heard. Henry Brewer and his son John were there, as were John Durst, Encarnacion Chireno, Jose and Juan Mora, Vicente Cordova, Adolphus Sterne, Frost Thorn and Haden Edwards, Lieutenant Juan Jose Gallardo, Lieutenant of Cavalry Jose Martinez, Sub-lieutenant Silvestre Leal and the army surgeon, Doctor Agustin Lejarza, and others.

Those who were regulars at Sim's felt distinctly overshadowed by the eminence around them.

"You've heard reports of the activities of Colonel Bradburn at Anahuac," Musquiz told Medina so that all could hear him. "Well, they were not exaggerated, not in the slightest. The man either went mad with power down there in his mosquito bogs, or had set out to conquer the world while no one was looking, who knows?

"To start, he let his soldiers do as they pleased with

140

the people of the area, and some of those *presidarios* were quick to take advantage. In the meantime Bradburn impressed the slaves of some of the settlers and made them do his work. When settlers complained, he locked them in the old brick kiln at the fort."

"The slaves?" Nathaniel Norris asked.

For protocol, Medina repeated the question. "The slaves?"

"No, the settlers." Musquiz sipped his whiskey and continued. "Then it got bad. An Anglo drifter, a worthless sort, got three soldiers drunk and they assaulted an Anglo settler's woman. Bradburn refused their complaints."

"The soldiers complained?" John Brewer asked, wide-eyed.

"No, *estupido,*" Musquiz growled at the young man, "the settlers complained. *Por Dios.* Anyway, the settlers took matters into their own hands. They visited justice upon the Anglo who did it, but as soon as they laid hands on one of the soldiers, Bradburn sent his troops in and jailed a lot of the leaders. The soldiers have gone free."

He paused for the shaking of heads and the muttering of oaths. Any man, uniformed or not, who molested a woman—any woman—deserved the severest punishment. It was a code upon which all agreed.

"So then what happened?" Chireno asked.

Protocol in mind, Musquiz looked at Medina. His report, after all, was to his fellow captain.

"What happened then?" Medina asked.

"Ah." Musquiz leaned back, stretching trail-kinked muscles. "Then the unexpected occurred. Militia units from Liberty and Brazoria came in, captured one of Bradburn's patrols, and offered to trade prisoners. And you won't believe this, but it is so. Bradburn's brave *soldados* abandoned the town, took refuge in the fort, and left all their powder and shot in the town."

Medina's mouth hung open for a moment, then he shook his head. "Incredible."

"Indeed." Musquiz leaned forward, slapping palm on planking. "But it gets worse. The great Colonel Bradburn made an agreement with the settlers. He would exchange his prisoners for theirs. Then when they withdrew—and after all, they had his word, did they not?— he moved in force and retook the town. And he kept his prisoners."

"He lied?" Sub-lieutenant Leal was aghast. "He gave his word of honor, and lied?"

Musquiz nodded, suddenly looking very tired. "He broke his word. The document you heard of, these 'Turtle Bayou Resolutions,' they were drawn up after that."

"Small wonder," Haden Edwards proclaimed.

"The two militias laid seige to the fort at Anahuac," Musquiz continued. "And some of them went to Brazoria for cannon."

"Civilians are not allowed to have cannon," Leal blurted out. Medina cocked an eyebrow at him and the junior officer reddened. "Well, it *is* regulation."

"At Velasco," Musquiz said, "Colonel Ugartechea tried to stop them, and they fought. The Texians, as they call themselves down there now, took the fort."

"What happened to Bradburn?"

"He was relieved by Piedras. Colonel Suverano has temporary command. Bradburn . . ." Musquiz shrugged eloquently. "It seems he had business in New Orleans. He did not return with us."

Nathaniel Norris had met Bradburn. He said in English, to no one in particular, "Sonuvabitch should'a been hanged."

Captain Musquiz, his cup halfway to his lips, stopped and cocked an eyebrow in Norris's direction. "Bear in mind," he said, also in English, "that sonuvabitch is a colonel in the Mexican Army."

"He ain't the only sonuvabitch that's a colonel in the Mexican Army," Brewer pointed out. "What did Piedras do about that mess down there?"

"What could he do?" Musquiz lapsed into Spanish again. "The civil authorities of the area upheld what had taken place as just and legal. They stood on the resolutions drawn by the civilians at Turtle Bayou, and they had enough combined militia strength to back us down. Our colonel raved, but there was no one he could punish."

"They've all declared for Santa Anna," Lieutenant Martinez added.

"And rightly so." Edwards thumped an empty cup down on the table. "High time we all did."

"That kind of talk," Medina said mildly, "is what throws our commandant into a rage. He sees General Santa Anna as a traitor. He hates him, *señores*. He is a legitimate candidate for the presidency."

"Agreed." Chireno nodded. "But that is no election taking place. It is a revolution."

"Certainly it is a revolution. How else can a royalist be cast out? Kings don't subject their thrones to electoral process, you know."

Musquiz ignored the political fervor venting itself around him. He had no use for politics. He was a soldier. When there was a lull, he spoke again to Medina. "It was a relief, my friend, when Colonel Suverano took over at Anahuac and we started home."

He wanted to say more, but could not. The veteran captain could not bring himself to tell of the shame he felt for the way his superior officer had conducted himself among civilians. He just added, "Most of the time we were there I kept my company out on patrol maneuvers."

Most of them read the unspoken. They all knew Pie-

143

dras.

Norris leaned forward. "Captain Musquiz, what do you expect the colonel will do now?"

Musquiz frowned. "Colonel Piedras is my commanding officer, *señor*. I would not predict what his decisions may be."

Frost Thorn understood the point of honor. He reversed the question. "Then tell us, Renaldo, if you were not a soldier . . . if you were one of us—a civilian citizen in this place now—what would you do?"

"I can answer that. I would walk very lightly, *señores*. I would be very careful, and I would have someone stay awake in my house when I slept."

CHAPTER XIII

*"Martyrs are dead. They can't dispute claims
of what they lived for."*
—Captain Francisco Medina

"And just where in hell have you been?" Alexander
Horton demanded. The drenched scarecrow standing before him on the short porch of James Bullock's main
house at "The Island" on the Attoyac River was about
the sorriest specimen of humanity he had seen. Coop
Willoughby was unwashed, unshaven, slouched, and
beat-out as he stood hunched in scant protection from
the screen of rain sheeting off Bullock's porch over-
hang.

"I been busy," he told the sheriff in a voice that said
he didn't give a bent horseshoe nail what Horton's reaction was. "Are you gonna let me in, or not?"

Horton stepped back and Willoughby pushed past
him, dripping rainwater on Elizabeth Bullock's clean
floor. With one arm laden with saddle packs and the
other holding his rifle muzzle-down against the rain, he
had to struggle to remove his sodden hat so he could
howdy Mrs. Bullock and her sister, Sarah. Setting some
of his burden down by the door, Willoughby turned a
weary face to the master of the house, who was just

coming in from the back room.

"Sorry to drop in on you like this, Mr. Bullock," he said. "But if you've got a place I could sleep for a few hours, I'd be mighty obliged."

Bullock stared at him, then nodded. "There's a bed yonder in the loft. Help yourself. Damned if it didn't take me a minute to know who you was, Coop."

Elizabeth Bullock, without a word, crossed to Willoughby and handed him a length of toweling. He stared at it dumbly, unsure where to start. He was soaked to the bone. One of the things he had lost to the Kickapoos was his slicker.

Sheriff Alexander Horton closed the door and said to his sister, "It's gonna take more than that to dry this jaybird off, Liz. Let's get a fire goin' and see if we can find him some dry clothes. James, you got some britches and a shirt my deputy could use?"

With the patience of exhaustion Willoughby let himself be bullied into dry garb and hot tea by Horton's two sisters while Bullock expounded on how bad he looked and the sheriff stood stolidly by, waiting for an explanation. When the refreshing was done and the smuggler lounged before a catching fire, he told Horton, "It ain't a matter for the ladies, Sandy."

Elizabeth and Sarah were unceremoniously hustled out of the room. When Bullock closed the door behind them Willoughby turned to Horton. "I got to find Anton Moro, or there's gonna be Indian trouble. The bastard tried to shoot Diwali. He shot Utsada."

The mouth behind Bullock's whiskers dropped open. Horton just stared for a moment. Then he managed, "Why?"

"Best I can calculate, he must have figured he could set the Cherokee to war against the Anglos if he killed Diwali." Willoughby shrugged. "How'n hell would I know why Moro does anything?"

146

Bit by bit, with many interruptions, he managed to fill them in on events since the day he left Horton in Nacogdoches. Outside, the reds and greens of East Texas were muted in the steady, silver screen of summer rain. Droplets negotiating the chimney sputtered and popped on the crackling pitch-pine blazing there, and rosy shadows danced on the gray log walls.

"Last couple of days now, since I left Nacogdoches, I guess I've covered about half of East Texas trying to get a line on Moro. I thought I knew where he'd be . . . figured the old Burton place on the Sabine, where he holed up after that ruckus two years ago. But I couldn't find any sign of him. Now I just don't know."

Horton's eyes narrowed even more. "If you knew where he was after the Perez thing, why in hell didn't you tell somebody? If we could'a found him then we could'a hanged him."

Willoughby looked at him disdainfully. "No, you couldn't. You just think it was him did that, Sandy Horton. Nobody ever knew for sure." In his tired euphoria he started to add that the Perez girl surely wasn't in any condition to say who had been at her, and nobody else had been home. But he held his tongue. Horton had suffered that knowledge enough. He had been sweet on Lola Perez. Now the whole Perez family was gone and there wasn't anything to be done about it. It was just one of the things that had gone into making a tough, hard man of Sandy Horton before his twenty-second year.

Willoughby, approaching the grand old age of thirty, had seen enough in his own life to understand the bitter helplessness of losing a sweet girl to a brute who, by the law, was beyond your reach.

As he saw similar thoughts playing across the young sheriff's face Coop added, "You'll always go by the letter of the law, Sandy. You're just built that way."

147

"And you ain't?" Horton demanded.

"Not near so much." Willoughby shrugged. "That's why I guess I can go get Moro now, before we get ourselves fetched up in an Indian war."

Bullock had been listening phlegmatically, chewing on his mustache. "You'll just get yourself killed, is all, Coop. Ain't no way under the sun you can take Moro even if you find him. No offense to you, Coop, but it'd take a dozen good men to take out that big curly wolf, and some of 'em wouldn't come back from tryin'. Besides, you don't even know where he is."

"He's around someplace. I been thinking about that. I been looking for where he might hole up, but I'm not sure he's hid at all. Moro wouldn't hide out just over killing an Indian. It wouldn't strike him to. So I got to look for him like he ain't hidin'."

Bullock was confused. "So where does that mean?"

"I don't know. All the places I know are hidin' places."

Bullock looked helplessly at Horton, who was nodding. The sheriff understood the devious thinking of his prisoner/deputy. "There's no law," he said flatly, "that says I can't help you find him."

"No. But then what, Sandy? The Indians want him back. You can't give him back, can you?"

"If he's dead, I can." Horton's eyes were flat and hard. None of them had any doubt that Alexander Horton might be a fair match for Anton Moro. There was just one catch. Horton was hampered by his stiff-backed insistence upon honor and the law. Moro had never known any such constraints.

Willoughby shrugged. "I guess if you help me find him that would be a blessing. Then we can think about what to do with him when we know where he is."

Horton looked askance at the tired, stubbled face in the firelight. "You *are* planning to take him out, aren't you, Coop? All by yourself, you're figurin' to take Anton Moro back to the Cherokee."

Willoughby's chin was slumped onto his bony chest. His words were slurred by irresistible sleep. "Yeah. He shot Utsada."

The stomping of James Bullock's muddy boots on the doorstep awakened Willoughby to a new day. An evening and a night had passed since he climbed into Bullock's loft, and the rain had passed with it. Bullock had been out in the fields looking to his crops. Elizabeth and Sarah, who was staying over while her own husband was away, had coffee on and ham and corncakes making.

Bullock came in as Willoughby climbed down the ladder. "Rain was just what the doctor ordered," he told everybody in general. "Them fields look alive again this mornin'." Spotting Willoughby he added, "Mornin', Coop. You sleep well?"

"I reckon, 'cause I don't remember it at all. Mornin', ladies."

Sarah smiled at him and Elizabeth handed him soap and a towel. "Breakfast is makin', Mister Willoughby. You can wash up out back. James's razor is there on the shelf and you can use it to shave."

"Obliged. Where's your brother this mornin'?"

"Oh," Bullock put in, hanging his hat on a peg. "Sandy left yesterday. Said he had places to go. Said for you not to worry, just plan to meet up with him at Ayish in two-three days."

Coop shot him a glance. "Gone to do some scoutin', has he?"

"I reckon. Sandy's been movin' right fast these days, with the stink that's been raised down south. Ben Lindsay, Wyatt Hanks, and Hiram Brown an' their folks is all throwin' in on Santa Anna's side, signin' up pledges to support the Turtle Bayou Resolutions an' all. Sandy's been all over the country talkin' to folks, gettin' a feel as to how things is shapin' up out here."

Willoughby peered at him. "Why?"

"Huh!" Bullock plopped down in a handy chair. "If you mean why are folks swingin' to Santa Anna, there's about three main reasons. Some of 'em are just naturally inclined that way . . . guess I should say some of 'us' are, 'cause I'm one. Never did have any use for Bustamente, an' Santa Anna sure won't be any worse. Then, a lot of folks been so ticked at ol' Colonel Piedras for so long that they'd jump on any wagon goin' some other way besides his'n.

"And mainly, word's got around about Colonel Mexia's visit to Brazoria . . . maybe you ain't heard about that? Well, Mexia put five gunboats in at Velasco after he got word on the fight down there, and he talked to the Austins and Henry Brown and McKinstry and some, and they taken him up to Brazoria and fed him and likkered him and convinced him what fine Mescans us Texians is, and he was so impressed he commissioned that militia down there to take charge of things and ordered all the troops home."

"All what troops?" Willoughby was tying into a heaping plate of ham and corncakes.

"Why, all of 'em. They need 'em down in Mexico to help fight the war."

"All of 'em?"

"Ever' last one." Bullock hitched his chair up to the table as Elizabeth put another plate on. "Lay down that damn fork, Coop. Ain't you got good manners? Now bow your head. God bless this food an' them that's partakin' of it, an' keep a eye on them crops out there so's there'll be more where this come from. In Jesus' name we ask it. Amen. Now you can eat. Course they ain't all goin' to go, because Mexia's a Santa Anna man and them that ain't on that side won't take no orders from him, like ol' Piedras. He ain't gonna answer to no Colonel Mexia even if they was on the same side of the fence because Mexia is junior to him."

For long moments there was silence. Bullock and Willoughby ate ravenously while Elizabeth Bullock and her sister stood aside and watched with the mixed emotions of women watching men devour the food they have worked to prepare. That's what it's for, but that isn't how it should be done.

"Piedras is crazy," Willoughby allowed, coming up for breath. "I figure the only thing keeping him from goin' off the deep end is General Teran. Teran is the only real power in Mexico that isn't Bustamente or Santa Anna either one. He's stayed neutral, and he won't stand for any nonsense."

Bullock bolted down a mouthful and looked squarely, soberly at his guest. "I guess you ain't heard, then, Coop. Teran is dead. He killed himself. There isn't anything holdin' Piedras anymore."

CHAPTER XIV

*"Anybody knows when you hear thunder
it's time to take in the wash."*
— Jane Norris

Nine miles south of Almazon Huston's Inn on El Camino Real, Alexander Horton reined his lathered mount to a halt on the bank of Ayish Bayou, dismounted, and led the horse to, and into, the cool water. It was a fresh, hot morning, with a high scent of pine in the air as the forest dried from the previous night's rain and began to bake under the sun.

He stood a few moments in knee-deep water, letting the horse drink and blow, then urged it into deeper water and swam it across the narrow stream. On the far side he found shade under the pine boughs, rubbed down his animal's neck, back, and flanks — leaving the light saddle in place — and set it to grazing for a few minutes while he poured water from his mule-hide boots and cleaned his weapons. Remounting, he turned north, following the bayou's twisting course.

He knew Donald McDonald would be home on this day. It had rained and the Ayish was flowing, and McDonald would not miss such an opportunity to use the waterwheel he had constructed for his grist mill. Of late, the Scotch-Canadian's mill had been mule-powered while the errant Ayish stream sat idle under the paddle wheel's dry blades.

By hard riding this morning Horton had managed to stop and inquire at four homesteads south of the Royal Road, so far without result. None knew the whereabouts of Moro. But at the last place, the widow Simmet's, he had a message waiting. Her oldest boy, George, had been up Ayish the day before. McDonald wanted to see him. There had been outlawry to the east.

Life would be a sight easier, Horton told himself, if a man could tend to one thing at a time. Only a few months before, he had sorted out his pressing projects and found them manageable: There was a crop to put into the ground for his mother and the younger ones still at home; there was some more education to get — he had been learning to read for two years now, and thought he might take up the law if he could learn proper grammar; there was pretty Patsy Mullen to court — and in case that didn't work out he planned also to court Rosemary Gaines, and just to be on the safe side he was thinking about sparkling young Becky Tice as well; and he had a nest of thieves spotted over in the Neutral Zone that he intended to clean out. From the vantage point of late spring this had looked to be making up for a nice, pleasant summer.

It hadn't stayed that way. First that knot-headed colonel at Anahuac had tried to take over the world and gotten folks down there all upset. Then word had come that there was another revolution making up down in Mexico, and that had folks upset too. Then that John Austin bunch had gone and taken the fort at Velasco, and that and the Anahuac business had gotten that slantwise Colonel Piedras all upset, and he had managed to get the Indians all upset, and that upset everybody else even more. Now his deputy, whom he planned to use to clean out that nest of thieves in the neutral zone, was all upset, and Anton Moro was out running around somewhere shooting at Indians, and Egg and Gu'nasoquo were upset and fixing to upset the whole country.

And now there was more trouble to the east. Horton's angry snort brought his horse's ears around. The way things were going he might not get any serious courting done this summer at all.

He thought of sunny-faced Patsy Mullen, and shy, dark-eyed Rosemary Gaines, and the way little Becky Tice was filling out her dress lately. For good measure he gave some thought to Annabel Owens too. And then there was Susanna Willis. And Helen and Ellen Murcheson. Aye, and Anna Maria Valdez, for that matter.

By the time he rode into the clearing at McDonald's, Sheriff Alexander Horton was feeling very put-upon.

The paddle wheel turned to the Ayish flow, sheets of bright water cascading from its blades as they rose. McDonald and his black helper, both soaked with sweat, were working the mill.

"Weel, noo, if it wa'nt the high sheriff." McDonald drew a sleeve across his brow and extended a hand. "How be ye, Sandy, lad? Coom find a spot of shade and rest ye'self."

"I'm tolerable, Cap'n. How you?"

"An' it weren't sae bloody hot I would be better. But see" — he waved toward the paddle wheel — "when the stream's up she turns strong and grinds fine. Things could be worse."

"Heard there was trouble over this way."

In the noon shade near the mill McDonald had cut down two crowding pines and shaped the stumps into chairs. They sat there, and McDonald pulled out his

154

pipe. The black man had taken Horton's mount.

"Ye might say so. There was a killin'."

Horton waited while his host got the pipe stoked and lit.

"East it was, day before yestidday. But this side of the Neutral Ground, aboot a mile from the river where the old heathen trail goes. Feller said 'twas Mescan soldiers done it."

"Soldiers?"

"What he said. Pair of 'em in ragtag army issue, one wi' a musket and t'other sportin' a fine rifle. Mean ones they wa', he said."

"Who said?"

"Feller as got away from 'em. Greener he was, name of Waverly, come wi' another feller an' his boy to find land in Texas. They two Mescans laid out to rob 'em, an' didna' even rob decint, just started in shootin' when they showed. Waverly lit out and got to here. Me an' Ben gone back wi' him and found th' bodies of t'other two, stripped clean of all they carried. One was but a wee lad, Sandy. A wee lad."

"Where's Waverly now?"

McDonald shrugged. "Na'a blessed he could do but go on, so he did."

Horton shook his head. One trouble with border outlawry against illegal immigrants was that the witnesses never stayed around to witness.

Something else was bothering McDonald. "A mon expects outlaws on the way into Mexico, Sandy. But he dinna expect them to be Mescans. Calls ye to wonder what things're comin' to."

"What did they get?"

"Oh, horses, tools, supplies, a bit o' coin."

Well, Horton thought, add two more to the list needing cleaned out of the Neutral Strip. These two were probably runaway *presidarios* from one of the garrisons. With a little luck, some of those tough characters laying out in the thickets over there might find them and save him the trouble. But he would need to go and look.

"Mac, I don't suppose you've seen anything of that Basque, Anton Moro?"

McDonald scowled. "Neither have nor wish to, lad. I've no business wi' that 'un. He's a bad 'un, he is."

"Yeah, well, I need to find him. Any ideas?"

The Scot sucked on his pipe. "There's few around will have dealin's wi' Moro. That addle-brained colonel at Nacogdoches, o' course, but wa' he there ye wouldna be askin' aboot him. Then maybe some o' them hot-heads on the Neches . . . Sam Looney an' them. Ha' ye asked o'er there?"

"Not yet. I heard he was comin' this way."

"If I hear aught I'll let ye know." McDonald glanced up. The sun was near its zenith. "My Louisa will be settin' dinner on the board soon. Can ye coom and ha' a bite wi' us, lad? There's cabbage from Louisa's garden, an' pork an' peas."

It was near two o'clock when Alexander Horton saddled his gray and headed north again, along Ayish Bayou.

He could hear Wyatt Hanks's sawmill long before he reached it. The long, hand-drawn saw sent its song bounding through the forest. He followed the sound down the narrow trail. In the mill clearing, two black workers were ripping a great pine log down its center. The saw they used was fifteen feet long. One of them stood on a platform above the log, the other in a pit below. The one in the pit was covered with sawdust, coating his sweating body in a blanket patterned by rivulets of moisture on his dark skin. The two glanced at Horton and grinned as he dismounted, but did not break the rhythm of their sweeping pulls at the great

156

saw.

Hanks himself was working nearby with another black man. They were at the two ends of a large beam, wielding hewing axes, squaring opposite faces of it as it rested upon cross-timbers. Seeing the sheriff arrive, Hanks signaled to another black who was stacking planks nearby. The man approached and Hanks tossed his ax to him. "Take over here, Hob. I be back directly."

Wyatt Hanks, at thirty-eight, was a lean, quick man who looked to be all bone and leather. He was known to describe himself as "a Sawyer by bornin', a Kaintuck by raisin', and a Texian for lack of better sense." Of him and his brothers, James and Horatio, it was said, "There's two things no Hanks is afraid of: another man, or ever being wrong."

Fiesty and determined, Wyatt Hanks intended to carve himself a life out of this Texas wilderness if it hamstrung half of Mexico.

"Ye're right on time, Sandy," he called. "Gimme a minute to get a shirt on my back and we'll head for Huston's."

"Huston's? What for?"

Hanks stopped. "Ain't you goin' to the meetin'?"

"I didn't know there was one."

"Well, hell, ye should'a knowed. Got the word out last day or two. There's to be a meetin' at Huston's. Ye'll be wanted there." Before he could explain further James and Horatio Hanks came into view on a side trail, James leading a mule hitched to a fallen log and Horatio and one of the black workmen walking beside it, guiding it with tongs and picks.

Wyatt Hanks called out, "James, when was it you tol' James Bullock 'bout the meetin'?"

The younger Hanks urged the mule into the clearing and sidled it over toward a log pile. "I didn't get that

157

far," he said. "I give the word to Will Russey an' he said he'd get them up there advised this mornin'."

"That's why I didn't know about it," Horton said. "I been out movin' around."

"Well," Wyatt Hanks recited, "there's to be a meetin' at Almazon Huston's this evenin' to con-sider the proper locatin' of a townsite, name of such yet to be determined upon by them present."

Horton groaned. "Is that all?"

"I doubt if that's all, cause they said 'God an' Liberty' whilst they's at it."

Horton pursed his lips and looked at the sun, now quartering into the west. "In that case, Wyatt, what you standin' here talkin' for? Get your shirt on and let's go. Horatio and James goin' with us?"

"Just Horatio. We'll leave baby brother here to keep things movin' along."

"How come Mac McDonald didn't tell me there was a 'God and Liberty' meetin' called?"

Horatio Hanks had come up to him. "I reckon he didn't know about it, Sandy. When James went down that way yest'day he was out buryin' a pilgrim or somethin'. You know what that was all about?"

"Yeah. We got us some new brush-poppers over in the thicket."

"Then how come the sheriff ain't out after 'em?"

Horton bristled. He liked the easygoing Wyatt Hanks, but his middle brother Horatio was an enigma. A man never knew whether he was joking or not. "Because the sheriff has other things to do too, Horatio. Or maybe you'd like to be deputized to go find a man about an Indian for me? Or figure how to put a stop to Willis's road-agentin'? Or keep an eye on what Sam Looney is haulin' across the Ayzes district? Or make me a list of greeners comin' through, or try to keep track of what that damn Piedras is gonna do next, or go to

158

this here 'God and Liberty' meetin' in my place?"

Wyatt Hanks grinned at the outburst. Horatio just shrugged.

"I'm already fixin' to go to the meeting. 'Sides, I heard you already got yourself a deputy. Where's he at?"

"He's out headin' off an Indian war, that's where."

"Smuggler, ain't he?"

Wyatt stepped in at that point. "Horatio, you get yourself around there an' get our horses for us. We can't jaw all evenin'."

As Horatio turned away Horton shot after him, "Hell, yes, he's a smuggler! An' one of the best!"

When Horatio was gone Wyatt Hanks turned to the sheriff. "Sandy, how come you don't like my brother?"

Horton looked at him in real surprise. "Horatio? Why, I like him just fine, Wyatt. I just can't tolerate talkin' to him, is all."

As the three rode away from the Hanks clearing, toward Almazon Huston's place, Wyatt Hanks took it on himself to ride in the middle, between the phlegmatic Horatio and the irritable high sheriff. That way if either one had talking to do, they could talk to him.

Huston's Inn was on the Camino Real not far from the collection of buildings at the Ayish crossing. When it came down to discussion of where a new townsite should be, there was little doubt in anyone's mind. The makings were already in place. But such decisions are never approached without constraint. The people involved were Texians, and more specifically East Texas Redlanders, and procedure was a code among them. Lesser matters such as going to war or politicking, or char-clearing a forest or seceding, might be decided in a whirlwind of emotion and whim. But when it came to such things as settling a will, staking a townsite, planning a wedding, or naming a child, there was due process to be observed. Adolphus Sterne had once commented on procedure: "You begin with a common knowledge of what you will do, then pretend you don't know and pose the question, and call a meeting to talk about all the wrong answers so that when you get around to the right one everyone can agree in good conscience. And what you will do is exactly what all of you knew you would do before you discussed it."

His audience had found nothing humorous in his comment. It was the way things were done.

It was that way now. Everyone knew where the new townsite would be, and while there was some question whether to call it Ayish of San Augustine, that was a minor point. But they met at Huston's Inn and solemnly recited possible townsites throughout the Ayzes District, considered every name except the two most likely, then appointed a committee to bring back a recommendation.

While they were about it, the committee also was to recommend who might serve as *Alcalde, Regidores, Alguazil,* and *Fiscales.* At the moment, Ben Lindsay was *Alcalde* for the district, and no one else spoke up wanting the job. Along the line they would talk to Lindsay about it. When Bullock asked his brother-in-law if he wanted to keep on being *Alguazil,* Horton's answer was short and to the point.

"Hell, yes. Who else you think could do the job?"

The *Regidores,* who would serve as town council, would be selected later, as would the fiscal overseers.

Achilles Edmond Challis Johnson, who answered to "Ed," was one of the committee chosen to work on the details when they got around to it. Throughout the ritual of the formal meeting he had sat impatiently, waiting for the agenda to run its course. He breathed a sigh of relief when adjournment was called, stood up, and took off his coat, waistcoat, and tie. He hiked the sleeves of his sweat-soaked linen shirt up over muscled forearms and said, "All right, that's it. Now let's go out where there's some air movin' and talk war."

The suggestion met with general approval. It was close and hot in the common room of Huston's Inn, and no place for serious conversation. It was, however, the proper trapping for public business.

Johnson, a Virginian, was another of the old-timers in East Texas. Like the Hanks brothers, and Bullock and Horton, he had been a Texican for more than five years. That, to the Anglo-Texas way of thinking, was akin to being a native.

Squatting under a pine tree in the late afternoon, Ed Johnson looked around him. Most of the members of the Ayish Committee for Peace and Harmony were present. The same men also were the leaders of the Ayish militia.

"Been nigh a month," Johnson said emphatically, "since we passed our resolution, and things haven't got better, they've got worse. Piedras shouldn't have took a hand in the doin's at Anahuac, but he done it anyway. Ugartechea shouldn't have tried to fight off them Austin folks down at Velasco, but he done it."

"And got whipped in the process," Bullock pointed out.

"Course he got whipped. Point is he shouldn'ta tried to stop them in the first place. Now Piedras is back and he's got the folks over at Nacogdoches all stirred up, and he's got the Indians all stirred up, and we got trouble.

"We told 'em straight. We stand for peace and harmony, even if we have to fight and raise hell to get it. But Piedras an' them aren't gonna leave it alone. That little colonel's out for trouble, and it's gonna come our way sure's hell."

"Seems to me if he'd just let things be there's no

161

need for trouble anywhere up here," Wyatt Hanks said.

"But 'bout everybody up this way favors Santa Anna in the war down there, an' he cain't tolerate that, Wyatt." Horton, who rode the countryside regularly, was the authority among them on what people were thinking.

"Yeah," Bullock said. "But like you just said, Sandy, the war's 'way down there, it ain't up here."

"Gettin' mighty close, though," Horatio Hanks allowed.

"Point is," Horton said to Bullock, "Piedras has already chose up sides, and he's determined that the war's right here, right now."

"I don't know as I particularly favor Santa Anna," Barney Lowe put in. "He's just another Mescan so'jer, like the other'ns."

Iredell Thomas turned a questioning face to him. "Then do you favor Bustamente?"

"Well, hell, no. I just don't think it's any of our concern up here, is all."

"Piedras," Horton said stolidly, "reckons it is."

"He brung the Indians in on it," Thomas pointed out. "Or at least he's tryin' to."

"Yeah," Lowe admitted. "I guess I can't tolerate that."

The Bailey Andersons, senior and junior, nodded assent. Cut from the same mold, they were solid, quiet men with gray eyes so light in color they looked white. Many people found the Andersons disconcerting. If there was humor in them, few could find it.

"I been askin' everyone I see," Horton said. "Has anybody seen Anton Moro just lately? I need to find him and he ain't in Nacogdoches."

James Bullock, who knew why Horton was asking for Moro, glanced quickly at him and then studied the others. The expressions were blank, but for one. Dan

Vail was slouched against a pine stump, digging tobacco and pipe from his possible pouch. He looked up.

"Sure, I seen him, Sandy. He stopped by my place for water. He was headed east. Ain't seen him since, though."

"Did he say where he was going?"

"Shoot." Vail brought out a tinder box. "You know Moro better'n I do. Would you go askin' him his business?"

"Damn right I would," Horton said. He snapped his fingers. "Like that."

"Well, you're the Sheriff. I ain't. I ain't gonna ask Moro about nothin'. That hawg-nosed bastid soon shoot a man as look at him. I hear he cut up a fella real bad over'n Nag-dish just fer bein' cross-eyed."

"I reckon." Lowe nodded. "I heard the same story."

Bailey Anderson Junior was listening curiously, pale eyes darting from one to another, then holding on Horton. "Why you want to find Moro, Sheriff?"

Horton shrugged. "My deputy and I need to talk to him about somethin'."

Horatio Hanks put in, "Seems to me you made a remark about that deputy of your'n bein' out to stop a Indian war, Sheriff."

Horton looked at him crossly. "I may have."

There was a long silence. James Bullock began to fidget. "Y'all know," he said finally, "if there's fightin' comin' up—Piedras an' all—it'll be different than it was five year ago in the Fredonia deal. Anybody wanted to stay outta that'n just moved back east for a while, got outta Texas an' waited it out. Won't be like that this time."

"How's that?" Wyatt Hanks asked.

"Y'all seen all these drifters and greeners comin' in lately. If we was to leave, there'd be folks jumpin' our holdin's within a week. We wouldn't have anything to come back to, likely."

There was general agreement to that. It wasn't likely anyone in East Texas would skip out to avoid trouble. It wouldn't pay.

As the sun disappeared behind pine thickets they talked of Santa Anna's revolution, of Anahuac and Velasco, of Colonel Mexia's carte blanche to the Austin colony settlers to send the soldiers home, and of the unpredictability of Colonel Piedras. To a man, they knew there would be trouble. They were about split on whether to wait it out or go ahead and start it and get it over with.

As the talk went on Sheriff Alexander Horton eased closer to James Bullock and asked quietly, "When Coop left your place today, James, where was he headin'?"

"East, I reckon." Bullock was worried. "Into the thickets."

As evening's shadows crept over the lowlands along the Sabine valley, there was a stillness in the area where a remote trail, scarcely used, wound down toward the river. For a time there was silence. Then a nightingale sang a tentative call. And again. And then there was an answer. A flock of passenger pigeons homing in toward their evening roost took up the sounds and added their chorus. A few larks twittered, and in the deep shadows of a thicket wood an owl greeted the ascending darkness.

On the ground a fox trotted along the path, nose up and ears perked. Rounding a bend it stopped, stood nervously for a moment, and shivered as its keen nose caught the dreaded man-smell and the pungent odor of fresh blood. Nothing moved. Cautiously, tentatively, it stalked forward, nose low and outthrust. With every sense at the alert it sidled around a copse of tall grass and stopped again, big eyes watchful and fearful. A man lay face down, half across the trail. He wasn't moving.

Only the eyes of the evening forest saw where Cooper Willoughby lay. He had gone after Anton Moro, and he had found him.

PART THREE
GOD AND LIBERTY

CHAPTER XV

*"I think only you and I, alone, have
understood Texas."*
— General Manuel Mier y Teran
to Stephen F. Austin

Directly outside the Red House, facing the square, was a notice board built of that same lumber which Colonel Piedras had acquired for the building of his quarters. Two sturdy posts set in the ground held planking on both sides, forming an impressive *signatorio* more than four feet square, its top six feet above the ground. The side facing the Red House was reserved for notices, ordinances, and regulations directed to the military. The side facing the square was for public notices issued by the garrison's commanding officer.

Since Piedras's return from Anahuac the board had stood vacant. But now, on a hot Thursday morning, a sergeant and two armed privates issued from the Red House and marched the few steps to the board, and the sergeant gravely tacked a large sheet of penned paper precisely in its center.

As he tacked it up the two privates stood at rigid attention. When it was in place the sergeant barked a command, turned, and marched back into the Red House. The two privates remained standing at attention,

169

flanking the notice.

A short distance away Vicente Cordova, Captain of the Nacogdoches Civil Militia, stopped to watch. Arms folded, lips pursed, he shook his head slowly from one side to the other at the display. Antonio Menchaca, carrying a bolt of brown cloth from Charles Taylor's store, stopped beside him. Rumpled and lumpy in outsized work clothes, the young tailor appeared frail beside the trim, muscular presence of the dashing Cordova, an illusion partly resulting from the fact that Menchaca had tailored the clothing Cordova wore, but not his own.

"Mira, Capitán." He displayed the bolt of cloth. "From this will be born your new tailed coat . . . what are they doing over there?"

Cordova looked appreciatively at the cloth, fingers tracing its fine texture. He nodded. "Handsome indeed. It appears our colonel has something to say. Let us have a look."

As the sergeant disappeared into the Red House the two crossed the narrow street and peered at the fresh notice. As Menchaca read it his thin face paled. He glanced up at first one and then the other of the stolid soldiers flanking the board. Neither would meet his eye. He turned back to the notice and read further. Beside him he was aware that Vicente Cordova was cursing under his breath.

The notice was dated and sealed below the signature of Colonel Jose de las Piedras, commanding, military district of East Texas.

To the Citizens of Nacogdoches District and surrounding districts:

By order of the Commandant, the following ordinances are herewith placed into effect and shall be considered law for the duration of the present emergency:

170

First—It being known that various agents of foreign interests are present in these districts and conspiring with certain residents toward treasonous ends, public meetings and gatherings of civilian personnel are herewith forbidden. Groups of more than five persons, with the exception of families, may not gather in any public building and private home, or at any place within the command of the Commandant of East Texas.

Second—All meetings and activities of civilian organizations are suspended until further notice, this order expressly including fraternal orders, civic meetings of non-official nature, and activities of the Church except for regular Mass.

Third—All militia organizations and all other civilian activities involving armament and organized drill are hereby suspended, and all arms, equipment, and stores held by any militia as common holding are to be tendered to the military authority at Nacogdoches as immediately as they can be gathered and transported.

Fourth—All civilians owning or having firearms of any description in their possession are instructed to deliver all such firearms to the military authority at Nacogdoches, such firearms to be held until such time as the Commandant declares an end to the present emergency, whereupon they will be returned to their owners. Those employed for necessary hunting may be excepted by obtaining written permission from the Commandant.

Fifth—Any and all structures, places, and holdings within the jurisdiction of the military district of East Texas shall be subject to search and inspection by delegates of the Commandant, and the finding of any contraband of any description shall be grounds for the arrest of such persons as may be present there, and of those deemed responsible.

Sixth — Civilian authorities and bodies may meet to conduct their proper business provided permission is given for each such meeting by the Commandant, and provided that such meetings may be attended at discretion by persons so assigned by the Commandant.

Failure of any resident, citizen or indigent, to comply with the above ordinances shall constitute a crime punishable by military tribunal in accordance with the articles of war."

When Antonio Menchaca, ashen-faced, looked up from the notice board, Vicente Cordova was gone. Turning, the tailor saw Cordova striding stiff-shouldered toward the house of the *Alcalde* Chireno. Hesitantly, and then purposefully, he followed. He passed others coming toward the notice board to see what had been posted there. Those who noticed his expression quickened their steps as they passed.

From a window in the Red House Colonel Piedras watched the sign being posted, and watched as first two, and then more, of his subjects came to read it. He saw the expressions of anger, of disbelief, of uncertainty, and allowed a tight-lipped smile to linger for a moment on his face. Then he turned and strode to the inner door. "Sergeant! Send for Captain Medina, immediately."

On his desk lay the report of General Teran's death. Piedras knew now, beyond doubt, that the structure of authority had collapsed and that war was at hand. He knew there would be no assistance coming from the interior. He knew he was on his own, and he would take the steps necessary to win his war. He would not wait to go on the defensive when his enemies struck. He would take the offensive. The war was here.

He was fairly certain that he would not have to go to such lengths as house-to-house search to enforce his civilian directives. A few examples should suffice. In him was the excitement of the commander in the field — the old, heady pleasure of combat at hand, of initiative and strategy begun. First he would subdue the population. Then he would remove his enemies one by one. His would be the line that held Texas when all else fell apart. Let others attend to the upstart Santa Anna. When it was done they would find East Texas in firm control, awaiting their pleasure. Then the Platonian structure would heal itself and there would be honor for Jose de las Piedras.

When Captain Medina arrived a few minutes later, hurrying toward the Red House in response to his sergeant's urgent message, he paused at the notice board to read what was posted there, stood motionless for a moment, and read parts of it again. Oblivious of the several citizens around him, some of them watching him for reaction, he straightened slowly and turned his eyes toward the heavens. *"Madre Maria, alivie a nosotros."* He would have called on some of the saints as well, had there been time. Entering the outer office he saw the abashed face of the sergeant there, felt the silence of the room, and beyond it, beyond the closed door, heard the steady, vigorous pacing of the colonel's boots.

"Is it safe to go in?"

The sergeant kept his eyes fixed on his desktop. "Only for the brave, *mi capitán.*"

Squaring his shoulders, Medina walked into the colonel's office, closing the door behind him. Piedras was completing a pass to the far end of the room, hands behind his back. He turned without breaking stride, then fixed the captain with glistening eyes. "I have been waiting for you."

"I came as soon as I was informed of your order,

173

Colonel."

"But not before reading my pronouncements, eh? Very well. Captain, I have determined that the insurrection of Santa Anna has spread to East Texas. I am taking steps to end it here. Further, I have learned that for the moment the chain of command in Texas and Coahuila has been broken. Therefore I have assumed full field command in this district and will hold it until relieved by proper authority."

At the captain's silence he raised his head, nostrils flaring. "Do you understand me, Captain?"

"*Sí, mi coronel.*"

"Very well, I am surrounded here by traitors. They are everywhere. I can trust no one." Pausing, he looked closely at Medina, commander of the 12th Battalion and second in command of the military forces of Nacogdoches. "Are you to be trusted, Captain?"

Medina took the question as he would take a blow in the face. For a moment he was too stunned to speak. Then the blood drained from his face and a cold anger grew within him. Holding himself rigidly at attention he answered between clenched teeth, "Colonel, I am a soldier of the Army of Mexico. I carry its sword with honor. I serve my country and my honor . . ." He almost bit his tongue to still the rest of it.

"Fine speeches," Piedras said distantly, already moving to other points. "We are past the point of speeches now, you see—"

"Do not condescend to me, Colonel," Medina said, cutting him off. "My honor is questioned by no man. Is that understood, Colonel? No man."

Mild surprise showed on Piedras's chiseled features, nothing more. "Well, of course, Captain. Of course."

Medina realized with a shock that the colonel had entirely forgotten his question.

The colonel turned away and resumed his restless

pacing, head down. "What of the others in my command, Captain?"

"The . . . others?"

"Speak up, man! My other officers. Are they loyal to me?"

"They have taken the same oath as you and I, Colonel. They are all honorable—"

"Yes, yes, of course, no question of that, of course. My orders, Captain. The guard and patrols are to be doubled immediately. I want every man of this garrison armed and on full alert. Patrols at intervals on the streets. A defense perimeter around the town. Yes, and I want patrols in the field—send the first to Ayish Bayou, Captain. I have word the citizens there have declared for Santa Anna. Then to the Neches. Report back to me. What are their forces, what are their arms, what are their supply lines . . . everything.

"I want an immediate report on any civilian meetings held, and on all rumors of rebellion, no matter how slight. We are at war, Captain. We will conduct ourselves accordingly. You are dismissed."

At war? Captain Medina's confusion was beginning to resolve itself into a bleak understanding of what was going on. Of course we are at war, he thought. It has just been declared, on that signpost outside the door. Muscles rippled along his jaws as he clamped his teeth tight to keep words in. The hopelessness of reason hit him like a pall. The colonel had gone beyond reason.

Piedras had already turned from him and gone to the door. "Sergeant!"

Medina squared his shoulders, took a deep breath, and raised his arm in a long salute, focused across the colonel's vacant desk to the flag of Mexico beyond. With sinking heart, Captain Medina saluted his flag.

Then he turned and marched from the office. The sergeant entered as he left. Behind him, Captain Medina heard the colonel instructing, "Sergeant, send an escort for the blacksmith, Will Goyens. I want him here immediately."

Outside, a cluster of citizens had gathered around the signboard. As he passed, Medina felt hard eyes upon him. Anger and hatred. He wore the uniform of Mexico.

Approaching the Quartel the striding captain, head down and eyes narrowed, heard running footsteps and looked up just in time to avoid being bumped by a man hurrying from a house. It was Mall Doya, and the house he came from was that of Adolphus Sterne. Doya skidded to a halt, looked up into the captain's eyes, and backed up a step, plainly embarrassed. After an instant's hesitation he mumbled, *"Perdoneme por favor,"* and hurried away. Across the square Medina saw the tailor, Antonio Menchaca, hurrying toward the house shared by Jose and Juan Mora and their families. He stopped, looked around, and then angled toward the intersecting corner. Down the block he saw Vicente Cordova pounding at the door of Juan Lazatin.

Medina smiled bitterly. The Nacogdoches militia had a captain and six lieutenants. In the space of two minutes, he had accounted for all seven of the militia officers. They move rapidly, he thought, and felt a sort of perverse pride. They were good militia. For civilians, they were good soldiers.

Medina also was a good soldier. Like it or not, orders were orders. He hurried on to the Quartel. Sublieutenant Silvestre Leal was at the main entrance, looking around.

"Lieutenant!" the captain barked without preamble. "Assemble two squads. You take one group, Sergeant Sanchez the other. Send the sergeant's squad to Will Goyens's gunshop. Your squad will go to the village armory. Mount guard on those places. No one is to remove any weapon from either place without my express order."

Leal snapped a quick *"Si, mi capitán,"* and hurried inside. Medina followed. He was in his office and giving orders to Lieutenant Juan Jose Gallardo and two sergeants when he heard Leal and Sanchez quick-stepping their squads out of the Quartel.

Sanchez and his men were the first to reach their objective. Goyens's shop was locked. It had not been attended regularly since the episode of the *presidarios*. Sanchez posted two of his men at the front door and sent the other two around to the back. There was much activity along the streets, and Sanchez watched curiously. He had not yet learned of the colonel's posted orders. He knew only that he was to guard this place and that no weapons were to leave here. He was watching people hurrying along the street when one of the men he had sent to the back returned.

"Sergeant, the back door of this place stands open. There is no one around. Mano and me, we looked inside. There are no guns in there, Sergeant. None at all."

At about the same time, Lieutenant Silvestre Leal and his four men arrived at the small, heavily built blockhouse in the field behind the three Ybarbo houses, which served the Nacogdoches militia as its main armory and storehouse. A rumbling wagon was pulling away from the place, its bed loaded half full of objects covered with a sailcloth tarp. The man in the box seat was whipping his horse with its reins, shouting as the vehicle picked up speed across the open field. Leal shouted for the man to halt, but it was already too late. He could not even see who drove the wagon. In a moment the careening wagon was into the forest across the field, and gone. Taking two of his men, Leal hurried into the armory. Some harness and miscellaneous paraphernalia hung on the walls, and a rusty saber lay on the dirt floor where it had fallen. Otherwise, the place had been stripped clean. Guns, powder, ball, swords, even the emblazoned green banner of the Nacogdoches militia and its guidon—all were gone.

In the early afternoon, two miles from the village of Nacogdoches, men assembled in a small clearing among tall pines. Captain Vicente Cordova and his six militia lieutenants were there, along with a dozen or so other citizen soldiers. A wagon load of guns and ammunition and a mule and a horse with rifles and muskets strapped to their pack mounts were held at the head of a trail which angled northeastward from the clearing. Cordova sent the militiamen to form a cordon around the clearing, then gathered his lieutenants. Briefly, he explained what had happened. None of them except Menchaca and Sterne had read the pronouncements on Piedras's *signatorio*. The rest had been told only, "God and Liberty . . . station three . . . now!" None had hesitated.

"Each of you," Cordova told them, "take the men you trust the most, collect all your extra powder and ball and all your personal weapons, and go to the Carrizo Creek crossing. From there I will lead you to a place where these things can be secreted. Be very careful, use the routes you know best, and avoid being seen. There will be patrols out before this day is done, and extra guards in town."

Antonio Menchaca still bore the bolt of brown cloth under his arm. He had forgotten all about it. Noticing it now, he grinned sheepishly and placed it in the wagon with the guns. "There will be a fight, Captain? Is it certain?"

Cordova nodded solemnly. "Yes. There will be a fight."

Juan Mora's eyes were flashing with excitement.

178

"Bravo! The revolution of Santa Anna will not pass us by."

"No, we will not be passed by. Now we have no choice." Anger deepened the color of his face above his bleached linen collar. "Colonel Piedras has declared war on his neighbors. He has drawn the line, and declared who shall be on which side. Very well, I accept his judgment. Here and now, with you men as my witnesses, I declare my support for General Santa Anna and the Constitution of 1824."

There was silence. Then Juan Mora raised his hand. "And I. I also declare."

Jose Mora looked at his son and shrugged. "I too," he said.

"And I." Lazatin and Doya spoke together.

Antonio Menchaca looked to the north. Over there, in the village, his wife and children awaited him. He took a deep breath and clenched his jaws. "I so declare," he said.

Adolphus Sterne stood slightly apart from the rest, his face troubled. He turned to Cordova. "You know," he said, "of the pledge I took after the Fredonia incident. I gave my word never to take up arms against the flag of Mexico."

"It was the thing that saved your life," Cordova nodded. "You had no choice in the matter."

"I had no choice, no. But I took an oath, Captain. A solemn oath." He looked around at the others, seeking understanding. Cordova's stern countenance softened, just a bit.

"The flag of Mexico, *Don* Adolphus. Who bears the flag of Mexico? Bustamente bears it. Santa Anna bears it. Colonel Piedras bears it. You saw the pronouncements. How can you not declare?"

"*Ja,* I can declare," Sterne told them. "I declared for Santa Anna and the Constitution before any of you. I

179

declare, and gladly. But I cannot fight against the flag of Mexico, no matter who bears it."

"But you are with us now," Cordova pointed out.

"*Ja,* I am with you. And will be, until there is actual fighting. But then I will not take part."

Cordova nodded. "Agreed."

Juan Mora raised a clenched fist, his muscled forearm gleaming in the sunlight. "For God and Liberty!" It became a cheer.

Antonio Menchaca was gazing again toward the town. "For God and Liberty," he murmured.

CHAPTER XVI

*"If men had babies, they still might fight. But
they would not enjoy it so much."*
—*Doña* Candida Chireno

Charles Stanfield Taylor stood in the doorway of his
small mercantile business, for a moment putting behind
him the shelves and bins of everything there was to sell,
getting a breath of fresh air before beginning his
monthly inventory. It was around noon—he hadn't
looked at a clock lately—and foot traffic on the red-
packed street before him was thinning. Antonio Menchaca had been in to pick up some cloth, but now the
store was empty. A rider in work clothes passed, tip-
ping his hand in a desultory wave. Across the street the
little gunshop owned by Will Goyens was closed, although he understood it would reopen again soon. Goyens planned to send back the black boy who had run it
and train him in the business. A pair of soldiers
passed, walking toward the square. A man on foot cut
diagonally across the street, heading for the eating establishment just down from the gunshop.

Down the street, where streets crossed, Taylor saw Padre de Leon hurrying along in his dusty robes, trailed
by a pair of Caddo Indians who had been helping him

repair the weather-beaten cross set in stones at the point where the Camino Real entered the village.

Coming from the other direction were three Indians, and Taylor let his gaze linger on these. They were not Caddo. He had seen the same three around town earlier, once at a distance, over in the square, and again when they passed by his door an hour or so earlier. He did not recall seeing any of them before.

He was sure they were Cherokee. One of the men was a slender, handsome youth who walked with a limp. The other was shorter, stockier, and darker. The woman was a beauty.

Admiring her as they came toward him, Taylor noted that her skin was fair for an Indian, and he thought her eyes were deep blue. There was much white blood among the Cherokee. The handsome young man beside her might be her brother. They both had the chiseled features that spelled white ancestry.

As they approached he turned away—it was not proper to stare. But when they reached him they stopped. They seemed embarrassed and unsure, but determined to address him. He smiled at them. *"Buenos dias."*

The shorter of the men, the dark, stocky one, returned his smile with a dazzling display of white teeth. *"Buenos dias, señor. Por favor,¿ sabe usted de un hombre se llama Willow-bee?"*

Even with his poor command of Spanish, Taylor recognized that the Indian was having a hard time with the tongue. He asked, *"¿Habla usted Ingles?"*

"No, señor." The man shook his head. *"Pa'sda Tsalagi?"*

"No." He smiled. "I'm so sorry. I suppose we had better try it in Spanish." At the Indians' blank expression he shifted as best he could to Spanish. "Who is it you seek?"

"We seek the one called Willow-bee. We do not know where he is. Do you know him?"

"Willow . . . do you mean Willoughby? The trader?"

Their eyes lit with agreement, and now the other two smiled also. For a moment Taylor found himself breathless at the dazzling smile of the young woman. The Englishman had never realized that an Indian girl could be so pretty. With an effort he forced his attention back to the speaker. "I know him, yes. He comes here from time to time. But I do not know where he is now." Catching the girl's crestfallen expression, he wished he had not said it. He would have liked for that smile to remain in place. Now, suddenly, she looked as if she would cry. The stocky one mumbled a garbled *"Gracias, adios,"* and turned away, the others following.

"Wait!" Taylor said, and then in Spanish. *"Alto, por favor.* Can I help you? What are your names?"

The three turned back. "I am Tenuto," the speaker said, finger on his chest. "This is my friend . . . *a's gaqui* . . . Atasi, and his sister, Udali. She is . . . much afraid . . ." His faulty command of Spanish seemed to run out and he stood, confused. Taylor had the feeling that something was very much wrong.

"Wait," he said, his hands speaking better than his tongue. He turned back into the mercantile, and walked through to the living space behind. "Anna Marie?"

She was sewing. "Yes, Charles?"

"Can you come here, please. There are people here with a problem."

Charles Stanfield Taylor was an Englishman. His wife was German. After two years he was still struggling with the Spanish tongue. She had mastered it.

The Indians had come in out of the sun and were waiting, the men staring around in appreciation at all the fine things displayed in the store. Taylor introduced Anna Marie to them as best he could, explained what

183

he had caught from the conversation, and she took over. After a moment she shook her head.

"Charles, he speaks so little Spanish, and the others even less. I don't know what their problem is, really."

"Well, I don't either, but I'd like to help them. They seem so . . . so . . ."

Anna Marie glanced around at them, her eyes lingering on the lovely, solemn girl. With an understanding smile at her husband she said, "Yes, dear, I know. Well, we need someone who speaks their language, don't we?"

"Yes. Ah. Frost does. I think he is at Dolph's store."

"Then I'll tend things here while you take them to Frost. Oh, and Charles." She glanced again at the girl. "You come right back."

Taylor grinned. It is pleasant to have a wife who understands her husband very well. "Come on, then," he said to the Indians, beckoning as he went out. Puzzled, they followed him.

Taylor found his brother-in-law, Adolphus Sterne, at his store talking with Frost Thorn. When they looked up Thorn blinked. "Tenuto? Atasi . . . Udali."

Thorn shook hands with Atasi and smiled at the girl. Taylor said, "Frost, they have some sort of problem but we can't understand them. This one has some Spanish, but not enough."

"I see. Well, then . . ." In rapid Cherokee he got them herded across to where there was a bench and chairs. Taylor propped himself on the counter beside Sterne. "Waifs," he explained.

"And you could not resist a pretty face," Sterne agreed.

"No more than can you, my Prussian friend."

The conversation in lilting Cherokee went on for a while, then Thorn came across and joined them.

"They came looking for Cooper Willoughby," he told

Taylor. "The young lady is . . . betrothed to him, and he has disappeared."

Taylor and Sterne looked across at the face of Udali. "The man's a scoundrel," Taylor said.

"The man's an idiot," Sterne said.

"No," Thorn corrected. "They got word he is in serious trouble somewhere, but they don't know where. The girl is worried half to death. The other two are with her because if they hadn't come she would have come alone."

"Got word? How?"

"Heaven only knows. If we could emulate the way Indian messages are spread we could . . . anyway, they didn't know where to start looking for him but here. I'm concerned too. You heard about the shooting up at the Indian village? One of their warriors? Well, the last time I saw Willoughby, several days ago—no, longer than that, I suppose—he was setting out to find the man who fired the shot."

Sterne's long face whitened. "Moro," he breathed.

"Moro? What about him?"

"Frost, Antonio Menchaca believes it was Anton Moro who shot that Indian up there. We discussed it in council." Quickly, he told them of Menchaca's suspicion, the odd remark about Diwali's death that Piedras had made, the fact Moro had been acting for Piedras, the conclusions. Thorn looked at him for a long moment. "Yes. It explains a great deal. A very great deal. For God's sake, though, don't tell *them* that." Briskly he turned to the waiting Cherokees. "Have you eaten today?"

Tenuto spread his hands in the palms-down negative. "Not today, Frost Thorn. We are strangers to the village of the *a'sgaya'unega*. We do not know where there is food, nor the custom of receiving it."

Without further conversation Thorn set out to take

185

them to his house. Susan would feed them, then he could decide what should be done about them.

Taylor visited a few minutes more with Sterne, then went back to his store. Before turning the corner he noticed a small crowd gathering in the vicinity of the Red House, and saw Vicente Cordova and Antonio Menchaca hurrying away from there. Curiously, he noted that Menchaca still carried the bolt of brown stuff he had picked up earlier. Odd, he thought, but paid it no more mind. The anxious face of the pretty Cherokee girl was much on his mind. Taylor barely knew Cooper Willoughby, but he hoped he was alive and well. He didn't like to think of tears in those big, dark eyes.

There was a pair of mules hitched in front of Goyens's shop across the street, and he crossed over. The door was open. Ambrose and a large aging black man were inside, the younger black still carrying his arm in a sling but looking fit enough.

"Going to open for business again, Ambrose?"

"Yessuh, Mistah Taylor. Soon's we gets this mess clean up. Mistah Goyens, he send me and Samson here to put it right." Samson was already at work, brushing dust off the shelves and benches to the floor, where it could be swept.

"Might be best if you lock the front door until you're ready to open," Taylor suggested. "Never attract customers unless you're ready to do business."

Ambrose nodded. "Yessuh. That soun' right. Samson, I'll haul them mules aroun' back. You close up after me an' then let me in the back door."

Samson made a face at him and then grinned at Taylor. "Don' that boy soun' jes lak Mistah Goyens when he start givin' orders?"

Chuckling, Taylor headed across to his own store. The ruckus over in the square had increased somewhat, and he noticed that there was more activity than was usual for the early hour of siesta. There were even a few men running here and there. He stopped to watch, but Anna Marie's voice came from the store. "Well, don't stand out there all day, Charles. Come tell me what that was all about."

Inside, he told her what he could of it, not mentioning the part about Moro.

"The poor little thing," she said. "She must be terribly worried, to come all the way down here." Inquisitive, humorous eyes tilted toward him. "She is very pretty, isn't she?"

"Yes. Very. If she were German, she would be nearly as pretty as you."

Outside, there were running feet. He saw a man run to Goyens's shop, peer through the crack at the locked door, and then hurry around toward the back.

"Now what in the world?" Taylor strode to the door, looked down the street toward the square. There was even more activity there now. It had a frenzied look about it. Anna Marie came up beside him. "What is it, Charles?"

"I don't know. Something's going on. I expect I'd better go see." A man came past, hurrying. "Joe? What is it? What's happening?"

"You just go take a look at the colonel's signboard, Mister Taylor. Then you'll know." The man shook his head and hurried on. Charles Taylor went to look at the signboard. When he returned he was white-faced and shaken. Anna Marie was waiting at the door, and Samson was coming across the street.

"Be all right if I wait here a while, Mistah Taylor?" the black man asked. "Ambrose, he say don' stay aroun' that shop."

"Where is Ambrose?"

"He gone, suh. He takes them mules an' ever'thing

187

inside that shop, an' he gone. He be back direc'ly, but he say don' stay aroun' the shop. Is they trouble, Mistah Taylor?"

"Come on in, Samson. Yes." He turned to his wife "Yes, there is indeed trouble."

CHAPTER XVII

*"One must envy the Anglos. They never look back,
only forward. Where one has been can be more
frightening than where one is going."*
— Fray Jose Antonio Diaz de Leon

While they ate, Frost Thorn explained to his Cherokee guests that Cooper Willoughby had been working
with the *Alguazil* of Ayish, Alexander Horton. Possibly
Willoughby was over there, but it would take a day or
two to get word. None of the Ayish crowd had been in
to Nacogdoches lately.

"Don't send word," Tenuto stated flatly. "Too slow,
these *a'sgaya-unega* plodders. Tenuto will go."

"Atasi will go," the other brave said, but it was only
a gesture. Their trip down from the Indian lands had
been slow, because Atasi was still too sore from his hu-
miliating snakebite to sit a saddle properly.

Tenuto handled it delicately. "Atasi must remain with
Udali," he pointed out. "It would not be right for a
Tsalagi maiden to be unescorted among barbarians."
(Thorn concealed a grin at the word—it was the proper
word in Cherokee, for any who were not Cherokee.)
"And of us, only Atasi is Udali's brother."

Susan Thorn sat to one side, making sure her hungry
guests got enough to eat but not understanding a word

of the Indian tongue her husband spoke so freely. She felt a kinship for the pretty Indian girl. She was not many years older than Udali, and felt an admiration for the determined young woman who, concerned about her man, had set off into the unknown European lands and finagled two braves into going with her. Had the roles been reversed, had it been her man who was missing, Susan Thorn would not have hesitated to do the same thing.

Frost was doing his best to keep her informed of the conversation, translating bits and pieces as the Indians ate. Now she said, "But Frost, he can't go out there alone. You know how some of those people feel about Indians. And how would he talk to any of them? Most of those new settlers don't even speak Spanish, much less Cherokee."

"Quite right," Thorn agreed, and translated for the Indians.

"The thing to do," he added in Cherokee—and then in English for Susan, "is to send someone along with you."

"Too slow," Tenuto repeated firmly. "White men move slow, take all day to get someplace. I have my best horse, Rides-the-Morning. No white man can keep up."

"Adolphus Sterne has racing horses," Thorn said, "to match any you have seen."

"No horse is a match for Rides-the-Morning."

There was a thunder from the front of the house, and men entered before Jaren could announce them. Adolphus Sterne was first, followed by a breathless Juan Lazatin.

"*Herr* Thorn, have you seen the notice?"

"Notice?" Thorn was on his feet.

"*Die coronel bist* . . . pardon, the colonel has done it. All civilians are restricted. State of emergency. All firearms to be confiscated—"

"And the meetings, *señor*," Lazatin blurted out. "There are to be no meetings. It is quarantine. It is—"

"It is war," Sterne announced.

"Now hold on." Thorn raised a pleading hand. "What is happening?"

"Piedras, *das dunderhead,* has posted a notice. He has declared war!"

"War on whom?"

"On us, Frost. All of us. You must go read the signboard. Then you will know."

In the excitement mounting in the room the three Indians looked around at one another. Then Tenuto arose. To Thorn he said, in Cherokee, "Thank you for your kindness, Frost Thorn. We will go now."

"You will . . . Dolf, wait a moment, please. Tenuto, where will you go?"

"We will go east, Frost Thorn, to the Ayish. Tenuto will go like the wind. Atasi and Udali will follow. We must find Willow-bee."

Caught between urgencies, Thorn looked around at Susan. She too was on her feet. "They're going, Frost? You can't let them go now. This girl can't go into those greener areas with all this stirred up. You know what could happen."

"Yes." Thorn looked back to Sterne, standing impatiently. Juan Lazatin was already heading for the door. "Dolph, I'll go with you to read the *signatorio,* but first, have you a horse I can borrow, a fast horse?"

"Of course. Take the black. Take even Die Fraulein if you want. Frost, I must go. The militia—"

"Dolph, you can't take up arms. You can't fight. No more than I can."

"No, I cannot fight, but I can help to that point. If you need a fast horse you take Die Fraulein. There is none faster, as you know. Who will ride her?" His eyes turned, with quick dread, to the anxious Indian at

Thorn's elbow.

"No," Thorn said. "Tenuto has a racer of his own. I don't know. Maybe Jaren."

The black servant had just entered the room, Peter Ellis Bean trailing behind him. The Negro's eyes widened as he caught the tail of the conversation. "Ah, nossah, Mistah Thorn. I's a boy of th' big house. I cain' ride no Dee Froyline hoss, no way, suh. I kin ride dat ol' mule, suh, but da's about all."

Bean stood in the parlor door, hands on hips. "What in God's name is going on around here?"

Sterne asked, "Have you seen the colonel's sighboard?"

Thorn said, "These Cherokee are looking for Willoughby. He's in trouble someplace. They know. Tenuto wants to go to Ayish."

Susan stamped her foot insistently. "Frost, that girl can't go to Ayish. Not now. You know how some of them feel about Indians."

To Bean, Tenuto said in Cherokee, "Tenuto must ride like the wind to find Willow-bee. He is Udali's *a'sga-memenete-sdo*. We must find him."

Sterne was beyond patience. "I have to go, Frost. The militia, it is God and Liberty now. Take Die Fraulein if you have someone to ride her." Without a further word he about-faced and hurried to the door. He was running as he hit the porch.

"Good God almighty," Bean declared, then raised both hands to still further talk as he tried to sort things out. He shook his head hard, trying to clear out the cobwebs of garble. A moment's silence, and they started talking again. Bean roared, "Sit!"

The authority of it was such that even Jaren sat down, and Haden Edwards, who had just entered the front door, looked around for a chair.

With the calm precision of a hounded field officer,

Bean sorted it out. Holding the others at bay he spoke first to Tenuto, then to Thorn, and decided to take one problem at a time.

"Udali, you and Atasi will remain here, at least until I tell you. Something is happening, and it might not be safe. Tenuto . . . wait." He strode through the parlor to Frost Thorn's front door, pulled it open, and roared, "Samuel!"

When his oldest son reached the porch, Bean said, "Can you ride a racing horse?" Seeing the youngster's eyes light up, he didn't wait for an answer. "Then you hotfoot over to Mr. Sterne's stable and get a horse called Die Fraulein. Saddle her and bring her back here. Now, boy!"

Back in the house he said, "Tenuto, go and get your horse. Bring him here. Samuel, my son, will ride with you to Ayish."

"Only if he can keep up," Tenuto said stolidly, and hurried out past Haden Edwards, who sat wide-eyed and alone in the parlor.

"Now, that's settled," Bean said. "Mrs. Thorn, it would be a mercy if these two can stay here with you for a little while."

"Of course." Susan was relieved. She looked accusingly at her husband.

"I don't have a Samuel," was all he had to say.

Edwards appeared at the parlor door. "What in thunder is going on here?"

Thorn shrugged. "I don't think any of us know, Papa. But I guess we should go and find out."

Bean, Thorn, and Edwards met Tenuto with his Rides-the-Morning and Samuel Bean with Sterne's prized Die Fraulein outside. Tenuto was glaring at the white man's horse. "Never make it," he grumbled in Cherokee. "Body is too long. Head too narrow."

"I got a notion." The younger Bean glared back at

193

him, then switched to the Cherokee tongue. "A spirit tells me this one can run better than yours."

"Now cut that out," Bean ordered his son. "Samuel, I want you to go to Ayish with Tenuto. He's looking for the smuggler, Willoughby. You help him, you hear?"

"I hear, Pa. And say, you ought to read that sign in front of the Red House. You won't like it, Pa."

"All right. I will. Now, go!"

At the word the two young men bounded into saddles. Die Fraulein pitched and Samuel clung, muttering curses he didn't want his father to hear. At the ruckus Tenuto's horse shied and started to pitch. The Indian calmly swatted his steed between the ears with his rifle barrel. Then they were off, and the dust of Nacogdoches rose behind them as citizens, soldiers, and drifters scampered to get out of the way.

"Going to have to have a talk with that boy," Bean grumbled. Then he, Frost Thorn, and Haden Edwards headed across to read the colonel's pronouncements on the signboard.

The mounted patrol led by Lieutenant Domingo Espasa was just three miles out of Nacogdoches on El Camino Real, heading for the Ayish settlements in accordance with the orders of Colonel Piedras. Youngest of the lieutenants in Captain Renaldo Musquiz's proud Company of Monclova, Espasa was acutely aware of his youth, yet very proud to be a part of that grand cavalry company that had so distinguished itself in the earlier wars in Mexico. He sat lightly the saddle of his fine steed and rode with head erect at the head of his patrol of nine men. Just behind and to his side, face deeply lined from many years of service, Sergeant Jimenez glanced back now and then to keep an eye on the patrol, but mostly watched the young lieutenant as

he rode, and stolidly kept from his face any trace of
the smile that tried to creep there. A good boy, he
thought. Maybe a good officer, but how could one tell
at this age? One thing about Lieutenant Espasa he did
admire. The youngster had brains enough to let his sergeant make the vital decisions, and style enough that
the men did not know it. With time, this could be a
good officer.

He glanced back again and frowned. Those imbeciles
of the 12th were lagging again. He barked an order and
three or four stragglers at the back closed up the
column. Sergeant Jimenez did not approve of mixed
units. In fact, he did not approve of mounted infantry
at all. Of the patrol, only he and the lieutenant and
three men were cavalry. The rest were mounted infantry,
soldiers chosen from the 12th Battalion to augment the
garrison's *caballero* forces because — supposedly — they
could ride. Sergeant Jimenez had his doubts about that.

The Camino Real here was no more than a hard-
packed, narrow trace through heavy forest, and at each
bend, where the trail made its way around rises and
gullies following the course of least resistance, the front
of the column lost sight of the back of the column.

"Por Dios," Jimenez grumbled, "we are only nine.
How can we occupy a half mile of road?" With a muttered *"Perdoneme"* to his lieutenant, he wheeled his
mount and headed back down the line. He would close
up this patrol if he had to horsewhip every "mounted
infantry" *bastardo* in it. The three regular cavalrymen
pacing the lieutenant smiled smugly as they saw their
sergeant depart.

Reaching the stragglers, Jimenez berated them.
"Columns of three, idiots! Three columns of three! *Por
Dios,* is that so difficult? Now move up there and close
ranks!"

As they spurred their mounts he wheeled in behind

them, crowding them on. In the noise and heat he failed to hear the sound behind him, until suddenly he was passed by two streaks of fury, one on each side. He had only a glance at the low-crouched backs of two riders on flying horses before they were gone, scattering clumsy infantrymen on pitching horses right and left into the woods on both sides of the trail.

With a curse the sergeant spurred his own mount forward, and rounded the bend in time to see chaos ahead of him. The lieutenant was clinging to a bucking, twirling mount dancing in mid-trail. Another infantryman was down, sprawled in the dust, his horse nowhere in sight. One of the cavalrymen was dismounting, while the other two tried to get their mounts out of heavy brush beside the trail. Far ahead, going up a rise, were the two devils who had caused the disaster. Small with distance, two faces turned back, curiously. One was an Anglo, the other dark. In a moment they were gone.

Belatedly, a mounted soldier of the 12th—apparently the only one besides Jimenez still in command of his horse—raised his musket and fired. The shot's only effect was to further startle the lieutenant's pitching mount, which went into another frenzy of bucking.

Beyond the rise Samuel Bean and Tenuto hauled their racers to a skidding halt. In Cherokee, the young Bean asked, "What was that?"

Tenuto shrugged. "Soldiers."

By common curiosity they trotted back up the rise they had just descended. From the top they could see what was going on. They watched as the patrol got itself reorganized. It seemed to take a long time.

"Anglo soldiers," Tenuto allowed. "They have a hard time."

"They're not Anglo," Samuel said. "They're Spanish."

"Same thing."

"They see us. Look. What are they doing now?" The small figures in the distance were forming in column. One led a horse out of the woods and mounted, joining the others. The one in front, an officer, drew his sword and held it high, then the column started moving toward them at a trot and then at a gallop.

"I think they are going to chase us," Tenuto said.

"Why would they do that?"

"Who knows? But this is what they are doing. We could wait for them and let them chase us. It might be good sport. But I don't have time. I must go to Ayyeesh to find Willow-bee. Are you coming?"

"I'll be there waiting when you get there, Indian."

When the charging, sweating patrol topped the rise where the young men had sat moments before, they were gone. Lieutenant Espasa reined to a halt, disappointment plain on his young face. Sergeant Jiminez pulled up beside him. "It is no use, Lieutenant. They are on racing horses. We will not catch them."

"No. Did you see who they were?"

"No, *mi teniente*. Only I think one was white and one *Indio*."

Espasa sheathed his blade. "Very well. We have a mission. We will go on."

He put his mount forward at a canter and the sergeant signaled the men in behind him. A good boy, he thought. A sensible lieutenant. But when they stopped to rest their horses, Sergeant Jiminez would have a few things to say to some of those bumbling clowns behind him.

CHAPTER XVIII

*"Texas is a poor man's land. A poor man can be-
come rich here."*
—Wyatt Hanks

Where men have need of law, and none is at hand,
they create it for themselves. In the early summer of
1832 in the Neutral Strip bordering East Texas, and in
the piney woods inside Texas's border, this was taking
place. The great western migration was in progress, and
all of Texas lay sprawled across its path. Of the thousands arriving there, some—the lone ones and the root-
less ones—crossed over into Texas because their need to
be there exceeded their fear of Mexican law. But many
of them stopped when they reached the Strip. They
waited there, expecting that something would change,
and while they waited they went about their business
day to day and protected themselves as best they could.

No law penetrated the Neutral Strip, but in the parts
of it where numbers of emigrants waited, a sort of law
took hold. A hundred encamped families can muster a
dozen fighting men full time, or half a hundred in
emergency.

The outlaws infesting the Strip, raiding occasionally
east into Louisiana and west into Texas, were a danger

to the waiting emigrants, and they reacted. Occasional cordons of armed men swept sections of the neutral ground, cleaning several miles at a time of outlaws and turning back those who tried to return. It was make-shift policing at best, but it kept the criminal elements scattered and disorganized, and it kept the little camps of Texas-bound Americans relatively safe for a few days at a time. It was temporary, but it was enough. The emigrants themselves were temporary. They were bound for Texas, and just waiting for an opportunity to go on.

It was such a cordon that Anton Moro encountered east and south of Ayish when he crossed the Sabine River.

Moro had not intended to go east. Were it not for those damned Indians he would have been at Bevil's Diggings by now, or at some other point where he might rest a few days until Piedras cooled off, when he could return to Nacogdoches.

Moro resented the manner in which Piedras had sent him away, after Moro had spent several days arranging events in the colonel's best interests. Piedras had sent him to the Indian villages, with instructions to persuade the Cherokee to support Piedras in his conflicts with the Anglo immigrants. To Moro, the manner in which he had gone about the task was direct and brilliant. Old Diwali stood in his way. He had disposed of Diwali, and done so in such a way that the Indians would blame white men for it. If the colonel could only see the simple logic of it.

Moro had no liking for the strutting Colonel Piedras. He would as soon have killed him, had it served his purpose. But in the shrewd, small mind of Anton Moro it was clear that his alliance with Piedras, as the colonel's agent, was an advantage. Moro was a hunted man to the east. Robbery and murder had too long been his way. But in Texas, so long as he committed no provable crime in Texas, he was protected.

Of Basque descent, Anton Moro had come of age in the Louisiana lowlands. He spoke Spanish, English, and French as well as several of the Indian tongues, and had lived among the Shawnee and eastern Cherokee for many years. Moro was an arrogant man, and his arrogance was based on ability. A competent woodsman, an excellent marksman with the 50-caliber long rifle he had acquired years ago, he was also a large, burly brute of a man and few could stand before him. It was Anton Moro's custom to take what he wanted and to do as he pleased.

Few things could strike Anton Moro as being funny, but he had laughed aloud when that skinny trader came upon him in the forest and told him to lay down his rifle. The man had proposed to arrest him, he said, with the purpose of taking him to stand trial among the Cherokee.

It irritated Moro that the trader had managed to track him down and approach closely enough to have the drop on him, but still he had laughed at what the man said. The idea was funny. But Anton Moro had not laughed for very long. With the trader's gun pointed at him Moro had stooped to lay down his rifle, then, cat-quick, had rolled to the side and come up with it at his shoulder. The trader was quick. His shot had gouged the flesh on Moro's hip. But after that he had no other shot. Methodically, Moro had stood, shouldered his weapon, and fired as the trader turned to run.

If it had not been for those Indians . . . even as he lowered his rifle Moro suddenly saw movement in the brush beyond, and then three Indians appeared. They were men of one of the dark tribes—at a glance he could not tell which one, although he noted their hair was unbraided and their leggings long. One carried an old musket. The others had bows. Another appeared, and then he heard sound behind him. They were after his horse, the bay racer he had taken from that greener above Nacogdoches.

His rifle empty, he drew his knife and charged the two who had appeared behind him. As one dodged his knife-stroke, he caught the other with his rifle barrel, bowling him over. Then he was on his horse, and bounding away through the brush as the old musket spoke behind him. He had been unharmed.

The Indians might have been Osage, although this was far south for them. They might have been Tuscaroras or Coushattas, or even Kickapoos. At any rate, they had cost him whatever valuables the trader might have carried and the horse he must have had staked somewhere in the brush.

But the scrape had changed Moro's mind about remaining in Texas, for the time being. He decided instead to go into the Strip. There were few Indians in the Strip this far south. And there might be something of value over there that he could pick up while he waited for Piedras's temper to cool.

When he crossed the Sabine he found armed men waiting for him on the other side. They looked like farmers, but the rifles they carried were held steady. They ordered him away, and he went, back across the river, back into Texas. But he didn't go far. Out of sight in bordering woods he watched the far side, the Strip side, and eventually saw the emigrant cordon emerge from forest into a clearing, moving south. There, then, would be their camp, and they were moving back toward it.

Easily keeping out of sight he moved south with them, keeping occasional watch on them across the river. They had gone less than a mile when the pattern of activity changed. Some of the dozen or so gathered briefly and then hurried away from the river, out of sight. With the instincts of a hunter Anton Moro urged his mount forward and pulled into a copse two hundred yards downstream from where he had lost sight of the emigrants. From where he sat, hidden, he could see a long section of the Sabine River and, just below him, a stretch where the waters widened and churned over a shallow bed. Across the river, seeming far away in the screening brush, he heard a gunshot. And then another. For a while there was silence. Another shot sounded, closer now, and he smiled thinly.

He was watching the point where the two men broke cover when they came. The cordon across the river had flushed a pair of birds, and Anton Moro waited to see if they had anything of value to him.

They pounded out of the screening brush and into the river, their mounts breasting the swelling water and throwing spray, the riders urging them on. When they were in midstream, several of the mounted emigrants appeared on the bank behind them, shouting. One fired over their heads to hurry them on.

Moro now had a better look at them. They were *mestizos,* and both wore remnants of clothing recognizable as Mexican army uniforms. The smaller of the two was poorly mounted and carried a musket, a battered Charlesville. The other, a husky, wide-cheeked man, had a good horse and carried a long rifle. Both had makeshift packs slung to their saddles.

Moro's casual curiosity quickened a bit. A *presidario* renegade capable of acquiring a good horse and rifle might have other things as well. He might even have money.

He watched in silence as the two spurred their lunging horses up the bank on the Texas side, the husky one leaping the shoulder and disappearing into the brush while his partner, his mount tiring, lagged behind. After both were gone he watched the far bank until the emigrants had gone away. Then he put heels to his horse, angling to the west to intercept the *presidarios*. Anton Moro would see if the birds were fat enough for plucking.

They didn't go far. In a wooded hollow he found them, standing and holding their horses' reins, both facing back toward the river. Picketing his mount he crept in close, where he could hear their voices. The larger of the two was haranguing the smaller, in guttural mountain Spanish.

"No more brains than a chicken, you Santos, *hijo de perra,* no more guts than a squawking chicken too. Why you think I said to be still? They would have ridden past. Now you have lamed your horse. You think I will wait for you? Me, Ruiz, you think I stay around clean your *niño de puta* nose for you? I don' need you anymore, Santos. I never needed you."

"Ruiz, don' say that. I didn' think . . . I am hungry, Ruiz. I am too hungry to think. Please."

"Shut up!" Ruiz whirled on him. *"Basta!* Was it me lost the food we got from those fat Anglos? Who was it lost all our food, Santos? Was it me? Now shut your mouth. I must think."

Leaning his rifle against a dogwood branch the husky one turned to tend his horse. The smaller one, Santos, stood shaking with fear and anger, still holding his old musket. Watching, Moro wondered if he would kill his partner. He was intrigued by the way the larger one, Ruiz, turned his back, ignoring this possibility. A tough one, that, he thought. Or else just stupid. Probably both. Well, it didn't matter. So they had no food. But maybe they still had some money. He waited for the second one to lay down his gun, as the first had, then decided he wasn't going to. The little man just stood there, shaking. Anton Moro slipped his knife from its sheath and padded a few steps forward, angling to get behind the two *presidarios*.

When he was within twenty feet of Santos he hefted the knife, paused for an instant to feel the distance, then hurled it with a sweeping overhand motion. The heavy blade whistled, and thumped as it imbedded itself between Santos's shoulders. The *presidario* stood rigidly upright in shock. His musket clattered to the ground and futile hands clawed backward, trying to reach the hilt of the knife. At the noise Ruiz spun around, crouching, and found himself staring into Moro's rifle barrel while Santos went to his knees, pleading face gone white, then pitched forward and lay still.

Moro glanced at the fallen man, then turned his attention to Ruiz. "You, *hombre*. What have you got in those packs?"

Ruiz, still crouching, snarled an answer in mountain *mestizo* dialect and spat. Indifferently Moro strode forward, rifle in one hand, raised his arm, and delivered a quick, hard backhand blow downward across the *presidario*'s head. Ruiz went to his knees, dazed and hurt. Moro stood for a moment observing him, then kicked him in the belly. Ruiz doubled over, wretching and strangling, sobbing as he tried to breathe. Curiously, Moro prodded him with his toe, and when Ruiz whispered a sobbing curse and tried to grab his foot, Moro kicked him again.

"Tough *presidario*, eh?" he muttered. "One tough *soldado, verdad,* but not tough enough, *hombre*." He spat on the shuddering form at his feet, then walked to where the man's horse had backed away and jerked the lashings loose on the pack, letting its contents spill to the ground. A half-full powder sack, a handful of jerky wrapped in soiled cloth, a hatchet, and a gold watch were there. Nothing more. Moro picked up the watch.

It had a name engraved on it, an Anglo name. He dropped it in his pouch.

He inspected the hatchet and tossed it into the brush. Trash. He poured powder out of the sack and found it moist. He tossed it aside, picked up the jerky, and walked across to the other soldier's horse, standing with one forefoot drawn up, obviously lame. In this pack there was nothing but a soiled blanket.

He retrieved his knife from Santos's body, holding the corpse down with his foot while he tugged the blade free. He wiped it on the soldier's blanket and returned it to its sheath. He retrieved Ruiz's rifle, inspected it, and tossed it aside. It was of smaller caliber and badly tended. Santos's musket he left lying where it had fallen. He was irritated. The watch might be worth a few American dollars. One horse worth something. The rest, nothing. Walking across to where Ruiz was trying to get to his knees, he kicked him again, then leaned against a tree trunk and began eating the jerky. Ruiz lay in the dirt, half-conscious and suffering. Moro watched him curiously. A tough *soldado, si.*

The sun was lowering when Anton Moro finished his jerky and strode across to take the reins of Ruiz's horse. The animal drew back and he hauled savagely at it, forcing it to follow. He was halfway across the little clearing when he heard a voice behind him.

"Señor!"

Moro turned, bringing his rifle up. Ruiz was on his knees, pale and bleeding, but upright.

"Señor," the *presidario* said. "Let me go with you."

Several miles away, in a willow thicket near a slough, a torn and tattered man whose face was stiff with dried blood pulled himself up on weak legs, stood unsupported for a moment, and then grabbed a branch to

205

steady himself when his knees started to buckle.

He stood patiently there, suffering while the world reeled around him and then righted itself. His only memory at the moment was of fierce pain throbbing in his protesting skull, and a driving need to move . . . to move and get away.

The pain had receded to a dull ache, sheathed in fog, but now the fog lifted for moments of lucidity and his surroundings appeared more real.

"Why in hell am I standing out here in a willow-wash?" he asked himself, and heard his voice hoarse and broken, hardly more than a whisper. With heroic effort he cast off from the branch and stood alone. That accomplished, he moved first one foot, then the other, and found himself walking. To focus his attention, to keep from falling, he chanted in a hoarse whisper, "Take a step, take a step, take a step, take another step . . ." As he came clear of the willows he added, "And pretty soon you notice you ain't standing still." Something about that struck him funny, but he knew if he laughed his head would hurt again. And he couldn't think why he would want to laugh, anyway. Not after . . . what?

That pain in his head, it seemed as though that had gone on forever, but there had been other things too. He had crawled . . . once, twice, a thousand times? Yet he had been moving. Sometimes upright, sometimes crawling, he recalled moving. Through woods, through a gully, across a clearing, into and out of a thicket, he recalled scenery like pictures in a fog, disjointed snatches of awareness. There had been something laughing at him. No, he decided, not laughing. Timid, grinning . . . a fox. There had been a fox looking him in the eye, but when he spoke to it the creature ran away.

Eye to eye with a fox? "You sunk low that time,

son," he whispered, and again thought about laughing and decided against it.

The sun, slanting from the . . . (west? Yes, it smelled like afternoon) . . . west was warm on his head and he realized he had no hat. That brought him to realize he had no gun, though he was wearing his pouch and horn. And for that matter, where had he left his horse? He scowled, and the scowl made his head hurt. Gingerly he felt there and found encrusted blood, a scab forming along a wound that seemed as big as the palm of his hand. He winced, and that hurt too.

Where had he left his horse? Dammit, that's a good horse, he told himself, and only a damn fool would leave it laying around somewhere, and . . . (who? Somebody) . . . was no damn fool. He concentrated on the horse. He had tied it to a branch in the woods, and left it while he went forward. Forward to where?

Thinking hurt. He postponed it. He was thirsty. Ahead, there was a rise with the tops of big trees just beyond. On steadying legs he made his way there, down the other side, and came to a stream. It was no more than a ribbon of water, but it ran clear over red sand and dark stone, and he drank a little, then a little more. Carefully he washed his face, getting some of the crusted blood off it. He peered curiously into the water, but its ripples gave no clear reflection. "I certainly do look familiar, though," he told himself in a drawl that, his thirst quenched, now also sounded familiar.

He sat back against a tree and slept for a while. When he awoke he felt better. He drank again from the stream, and the water made him hungry. He felt weak and faintly distant, but not too bad considering how he recalled feeling before. He looked around for his rifle and remembered he didn't have it.

"Where the hell did I leave my horse?" he asked irritably.

Carefully, methodically, he started digging back. The pain, the places, the fox, the pain, Indians.

There had been several of them. They ran past where he lay, and one of them paused to peer at him for a moment, then went on. He heard a shot, the bellow of a musket, a horse crashing through brush, voices going away. He had moved then, and kept on moving as best he could.

He searched back again, seeking a clue, and a voice came to him, his own voice, speaking bitterly, "I do."

I do what?

"Do you," another remembered voice said, "swear to uphold the laws and ordinances of the Ayzes District? Say, 'I do.'"

"Hell I will," he swore, and that was familiar too. "That goddamned Sandy Horton . . ."

With that it came back. He sat a few moments longer reviewing it, putting it in order, then got another drink of water, looked at the graying of evening around him, and rose on steady feet. Hungry, hurt, and harried, but feeling better, thank you, Cooper Willoughby set out in the evening light to backtrack himself.

In the dappled brightness of woodland mid-morning he made his way north by west, keeping the sun at his right shoulder, stout stick in his hand thumping the rocky soil when he climbed low hills, swinging with his stride when he descended.

He had found the place, but there was nothing there now. His horse and rifle were gone. Painstakingly he had read the sign. He saw where Moro had made his escape, and where he himself had lain. He saw where his horse had gone, but there were moccasined tracks with it, too many for a cautious man to follow. So, knowing now where he was, he set off on foot angling west of north. With his knife he cut a sapling and made himself a stick. A man feels better when he carries something in his hand. With the stick, in the evening hours, he had waylaid a careless rabbit at a seep. The rabbit and a handful of berries had been both supper and breakfast, coupled with some tea made from sassafras root and boiled in his drinking cup. Though his head still hurt, the weakness was abated and he felt better.

Up hill and down, along ridges and gullies, through sunlight and pineshade he made his way, judging the slow passing of miles. Where a game trail went his way he followed it, because animals knew where the going was best.

West of him some miles was the Ayish Bayou. North along its course, several miles away, the settlements began. He had to have help, and there he could find it. He knew where there was a trail too, but it was too far out of his way to find it.

Through deep woods he walked, forest carpet and long habit combining to make his steps silent, and through the trees he saw bright sunlight ahead, a pocket glade in the woodlands where the climbing sun bathed a tiny, hidden prairie in its warmth. He passed the trees and stepped out, then stopped, frozen in place. Barely ten yards away and just to his right lay a panther, stretched out in the sun, for all the world like a huge housecat warming itself on the kitchen stoop. Sunlight glistened on dark cinnamon pelt. Ears four inches apart were up, questioning, and great almond eyes stared at him through pupils closed to slits. The animal's heavy tail swung slowly back and forth, stirring the grass.

Just beyond were two kittens tangled in drowsy conflict but discovering him now, following their mother's signals. They rolled apart and stood, intense and curious, unable to identify the strange creature before them.

As one of the kittens ambled forward for a closer look the great cat rumbled and muscles bunched as she started to rise.

Under his breath Willoughby muttered, "Pardon," then carefully backed away, one slow step at a time. The panther was on her feet now, but stood her ground as Willoughby retreated. He eased back through the trees, then backed further until he was out of sight. From there he turned and hurried away.

Overriding the tension of having come that close to a creature that big—and that lethal—was an odd embarrassment. He felt as though he had walked into a fine lady's parlor with mud on his boots.

Circling wide around the hidden clearing, Cooper Willoughby set his course again north by west, and kept walking.

He had thought the weakness was gone, thought so more as the sun rose higher and his spirits lifted with it, and kept lifting. He was light-headed before he discovered he was dizzy, before he missed a step and tumbled down a draw to fetch up against a tree stump and lie dazed as the world whirled around him.

"Damn, son," he panted, focusing on his words, "you ain't quite ready for travelin' just yet."

His head still throbbed, and now the skin around the wound felt hot and swollen. Regaining his balance, he found tree moss and tucked slabs of it into his shirt, then staggered on, one knee now sore from the fall, until he found a sumphole at the bottom of a deep-wooded hollow. He gathered willow bark and dark mud, mixed these in his cup with the tree moss, and got a hatful of fire going. Adding a bit of water to the mixture, he set it to boil. In an hour he had a thick, dark poultice wrapped in the sliced-off tail of his shirt and bound around his head. Rinsing the cup, he filled it with turgid water, got that boiling and crumped the last of his sassafras root bark into it, let it steep for a while, then drank it down rapidly.

Through the afternoon he slept there in the shade, waking often as fever and chills hit him. With nightfall he was cold, and managed another fire, but had not the strength to tend it. As its comfort dwindled, he wormed his way among the pine needles and buried himself in the forest floor.

Thoughts that had been lucid earlier in the day now tumbled around in his head without order. Annoyed, he tried to identify those that made sense and hang onto them.

Back and back again came the sweet face of Udali, little Mistletoe of the Cherokee, and her voice called him. Then overlaying it came the laughing face of Utsada the *unegadihi,* his friend, and Utsada had no voice. It was gone.

"Damn it," he whispered. "Damn it all." In a clear moment he reckoned that McDonald's stead was no more than four or five miles from where he lay now. But the shape he was in, he'd never make it.

"A dollar a day and keep," Sandy Horton's voice told him.

"So pay me," Willoughby muttered, his teeth chattering. "I quit."

CHAPTER XIX

*"It is glory that's golden. Duty is red, like
flowing blood."*
— Captain Renaldo Musquiz

When Colonel Peter Ellis Bean turned from the signboard his face was bleak. "He's doing it," he muttered
to no one in particular. "The crazy bastard is doing it,
sure as hell."

"Doing what?" Edwards asked.

"He is starting a war." Bean pointed toward the pronouncements. "He has decided there is going to be one,
so he's starting it."

Edwards's brow was like a thundercloud, but he
gazed at Bean without understanding. "Of course he is.
I thought everybody already knew that. This . . ." He
waved at the notice. "This garbage is just the latest
thing, not the whole thing. This is one of many provo-
cations. I have some thoughts" — he turned to Frost
Thorn — "about how we might respond to this."

"I gather," Thorn said, deep in thought, "that there
already is ample response. The militia — "

"Gathered its weapons, that's all. That's no response.
That's just a defense. These latest effronteries demand a
counteraction."

212

Frost, head low and his mouth pursed in thought, turned toward his house. The scolding, fiery Edwards fell in alongside him, talking war. Bean shook his head. Piedras and Edwards were a perfect match, in a way. Like instruments in an orchestra, they might not play the same note but they did play the same tune. And each could be counted on to respond in form to the tone of the other.

Thorn paused and looked back. "You coming, Pete?"

"Later." He waved absently. "I have business to attend to."

His expression thunderous, Peter Ellis Bean turned toward the Red House, but stopped when a hand plucked at his sleeve and his name was called, softly.

Fray Jose Antonio Diaz de Leon had long since reached an age and eminence entitling him to spend the rest of his days on earth in surroundings more comfortable than the harsh demands of a turbulent frontier parish. The Church would not have sent him to East Texas had he not insisted. Of the sixty-eight years he counted, all but fifteen had been spent in the service of the Church.

Recently, though, Bean had seen the fires of purpose burn dim within the old priest. It was his nature that the victories of all those years had not been cumulative. Those thousands he had brought into the Church—Indians, mostly, but also scores of the "Muldoon Catholics" among the Anglos—failed to give the old priest a defense against the fears and disappointments he had accumulated during those same years. The Church should have refused the old man this last mission, Bean thought. He was no longer strong enough.

"I have been hoping you might come to town soon, Peter," the padre said. "Can we talk while you are here?"

"Of course, Padre." Bean smiled his affection for the

213

aging priest. "I will come and see you later today if you like."

"I will be waiting." The priest turned away, bent and worried in his robes, and his two Caddo helpers plodded along behind him as he went down the street.

The garrison, Bean noticed, was out in force. He saw soldiers everywhere. And the only Indians he had seen so far, aside from the priest's acolytes, were those at Frost Thorn's house. Across the way he saw the *Alcalde, Don* Francisco Encarnacion Chireno, beckoning him. He strode across.

"Have more soldiers come to town, *Don* Nacio?"

"No. But today we are seeing all of what we have. It is disconcerting, isn't it?"

"Have you talked with Piedras?"

"Since he posted his notice? No. I suppose I will have to, but I don't know what good it will do."

"Probably none. Nacio, you know of the incident some time back at the Cherokee village. One of their people was assassinated."

"*Si,* I know. And I stood there before the square the day Gu'nasoquo and his warriors came looking for the assassin. I was frightened, *Señor* Bean. I think until that moment I had never really seen the Cherokee. Not like that."

"No. I don't suppose many have. My friend, take some advice. The Cherokee are a good people. Respect them, appreciate their friendship when you have it, but don't underestimate them. Do you know, for instance, that every Cherokee over the age of five can read and write? How many of our own can do that?"

Chireno wasn't concerned with literacy at the moment. "When you and Thorn and Goyens returned from the Cherokee, we were told the tribe would remain neutral if trouble comes. But then those warriors came. Peter Bean, which way will the Indians go? We must

214

know something. That idiot"—he pointed an extended finger toward the Red House—"is going to cause fighting here. I can see it beginning. And I cannot stop it. But *Señor*, look." He turned and indicated his house across the way.

"In that house," he said softly, "is my life. My Candida waits there for me. My children. All I have in the world. And look at all these other houses. Each is to someone what mine is to me. I am the *Alcalde*, so I can't look only upon my own house when trouble comes. I have to look at all.

"With Piedras on a rampage, we have a course to follow. We pray to God, protect our families and hide our valuables. But if Gu'nasoquo comes here again, and Nunnehidihi . . . if Egg should come in war paint, *Señor*, then there is no hope and no course to follow."

When he turned back to Bean the *Alcalde*'s face was bleak, his eyes haunted.

Bean shook his head. Chireno had said, without the words, "You are the Indian agent. Do something."

"They are not like us," Bean repeated. "The tribe serves its members. It does not control them. We have Diwali's word. The tribe will be neutral. But the warriors may act on their own, unless they can be appeased. And that's why I'm here today, Nacio. Tell me, the story I heard about what Colonel Piedras said to the tailor. Is it true?"

"I believe it," Chireno said. "Antonio Menchaca is a young man, but he is wise for his years. If he says a thing was said, it was said. And if he gives a meaning to it, I trust that meaning."

Bean nodded. "What I thought," he muttered.

When he left Chireno, Bean retraced his steps to the Red House, brushing unceremoniously past the soldiers at the door, waved down the sergeant in the outer office, banged on Piedras's door, and then strode in with-

215

out waiting for an invitation. At his desk, Piedras scowled, but kept his tongue. This imperious frontiersman had military rank equal to his own.

Without preamble Bean planted his feet solidly on the floor of Piedras's inner sanctum, crossed his arms, and asked, "Where is Anton Moro?"

Standing, the dapper Piedras let his eyes run over the solid, muscular form before him, his distaste plain. Clad in the broadcloth shirt, leather pants, knee-high moccasins, and floppy hat of the Texas frontier, Peter Ellis Bean looked far more like one of the Anglo colonists than he did an officer of Mexico.

"Nice of you to call, Colonel Bean," Piedras said thinly. "I did not realize you were in Nacogdoches."

"I wasn't, until I got word that brought me here. And when I got here I read the notice out there on the *signatorio*. Colonel, don't you think you have exceeded the occasion?"

"It is quite possible you don't understand the occasion, Colonel Bean. Your responsibilities being what they are, and mine being what they are—"

"Your responsibilities, like mine, have some limits, Colonel. Authority has the same limits as responsibility. Were I one of your civilian neighbors here, I would deeply resent that instrument posted before your house."

Piedras paled as he fought back an angry retort. Peter Ellis Bean was not one to be casually crossed. Even Piedras realized that. With an effort he kept his voice calm, his tone civil, and clasped his hands behind him so that they would not betray his anger by trembling.

"I do not care what they resent, Colonel Bean. That is not my concern. I am in command here, and I will act as I see fit. Do you not realize that the Anglo settlers at this very moment are preparing to break away from Mexico? They intend rebellion. They have *always*

216

intended to separate Texas from Mexico, and now they are preparing to do so."

"Bull!" Bean exploded in English, and Piedras's cheeks darkened.

"I know it to be true," the commandant said through clenched teeth.

Bean shook his head, sadly. "Then you are the only one who knows it, Jose. No one else does." Their eyes met and held across the span of the desk, and for a long moment neither spoke. Bean noticed, oddly, that the carefully mounted flag of Mexico on the wall behind Piedras was tilted slightly, slanted as though someone had brushed past its frame and left it ajar. He wondered vaguely how long it had been that way. It was a discordancy in the neat, orderly surroundings in which the little colonel prided himself. Unless, he thought, the man who viewed it also was that far off center, in which case it might still look straight. The thought brought a fleeting sympathy to him and he lowered his voice as he spoke.

"Listen to me, Jose. You have misinterpreted what happened at Anahuac. Bradburn asked for trouble down there, and he got it. He impressed the servants of civilians. He took supplies for his troops and refused to pay. He encouraged runaways, harbored them and worked them. Then he arrested those who complained. He turned his soldiers loose on the citizenry and refused to discipline them. He used the people he was supposed to protect, Jose, and when those people rose up to object, he punished them.

"General Teran himself warned Bradburn to straighten out his affairs, Jose. You know that as well as I do. But Bradburn ignored it."

"The General is dead," Piedras said, interrupting.

"Yes, and that is unfortunate. General Teran was a wise man, Jose. He was a calming influence in troubled

217

times."

"At Velasco they rebelled."

"At Velasco they simply stood up for their rights. Do you know what flag the settlers carried at Velasco, Jose? It was the flag of Mexico. The same flag we both follow. Do you know Stephen Austin has written his people's pledge that they will not consent to the secession of Texas . . . so long as the government of Mexico upholds the Constitution? Colonel Mexia has been to Velasco. He has talked with the settlers there. He is satisfied."

"Mexia is a *Santanista!*" Piedras exploded. "His word means nothing. He is a rebel, just like those Anglos. He has declared for Santa Anna, just as they have."

Bean tried to keep his voice calm. It was like talking to a snapping turtle. "They have declared for our country. That is what matters. Why must you bring politics up here? Why can't you leave it alone?"

Piedras squared his shoulders. "We are at war, Colonel. The Anglos are preparing to attack. I have no choice in the matter."

Bean took a long look at the colonel's face, then swore, both in Spanish and English. He found English better adapted to the purpose.

Piedras leaned forward, placing his hands upon his desktop. "Whose side are you on, Colonel Bean?" he asked intently. "For whom do you declare?"

With an effort Bean kept his answer civil. Without hesitation he stated, "I declare for Mexico and for the Constitution of 1824."

"The answer of a *Santanista,*" Piedras hissed. "I declare for Bustamente. Bustamente is Mexico."

Bean rubbed a callused hand over his chin, then clasped his hands behind him. He was afraid he might reach out and swat the imperious little commandant if he did not control himself.

"When I came in," he said, "I asked you a simple question. I have not received an answer."

Piedras hesitated. "What question was that?"

"Where is Anton Moro?"

Piedras's eyes darted away in surprise, then dropped to the desk before him. "How would I know where Anton Moro is? He no longer works for me. He has gone."

Bean counted slowly to ten in his mind. "And how long has he not worked for you, Colonel Piedras? Since before or after his recent visit to the Cherokee?"

"What does that have to do with where he is? I told you, I don't know where he is."

"Very well, I suppose that is all I'll learn here. But before I go, I suspect there is a thing no one has thought to tell you, Colonel. I'm sure you will be delighted to know that Chief Diwali is alive and well. Moro missed him."

Without another word, Bean strode from the office, slamming the door behind him. To the sergeant orderly in the outer office he said, "This would be a very good time for you to go deliver papers or something. There is about to be an explosion beyond that door."

Outside he pushed his way through the crowd that was still growing in front of the signboard. Chireno was still standing beyond, by the square. Frost Thorn had joined him and they seemed to be waiting for Bean to come out. As he approached them he read the questions in their eyes and shook his head.

"That used to be a good soldier in there. Something has gone wrong. He surely doesn't wake up in the same world we do."

Thorn asked him, "Is there anything you can do? Or the commandant over at Tenoxtitlan?"

"Nothing. We are all colonels, but each has his own job. I am the senior colonel in East Texas, even ahead of Piedras, but my assignment has to do with the Indians, not with the garrison here. That is strictly his command.

"I've had a runner from Tenoxtitlan. Steve Austin has made a statement, and notified all commands. He said, 'Let the Constitution of the nation and state be observed, and we will never consent to secession.' I told Piedras about it . . . I'm fairly sure he already knew it . . . but it made no difference. Piedras is beyond reason."

"You read the pronouncements, Pete," Thorn said. "I guess you have an idea of what has to happen now."

"I know a lot of people who are ready to stick Piedras's head right up on a pole alongside Bustamente's. When the word gets around of these new orders . . ." Bean shook his head sadly. "Well, I guess that's gonna be just about all the reason they're going to need."

Bean went to find Padre de Leon. The old priest was at the church, and as he rapped at the door, Bean suspected what was troubling the old man. His dragons were ripping at him again.

The padre opened the door a crack and peered at him for a moment as though he didn't know him. Then his eyes cleared and he pulled the door open enough for Bean to enter. "Hurry," he said. "Come in, hurry." As Bean edged past, the priest glanced out the door, then closed it quickly. Bean's eyes narrowed in pity and sorrow.

"Did you know that someone is trying to kill me?" the old man's voice quavered.

"I know you sometimes think so." Bean shrugged. "You have told me before." He took the old man's elbow and guided him to a chair. "Why don't we sit down and talk."

"I know who it is," Padre Leon said urgently. "One of the Anglos. The Anglos want to destroy Mexico and they want to destroy the Church. They want to kill me because I am the Church, to them." He let Bean ease him into his best chair, then he put his face in his hands. "Oh, I know. I know. It is not reasonable to think such things. But sometimes I do and I cannot help myself. I pray to God for relief. I appeal to Mother Mary. But then the bad dreams come again, and now Colonel Piedras tells me . . . he tells me . . ."

"Easy, Father. It is all right. What did Colonel Piedras tell you?"

The priest raised his head. His eyes were bright in a pale face. "Why, that the Anglos are coming to destroy Mexico, Peter. Didn't you know?" He was breathing hard, and Bean could see the veins throb in his temples. He realized the old man was terrified, and a hard lump formed in his throat.

"You are in your church, Padre. Everything is all right. No one would hurt you." Tenderly, he lifted the priest's feet to the wicker hassock and removed his sandals. Then he went to the sideboard, found whiskey, and poured a stiff shot into a silver cup. He had to steady the padre's hand so that he could sip it.

Most people in Nacogdoches knew of Padre de Leon's "spells." Few knew the nature of them. Silently, Bean cursed Colonel Piedras. The commandant could have shielded this old man. He could have placated him, calmed him, but no. Not Piedras. He had not only taunted the priest's private dragons, he had added to their number. Bean didn't care what sort of delusions Piedras lost sleep over, but he resented what the colonel had done to this gentle, sad old man.

He wished there were brandy. It would be better for him than whiskey. But there was none.

After a time the padre finished his whiskey and handed back the cup. "I will rest easier now, Peter. Thank you. It was good of you to come. Bless you, my

221

son."

The old man's eyes were closed, and he rested easily in his comfortable chair. Bean stood and walked lightly to the door. As he reached for the latch the padre spoke again, seemingly to no one in particular.

"One really should envy the Anglos. They never look back, only ahead. Always ahead. As though they realize what we have always known—that where one has been can be far more frightening than where one is going."

Bean waited, but there was no more. After a time the shallow breathing of the old man was punctuated by light snores.

Peter Ellis Bean was not a man given to philosophy, but as he crossed the square toward Frost Thorn's house he asked himself: What kind of world has this become, where a rough soldier comforts a priest, where men prepare to defend themselves against their own leaders, where a revolution so far away could so affect the lives of so many here where there was no reason for revolution?

What did Texas do to people? Padre de Leon's predecessor, Father Feliz, had been called away because of aberrations. There were reports of his involvement with women. General Teran, one of the strongest men in Mexico, had become involved with Texas and had taken his own life. Colonel Bradburn, once a fair soldier, had become a tyrant and caused a revolt. Now Colonel Piedras, once an excellent soldier, had become despotic and so determined that his enemies were real that he was rapidly making them real. And Padre de Leon, of all people, now suffered from an illusion so bleak as to terrify him.

Bean could not understand it. Of all the places he had been, he considered Texas by far the most beautiful, especially this eastern portion with its piney woods and ruddy breaks, its abundant game and its laughing streams, its somber glens and brilliant prairies.

A vagrant thought crossed his mind and he puzzled with it: Those who were scarred by Texas were those who tried to change it. Peter Ellis Bean had never tried to change Texas. He loved it, and accepted it as it was.

CHAPTER XX

"The manner of containing depends on whether you want to keep something in or out."
—Will Goyens

Riders had been sent to all the outlying settlements, carrying word of Piedras's pronouncements. Captain of Militia Vicente Cordova made it an early order of business to advise all the other militia units he could reach. But though the Texian riders were fast, they were not the first to bring news to Ayish. Nobody on horseback could have matched the time of two young adventurers on racing stock when each decided to outdo the other.

Samuel Bean on Adolphus Sterne's prized Die Fraulein and Tenuto on his own beloved Rides-the-Morning were neck and neck as they crossed the west-bank pass and skidded to a halt in front of Almazon Huston's place. The abrupt arrival was unfortunate, because the committee to select a name for the new town was at the moment adjourning from Huston's, and several of them were stung by the gravel of the youths' sudden stop.

Alexander Horton and Ed Johnson, in particular, caught the brunt of the flying debris as they stepped out the door. Horton swore and ducked, Johnson hollered and ducked, and then they turned to see where the assault had come from. Ed Johnson was a decent man in many ways, but he could not abide Indians, and the first thing he saw was Tenuto grinning at him from the back of a lathered horse.

"Well now, by damn," he roared and started forward, fists clenched and ready to swing. Young Samuel Bean leaped from his horse and stepped squarely in front of the infuriated Johnson.

"No disrespect, sir, but if you're going after Tenuto you got me to whip first, and if you whip me you'll probably have to answer to my pa, an' you wouldn't want to have to do that."

Johnson stopped in astonishment, his face a foot from the boy's. The man's mouth hung open in surprise. The boy's was clenched shut in frightened determination. Samuel Bean was as tall as Ed Johnson, but Johnson would have made two of him in bulk.

The scene brought grins to the faces of some of the other men now gathering around.

Johnson asked, "Do I know you, boy?"

"No, sir. My name is Samuel Bean. My pa is Peter Ellis Bean, and he told me to take care of Tenuto here, so I'm obliged to do that."

"You're Pete Bean's boy?"

"Yes, sir."

Johnson was beginning to enjoy the situation now. He considered Bean a friend, and if he could help one of his boys get the measure of himself as a man, he would do so.

"You'd fight me, boy?"

"If I had to, sir, though you sure enough would make me hurt, I can see that."

Johnson shrugged. "Expect I would, but I wouldn't feel right about it. You come back when you get some meat on your bones." He cast a glare at the Indian behind young Bean, but his temper had worn off by now. "Just don't come busting up to folks' doors like that anymore or somebody sure enough will take issue with you."

"Yes, sir. I'll remember. But we was in a hurry. Tenuto here's looking for somebody, and Colonel Piedras has declared war on y'all, and there's soldiers coming up the road behind us, and Tenuto's friends are waiting for us back at Mister Thorn's house, and they're pretty upset, and—"

"Ho," Horton interjected. "Whoa up there, Samuel. What was that you just said?"

"I said Tenuto's looking for somebody and his friends are waiting—"

"No. The other part."

"Oh, yeah. Colonel Piedras has declared war on y'all and there's some soldiers coming up behind us. Do you know where Mister Willoughby is, by any chance?"

The Ayish Committee for Peace and Harmony was a competent organization. Its thirty-odd members were essentially the same as the Ayish militia, and a third of them already were at the crossing as members of the committee to name the new townsite. The news brought by young Bean and his Indian for the moment outweighed whether the crossing of the Bayou and the Camino Real would be called Ayish or San Augustine. That matter was tabled and a long dozen Redlanders checked their priming, saddled their mounts, and set out to meet the enemy.

The meeting wasn't long in coming. The enemy, in the form of *Teniente* Domingo Espasa of the Company of Monclova, accompanied by a sergeant, three cavalrymen, and a handful of mounted infantry, was approaching Ayish Bayou as the militia rode out. The Battle of Merrivale Field was no battle at all, as it turned out. It was simply a taking by force.

John Merrivale was one of those who had filtered into East Texas shortly after the Fredonian incident, in that forgotten time between the end of a rebellion and the beginnings of redress.

He built a shanty cabin and cleared a patch of bottom land on the Camino Real between two forested hills. He kept a handful of gold coin in a pouch beneath his hearth and was not always sober. Someone in the Strip learned of what he had there.

John Merrivale was gone now, and so was most of his cabin and his works. But the lowland field he cleared remained, and the road at that point was open to view from the flanking hills.

Of the quickly formed militia company from Ayish, Ed Johnson was ranking officer, with Alexander Horton as his second. From the rise east of Merrivale's they watched Lieutenant Espasa and his patrol straggle across the open stretch, and formed a plan.

Horton, with most of the militia, eased off into the woods beside the trail. Johnson and three men turned and rode back a hundred yards or so, then pulled off the trail.

The army patrol was a double cluster of mounted men. Sergeant Jimenez had about given up on trying to keep his saddle-weary mounted infantry charges in a disciplined column. They straggled behind, and the sergeant cursed under his breath, wondering if it would be worth the effort to go and herd them forward one more time. He decided to make one more effort when they approached Ayish, a mile or so further on. In the meantime, let the idiots follow along as best they could. He was disgusted with them.

The lieutenant, the sergeant, and their three cavalrymen crested the low, forested hill and started down the long incline beyond it. They had gone a hundred yards

227

when the brush burst open just before them and mounted, armed settlers wheeled into the road, facing them. The men all carried long rifles, and the rifles were leveled at the soldiers. Jimenez counted four men. He had no idea how many more might be on their flanks, in the brush. Lieutenant Espasa raised a hand to halt his column, and Sergeant Jimenez looked back wildly, up the hill, for his mounted infantry. They were nowhere in sight.

Ed Johnson stepped his mount forward. "You are taken, Lieutenant. Tell your men to set their muskets on the ground."

Teniente Espasa was astonished. "What does this mean, sir? Get out of our way."

"What it means is, we're at war and your company has just been taken in the field."

"You men have declared war on the Army of Mexico?"

"No, son, the Army of Mexico has declared war on us, by action of Colonel Piedras, and we are responding appropriately."

"But Colonel Piedras has not 'declared war,' as you put it."

"Then why are you and these soldiers here?"

Jimenez looked again toward the top of the hill. Still no troops in sight. He felt a cold uneasiness forming on the back of his neck. He looked again, and now there were riders, but they were not his. Four more Texians were coming down the hill behind them.

Espasa was saying, "My orders are to direct the collecting of civilian arms, sir. For the duration of the emergency."

"You came here to take our guns from us?"

"It is the colonel's order, sir."

"Well, *Teniente,* I'll make it clear. What you just said is a declaration of war, and you'll never hear a better.

Now, get them musket butts on the ground."

Helpless, surrounded, the cavalrymen were disarmed. Some of the men were for taking their horses too, but Horton intervened from the rear.

"We ain't here to steal horses, boys. Their guns'll do. Besides, these boys here are Musquiz's troops."

Ed Johnson had been reaching for the young lieutenant's sword. He stopped and considered Horton's words. "Yeah, well, I've had a drink or two with the captain." In Spanish he told Espasa, "All right, *Teniente*, your patrol has been captured and disarmed. It is not possible now for you to carry out your orders. I'll turn you loose on your parole that you'll turn this bunch around, go back to Nacogdoches, and never come to this part of Texas again."

The young lieutenant's chin quivered, but his voice was steady when he answered. "I agree, sir, my mission here is impossible. I will return to Nacogdoches now. But I cannot promise what I will or will not do another day. I am at the command of my superiors."

Johnson nodded. "I guess that'll do, all right. Well, then, turn around and head back. We will keep your guns here. For the duration of the emergency."

Across the hilltop five more Texians waited with a confused and outmaneuvered cluster of saddle-weary mounted infantry. The more astute among these dreaded the trip home. Sergeant Jimenez was not going to be an easy man to travel with.

The first *Santanista* encounter of the Redlands had been decisive, and the Texians thoroughly enjoyed it. There was a strong temptation to treat it as a lark, a funny story complete in itself to tell to their families and their neighbors. But they knew it was no lark. There was little resemblance between the episode of the little patrol at Merrivale's and an encounter with real, at-war troops.

"Hell," Wyatt Hanks said, "them boys was ducks on the water. For sure nobody took time to explain to that kid lieutenant what was gonna happen when he come for our guns. He probably didn't even know what Piedras has been up to."

"None of them knew they were at war, that's for sure," Horton agreed. "But the next time, they'll know. Then it'll be troops in the field, not a half-asleep gaggle like that'n."

"Y'all see that old sergeant's eyes when we disarmed them fellers? Been different if that bunch had been nine or ten like him. Been a different story altogether."

"You faced troops before, Joey?" one of the group asked another. "Well, I have, and when they know they're at war they ain't easy anymore. And now they'll know."

Several of the younger men volunteered to carry the word to the surrounding settlements that the colony was now definitely at war, and to call in the militia. With Johnson's nod, they set off in three directions. Johnson, Horton, and the rest gathered up the captured ordnance of the army patrol and headed back down the road to Ayish.

"San Augustine," Horatio Hanks declared, to no one in particular.

"What?"

"I said I favor San Augustine for a name. Got a ring to it."

"Ayish is better," Horton said. "Everybody knows where Ayish is. Nobody ever heard of San Augustine."

Johnson swung around in his saddle to study both of them. "Just what brought that up, anyway?"

"It was always up," Horatio Hanks pointed out. "We just tabled it to come fight Meskins. Now we done that, so let's get back to it."

"But the table we tabled it on is settin' in Almazon

Huston's main room. We can't conduct business out here on the road. It isn't proper. If we're gonna be a committee, then let's proceed like a committee. We'll talk about it later."

Cocking a phlegmatic eyebrow at Horton, Horatio asked, "If I'd said Ayish, what would you have said?"

"San Augustine, probably."

Dan Vail asked, "What you gonna do about your Indian, Sandy?"

"What Indian?"

"The one the Bean kid brought you."

"That isn't my Indian. That's just an Indian looking for my deputy."

"What you suppose an Indian wants with your deputy?" They were coming in sight of the inn now, and they could see Tenuto and young Bean sitting on the bench out front, waiting for their return.

Annoyed, Horton shrugged. "I don't have any idea what he wants with him. I don't even know where the devil Willoughby is."

There was a moment of silence. Then Horatio Hanks needled him. "Seems to me a high sheriff would keep better track of his deputies than that. Anyhow you ain't got but one."

Horton had had all he could take. "You're plumb wrong about that, Horatio. I got me two deputies, and the other one is you. Raise up your hand."

"Aw, now, Sandy . . ."

"Raise up your hand!"

Horatio did as he was told, and as they pulled up in front of Almazon Huston's he was sworn in as a deputy sheriff (*alguazil segundo* to make it legal) of the Ayzes District.

"Pay's a dollar a day. Would you rather go lookin' for Coop Willoughby or Anton Moro?"

Some of the other settlers in the area, those who had

231

gotten the word too late to join Johnson's militia company, were beginning to arrive now at Huston's. Among them was the *Alcalde*, Benjamin Lindsay. James Bullock arrived just behind him, and Ed Johnson turned over command of the militia company. None of the men, however, were dismissed.

Lindsay's first action was to call a council of war.

Tenuto was growing irritated with the delays. He was anxious to get on with locating Willoughby, which after all was why he had come here among these barbarians, and he kept Samuel Bean as his interpreter busy interrupting and pestering the hurrying men coming and going around Huston's. Alexander Horton explained to the Indian, through Samuel, that his mission would have to wait. There were more important things afoot. Tenuto explained through Samuel that he didn't give a hang about the white men's war, he expected some assistance, and promptly.

In exasperation Horton told James Bullock that he needed to have Horatio Hanks furloughed to take care of deputy duties. Bullock balked at losing any of his men before the militia received its orders, but finally relented. Tenuto and Samuel Bean were already saddling their mounts.

When Horatio Hanks was called out Horton told him, "You take these two and go find Coop Willoughby. Bring him back here, or if I ain't here you can take the lot of them to Frost Thorn's house in Nacogdoches."

Hanks shrugged. "Where do I look for him?"

"Hell, if I knew that I'd go myself. Just start lookin'."

Hanks went for his horse, cursing valiantly.

There were more riders coming in. Donald McDonald and two men from Bevil's Diggings to the south, who had been at McDonald's when Johnson's rider passed there.

"Light down and come in," Ed Johnson called to the Scot. "We're at war, and fixin' to talk about it."

McDonald swung down off the sturdy gray mare he favored. "At war, is it?" He turned to Horton. "How do, Sandy lad. I've been a bit busy or I'd ha' coom to find ye two days since. I ha' somethin' o' yours down to my place."

"Somethin' of mine?"

"Aye. 'Tis that smuggler o' yours, that Willoughby. I fetched him in and tended him. I'll be lookin' to you for payment. The man eats like there was two of him."

"What happened to him, Mac?"

"Robbed by Indians and shot in the head by a renegade, is how he tells it. Ye can go fetch him do ye want, but take along a horse. He dinna' have one, nor a rifle neither."

Horton's shoulders sagged in resignation. He shook his head.

Finally he called Samuel Bean and Tenuto over. "Samuel, do you know where Mr. McDonald's place is, where there's the mill?"

"Sure. I been there with Pa. Why?"

"Well, that's where Cooper Willoughby is, and you and Tenuto can go get him. Take an extra horse with you, though." He looked around. Horatio Hanks was just coming from the corral with his saddled mount. "There, take that one Mr. Hanks is bringing. It's saddled and ready to go."

Samuel translated for Tenuto, who nodded and dug heels into his racer. Samuel yelled, "Hey! Wait for me!" In the mist of sand and dust they raised departing, Horatio never was quite sure which one had grabbed the reins from him. All he saw was careening horseflesh going by, and then three horses with two riders racing away down the high bank trail. The empty horse was his.

Horton wandered over to him. "You're dismissed from deputying, Horatio. Report back to Cap'n Bullock for militia duty. We got a war on our hands."

A few minutes later Ed Johnson collared Horton and Ben Lindsay. "I been thinkin'," he said. "What you said back there on the road, Sandy, about those boys bein' mostly Musquiz's troops, and all. We don't need them guns we got from them, do we?"

Horton looked at Lindsay. Lindsay considered it and shook his head. "No, we have all we can use, I guess."

"Then I think we ought to give 'em back. You know, when those fellers get back to Nacogdoches, they gonna have a lot of explainin' to do, especially if they come in without their guns. And Musquiz will have to report to the colonel, and he's gonna be awful embarrassed doin' that."

"He'll have to report anyway."

"Yeah, but I don't like to think of him explainin' to that nutty colonel how it is his patrol came back disarmed."

Lindsay thought it over. Musquiz was a good man, and a friend. A few guns weren't going to make any difference, and just might make things worse. "I believe you're right. Do you suppose a couple of the boys on fast horses might get around ahead of the patrol before it gets to town, and leave all their stuff where they can find it?"

"Could sure try," Johnson said. "And maybe that part of it wouldn't ever have to get reported at all, past just Musquiz, Sandy."

"I reckon we owe him that much."

CHAPTER XXI

"Some fear the earth because it is a million miles wide; others because it is six feet deep."
— Donald McDonald

Will Goyens had been in no hurry to answer Colonel Piedras's summons. He had other, better things to do, and after seeing the message posted on the *signatorio* he really wanted nothing more to do with the man.

The second time the message came he had no choice. Two armed soldiers accosted him just outside Nacogdoches and escorted him back into town, to the Red House. When he dismounted they handed his horse over to the guard stationed there and walked him in through the outer office to the commandant's door. He was announced and the door closed behind him.

Piedras glanced up from his desk, then tilted his head far back to look down his nose at Goyens. Will had seen the look before, usually from white men looking at a black. It was the same expression, but this was from *El Comandante* looking at a civilian.

"You sent for me, Colonel?"

"I sent for you, blacksmith. Twice. Where have you been?"

Goyens shrugged. "Around. I was busy."

"Henceforth, blacksmith, when your *comandante* sends for you you will not be busy. Do you know I could have you whipped?"

Head tilted, Goyens studied the man behind the desk.

235

He saw something new there, something he had not seen before. Maybe it was a trick of the light, but Piedras looked smaller than he had before. The spotless uniform still fit as perfectly as it always had, but there remained the impression of shrunkenness. The colonel's manner, once the arrogance of a small man in authority, now seemed the desperation of a small man in a corner. Eyes that had flashed command now glittered furtively. Subtle as it was, the change shocked Goyens.

"Let me assure you, Colonel," he said evenly, "you don't ever want to do that."

Piedras's eyes held his for a moment, then dropped away. "Did you bring my barrels with you, blacksmith?"

"What barrels?"

"My barrels. My two small barrels, as ordered."

Completely baffled, Goyens spread his hands. "I don't know about any barrels, Colonel. What kind of barrels do you want?"

Piedras clamped his jaw tight and breathed deeply. "Why do you think I called you here?"

"I don't know. You haven't told me yet. You want some barrels?"

"Of course I want some barrels. Two of them. Immediately!"

"Small ones, you said."

"Yes, small ones."

Goyens sensed an advantage. The threat of whipping had been unwarranted, and he didn't appreciate it a bit. When Will Goyens set his mind to it he could be as thick-headed as any white man, and he set his mind to it now. "What do you want them for?"

Piedras bristled. "That is of no concern to you, blacksmith. This is military business."

"All right," Goyens shrugged. "But I can't give you the right kind of barrels if I don't know what they'll be used for. Do you want barrels that will keep out moisture, or do you want barrels that will hold water? Or do you want barrels just to keep things tidy and it doesn't matter how tight they are?"

A trace of bafflement crossed the malign face that was raised again from the papers on the desktop. "What, pray tell, is the difference between a barrel that keeps out moisture and one that holds water?"

"Well, there is a whole lot of difference. A barrel to hold water has to be tight and made of some wood that will expand when it's wet and get even tighter. It has to seal its own seams when it's full. Barrels for spirits are the same way, except you can char the insides of them, and that cuts down evaporation seepage in case they're not quite full and the top edge gets dry. Either one ought to be a good oak barrel.

"A barrel that keeps out moisture has to be built even tighter, because it does not actually hold liquid to seal it. So the barrel has to be tight as everything to begin with. A barrel of Osage Orange—some call it bois d'arc—is about the best for that, and it won't rot either. However, it shouldn't be set too long on the bare ground or the waxworms will bore it, and if some of them bore all the way through, which they will eventually, then you have holes and your barrel won't keep out moisture. In fact, then your tight wood works against you, because your barrel won't breathe . . ."

Piedras half stood, holding up a hand. Goyens noticed that his eyes had a glazed look, and was content.

"Please bring me two small barrels," Piedras said, "that are moisture proof, rot proof, and worm proof. I need them right away."

"Yes, sir," Goyens said, happily. "Will you be paying for them now, or when I bring them?"

Quick anger darkened the colonel's features. "You will receive your payment at my pleasure, blacksmith."

"In coin?"

"You will receive *boletas* payable by the government of Mexico."

"Sorry, Colonel. I can't use them."

Piedras looked about to explode. Goyens stood his ground. The easygoing, phlegmatic blacksmith was not now apparent. He would do business with Piedras, but he would have his money.

After a chill silence Piedras again dropped his eyes. He leaned down, dug around under his desk, and came up with a handful of coins. He slapped it down. Goyens counted out a fair price for two good barrels. "That'll do." He smiled at the colonel. "I'll bring them around some time next week."

He started to turn, but the shriek of fury brought him around again.

"Not next week!" Piedras was on his feet, fists clenched at his sides. "Not tomorrow! Now! I need them now!"

Goyens propped his chin in one hand, the elbow resting in the other hand. "Now you know I've moved my whole shop out to my place, Colonel. It will take me a little while just to go out there and back, much less come up with the kind of barrels you want. Maybe I can have them back here today, maybe not."

Piedras settled into his chair as though exhausted. "Bring me my barrels," he said, not looking at the blacksmith. "Just bring them."

Goyens grinned maliciously. "Sure thing, Colonel. It won't take long. I move a lot faster when I don't have soldiers with me."

As he left the Red House, Will Goyens was satisfied. Piedras had caused him inconvenience. The debt was paid. Now his artisan's mind turned to the question of the barrels. He had none on hand that would meet the requirements, but he was thinking of those new copper kettles hanging in his shed—kettles he had made during bad weather when there was nothing better to do. Two of those kettles, rim to rim, would be the size of a small barrel. They certainly would be moisture proof, rot proof, and worm proof. A barrel like that would last forever.

As he rode out of town, he was already resolving the problems of how to join and cap copper kettles to make copper barrels.

As Goyens rode out, a man on a tired horse paused in the shadows off the road to watch him pass. Smoke-stained buckskin breeches and a darkened homespun shirt with sleeves rolled up over muscular forearms blended into the pattern of the woods behind him. Level, humorless gray eyes regarded the passing mulatto from under a flat-crowned slouch hat. The man sat his horse easily, comfortably, and in no apparent hurry to move on. Goyens passed within fifteen yards of him and did not notice him there.

When the mounted mulatto was gone from sight, the man nudged heels into the horse's flanks and reined to the right, into the town of Nacogdoches.

He pulled up short of the first crossing in the town and studied the place. The usual bustle of post-siesta time was missing. The town seemed subdued. Ahead, a squad of five armed soldiers marched across the inter-section and disappeared behind buildings. A man standing on a shaded porch watched them cross, then leaned forward to spit on the ground when they had passed. He saw no women or children on the streets.

Moving on, he passed a row of near-silent houses, a few men visible watching him, nothing more. At the next street he looked right and saw more soldiers in the distance, all armed, and a few other men. He noticed that none of the civilians, either Spanish or Anglo, carried weapons. He looked again. Not one that he saw or had seen carried a rifle. Not so much as a pistol. His own rifle, a long-barreled, gold-hued flintlock of the Kentucky design, rested across his saddle and his right hand never strayed from it.

Thomas Bell, "Tecumseh" Bell to those few who knew him, and those many who knew of him, had come a long way from his last battle, but he would never have assumed he was far from his next one.

There was activity in the middle of the little town. Just off the square several people were gathered around a signboard in front of the rust-red building that he knew housed the *Comandante* of Nacogdoches. Bell watched them from a distance, then walked his horse forward, shouldering some people aside, and leaned down to read the notice posted there. Weather had dimmed the letters, but the message was still clear. He ignored the soldiers standing at both sides watching him, muskets lowered hesitantly from their shoulders.

The one nearest him cleared his throat, then spoke.
"*Señor, por favor,* it is the *Comandante*'s order, I must ask you for your rifle . . ."

The hat brim came up and cold gray eyes fixed on the youth. His voice trailed off and he swallowed. Private Gomez had never before seen eyes like those. When they turned on him his skin felt cold, as though someone were going to die. It was a reflex that lowered his musket and trained it on the man only yards away from him. With nerveless fingers he pulled back the hammer and tried to repeat his statement. His voice sounded thin. "*Señor,* it is *El Comandante*'s order . . ."

Bell didn't move, but ice-gray eyes under a wide hat brim bored into the young soldier.

"Sonny," he said, almost a whisper, "if you pull that trigger you better pull it hard, 'cause if you don't drop

240

me with that shot I'll kill you, sure as hell."

The musket barrel wavered and the cold eyes bored in. Private Gomez swallowed again, and the musket sagged. "Please, *Señor* . . ."

Bell peered at him a moment longer, then appeared to forget him entirely. Glancing once again at the posted pronouncements, he turned his animal and walked it away across the square, never looking back. Gomez shifted from one foot to the other, holding his musket awkwardly, embarrassed and unsure what to do next. His companion, another private of the guard, stood at rigid attention throughout the incident, his attention fixed on something far away. Looking around, Gomez saw Sergeant Marcos Sanchez standing before the Red House. The sergeant motioned, and Gomez went to him.

"That was not done well," Sanchez said.

"No, Sergeant. *Por favor,* what could I do? I did not know what to do."

Sanchez studied the youngster for long moments. When he spoke, his voice was mild. "Ah, *niño,* nobody knows what to do these days. We just do our best, and we follow our orders, and we try not to make too many mistakes. You made a mistake a moment ago. You should either have shot that man or never have pointed your weapon at him."

"*Sí,* Sergeant, I know."

"Next time, *niño,* when you are set to guard the sign you guard the sign. Let others worry about doing what it says."

"*Sí,* Sergeant."

At a secret place on Carrizo Creek Vicente Cordova met again with a trusted few and inventoried the arsenal assembled there. All of the militia's guns were stockpiled now in this place, safe for a time from the spies of Piedras. They would not have to remain hidden very long. Soon they would be put to use.

The arsenal was a motley assemblage of weapons. Most of the militia arms, spirited from their repository just ahead of the military's arrival, were muskets—some Charlesvilles, a few Austrian big-bores, and four old English Brown Bess types. Some had been converted to caplock, most remained flintlock-fired. Most of the Spanish settlers preferred muskets for their ease of loading, their versatility, and their awesome power. Few of the Spanish were hunters.

Alongside the muskets were arrayed the guns of some of the Anglo settlers, caught up in the evacuation of weapons from Nacogdoches. Some had been in Goyens's gunshop. Several had been delivered to the militia by their owners, for safekeeping. Most of these were long rifles of the Pennsylvania or Kentucky style. Bore sizes ranged from 30-caliber squirrel rifles to 50- and 58-caliber game rifles. Slim, sleek, and deadly accurate, the long rifles were like fine ladies among the coarser musketry surrounding them. They were virtually the trademark of the Anglo emigrants to Texas. Men who had grown up with one of these at hand could bark a squirrel at 50 yards or drop a deer at 200. As Robert Hester had said once of his prized *Vinnie*, "Happen a man need her to, she can thread needles for the lady down the road."

They counted and tallied them all, and made a careful list. They entered Antonio Menchaca's two-barreled fowler, Norris's short Austrian percussion smoothbore and his *Meat-in-the-Pot*, a 50-caliber Kentucky, Ham Borden's *Diana Swift*, and Emilio Sato's much-abused old Charlesville. Silas Brown's *Old Spit* was there, alongside a nondescript flintlock smokepole belonging to one of Goyens's overseers and listed simply as "one of Mr. Goyens' guns." There was a fox-in-the-circle Leman, and several Plainer rifles.

The inventory completed, Cordova assigned a guard to the cache and took the rest of his company by circuitous routes back to Nacogdoches. In a way, the militia captain was more bothered by the responsibility of protecting those guns than by the fight he saw coming. Particularly the guns of the Anglos. He had watched the faces of some of those who had delivered their precious long rifles to him for safekeeping. Some would rather have deposited their wives.

Nacogdoches lay quiet now, waiting. Hostility and sullen anger hung in the air like swamp mist. The long-festering annoyance with Colonel Piedras had evolved into a new thing. The men of Nacogdoches were past irritation with the erratic colonel. To a man, they felt degraded and insulted. Dislike for Piedras had become hatred.

Cordova stabled his mount and walked along the street toward his house. Across the way Captains Musquiz and Medina stood outside the Quartel in earnest conversation. They looked up as Cordova passed and all three nodded curtly. The ease of familiarity was gone. You don't pass the time with a man you may be trying to kill tomorrow.

A shame, Cordova thought. A terrible shame.

In the twilight he saw a cluster of bright forms at the dooryard of Frost Thorn's big house, and heard the chatter of feminine voices. A dozen ladies were assembled there, the remains of . . . what? A tea party? A meeting? A gossip session? He suspected the occasion was more serious than trivial. He paused to doff his hat, bow, and smile at the lovely cluster. Ladies of all shapes and sizes, ladies of all stations and ages, and at this moment he loved them all. How were they to fare in what would come? What was their part in this thing of men that was building around them?

The bright smile of Susan Thorn, the imperious glance of *Señora* Ybarbo, the sweet gaze of Antonio Menchaca's little wife, the dark eyes of Candida Chireno haunted him as he went along his way.

With a knowledge born of experience, he knew. The ladies were planning their part of a war, the plans that women must make when their men will fight. Did they know *why* their men would fight? Probably not. Yet they understood. They accepted. And they would make their plans.

The tough, proud veteran, the captain of militia, ducked his head aside as he entered his own house so that his own wife might not see that his eyes were moist.

In the third village of the Tsalagi where crippled Nicolet was chief, Gu'nasoquo and Nunnehidihi assembled the men of their two clans and such young warriors as would follow them, and old Diwali came to them there with John Bowles and Egg riding beside him.

Dita-staye-sgi, the father of Udali and Atasi, followed close behind them, scowling and fussing.

As he dismounted, Diwali took from his saddle pouch a fan of eagle feathers, which he spread and offered to the winds in succession—south and north, west and east. Then he handed it to Egg, who strode to the center of the village circle and held the fan high. With this the circle became council grounds and the men assembled. When all were seated Diwali walked forward and stood among them. Women came and joined them. This was tribal business, the business of war. Each person sat with his clan.

Nicolet started to rise, a long pipe in his hand, but Diwali motioned him down. The old chief stood tall and turned a full, slow circle, pale blue eyes lingering on every face around him. He stopped when he faced Gu'nasoquo and Nunnehidihi.

"Some among us are very anxious to take up the war club," he said. "Not only the young warriors, who are always anxious to fight, but some whose years should give them wisdom."

Under the old man's level gaze Gu'nasoquo sat silent for a moment, only his scarred left cheek twitching, as it always did. Then he responded, "Old chief, you know that our brother Utsada is dead."

"All men die," Diwali told him, "at one time or another."

"Not all men die with holes in their backs, in the middle of their own village."

"Men die all sorts of ways, Gu'nasoquo. You cannot bring Utsada back."

"Anglos killed him. Vengeance is demanded. Is this not clan law? Since when have the Tsalagi hesitated to take revenge, Diwali?"

Diwali raised a hand in disagreement. "Not Anglos. One man killed Utsada. Only one. And you do not know he was an Anglo. Who here has a nose that can tell the smell of Anglo from the smell of Spanish?"

"One man then," Gu'nasoquo persisted. "But we will find him."

"Did not Willow-bee promise to find the man for you? Did you not agree?"

From the side Dita-staye-sgi interrupted, his voice querulous. "Willow-bee has failed. Everyone knows that. Willow-bee may be dead. He has failed."

"Have your children come home then, Dita-staye-sgi?" Diwali's thrust deflated the irascible Cutter for a moment. He was sensitive about the fact his son and daughter had gone off looking for the white trader. His dignity was ruffled by their concern, and his pride was

245

hurt that they had gone despite his disapproval. "My children have bees in their heads!" He spat. "A young woman should not go among the whites. They are savages."

Diwali raised a hand to placate the truculent Cutter. He had not meant to wound him, only to shut him up. "Your daughter is safe, Dita-staye-sgi. She is with Frost Thorn, and Atasi and Tenuto are with her."

Broad-shouldered Nunnehidihi, the silent one, asked, "Does Diwali know what man killed Utsada?"

The old chief paused, unwilling to lie to his people. "Yes," he said.

"Then will you tell who he is?"

"No. I see too many axes here, too many war clubs. The man is in the white lands south of the Spanish road. If warriors go there after him they will have to fight the Anglos. And if our warriors fight, then our tribe must fight. And if the Ani-Tsalagi fight the Anglo, the Ani-Tasalagi will perish."

"If the Ani-Tsalagi do not fight the Anglo, sooner or later, the Ani-Tsalagi will be overrun again," *Gu'nasoquo* growled. "Diwali knows this will happen."

"We must wait and see," the old chief said. "But now there is bad blood between the whites and their soldiers. Now if some of the *Aniyunwiya* fight, all must fight. So none should fight now."

"Since when"—Dita-staye-sgi's dark eyes were slitted—"does the tribe . . . or its war chief . . . tell any man when he can fight and when not? Has the law been changed, Diwali? Have we chosen a new kind of law, like white man's law?"

"The law has not changed. The tribe does not tell. But the chief requests patience of each of you. It is a bad time. It is a time to be united."

"Pfaw! When have the Tsalagi ever been united, Diwali?"

246

The old chief ignored the outburst, turned again to look at all of them, and raised his hands. "I tell you this. Before the moon comes full again, the whites will have fought among themselves. The soldiers will be gone or the Anglos will be tamed. When it is over we will know what we might do. For now it is a time to wait. I believe Willoughby will do as he told you, Gu'nasoquo. I say give him time to bring you the man who killed Utsada."

They spoke among themselves, then Gu'nasoquo arose. "Because Diwali bears the eagle fan we listen. We will wait, but we will not wait here. We go south, to see what it is the white men do. But know this, Diwali. If Willow-bee fails, if the backshooter is not delivered before the white men make their war, then some among us may join that war. And if the Tsalagi must go to war without their war chief, then maybe it is time we have a new war chief."

Diwali nodded. He retrieved the fan from Egg and strode away, the huge warrior at his heels. He had made the best deal he could. On the way upstream from Nicolet's village he conferred with John Bowles, then called Egg forward.

He had an errand for the big warrior.

PART FOUR

WIND IN THE PINES

CHAPTER XXII

*"Those who distrust their own government
are seldom wrong."*
—Frost Thorn

The festivities the ladies of Nacogdoches had been planning for August were in shambles. With things as they were in East Texas, the only ones constrained to celebrate were those few who somehow remained blithely unaware of what was going on around them. Susan Thorn, Candida Chireno, Jane Norris, and several of their friends, who had taken it upon themselves originally to plan a fiesta for the town, had put aside their plans as the split between Colonel Piedras and the settlers became more ominous. *Doña* Elena Ybarbo, on the other hand, proceeded with her planning as though nothing were amiss.

Doña Elena's function regarding local festivities, as she saw it, was to sanction them. The criterion for sanction was simple: Either she approved or she didn't. She had no hard and fast rules of propriety. An affair either was gracious or it wasn't.

Aware of the slacking of interest by the other women, *Doña* Elena happily took upon herself the entire responsibility for arranging Nacogdoches's Fiesta

Grande, knowing that in so doing, she was assuring its social success.

From the *escribador, Señor* Sepulveda, she acquired a list of the households in and near Nacogdoches. *Señor* Sepulveda still suffered from his encounter with the renegade *presidarios* who had roughed him up and taken his *pistolas,* but the gentleman was out and about again, and delivered the copied list in person when *Doña* Elena summoned him. He was curious. With his departing bow and a decorous cough, he inquired of the *señora,* "For what will the list be used?"

She was startled at the question, and her dark eyes widened. "Why, for the fiesta, of course, *señor.* I am planning the fiesta, you know."

The man looked blank. "The fiesta, *señora?*"

"Of course, *señor.*" As he did not seem to understand, she repeated it slowly. *"La Fiesta."*

"Yes, *señora.* And when will the fiesta be held?"

"The first Sunday in August, of course." Her tone was a bit sharp now. "That will be the fifth of August. You will, of course, be welcome, you and *Señora* Sepulveda.

"Ai, alas, *señora,* my beloved wife has been gone the past two years. The *señora* was kind enough to send her condolences."

"Yes, of course. My deepest sympathy, *señor.* But you must come anyway. We will have the entire plaza, I should imagine. I must notify Colonel Piedras that we require it. Good day, *señor.*"

By the time Sepulveda closed the door behind him, she was already on her way back to the parlor to have Nuni read the list to her. So many sheets of paper . . . she had not dreamed there were so many people in Nacogdoches these days. She really hadn't noticed so many. She felt a tug of sympathy of *Señor* Sepulveda. Apparently losing his wife had affected his memory.

She was sure he had been surprised to hear of the fiesta. Also, he had rather a bad limp.

From the back of the house she could hear children's voices, bright with play. The house of Domingo Ybarbo had never been short of children—first their own, and now grandchildren. There were the young ones at play, just hear their voices. And there was Maria now, her oldest daughter, singing to them, and Dorotea would be somewhere nearby helping to keep an eye on them.

Her husband, Domingo, would be out in the pastures beyond the town, counting his cattle, she supposed. Her other grown daughters, Estefania, Alejandra, and Barbara, were gone with their twelve-year-old brother Juan Batista out to where Alejandra's new husband was building his house. Her older sons, Juan Jose and Juan Antonio, had gone somewhere with their uncle Concepcion Ybarbo two—no, maybe three days ago. She worried sometimes about Concepcion's influence on the boys—no, not boys now, young men, but boys to her. Concepcion was a wild one sometimes, always running with the Anglos, in and out of town, speaking as often in English as he did in Spanish, carrying that long-barreled rifle of his, riding fast horses. He was connected in some way with Captain Cordova's militia organization, she thought.

When they left, the boys had been furtive. And they had taken most of the guns from the house, and had not brought them back. She had mentioned it that evening to Domingo, but he only nodded his grayed head and sighed. He had been very preoccupied of late.

"Nuni!" *Doña* Elena called, then tapped her foot and called again. "Nuni!" When there was no answer, *Doña* Elena went through to the back door and called to her daughter, "Maria! I cannot find Nuni. Have you seen her?"

Maria was squatting in the fenced court, wiping dirt

253

from the face of little Juana. "*Sí*, Mama. Nuni has gone again to the Thorn house to visit the Cherokee girl, Mistletoe. They are cousins or something, I think."

Turning back into the house, *Doña* Elena scowled. Nuni had been gone too much of late. She should be here when needed. She would have to be scolded. She remembered Padre de Leon urging her to be patient in dealing with Nuni—with all *Indios,* for that matter.

"Remember, they are like children," he had admonished.

Child or not, the Indian girl was the only one available right now who could read, and *Doña* Elena needed her census read to her. She didn't want to wait for evening, when Domingo could read it. She wanted to get busy now.

She returned to the back door. "Maria, please send Dorotea to the Thorn house to bring Nuni home. I need her."

When the youngster came through the house Elena repeated the instructions to her and added, "Now hurry, child, there is much to be done."

Dorotea cocked her head to the side, studying her mother. "But how can there be a fiesta, Mamacita? All the men are getting ready to fight."

Elena looked at her daughter and smiled. Ten years old. All big, dark eyes, long legs, and coltish wisdom. "The men are always talking, little one. It is the way men are. One cannot set aside the important things while the men talk of war. There will be a fiesta. Each year we have fiesta."

"Yes, *Mamacita*." After another moment's puzzling, Dorotea shrugged and went out the front door. Elena watched her depart, then went to the front veranda to look after her. Dorotea would be a pretty woman. Two more years, and the boys would be noticing her, two years after that and she would have the young men's attention. She would make a good marriage. Elena would see to it.

Dorotea made her way along the red-packed street to the corner of the plaza, past the houses fringing it, and around to North Road street, where she turned past the Norris house and the wide *jacale* of the Martines family, where Faustina Martines stood beside the front gate, chewing on a broomstraw. At Dorotea's wave the girl came out and fell in beside her.

"I have to go to the Thorn house to get Nuni," Dorotea told her. "My mama is planning the fiesta."

"My mama says there cannot be fiesta this summer. She says there will be fighting here." Faustina said it with the manner of one who knows all, but her eyes held a dread. She had caught the concern of her parents, but could not really grasp the significance of it. "I have never seen them fight."

"A long time ago, when I was just a baby, they fought. I was three years old. Papa and Mama took us all to Ayzes to wait until it was over."

Faustina inspected her broomstraw, bit off the chewed end of it, and started over on crisp straw. "Who was fighting?"

"Some of the men. They fought the Fredonians."

"Who are the Fredonians?"

"Some other of the men, I suppose. There weren't any soldiers here, then, but some of the *Indios* fought with them."

"Mama says the men will be hurt if they fight. She says to my papa that some will die."

Dorotea shrugged. "I don't think any of them died when they fought before. My papa says they just made a lot of noise."

"I've been watching the soldiers." Faustina gestured toward the plaza where a company was assembled for drill. "I never knew there were so many."

255

"These last few days, we see patrols go past our house all the time. They all have bayonets on their guns."

"Dorotea, are you frightened?"

"A little," she told her friend after hesitation. "I guess I am, a little."

Will Goyens pulled up his two-wheel cart at the intersection by Chireno's house and looked around. Two little girls, Dorotea Ybarbo and Faustina Martines, were approaching the Thorn house, turning in at the gate. They waved to him and he waved back. Beyond, in the plaza, a company of infantry was beginning drills, green coats and white bandoliers bright in the patchwork sunlight. A cavalry patrol was being formed outside the Quartel, where Captain Renaldo Musquiz was in conversation with one of his lieutenants, a sergeant standing by, listening. A few women were on the streets, and here and there were children. At the moment, no men were in sight except the soldiers.

Odd, he thought, that there should be no men on the streets of Nacogdoches. The absence imparted to the town a sense of imbalance, an ominous feeling of storms building up. Looking further, he noticed there were two men on the porch of his inn across the way, idling there, watching the soldiers drill. He didn't know either of them.

Flicking reins on the back of his mule, he drove across North Road street to the Red House, where a pair of armed sentries stood drowsily in the shade of the veranda roof. He pulled up, got down, snapped a tie-line to the mule's bit and looped it over the hitch rail. Then from the cart he unloaded four large copper pots, a pair of wide brass rings with serrated edges, and a large iron clamp wrench. Bearing these items he went to the door, ignoring the sentries there, and kicked at the bottom of it until an orderly admitted him.

Padre de Leon and Captain Francisco Medina were in the office of the Commandant of Nacogdoches. The old priest looked pale and angry. Medina smiled a greeting when Goyens entered and Colonel Piedras glanced at him, angered at the distraction, then turned back to his conversation with the priest. Padre de Leon had not looked around. When he had Piedras's attention again he said, "It simply is not right, Colonel. It is not just. The holy things, these belong to the Church, not to the State . . . and certainly not to the Army."

Piedras scowled, irritated. "Padre, you misunderstand. I am not asking you, I am ordering you. You are to bring everything to my office. Everything. It is my responsibility to protect and defend state property. I make it also my responsibility to protect the property of the Church. You will . . ."

The priest held up a trembling hand. "But who then is to protect the Church from the State? Who is to protect these properties from you, Colonel?"

Piedras half rose from his chair, his eyes flashing. "You dare question . . ." He got hold of himself with an effort and settled back into the chair. "Padre. Hear me. Do you think the State is not safer than these Anglo revolutionaries running through the streets planning revolt? Are you not better advised to put your trust in the representative of the Supreme Government of Mexico than to chance its loss to those rabble? Do you think they would hesitate a minute to pillage your poor church?" He paused, a sly expression pulling at the corners of his mouth. "Tell me, Padre, is it not you who has nightmares of an Anglo taking your life?"

Goyens, standing by the doorway, frowned. Captain Medina looked sharply at his colonel. The Commandant was toying with the old priest, playing upon his secret fears. Neither of the listeners approved.

Piedras glanced at Medina but ignored the look. "We

257

will have trouble here very soon," he told the Padre. "The Anglos will attack us. I know it. And if, during the trouble, you should be injured . . . maybe killed . . . who then would protect the property of the Church, Padre? That is why I must take the Church artifacts and protect them. They will be safe with me."

The old priest lowered his eyes. It galled him, clearly, to have to give cherished things over to the custody of the very man who had, those years before, commandeered the church building itself and turned it into a barracks for his rowdy troops. The Padre, against all his charitable nature, simply could not trust Piedras. But he had no choice. Armed men wield more power than the word of God. With a sigh of resignation he stood, not meeting Piedras's victorious stare.

The colonel arose, now the efficient, busy officer with no time to waste. "Captain, you will take some men and go with the priest to his church. Bring back here everything that is of value. Leave nothing there which might profit the Anglos. Bring all important documents as well."

Padre de Leon shook his head. "Not the church records."

"Everything of value," Piedras repeated. "Now go. There is no time to waste."

As they passed the doorway Will Goyens heard Captain Medina's whisper to the padre, "Don't worry, Father, I will look after your things."

"Ah." Piedras took notice of Goyens for the first time. "The blacksmith is here. Did you bring my barrels?"

"Do I look empty-handed to you, Colonel?" The mulatto shrugged, indicating his double armload of pots and brass bands.

"I plainly stipulated barrels, blacksmith, not kettles. Where are the barrels?"

"When I get done, these will be barrels. What you stipulated was something to keep moisture out. Where do you want them?"

Skeptically, Piedras strode past him to the anteroom and came back with his orderly and one of the sentries. A map table in the office had been cleared and was piled with valuables. There were documents, ledgers, several small rolled paintings, a pair of gold chalices, and a dagger with an ornate ruby-studded hilt. A leather pouch crammed with gold and silver coin was there, and several bits of jewelry. An ivory-inlaid rosewood box lay open on the table, displaying a pair of silver-mounted dueling pistols.

Goyens told them he would need a fire for soldering. He wondered how much of the treasure was state property and how much was Piedras's own. With Piedras supervising closely, the soldiers filled one of the copper kettles, piling things high above its rim. Then Goyens placed another kettle over it, rim down, and fitted a brass band down over the rims, which he had seated with lead gaskets. With his heavy clamp wrench he rolled and cinched the brass serrations down over the lower kettle rim, compressing the lead between them. Despite himself, Piedras looked on in admiration. "Remarkable," he said.

By the time Goyens was done, the soldiers had returned with Padre de Leon and the church relics. These, along with the remaining valuables in Piedras's pile, were placed into a second copper container and sealed. The priest stood by, resigned and beaten, his mouth working silently as he inventoried his precious charges and committed them again to memory.

When it was done, two copper barrels with brass belts sat on the colonel's map table. With an iron from the fire, Goyens soldered the rims.

Piedras nodded his satisfaction. "Now, should the

Anglo rabble take Texas, at least they will not profit by these. Captain, I want a full squad on guard around this building, immediately. I want a strong handcart brought here and set just outside the door. There must be a pick in it, and a spade. At sundown today I want a tight, armed curfew on the entire town. No one is to be on the streets. Absolutely no one, until morning. And tell Captain Musquiz to put patrols on all the roads at sundown, push outward one mile, and block the roads there until morning. Now, all of you, leave. Go about your business."

They left, and behind them they heard Piedras dropping bolts across his doors, barricading himself and the two copper barrels inside the stifling office.

"The man is crazy," Goyens told Medina.

The captain of infantry pursed his lips and shook his head.

"What do you suppose he plans to do with those things?"

"Who knows? Bury them somewhere tonight. No one but him will know where."

"He'll take them out and bury them, all alone?" Goyens couldn't quite picture the dapper colonel digging holes in the middle of the night.

"Of course," Medina said. "Do you think he would trust anyone else?"

It was the turn of Goyens to shake his head. "Things are beginning to fall apart, Captain. There's a bad time coming."

"Yes."

"There is nothing you can do? Or Musquiz?"

"You know there isn't, Will. As you say, things will now fall apart. And someone else will have to put them back together. I know the Anglos, my friend. Do you see any men out here on these streets? No, the men are out there somewhere, hiding their weapons, getting ready to revolt. The colonel has made his own predictions come true, I fear. Your Anglos will not tolerate the disarmament order. And for that matter, neither will my people. They know better."

Padre de Leon, standing with them, said nothing. He had a feeling he would not see his precious church properties again.

CHAPTER XXIII

*"War's different. When you shoot hell out of a
soldier it don't mean you mean
him any harm."*
—Ed Johnson

From a brushy ridge above a bend in the Camino
Real, Anton Moro and the renegade *presidario* Ruiz
watched a disarmed and disheartened file of mounted
soldiers come across the cache of arms left there minutes earlier by two Anglo riders. They watched as the
column halted, as a young lieutenant and a grizzled sergeant dismounted to inspect the pile of weapons, as the
weapons were distributed among the soldiers.

Ruiz's battered face was blank. "What are they doing,
señor?" he whispered.

"Shut up," Moro growled at him. "They play games,
these Anglos and these *soldados*. They play games like
children."

Long after the soldiers had gone on, toward Nacogdoches, Moro stared after them, brutal, slitted eyes
contemplative. The sight of the soldiers reminded him
of Colonel Piedras, and smoldering resentment arose in
him. Piedras had sent him to do a thing and he had
done it. Then Piedras had turned on him and cast him
out. He decided now he should have killed Piedras. He

could have then, certainly, but for all those soldiers camped around him. Piedras owed him. He decided Piedras owed him much more than he had been paid. He turned his mind to collecting.

Moro was sullen. Things had not gone as he wanted. After picking up Ruiz, he had headed back across the Sabine to where the greeners were camped. Silently, methodically, a wolf in timber, he had scouted several camps until he found one unguarded. With Ruiz behind him he had entered the camp and taken what he wanted—food, a few shabby valuables, and a young woman who wouldn't stop screaming until he knocked her senseless. He would have gone on from there, but the greeners came too soon. They found his trail and nearly caught him at the Sabine. Ruiz had been little help, though the *presidario* had alerted him before the mounted men came too close for them to escape.

The odds were wrong. Too much chance over there for too little gain. The odds were better on the Texas side, if he could just discover a good target.

Right now he was hungry again. He went to his mount, the fine racing horse he had taken from the man on the north road, and dug a large hand into the pouch on the saddle. It was empty. Ruiz had also gone to his horse, and Moro noticed he had a chunk of meat.

"Give that to me," he said.

Ruiz turned, wary. "But, *señor*, there is only a little."

Moro walked around his horse, then with a sudden, long step forward he backhanded the *presidario,* sending him sprawling. "Give it to me."

Ruiz had no gun, but as he came to his knees, eyes glinting with hatred and pain, his hand went to the knife at his belt. Moro crouched, arms spread at his sides. "You want to try me, eh, *soldado*? You want to try Anton Moro?"

Ruiz hesitated. Moro took a step toward him. "You pull the knife, tough *soldado*. Pull it now. Then I break your arms, and then I twist your head until your neck breaks. Pull it!"

Ruiz subsided. Lowering his gaze, he tossed the dried meat to Moro. He knew the big man could and would do exactly what he said. In his whole life, Ruiz had never met anyone like Anton Moro.

Moro ate the meat. It was not nearly enough. Casting around in his mind, he hit upon a plan to get more food. There was a house near Nacogdoches, but still away from the town, this way. It was a farm where a man kept milk cows, to sell milk in the town. It was an isolated place, off the road, not too far away.

Checking his rifle, Moro mounted the racing horse. Without a backward glance he put it down off the brushy ridge onto the road and swung westward. Behind him Ruiz wiped blood from his mouth, got to his feet, and climbed on his horse. He set off after Moro, a whipped dog following its master.

At the edge of Nacogdoches, on the old Indian water trail that entered the town from the northeast, Cooper Willoughby sat his borrowed horse and looked aghast at the scene in the distance before him.

"My God in Heaven," he declared as much to himself as to his three companions. "They're building breastworks."

They were at the edge of the cleared ground of the village, shaded in the fringe of woods that followed Brushy Creek almost to where it crossed the north road. From here they could see most of the town, and in the late afternoon sunlight the activity they witnessed seemed strangely out of place.

"They must have every soldier they've got out on the

streets," Alexander Horton commented. "Will you look at that! There are four foot patrols that I can see . . . no, there's another, over there."

"With their bayonets mounted," Samuel Bean added, his sharp young eyes missing nothing.

Tenuto, his dark face alive with excitement, said something in quick, sibilant Cherokee and Horton turned to Willoughby. "What did he say?"

"He said if there's going to be fighting he'd sure like to get in on it."

"On which side?"

"He didn't say, but I don't imagine it matters a whole lot. He'd just hate to miss a good fight."

"Looky there!" Samuel Bean pointed. The Quartel gate had opened and the Company of Monclova issued forth, spreading across the parade ground in precise military order, blue coats bright with trim of red and white, short muskets sheathed, lances and shields gleaming, tight-reined mounts high-stepping.

The cavalry assembled into a long line in the dappled evening sun, and an officer walked out to face and address them. Horton said, "Is that Musquiz?"

"It's him," Willoughby nodded.

As the four in the trees watched, the cavalry company was read off into five units, and each wheeled and set out, all in different directions. A squadron of ten cantered across the plaza and turned east on the Camino Real, passing an infantry group building barricades. Another unit went south, toward the Camino Sud trace, and another entered Camino Real and turned west. A smaller group galloped its mounts down a side street and disappeared into the forest on the old Indian road. The fifth patrol crossed the plaza, passed the houses of Thorn and Chireno, the lesser houses beyond them, swung past Goyens' Inn, and clattered across the bridge, heading north.

The four observers backed their mounts deeper into the shaded grove. The northbound patrol passed within fifty yards of them.

Except for the soldiers there were few people visible in the town. A man in work clothes appeared at the far corner of the plaza and a foot patrol turned his way and accosted him. Two soldiers paraded him across the plaza and along a side street to a small house, then watched as he went inside and closed the door. A patrol marched along the lane to Sim's Tavern and two remained at the door while the others entered. In a few moments several civilians, mostly Spanish but with a few Anglos among them, came out, milling about, prodded from behind by the soldiers. They were divided into groups and escorted off toward their various homes.

Horton looked off to the west. The sun was edging into the pines. "Curfew," he said. "They're cleanin' the streets."

At Goyens' Inn, close by, two men stepped off the porch and started toward the stables. Three soldiers intercepted them, motioning them back. One of the men, a tall, dark-faced Anglo in buckskins, carried a long rifle and one of the soldiers reached for it. In the next instant the soldier was flat on his back and the man was standing over him, still holding his rifle. The other two soldiers hesitated, muskets half-lowered.

"Smart boys," Horton mused. "That there is Bell. They best just leave him alone."

A sergeant shouted something from the intersection and then hurried forward. He spoke first to his soldiers, then to the two civilians, and there was considerable gesturing while the buckskinned man simply stood, rifle in hand, waiting. At last the sergeant conceded a point, bowed, and backed off. The second civilian turned and went back to the inn. Bell proceeded to the stables, two soldiers trailing behind him. A few moments later he reappeared, mounted now, and without a backward glance turned his horse north, crossed the bridge, and disappeared into the trees.

"Lettin' 'em leave," Horton commented, "but not lettin' 'em stay on the streets."

Evening shade was spreading across the village. From the Stone House a pair of soldiers walked to the cavalry barn, one of them carrying both muskets, and the other entered and came out pulling a light two-wheel cart with some tools in it. They crossed to the Red House and left the cart there, by the door. Willoughby noticed that Tenuto wasn't watching the scene. The Indian was turned away, his eyes alert, nostrils quivering. Willoughby followed his gaze and saw slight movement in the brush across the draw. A second later a horseman broke into the clear, jumped his mount down into the draw, and came up to join them. It was the buckskinned man they had seen in front of Goyens' Inn.

"Howdy, Sandy," he said. "Saw you fellers watchin' over here. Some show down there, ain't it?"

Horton grinned. "Howdy, Tecumseh. It is for a fact. What's goin' on?"

"Colonel's got the town on tight curfew tonight. I ain't heard why. You fellers goin' in?"

"Aim to."

"Then you better slip in careful an' find a place to light. Colonel don't allow anybody carryin' weapons these days."

"I notice you still got yours."

Bell made no response to this. It didn't deserve one. Cold gray eyes surveyed the other three, and he nodded slightly toward the Indian. " 'Siyo, Tenuto."

Tenuto's face was expressionless. "Osiyo, Tecumseh Bell."

Horton said, "That's Bean's boy, Samuel, and this

267

here's my deputy, Coop Willoughby."

Samuel howdied the man and Willoughby nodded. "I ain't anybody's deputy," he muttered. "I told you, I quit three days ago."

Horton ignored him. "You stayin' around, Tecumseh?"

"Not likely. I finished my business here. I just come by to tell Thorn and Sterne what happened at Velasco. Now I done it."

"Who was that fellow with you at the inn?"

Bell shrugged. "Name's Smith. Don't seem to have any good reason for bein' here and dressed too good for a greener, so I guess he's a spy."

Horton thought a moment. "Yeah, I guess so. Seems like he's the same one come in with Sam Looney a little bit back. Ain't he the same one we saw, Coop?"

"I reckon."

"Well, I hope he stays out of the colonel's way."

They sat their horses in silence for a minute or two, and then Bell said, "I mean it, Sandy. You fellers goin' in, you best slip around real quiet. Those soldiers got the itch. Come dark, they might be dangerous."

With that and a general nod, Bell turned his mount, crossed the draw, and was gone. Samuel Bean looked after him. "My pa talks about him. Now I know what he means. Man! Did you see those eyes?"

Tenuto said, "Tecumseh Bell *Sawamugidihi*."

"What did he say?"

"He says the Indians know Bell as He Who Kills Shawnee," Willoughby explained.

"Now." Horton turned back to look at the village, where long shadows were growing. "How do we get to Thorn's house?"

"That's no problem," Willoughby muttered. He turned is mount, jumped down into the draw, up the other side, and turned west in the deep pine shade,

Tenuto pacing him, the other two close behind.

With Willoughby and the Indian leading by turns, they made their way the short distance to the north road, edged north past the bend, looked both ways, and ghosted across. From there they headed west through pine forest, nearly a mile, then swung south to the Camino Real. They could see firelight where the cavalry patrol had blockaded the road. They went around them, crossed, and turned easterly again. At the edge of the clearing behind the Lopez house at the edge of town they dismounted, led their horses, and crept forward, using every scrap of cover in the deepening dusk. The slight sounds of their passage were eerie to Alexander Horton, because he could hear only two—himself and young Bean. He had to peer around repeatedly to reassure himself that Willoughby and the Indian were still with them.

At Frost Thorn's stable they unsaddled, rubbed down their horses, and put them into stalls, working in near-absolute darkness in the big shed. Once they froze, hands on horses' noses, as a patrol passed just outside.

At the back door of the house Horton rapped lightly and Jaren admitted them, his eyes big. "Y'all ain' supposed to be out there, suhs."

"We ain't," Horton said, laying his rifle on a cabinet and pulling off his hat. "We're in here."

Willoughby, not waiting on civility, had already gone through into the front of the house. When the others came up behind him, they had to go around. Cooper Willoughby stood in the lantern light, his mouth open, speechless. The room before him was full of people, but he saw only one.

She wore a soft white house dress with blue embroidery at the throat and waist. Her long midnight hair was rolled and piled upon her head, set in place with a silver comb. Great dark eyes sparkled in the lamplight

269

and a copper-pink flush spread across her full cheeks.

From his armchair beside the door, Haden Edwards laughed aloud. "You better do something about your friend, Sandy. Looks like rigor mortis has set in."

Udali, Mistletoe of the Tsalagi, took a tiny step toward her tired and scruffy intended, then smiled, curtsied, and struck a ladylike pose. With uncertain precision she said, "Good afternoon, Willow-bee. It is so nice of you to call."

"I'm not goin' to try that again." Cooper Willoughby shook his lowered head. "I may have thought I was man enough to bring in Anton Moro, but I'm not. I never had a chance. I'm damn lucky to be alive right now." He took another long sip of his brandy, settled lower in the armchair, crossed the legs thrust out before him, and looked around defiantly.

"I agree," Frost Thorn nodded. "We can't ask him to either. It's too much." He looked pointedly across the study at Alexander Horton, who raised a hand.

"Don't look at me, Mr. Thorn. I never asked him to go lookin' for Moro in the first place. It was his own idea."

They had finished a good, hot meal, and the men were enjoying the plush furniture of Frost Thorn's study. Atasi, Tenuto, and young Bean were prowling through the house somewhere, Atasi giving Tenuto a guided tour of how the white men lived, Bean tagging along trying to explain the impropriety of exploring other people's houses, and Jaren following nervously behind to pick up anything the Indians might drop.

With nightfall, heavy clouds had banked in from the south, and now a hard, determined rain was falling outside. Susan Thorn and Mistletoe were in the front living room, watching the rain through an unlighted window

270

and discussing mysterious things in improving English.

In the study, Haden Edwards stood at a draped window, parting the blinds and peering out. Occasional lightning flashes silhouetted him, and he chuckled now and then. At one point he burst into uncontrolled laughter.

Thorn looked around. "What's so funny, Papa?"

Edwards laughed again. "It's raining like hell."

"So?"

"So every damn soldier in town is out on the prowl tonight, and I'll wager there isn't a dry inch on a one of them."

It was infectious. The others grinned, except for Willoughby, who was deep in somber thought.

"Nice night for a curfew," Horton agreed. "I reckon we'll have to impose on your hospitality tonight, Mr. Thorn."

Thorn waved it off. "Of course, you'll stay the night. We've plenty of room."

"First thing in the morning, I've got to find *Señor* Chireno and Vicente Cordova, let them know the Ayish folks have decided for Santa Anna. Then I'll take my deputy and we'll get on back to Ayish. Lot to do the next few days. It looks to me like Piedras isn't going to let well enough alone."

"You ain't got a deputy, damn it," Willoughby muttered.

"I'm going to talk to Piedras in the morning," Thorn said. "The man may be crazy, but he has to see reason before he destroys this town."

"Wish you lots of luck," Horton said dryly.

At the window, Edwards was laughing again. "I just remembered what Will Goyens said." He coughed, almost choking. "Right this minute, Piedras is out there in the woods someplace, all by himself, trying to bury those damn barrels." His laughter welled up again, and

271

he leaned against the window frame.

Horton thought about it, then his shoulders shook and he burst out laughing, setting Edwards off even more. Thorn chuckled, and the chuckle grew. Willoughby, brought out of his morose thoughts, grinned. "I wonder if those things float."

That brought on increased merriment. "Can you picture it," Horton sputtered, "him trying to push them things down in a hole full of water so he can cover 'em up, and they keep bobbing back up again?"

"If he went uphill," Edwards allowed, "those barrels may get back to town before he does." The ensuing howls brought the women in from the front room. Jaren came hurrying to see if he was needed, and Samuel Bean and his Indians peered curiously from the head of the stairway.

"Jaren, bring us more brandy, please." Thorn looked around and saw Susan and Mistletoe. He stood, and the other men stood as well. "And bring some for the ladies, Jaren. Ladies, won't you join us?"

"Why, I thank you, sir," Susan drawled. "We'd be delighted."

Through the course of the evening, Willoughby had recovered from his astonishment at the change in Udali, but not from the enchantment of her. As they were seated, he couldn't tear his eyes from her. And when she smiled, a smile just for him, his knees felt weak. Edging close to him, the sheriff of Ayish Bayou muttered, "I don't blame you a bit, Coop. She really is something."

Straight and decorous in a high-backed chair, Mistletoe clasped her hands on her knees, pursed her lips in thought for a moment, then burst into a radiant smile. "My," she said. "Isn't it a beautiful evening." Susan Thorn nodded approval, Thorn and Edwards bowed cordially and smiled. Horton, who was facing the other

272

way, grinned broadly, and Willoughby sat down quickly to keep from falling. Except for the voice, a bit softer and huskier, she sounded for all the world like Susan Thorn.

Edwards went to the window, parted the blinds, peered out for a moment, and then turned. "Something's up, Frost. A foot patrol just hotfooted past here, coming from the back. They spread out when they got to the street. Looks like they're looking for someone."

Curiously, Thorn, Horton, and Willoughby went into the front room, to look through the unlighted window there. There was activity outside, several soldiers in ponchos hurrying back and forth, peering into the gloom, one holding a steaming, shaded lantern. As they watched, the soldiers dispersed in two directions and disappeared into the rain.

"Well," Horton allowed, "whoever it was, they lost him."

As they turned to go back to the study they heard, plain through the house, a knock at the back door. At a signal from Thorn, Jaren went to answer it and they followed him, Horton picking up his rifle.

Lightning flared as Jaren opened the door, and the black gasped and recoiled. There in the doorway, framed by sheet lightning, stood a huge, half-naked man, water sheeting down his bare shoulders and dripping from the two slanted eagle feathers in his hair.

The spectacle froze them all for an instant, then Horton's rifle came up. Thorn shoved the barrel aside and peered more closely. "By God," he exclaimed. "It's Egg." He tried to say something in Cherokee but the big warrior ignored him. In the gloom his eyes sought out Willoughby. Thunder rolled behind him as he raised a wet hand to point at the smuggler.

"'*Siyo,* Willoughby. I come from Diwali. Diwali says

you must hurry, to keep the promise you made to Gu'nasoquo. Diwali says the warriors will not wait much longer. Diwali says it is better for all of us if you bring us the killer of Utsada than if Gu'nasoquo and his warriors go searching for him. Diwali says for you to hurry." The speech was delivered without inflection; then Egg paused, lowered his arm, and grinned hugely, his teeth flashing wickedly in the light of Jaren's new-lit candle.

"I bring you something you have lost, Willoughby, to help you on your way." He brought a long rifle around from behind his back and thrust it out to Willoughby. "Try not to lose it again."

Willoughby took the rifle. It was his own. Egg turned, ducking through the open door, and was gone in the darkness and the rain. Jaren had handed his candle to Thorn, and was lighting a lantern. They crowded out into the wet patio and looked around. There was no sign of Egg, but in the patio stood Cooper Willoughby's horse, the one he had lost to the Kickapoos. Saddle, trappings, tools, and travel gear were all there, and the pouch was filled with jerked meat.

None of them had yet spoken. Now Horton said, "What did he say?"

Willoughby bowed his head, resignation drawing his shoulders down. "He said I got it to do, Sandy."

CHAPTER XXIV

"Sixty-six bold men went out.
Sixty-six came back.
Some were riding, some were walking,
Some were in a sack."
—From a Texas folk song

The morning of Tuesday, July 24, dawned clear and fresh-washed over Nacogdoches, and people of the town watched from dark windows as the night's tight curfew was lifted. One by one, the cavalry patrols came in, animals were stripped and led into corrals, men dispersed to the Quartel or the Stone House. When the last unit was in, the foot patrols were called off and the wet, tired soldiers of the 12th and their *presidario* companions slogged off to find a few hours' sleep, some at the Quartel, most at the old church.

There were long moments of silence, and then here and there citizens unbolted their doors and stepped outside to look around. John Sanford Smith stepped from the porch of Goyens' Inn, stretched, took a deep breath of morning air, and surveyed the town from where he stood. For the moment, there was not a soldier in sight.

Over by the Red House a two-wheel cart lay overturned by the *signatorio,* a spade and pick lying on the wet ground beside it. As he watched, two riders came

275

around a house down the street—the largest one—paused at the street to look around, then cantered their horses straight across the plaza and spurred to a gallop, eastbound on the Camino Real. He had seen them both before. One was the sheriff from Ayish Bayou. The second was the slender man who had been with him that interesting day over in the Neutral Strip. Both carried long rifles, and their saddles were tied and hung with traveling gear. A moment later two more riders appeared at the same place, turned north, and trotted their horses toward him. They were Indians, and as they came closer he saw they were young braves, probably Cherokee. As they passed, both of them glanced at him curiously, then went on, across the bridge and out the north road.

Smith strolled across to the stables, looked to his horse, then came out again. More people had shown up on the streets, hesitantly at first, then becoming a traffic that looked almost normal for the busy little town. Within minutes of each other, mail couriers rode in from the east and west on the Camino Real and deposited their packets at the Red House. Smith noticed that both of them then went into Sim's Tavern. Smith had not yet had his breakfast, and decided that Sim's would be a good place to try. Tired couriers from different points might be talkative, and a man can eat and listen at the same time.

At the east edge of town Horton and Willoughby stopped to look over the barricades being assembled there. It looked as though Piedras were building to withstand a cavalry charge . . . or a siege. Heavy, movable barricades of notched, tied logs were partially complete. When finished, these could be used either to close the road or to provide breastworks for line fire by

276

muskets. Horton shook his head and spat. No militia commander, he thought, would attack head-on at such an obvious obstacle. Much easier just to go around, or attack in concert from another point.

"He's fixin' to defend Nacogdoches. The whole town. Ain't no way that can be done. He's crazy as a loon."

They rode on, eastward on the Camino Real. At the road to Hugh Baker's farmstead they parted company, Horton to return to Ayish with reports to the militia assembling there, Willoughby to begin a methodical, zigzag search of the scattered homesites eastward from Nacogdoches, for sign or trail of the renegade, Anton Moro. Moro had been seen in the area two days before, and word of it had reached Chireno, who passed it along to Thorn. Whereas the big outlaw had been hiding before, now he seemed to disdain the back trails. He had been right out in the open, another man with him.

"It's as though he knows he's safe to come and go as he pleases," Thorn had said. "And he may have reason to feel so. He knows the army isn't going to bother him, and he knows the settlers have their hands full right now, and it is pretty certain he doesn't know anyone is looking for him."

"You'd think it would stand no reason he would know he's wanted," Horton said.

"No, not really. Moro is a bushwise and crafty man, but he has the mental processes of a brute. What's out of sight is out of mind."

Now at the Baker road Horton cautioned his erstwhile deputy, "Don't try to take him, Coop. If you can get a line on him, just hold the trail and get the word out . . . to me or Ben Lindsay if you're east, to Cordova or Chireno or some of them if you're over here by Nacogdoches, to Sam Looney or some of his boys if you're west. You'll have plenty of help if you ask for it."

"Yeah, I know, Sandy. I got a funny feeling, though."

"What's that?"

"I got a feeling Moro's around close here somewhere, and it won't take long to get a lead on him."

"Well, just don't pull some dumb stunt like last time then."

"You think I'm stupid?" Willoughby frowned. "Hell, I'm gonna have all the help I can get."

They shook hands . . . a gesture that surprised Willoughby, coming as it did from the dour young sheriff . . . and parted there. Willoughby turned south, riding the half-mile toward Baker's place, his plan firmly in mind. He would inquire at Baker's, then east to the dairy farm of Luis Ramos, then to the old Hernandez place where the Pritchards lived now with their great flock of children, then . . .

He found Hugh Baker in his field, plowing a gully through red mud to drain ponded water from a swaled corn patch. The man was muddy from the shoulders down, cursing at every other step and generally having a fine time this bright morning. One of his young sons plodded along behind him, carrying the rifle and learning some new words.

No, Baker had seen nothing of Anton Moro or anybody else, for that matter, but if Willoughby would like to light down and put in a day's work behind this gawdforsaken plow, Baker would pay him a dollar for it.

It was more than a mile from Baker's to Luis Ramos's isolated clearings, where Ramos kept a small herd of milk cows, and from which he and his son drove three times a week to sell milk and butter in Nacogdoches. The narrow wagon trail wound through tall timber. Willoughby had gone less than half the distance

278

and was rounding a shouldered curve when he heard a rustling in the brush behind and above him. Before he could turn his head a voice said in Spanish, "Stop there, *señor*. Do not move."

He had stopped. The voice was that of a child. Slowly, his hands plainly visible, he turned in the saddle. Crouched on the redrock shoulder behind him was Felipe Ramos, wide-eyed, smudged, and trembling as he fought to keep an ancient flintlock fowler on him. As Willoughby turned, the boy's shoulders sagged and he lowered the heavy old gun. *"Señor* Willoughby! *Perdoneme,* but I did not know you."

The boy looked exhausted. His eyes were bright with tears and long terror, there was a livid bruise on his cheek, and he stumbled and. nearly fell as he tried to stand up. Willoughby swung down from his horse, dropped the reins, and ran to catch the boy before he tumbled over the ledge onto the road.

Carefully, he helped him down and sat him on a grassy hummock at roadside, then brought his horse and got his canteen from the saddle, and some clean cloth.

Felipe Ramos was barely eight years old, and he had been having a bad time. Willoughby gave him water, cleaned his face carefully, and checked him for other injuries. His narrow back was heavily bruised and clotted with blood. He had been beaten or kicked, or both. As Willoughby worked over him, the small boy quivered again and again with uncontrollable sobs. Between them, he talked, his voice barely on the same side of hysteria.

"The men . . . bad men . . . they came to our house in the night . . . they killed a cow . . . they beat my father . . ." He gave way to sobbing, and Willoughby let him cry it out, not pressing. He pressed him close to his breast and felt the boy flinch as his fingers touched

279

the abrasions on his little back. A great, fire-red anger welled up in Willoughby. He clenched his teeth and found he was trembling almost as violently as the boy.

"Where is your father, Felipe?"

"My . . . he is in the house, *señor.* They hurt him . . . he cried and asked them to stop . . . they hurt him . . ." Again the collapse. The anger in Willoughby roared in his ears. Rage. Outrage . . . and something else. His vision blurred, and he felt moisture on his own cheeks. He put his arms around the child again and let him cry on his shoulder. The only sounds for several minutes were the little boy's sobs and, beyond them, birdcalls, the sounds of small things here and there, and the sigh of morning wind in the pines.

When Willoughby finally released him, he noticed that the boy still had a grip on the rusty old fowling piece, small fingers clenched and blue on the worn stock. He pried them loose and set the old gun down.

"They stayed all night in our house, *señor,*" Felipe told him when the sobbing had receded. "This morning, when they slept, I got away. I tried to get my father out, but I could not lift him. I took the gun and ran, and I watched from the bushes as they left. I tried to shoot them, *señor,* but the gun, it would not shoot, and they saw me, so I had to run again."

"Where are they now, Felipe?"

The boy shrugged. "Gone. I do not know."

Willoughby stood up. Hard, cold anger had replaced the burning rage, and he had things to do.

"Can you walk, Felipe?"

"*Si, señor,* I think so."

"All right. Do you know where *Señor* Baker's house is? Good. You go there, as fast as you can, and tell *Señor* Baker what happened. Tell him to come to your house, and send his boy for others to help. I'll go see what I can do for your father. Now go. Hurry!"

The boy blinked at him, nodded, and set off along the wagon road, moving at a limping run. So little, Willoughby thought. So goddamned little.

He grabbed his reins, swung aboard, and put heels to his horse.

Ramos's cabin was a modest, weathered *jacale* at the edge of a cleared pasture. The door hung open and there was a dead cow in the milking pen. Skidding his mount to a halt, Willoughby ran to the open door. Inside was a shambles. Luis Ramos lay against the back wall, and Willoughby knelt over him. The dairyman had been beaten badly, viciously. Willoughby could not begin to guess the extent of his injuries, but the gurgling sound of his faint breathing and the bright blood seeping from his lips and his nose were bad signs. He did what he could to ease him, tried to get a little water down his throat and gave up, got a fire started in the hearth, and then sat down beside Ramos and waited. When they came—Baker, his oldest boy, two Mexican men from the place adjoining Baker's, and a woman carrying clean cloth and a medicine bag—Willoughby was grateful that they had not let Felipe return with them. Luis Ramos was dead.

He left them there to do what must be done. He cast around the fresh-wet clearing for sign, and when he found it he mounted up and set out, south by west, along a game trail. He was half a mile away before he remembered Alexander Horton's word of caution. He had not remembered to send for help. Or maybe, he thought as the cold anger took him again and he recalled the bruised face of a frightened little child with a malfunctioning old gun, maybe he didn't want help. Maybe he just had it to do. Eyes on the fresh trail before him, he moved on.

In thin, damp sand at the bottom of a gully he read the situation: two horses, with riders. One mount was a racing horse, the other a short-coupled horse with a split shoe on the left forefoot.

They were in no hurry, just traveling. Further along, he found where they had stopped briefly beside a stream. He judged he was an hour behind them, maybe less. He picked up the pace.

Miles crept by, and he pressed on, his eyes finding and his mind cataloguing the faint signs, the occasional prints, broken limbs, brushed-aside grass, tiny mars on tree bark, that were all a tracker needed and all he would have in this rocky, rolling, forested land.

Mid-morning came and went, and the sign told him he was gaining. He found fresh droppings, the flies just now locating them. At a sandy bend there were hoofprints with the edges still clear and moist.

And then the sign was gone. For a hundred yards he found nothing, then another hundred. Nothing. After a quarter of a mile he reined in, looked around him, spat, and cursed. The game trail still wound before him, but his quarry was not on it. Somewhere back where they had turned off, and he had let his mind wander and missed it.

"We lost 'em, sport," he told the horse. "One of us done messed up, and it wasn't you."

When he loosed the reins the horse stood head-down, and he noticed the sag in its shoulders. He himself felt sore and stiff, top to bottom, from long hours of intense concentration. He swung stiffly down from the horse, stamped his feet and swung his arms to loosen his muscles, then patted the horse's neck and scratched behind its ears. He hadn't noticed the passage of time, but shadows across the trail where it widened in a hillside clearing told him it was mid-afternoon. He noticed too that his stomach was growling and his throat was dust-dry from thirst.

"Sorry, sport," he told the horse. "Some folks can't

think on more than one thing at a time, and I'm one. Let's rest us for awhile."

He led the animal back the way they had come to where they had crossed a little stream, and there he stripped off its saddle, rubbed it down with the corner of his blanket, and put a soft hobble on its feet.

He sat down, leaned back against a tree, put his hands behind his head, and gazed upward through laced pine needles at the blue Texas sky. "Utsada, you damned old *unegadihi,* what would you do now if you was me?" He sat for a while listening to the breeze play in the pines. "Yeah, I know, You'd take it a step at a time and just do whatever comes handy."

He drank a little water, ate a little jerky and hard bread, and slept for an hour while his horse grazed. When the sun was low beyond the forest and blue shadows lay on the land, he saddles, mounted, and started back the way he had come, searching for the missed trail. Scouting, swinging out left and right, he finally found it. They had turned right, turned westward across the Camino Sud, and their trail bore west beyond it.

On into the evening he followed, again reading the signs with care. They had passed this way some hours back, but still they seemed in no hurry.

The Ramos house had been stripped of food. They had provisions, probably would stay in the woods until they ran low. With last light he found the trail edging northward from west, and at the last clear sign he stopped for the night. With morning, he could make up some lost time.

He might have found them by now had he not lost the trail back there, but he accepted the deal with a woodsman's patience. He would find them. That awesome, cold anger he had felt when a hidden brute shot and killed his friend, the anger that there would be no more laughter from the prankish *unegadihi,* had come back tenfold when he held and comforted a small, hurt, brave, and terrified child. Outrage had thrown open all his private doors and anger had flooded it. It was part of him now, and he welcomed it. He would use it when he found Anton Moro. It would be the ally he needed.

As he stood in the gathering dusk, on a wooded hilltop southwest of Nacogdoches, he listened to the first night sounds and the background keening of wind in the pines. The world was going crazy, he decided. Off there to the north somewhere they were fortifying a sleepy little town, and most of the men of the town were slipping around caching arms and ammunition. Some of the women were planning evacuation and others, he had heard, were planning a fiesta. Crazy. Up north there were red people, good decent people, cleaning their war clubs and cooking their supper and bathing their children. And some of them were trying very hard to stay out of the white men's troubles, while others were itching to get into them. Crazy. Over to the east the militias were assembling, and he supposed they were doing the same thing to the west.

And a way off down south, so far away that it shouldn't really matter, a smooth, treacherous little general and a brutal royalist president were having at it to see which one could take supreme command of something neither one had the vaguest idea what to do with—Mexico. And in a crazy way, that was the root of all the other craziness going on.

If the people who have Texas could just get together, work together, he thought, they could keep Texas. But they aren't going to do that. They just have to fight among themselves, while over there on that east border a storm is building up. Those greeners are land-starved and they're piling up by the thousands. Give them a chance and they'll sweep this land like a howling east wind.

The keening in the pines was louder now. The wind was coming up. It was the time of summer storms in Texas and the east wind was rising.

CHAPTER XXV

"The only way the Spanish kept folks out of Texas as long as they did was by hidin' it from 'em."
—Samuel Looney

In his sleeping quarters in the north end of the Red House, Colonel Jose de las Piedras stood in his nightshirt and watched through his open window as the two armed Anglos, Horton and Willoughby, rode brazenly across the plaza, turned on the Camino Real, and disappeared beyond the buildings there. Slow anger mounted in his breast. He was quite aware that no citizens had so far complied with his explicit order regarding firearms. He was not surprised. It proved again that he was surrounded here by traitors and sympathizers. As commander of this town he had ordered all arms turned in. No arms had been turned in. It was direct and willful disobedience.

But he had expected more subtlety. Yet here, right in the middle of his command, Anglos paraded around carrying their guns in plain sight. Nor had his officers done anything about it. True, he had not yet ordered search and seizure, but his officers were aware of his orders to the citizenry. They should have exercised the initiative to see his orders carried out.

It was too quiet out there. Where were his soldiers? Where was the military presence to keep these renegades in line? Pulling on his boots, he strode to the door to his office, through it, and to the orderly room, where his hard hand on the bolt aroused a startled and sleepy-eyed corporal. The soldier came groggily to his feet, his hand fluttering as he tried to recall the etiquette of saluting a superior in nightclothes.

"What is going on here?" Piedras shouted. "Where are the foot patrols? Is this a holiday?"

"But, *mi colonel*," the soldier stammered, "the whole garrison was awake all night sir. I think they have gone to sleep."

"Sleep!" Piedras raged. "Corporal, I want this garrison aroused immediately. I want my horse brought around, and an escort standing ready in one half hour. I will be on inspection then for an hour, and when I return I want Captain Medina here in my office!" He slammed the door.

As he dressed himself he heard, through the open window, the commotion of his garrison being brought to life. When his orderly brought him tea and biscuits a few minutes later he was dressed and polished, his shoulders squared and his epaulets glittering. It angered him that he must always set an example for his entire garrison, but if he must, then so be it. He heard the bugle from the Quartel, the babble of soldiery turned out at the old church barracks, and the jangle of harness as his horse and his escort appeared in the common outside his door. He heard couriers arrive and deposit their packets. He sat straight in his chair, chewed slowly on his breakfast, and sipped his tea. When he was good and ready, he marched through the orderly room and out onto the common. He scowled at the appearance of his escort. Proud cavalry! The great Company of Monclova! The lieutenant and four cavalrymen looked half asleep, slouched beside their horses. Some of them had dried mud on their breeches and boots. One had forgotten his shako.

In exasperation he screamed at them, "Idiots! Dolts!

287

Are you what the Mexican Army has come to? Straighten yourselves! Lieutenant, when I dismiss you, you will put these four men on first report . . . and yourself as well."

There were civilians here and there on the streets, and he could feel them watching him. With a curse he strode to his horse, his orderly hurrying ahead to hold the stirrup for him. His horse tried to pitch, and he gritted his teeth, clamped his legs, and hauled on the reins, the wide shovel-bit spreading the animal's jaws until it squealed in agony. The lieutenant and his men turned away, then mounted their own horses. Piedras hauled his steed around viciously, and set off at a canter.

He inspected the barricades at the east edge of town, and cursed the soldiers working there, tongue-lashing them into a frenzy of labor. From there he rode to the north bridge. There were guards there, but he knew from their sleepy, disheveled appearance they had arrived only moments before him. In tight-lipped fury he ignored their salutes and reined south, then west, to inspect the western perimeter of the town, to ride hard for a bit in response to his fury.

The commotion he had triggered ran through the town, and curious citizenry came out to watch, uncertain what was going on now. The tight curfew of the night before had left them all uneasy.

Frost Thorn, standing on his front stoop to watch the show, shook his head slowly. It was an embarrassing, unnerving spectacle. When the Commandant of Nacogdoches and his escort had gone, Thorn walked down to his gate, through it, and met Encarnacion Chireno there. The *Alcalde* was shaken and tight-lipped. They stood for a while not speaking as the bedlam continued around them.

"Can you believe it?" Chireno asked finally. "Frost, I

don't know any more what is happening here. Mandates. Barricades on the roads. Church property confiscated. People not allowed to leave their own houses. And then . . . then . . . this! This sorry spectacle! Frost, the man is a lunatic. He has completely lost his mind."

"Yes." Thorn nodded. "I am afraid you are right."

"I have tried to talk with him. I got nowhere. Vicente Cordova has been to him. Even Colonel Bean has tried. But it doesn't get better. It gets worse by the hour."

Thorn was contemplative. "The colonel learned Sunday, as we did, that the Ayish Bayou district has refused his authority. He also knows they have decided to support Santa Anna and the Plan of Vera Cruz. He is reacting."

"He behaves as though the world is crumbling around him." Chireno spread his arms. "Look around you. Do you see anything crumbling here? The sun is in the sky. The people are prosperous. What is crumbling?"

"Piedras is crumbling, my friend. He himself is his own chaos. He is defending himself against attack."

"No one has attacked him. No one ever wanted to."

"No. But they will now. He has pushed it too far." He shook his head. "I will talk to him again today, Nacio. If he doesn't break his neck, and returns from whatever he is doing, I will go see him again. It will do no good, but I will try."

As they watched, two light wagons and a cart rolled past. Women and children walked beside them. The men driving averted their eyes and the little procession passed on.

Frost glanced at Chireno, then looked away quickly. There were tears in the *Alcalde*'s eyes.

"I know what is crumbling, Frost. My town. I saw some leaving Sunday after Mass, and I pretended it was nothing. I saw more leaving yesterday. Now I cannot pretend any more."

They watched the procession turn west on Camino Real. When it was some distance away, two more families joined it.

"It would be best if all of us pack today, Nacio," Thorn said as gently as he could. "Vincente Cordova has prepared a place on Carrizo Creek, and there is the old Bean place where our women and children can wait."

"When I get back to Tenoxtitlan," Pepe Vargas said decisively, "I am going to volunteer for courier duty one more time, but this time to go west. I don't want to come back here, and I don't want to stay there either. And anyway, we'll all be going west soon. Everybody is pulling out." Vargas sat sprawled on a bench in Sim's Tavern, one tired shoulder propped against the wall, his legs spread wide below the table. It had been a long, wet ride from Tenoxtitlan.

"What do you mean, 'everybody'?" Chico Reyes's ride had not been so hard. He had come only from Gaines' Crossing. The two couriers had arrived almost simultaneously, from opposite directions, had dumped their packets at the Red House, and had come here to hide and rest a bit before reporting back for responses.

Vargas cast wary eyes about the room. The only other person present was a well-dressed Anglo sitting apart from them, his back to them, waiting for his breakfast. With a furtive wink and raised finger to his lips, Vargas shook his head at Reyes. Then raising his voice slightly he said, "They are all out shooting Americans. Everybody is ordered to kill every damned Anglo greener they see, on sight." He watched the Anglo's back closely. There was no sign of reaction. He turned back to the startled Reyes. "It's all right, I just wondered if that one understands Spanish. What I mean is what I said. Everyone is leaving. The entire garrison from Anahuac set sail a week ago fro Tampico. Colonel Suverano took them. And Colonel Ugartechea's command is gone from Velasco. The settlers drove them out. They have sailed for Matamoros."

He sipped at his wine. "Not only that, *amigo*," he added, "but there are no soldiers left at Gonzales either, and I hear the troop at Goliad has pulled out for Bexar, to leave from there for Mexico to support General Santa Anna. All of them are going to help Santa Anna. You know, Chico . . ." He glanced around again and leaned closer. "The only commands left in East Texas — right now, this minute — are at Tenoxtitlan and here in Nacogdoches. And I bet you we leave Tenoxtitlan pretty soon."

Reyes cocked his head skeptically. "If everybody leaves, who is going to defend Texas?"

Vargas chuckled. "Ah, *amigo,* who cares about Texas? Let the Yanquis have it. Let the Comanche have it. Let the Cherokee have it. It isn't any good anyway. I say, let them all have it, and let us go home to Mexico. It is better there. Besides, that's where the war is being fought."

Reyes glanced down at his own 12th Battalion insignia. "What do you think then? You think we here will go home too?"

Vargas leaned back and sighed, knowingly. "*Si, amigo,* I think you will go home soon too. One way or another." He stopped talking when a man came in from the back, carrying plates of food.

At his own table John Sanford Smith smiled pleasantly at the waiter and accepted his breakfast. When the waiter had turned away he smiled again, at no one in particular.

Feliciana Menchaca wept as she wrapped and packaged her few precious possessions, and set them by the door for Antonio and his helper to carry out. Her two oldest daughters, Maria Concepcion and Maria Rafaela, ages five and four, sat wide-eyed and quiet on a bench, watching her. Little Maria Carmen was asleep in her blanket between them, while Maria Concepcion held the baby, Maria Juana, rocking her gently to keep her from crying.

Feliciana had steeled herself against this moment, had in fact helped plan for it along with Susan Thorn, Jane Norris, Candida Chireno, and several others. But now that it was here she found she was not ready for it, and no matter how she tried to hold them back, the tears kept coming.

Concepcion, her dark eyes wide and concerned, said, "Mama . . ."

Feliciana brushed again at her eyes and smiled. "Hush, little bird. It's all right. Everything will be all right."

She finished a wrap and looked around her. Nothing heavy could go. The furniture must remain, and most of the implements. Antonio had only a small cart, and only his poor old horse to pull it. She must allow for the children to ride.

Concepcion tried again. "Mama, why is Papa not going with us?"

Feliciana tried to hold back a new flow of tears, but they came anyway and she brushed angrily at her eyes. "Your papa must stay here, little bird. It is his duty. We will see him later, in just a short time."

She prayed it was true. Antonio Menchaca was no soldier. He could never have been a soldier. He was brave, yes, and loyal and determined, but he was a tailor, not a fighter. His proper tools were the needle,

292

thimble, and chalk, not the gun.

She turned to the wardrobe where her special clothes hung, and looked in at them. Beautiful, fine clothes, and each garment pieced together for her by her own husband, often working all night on a dress, because of his love for her. She closed the door and locked it. Holy Mother, what would she do if anything happened to her special clothes? Yet she could not take them. It would be too much.

Antonio came in, his face pale and worried, to get the last armload of packages. He glanced at the girls, then at her. "Are you ready, Feliciana? I hear them coming."

"*Si*, Antonio, I am ready." She crossed to the bench and picked up the sleeping Maria Carmen, folding the soft, tiny body to her. Somehow the tears had stopped, and she could look at her family with dry eyes. She spoke quietly now. Maria Carmen was just teething, and she didn't want to wake her up. "Come, girls. It is time to go. Concepcion, keep the baby well covered and don't jostle her. Rafaela, you can bring the food sack."

Outside the cart was loaded and the horse hitched, short reins attached so that she could walk and lead him. Antonio stowed the last few parcels, making a safe, soft nest for the babies, and climbed up to place them there. Then he helped the older girls aboard, then climbed down to look long into his young wife's red-rimmed eyes.

"You have been crying."

"No, it is just a touch of rash. I am just fine."

He put his arms around her and held her close, while she clung to him. Then he backed away and led her around to where she could take the horse's lead. Coming toward them was a caravan of wagons, carts, cabs, and barrows. Children and the old and infirm rode where they could. Women drove, led, or walked alongside. Only five men were with the cortege, three in front and two behind, all mounted and all well-armed. As they passed a platoon of soldiers the men stared at them, hard-faced, making it clear they must not interfere. The soldiers stared back, some curious, most indifferent, and went on their way.

As the caravan came to them Antonio helped Feliciana get the horse started and steered into the line. Then he backed away. He stood in the street for a long time, watching them go.

Colonel Piedras's temper had abated somewhat when he returned from his inspections. He could think more clearly now. He strode into his office, closed the door, and went to work with paper and pen. There was a courier standing by from Tenoxtitlan. He could take a communique, to be forwarded from there to the command garrisoned at the Mission San Antonio de Bexar.

Pausing only briefly to order his words, he wrote rapidly. The treacherous Anglo immigrants infesting Nacogdoches—and their traitorous Mexican accomplices—were on the verge of declaring for the rebel Santa Anna. He must have reinforcements and more supplies, as quickly as they could be dispatched. He was surrounded here by traitors, and could not even trust his own officers. He had received word that the Anglo settlers along the border, around Ayish Bayou, already had declared their treason, exempted themselves from military rule, and adopted the Plan of Vera Cruz. He was expecting attack from that quarter in a matter of days.

He folded and sealed the message and called for his orderly.

"This must go in the packet to Tenoxtitlan, for Bexar. Find the courier and set him on his way without delay.

Tell him he is ordered to make all possible speed."

"Yes, *mi colonel.*" The man saluted. Then, *"Señor* Frost Thorn waits to see you, *mi colonel.*"

Piedras drew his breath for an angry response, then sighed and shrugged. He hated Frost Thorn. He envied and despised him. But Thorn had great influence in Mexico, and represented great wealth. He shrugged. "Very well, send him in."

Thorn was angry, and went straight to the point. "What are you trying to do to this town, Colonel? Are you trying to destroy Nacogdoches?"

Piedras tensed, his face reddening. But he controlled it and his expression was evasive. "I don't know what you mean, *Don* Frost. I have done nothing to the town."

"Let's not play games, Colonel. Your military high-handedness, these ridiculous orders, these curfews and drills, have you seen what you are doing? People are leaving here, Colonel. They are sending their women and children to safety. The town is collapsing. You have frightened your own people away."

"Frightened? I? Why should any here fear me, *Don* Frost? Am I not their protector? I am not the one they should fear. I am here to defend them."

"Defend them against what? Why are you fortifying Nacogdoches? Why are you frightening everyone so?" Thorn clasped his hands behind him and stood, looking down at the dapper little colonel behind the desk. God, he thought, if only Teran had lived.

Piedras sat forward, his hands forming a pyramid above his desk, a mask of patient reason on his features. "Possibly you have not heard, *Don* Frost. I have learned that the settlers in the Ayish district have declared for the traitor, Santa Anna." He smiled thinly and spread his hands. That should explain all.

Thorn just looked at him, unmoved. "So?"

295

"So now they will attack me!" Piedras reddened again. "I am their enemy. They fear me, and they will attack. I must defend my command!"

"That makes no sense," Thorn stated flatly. "If they attack you . . . and they might, now that you have provoked them enough . . . it is entirely because of what you have done. Nothing more."

"No!" Piedras came to his feet, fists on the desk. "It is Mexico they will attack! They and the traitors right around me here in my own headquarters . . . traitors everywhere in Nacogdoches . . . They want to drive Mexico from Texas. But I, Jose de las Piedras, will not submit. I will stand before them. They will not take my command!"

Thorn pursed his lips and looked down at the floor, letting the fury and the futility of it wash over him. Piedras was trembling, staring, defying any answer.

"Jose," Thorn said, pleading, "back off. Call in your patrols. Rescind your orders on curfews and meetings. Lift the order on confiscation of people's private guns. Do it now, and maybe we can work all this out."

Piedras stared at him, pure, malignant hostility plain in his eyes. "No," he rasped, his voice hoarse with emotion. "That I will never do!" Stiffly, the officer turned his head, tearing his eyes from the Anglo before him. Then he turned half around, squared his shoulders, and stood for a long moment, staring at the flag of Mexico on his wall.

"*Señor* Thorn, I would arrest you if I could. Right this moment, I would have you taken away and thrown into prison. Because I think you are in league with the traitors to Mexico. But I cannot prove that. Not just yet." Silence for a moment more, then he turned again, sat himself in his chair, and looked up, his face calm and judicial. "*Señor,* I have of record that you took an oath never to take up arms against the flag of Mexico.

Is that correct?"

"Of course it is correct."

"And your friend, Adolphus Sterne. Did he not also take such an oath, after he was imprisoned for treason? After he helped your father-in-law and his brother try to overthrow Mexican rule?"

"You know he did."

"Then where do you stand now, *Señor* Thorn? And where does your accomplice Sterne stand now?"

"We stand by our honor, sir." Thorn's brow lowered. "Do you question my honor, Colonel? Or that of my friends?"

"But your friend Sterne is an officer of the militia, is he not?"

"The militia's purpose is to defend the citizens of Nacogdoches."

"The militia has taken away its arms, in direct violation of my orders."

"Your order was wrong."

"My order stands."

"Then we will have trouble, sir."

Piedras turned away, busying himself with items on his desk. "Good day, *Señor* Thorn. I have no more time."

As Thorn, his face dark with frustration and futility, stalked from the Red House his friend, Captain Renaldo Musquiz, commander of the Company of Monclova, waved a greeting.

CHAPTER XXVI

"I never seen a fight yet that couldn't have been avoided . . . but none of 'em I seen was."
—Henry Stockman, carpenter,
Nacogdoches, Texas, 1832

Piedras summoned the *Ayuntamiento*. Only Encarnacion Chireno and the Moras—Jose and Juan—responded. The colonel told them emphatically, "You and the people of Nacogdoches must protect this garrison. You must help defend against these ambitious foreigners who plan to attack us."

"What foreigners?" Jose asked.

"Protect you with what?" Juan put in.

"I had thought it was your purpose to protect us, not the other way around," Chireno said with acid in his voice.

"Those Anglos near the Neutral Strip," Piedras shouted at Jose. "The foreigners at Ayish Bayou. Yes, and at Bevil's, and on the Neches. All around us! I want it understood that all of you are to come to the defense of the military command when you are called upon. You have a militia, under Vicente Cordova as captain. You will assemble the militia and place yourselves at my disposal."

Chireno stood straight, his dark eyes glittering. "The

militia of Nacogdoches has one purpose, Colonel. That is to defend the citizens of Nacogdoches from our enemies. It seems to me there is a serious question at this point just where our enemies may be found."

Piedras glared. "It is for me to decide who and where are our enemies. I tell you this. Either you and your people give me aid or I will march to San Antonio de Bexar. And when I return it will be with a force large enough to punish every traitor who has failed to obey the commands of the Mexican Army. Am I understood?"

"You are abusive, Colonel." Chireno's face darkened. "You are also arrogant, threatening, and annoying, and you have forgotten your place . . . hold your tongue! I have not finished. We and the others of the *Ayuntamiento* are the legally elected leaders of the town and district of Nacogdoches. We are sworn to uphold the Constitution of Mexico. The people we serve are free people, in a free nation. You will either serve us, or you will leave us alone. Am *I* understood?"

Piedras drummed his fingers on his desktop. Then he stood, stared at Chireno for a moment, and drew his sword. The Moras drew back. Chireno stood his ground, meeting the colonel's stare until the commander's eyes fell away. Piedras paled, the sword quivering in his hand. "I am the law here!" he rasped. "I am Mexico! And I will remember you. Get out. Get out!" As they turned and walked out they could hear him behind them. "I know you! I know you all! I will remember you!"

On the plaza Chireno asked the Moras, "Are your families packed?"

"Nearly," Jose told him. "We will be ready soon."

"Bring them to my house," the *Alcalde* said. "Candida and the children should be ready soon. Others will gather there as well. It is a long road to the old Bean place, and women and children should travel in large parties."

"Some will stop at the Goyens place?" Juan asked.

"Yes. As many as they can make room for. But most will go to Bean's old place. There is shelter there for many."

As they parted, Jose Mora looked curiously at his son. "What will you do about that mother-in-law of yours?"

Juan shook his head. "We have the second wagon. We will put her younger children in that, and they can go with Carmen. But *Doña* Elena Ybarbo is her own husband's problem, not mine."

Chireno was halfway across to his house when he heard hoofbeats behind him and turned. Captain of Militia Vicente Cordova, flanked by two men, rode up. "I had hoped to find you, *Alcalde*. There are reports." He got down from his horse and they walked a few feet away, to stand under a tree. Cordova's men pulled into position on opposite sides of where they stood, eyeing the foot patrols passing on the nearby streets. Both of them were armed, and the patrols kept their distance.

"First," Cordova said, "it is official. The settlement at Ayish has declared for Santa Anna. They have also separated themselves and their area from Piedras's command."

"Ah." Chireno nodded.

"Second, there is word that militia units in other outlying settlements are assembling, to join the men of Ayish. I do not know whether the other settlements have declared for Santa Anna."

"If they have not, I expect they will."

"Yes. Third, there has been an outrage. Renegades entered the house of Luis Ramos, robbed him, and killed him."

Chireno's eyes widened with shock. "Ramos? Luis

300

Ramos?"

"The dairyman. Yes. His son Felipe escaped, and has described the outlaws. One of them is Anton Moro. It is certain."

"The trader, Willoughby . . . *Señor* Horton's *segundo* . . . he left here this morning searching for Anton Moro."

Cordova nodded. "Yes. He came to the Ramos house. He found Luis. Then he went off alone. I think he has gone after Moro."

"But he was to send word, send for help," Chireno protested. "We have heard nothing. Where is he?"

"No one knows, He is just gone, after Moro."

"You said there were more than one of them, the renegades?"

"Felipe said two."

"Mother of God! What else can happen?"

Cordova was grim. As if in answer he said, "Fourth. We are on Carrizo Creek, as agreed. We can cache arms there, as we have, and we can assemble there. But some of my men have seen Indians around there. Cherokee. One who was recognized is Gu'nasoquo, the one with the scar on his face."

Chireno looked ashen. "Will they attack?"

"So far they have not. They just stay off in the distance, watching. But they are many, *Alcalde*. Very many."

"Vicente, we are sending women and children out on the roads. Several groups already have left."

"Yes. We have found some of them, and taken them to Carrizo Creek. But tell the rest to go west. Do not let any more go east from here, *Alcalde*. We don't know what the Cherokee out there are going to do."

Chireno asked, "How many of the militia are with you on Carrizo Creek?"

"About a third of the men, either there or on patrol.

The rest will join us when they finish here. We wait for you to tell us how to move, *Alcalde*."

"I will tell you when I am sure. Colonel Piedras has ordered that I give the militia to him, to help defend his garrison."

Cordova's eyes narrowed and he grinned wickedly. "Tell him if the Nacogdoches militia comes to him he will not like it."

"I cannot tell him anything," Chireno spread his hands. "I don't think anyone can now."

The militiamen departed and Encarnacion Chireno, worried and sick at heart, went home.

Candida was directing the packing with an efficient hand. Their married daughter and two married sons were there with their families, helping with the packing and loading. Their own vehicles and pack animals drawn up in front of and beside the house. Little Jose, the youngest of the *Alcalde*'s sons at eight years, was struggling to carry a load too big for him, and Chireno relieved him of most of it, carried it out, placed it in a cart, and returned. Three-year-old Tomasa was clinging to her mother's skirt, wide-eyed at the unusual activity around her.

All up and down the street and on other streets visible across the plaza, similar activity was going on at many houses. Many others were silent, their women and children already gone.

Noon came and went, and the remaining families in the little town began to move toward the west of the plaza, where the Thorn house and the Chireno house stood. Those who had evacuated early and independently were gone. Those remaining had agreed to Susan Thorn's plan of a joint evacuation. Wagons, carts, pack animals, and their burdens waiting to be lashed on filled the street and spread across into the plaza. People hurried around doing last-minute things with their own possessions, trying to remember things they had forgotten, helping one another, getting in each other's way.

The men, those not occupying themselves with work, stood around looking lost, realizing that their families were about to leave.

Susan Thorn and her household had completed loading two wagons, and now Frost Thorn came across to where Chireno stood. "My wife has a good idea, Nacio. We have an extra wagon, empty. There are more small children in this crowd than there are vehicles to carry them. The servants can drive our supply wagons. Susan will take the empty one and as many small children as it will carry. It will make it much easier for them to travel."

Chireno nodded and moved among the crowd, spreading the word. Looking back over his shoulder, he stopped. Colonel Piedras was strolling across the plaza, two armed soldiers flanking him. As he approached the babble of voices quieted, then ceased. Chireno hurried out to the edge of the crowd, ready for anything. He wished he were armed.

Thorn joined him, and Piedras came up to them, hands behind his back, face bland and thoughtful, for all the world a man out for an innocent stroll.

"Ah, *Señor Alcalde,* I see you are getting your people organized."

Chireno didn't answer, and Piedras glanced at him oddly, then looked back toward the crowd.

"It is best," he nodded. "The women and children should not be here in times of trouble, and I am sure they will enjoy the outing. I am pleased. With our burdens removed, we of the town will be able to conduct ourselves as the situation may require. Very good. Good afternoon." Turning on his heel, he strolled off across the plaza, stopping now and then to watch his soldiers on patrol, stopping once to study the bark on a pine

303

tree where the banking sun gilded it.

Chireno and Thorn looked at each other. They both shook their heads.

Finally the evacuation was organized, and the long line of women, children, and aged people started on its way. Several men with rifles and muskets rode at the head of the column, several more waited to bring up the rear. Two or three families from beyond the east edge of town had come in and joined the caravan.

As the first movers started out, Susan Thorn and the Indian girl, Udali, disappeared again into Thorn's house, and came out a minute or two later. Udali, Mistletoe of the Cherokee, had changed into one of the bright dresses Susan had given her. Her hair was up, a bonnet on her head, and she flashed a dazzling smile toward those waiting for them. If Udali was going to travel, she would travel in style. Susan Thorn was carrying a double-barreled shotgun, and they had her beloved silver service between them. They climbed aboard the last wagon, a sideboard vehicle crammed with small children, the overflow of a dozen other vehicles, and Susan took the reins.

Before she could lift them a woman hurried over with a small boy in tow. *"Señora! Señora,* this little boy is Felipe Ramos. He is an orphan. I have no room for him in my cart."

Susan looked down at the small, smudged face, a wicked, crusted bruise on one cheek. "He has been hurt."

"Si, señora. Bad men came to his house. They killed his father. Have you room?"

"Of course we have room, *señora.* We will make room."

Udali had risen in the wagon box. She said, "Let me," and got down to help the boy aboard. Her fingers found the scrapes on his back, and she hesitated about putting him in the crowded bed. She remounted the wagon and took the child on her lap. *"U'sgu calana s'di,"* she said. "A brave boy. You stay here with me."

Again Susan lifted the reins and flicked them across the back of the mule. The wagon pulled out, and the waiting escort of three men pulled in behind it. As the wagon passed, Frost Thorn raised his hat, his eyes misting slightly. Susan smiled and waved back, then drove on. They had said everything they had to say.

A somber knot of husbands and fathers stood at the crossing of the Camino Real and the Camino Norte to watch them go. Finally Thorn turned to Chireno. "I guess we'd better look to our own preparations," he said, and Chireno nodded. Not a man in the street at the moment wanted to return to his house, because the houses all were empty.

"They were safe now," Chireno said, loudly enough for most of those around him to hear.

"The weather looks odd," Samuel Norris said. "East wind is comin' up. I hope it don't storm tonight."

Thorn shook his head. "They probably won't go further than Goyens's place tonight. They'll have shelter there. They can go on from there tomorrow."

At the door of his house, Thorn met Haden Edwards coming out. The older man was dressed in buckskin and leggings, and carried a shiny new rifle of the Hawken variety. Around the corner, beside the house, Thorn saw a good horse saddled, packed, and waiting.

"Papa, where are you going?"

"Where the militia is, of course. Carrizo Creek. Now that the women are gone, several of us are heading out there. Susan get gone all right?"

"Yes, they will all be fine. Papa, why don't you at least wait until tomorrow. I'll tell you the truth, I hate to be alone in that big, empty house tonight."

"You ain't alone." Haden grinned. "Jaren's in there,

305

sitting with a shotgun across his lap, black as the shadows he's in. Like to scared hell out of me when I first went in and saw him there."

Thorn frowned. "I told him to go with the women."

"Susan told him to stay with you. I guess that shows who's boss in the Thorn house."

"I suppose there never was any question of that, Papa. Still, I wish you'd stay—for a while at least. I don't think anything will happen for a few days yet."

Edwards shook his head. "No. Frost, there's something I've waited seven years to do, and at my age I won't have another chance. When our militia comes in on Nacogdoches, if it does, I'm going to be with it." The old man turned away, but not until Frost Thorn had noticed something. The long-gone fires of Haden Edwards, so long dulled in his dark eyes, were back again and burning as brightly as ever.

Edwards took a step and then turned back. "Frost, I want your promise that you'll stay out of the shooting. Don't get any further involved. I already got you into one mess here in Texas. I don't want you in another one. Promise me."

Thorn nodded. "I've done about all I can do, Papa, and still live up to my oath. But I tell you this. My rifle is loaded, and if things go wrong I'll have to decide then how much difference that oath makes."

It was all the promise Edwards was going to get. He knew it. Suddenly very solemn, he stepped toward his son-in-law and held out his hand. "Take care then, son. And take good care of my daughter."

"I will, Papa."

He watched Edwards ride away. He looked toward his house, then turned the other way, across the plaza. Damn Jaren's black hide, he thought, I am glad he stayed. He headed toward the store. There was packing to do there too, and tomorrow he and the others would

306

try to move their stores to safety. Family first, then property. It was the proper way of things.

The evacuation caravan moved slowly, with many stops. Some of the handcarts were heavily laden, mothers and daughters working to make any time at all with them. Within a mile the carefully ordered plan of march had collapsed. The men riding escort couldn't stand watching women work that way. Most of them were pulling carts, their horses tied on behind. Only two mounted escorts remained on duty, one front and one rear, and they paid more attention to the caravan than to the wilderness around them.

None passed any others on the narrow road. All held to the pace set by the slowest. But gradually the train became segmented, strung out in little knots and clusters.

Susan Thorn halted her wagon several times while she and Udali tended the needs of some of the younger of their cargo of children. The man riding behind them, the rear guard, chaffed at the delay. His eyes were on the group moving away, up ahead. His own family was up there, and his wife had no one to help with her driving.

"Oh, for heaven's sake, Juan," Susan told him. "Go on and look after them. We'll be right behind you. We have a gun, see?"

Skeptically the man held his position for a minute or so. Then as the rest of the train rounded a bend ahead and disappeared, he shrugged, nodded, passed around the wagon, and spurred ahead. He was out of sight by the time Susan lifted the reins again, and they were alone on the road.

She flicked the reins and they moved on. They had gone only a little way when one of the babies began crying again. Udali looked at her across the wagon seat, fumbled for words, found them and said, brightly, "Oh, hell!"

Susan was still laughing when she got the wagon halted.

It was nearly dark when the caravan completed the four miles to the house of William Goyens. Goyens and his wife had every available roofed space cleared, ready for them. There was food in the house, tubs of water to bathe children, lanterns filled and ready. It was hospitality of the first order. It was also mass confusion.

It was nearly full dark before one of the women, and then another and another, noticed that some of their children were missing. They looked around, questioned, and in the rising panic it was discovered that Susan Thorn's cargo was not among them. The last wagon had not come in. Men saddled quickly and headed back east. In the darkness of an overcast night they came back. They had ridden all the way to Nacogdoches, searching. The wagon had disappeared.

CHAPTER XXVII

*"In one way at least, Texians are like the
Lord God. It doesn't pay
to make them mad."*
—Samuel Norris

He slept fitfully, harassed by interwoven dreams. Utsada's laughing face became Gu'nasoquo's vengeful mask. Through them, a mist of tenderness, came the lovely face of Udali. A hurt little boy, a dying man all broken, vague recall of simpler times and simpler problems fading to determination . . . fear. The great bulk of Anton Moro . . . laughing . . . laughing at him . . . killing him . . .

It was still dark when he awoke, but there was a feel of morning. For a moment he lay unmoving, coming alert, letting his senses range. The hackles rose on his neck. His hand closed on his rifle. He freed his enwrapping blankets silently. Then, cat-quick, he was on his feet in the darkness, silent and wary. Nothing. Nearby his horse dozed and grazed. He could hear its quiet sounds. But something had interrupted his sleep. Some sound or sense had been, for a moment, out of place. Crouching, he moved away from his bedroll and into the forest, letting his ears and his nose guide him in the darkness. Silently he made a wide circle, ranging for a clue to what had awakened him. There was nothing. Finally he found his way back to where he had slept, his tension easing but still not gone. The sounds of sleepy, early-morning birds told him there would be a little light within an hour. All his senses remaining alert, he scratched around and found the little packet of tinder he had wrapped against the dew. In a tiny cove between a fallen log and a gravel bank he built a little fire—just a handful of flames—and boiled coffee in a tin cup. With this and dried meat he made his breakfast, adding a handful of berries for dessert, then waited for first light.

The initial tension of awakening was gone. He put it to the dreams that had tormented him. But as pale gray picked out the forest floor, as he saddled and moved out, a nagging uneasiness remained. Whether it was imagination or some odd sense alerting him, he had the feeling he was being followed.

He had the trail and he was on it. Within a mile he came upon the place where his quarry had slept. They were gone now, but their sign was fresh and the droppings of their horses were warm in the cool air of morning. Eagerness prodding him, pushing at his anger, he stepped up the pace.

Susan Thorn was exasperated with herself, and didn't mind showing it. Nobody but an idiot could have lost the road. Any fool could have followed it, stayed on it. The Camino Real was the best-marked road in East Texas. All anyone had to do was just follow it. Even in the narrow places the road was clear—packed earth here, grass beaten down by traffic there, underbrush cleared back. There were trails branching off at various places, of course, but none of them were deceptive. How anyone could have lost the Camino Real was absolutely beyond her, and she had no one to blame but herself. Only she had driven the wagon.

She had been distracted, of course, by the clamor, the never-ending fidgeting and constant little emergencies of the nine young children they carried. Of the nine, only the little bruised boy, Felipe, was more than three or four years old. That was why they had them in this wagon. All of them were too young to walk alongside their mothers in the evacuation from Nacogdoches, and none of them could be provided for in other vehicles.

Their various mothers would be worried sick, she knew, and she wouldn't blame every one of them for giving her a dressing-down when they got back to the caravan. She fully expected it.

By the time they had realized they were lost, it had been too dark to turn back. So they had spent the night here, on this narrow deep-forest trail, and Susan had sat up most of the night holding her shotgun across her lap. Udali had been up most of the night too, tending children.

Susan was impressed at the Indian girl's calm acceptance of the situation. With nothing more than some blankets, a hatchet and knife, and the things packed in the bag of provisions they carried, she, with some awkward help from Susan, had transformed this few yards of close-brushed trail into quite a comfortable campsite. She had even found water somewhere close by, and hauled it in, a bucket at a time. The children were safe, fed, and sleeping comfortably, and Udali had wrapped herself in a blanket to doze against a wagon wheel.

Susan noticed there was light enough now to see, and she stood, stretched cramped muscles, and looked around her. She judged it would take two or three hours to get back to where they had left the Camino Real, and then possibly an hour more to get to the

Goyens house. Then everything would be all right. She doubted if the mothers of her charges would trust them with her again, but that wasn't important. They would be reunited and safe. Oh, when Frost heard about this episode . . . she winced. Her husband was a gentle, understanding man, but he could be a terrible tease. It would be a long time before she lived this down.

Their fire had died, and she set about kindling a new one in the ashes. She wished she had the dexterity of Mistletoe. Well, she thought, it's time I learned. After several tries she had it going, and put water on the heat. There was no coffee in the provisions, but there was tea. And there was plenty of milled corn and oats to make a hot porridge for all of them when the children were awake. I got us lost, she chided herself, but at least we aren't hungry.

Birdcalls awoke Udali, and the Indian girl came to the fire to join her. She dipped a cloth in water, scrubbed her face, combed out her hair and pinned it up with the comb, and looked as though she were ready for a fine party. The dress she wore was not even smudged. Udali, Susan thought, I could learn to hate you. Udali finished her ritual and then smiled across the fire. "Good morning," she said.

Susan groaned. "Good morning, Udali. Interesting night, wasn't it?"

It took a moment for the irony of the words to penetrate two languages, then Udali grinned. "Yes. Interesting. Good night, wrong place."

Susan smiled in spite of herself. The water was hot, and she prepared tea for them. Udali watched her curiously, her lips pursed.

"One time I 'member . . . *sa'quo* . . . two? Yes, two summers pass. That time Tsula . . . you know Tsula? *Ani'taheik* . . . very wise one of Tsalagi, Tsula. Good hunt, good speak to corn make grow, good lead people.

That time Tsula go hunt, gone many day. Gone too many day. Men go to look for Tsula, he maybe die some place. When they find Tsula he not die, just go wrong way. Men find him in Arkansas." She paused, her dark eyes crinkling at the corners. "Susan, if Tsula get that much lost, anybody get lost. Anybody."

Susan stared into her cup. It was light enough to see the steam rising from the tea. Finally, composed, she said, "We must practice numbers." She held up a finger. "One."

"One." Udali nodded.

"Two."

With full light the children began waking up, and Susan got to work on breakfast. Felipe Ramos assisted her while Udali tended the little ones' morning needs. The Mexican boy was squatting beside the fire, a meal sack in his hands, when he looked up and froze. The next second, he screamed. Two men had come out of the woods and stood twenty feet away, grinning. They were both heavy, muscular men, both large, though one, the one with the mashed-up nose, was substantially larger than the other. The shorter of the two, a brown-skinned, stocky *mestizo*, grinned savagely and began to laugh. The other just smiled, and there was something in that smile that chilled Susan Thorn. Abruptly she realized that her shotgun was in the wagon, under a pile of blankets and sacks, far beyond reach. She stood, slowly, putting herself between the men and the terrified Felipe. A few yards away Udali was crouched, her eyes startled, several of the children behind her.

The biggest of the men, who carried a long rifle across his arm, looked coldly from Susan to the Indian girl and back. His gaze was rude, appraising. Susan suddenly realized she was very much afraid.

The *mestizo* said something in a rapid undertone and the big man hesitated, looking again from Susan to

Udali. Then he shrugged, spread a hand, and nodded.

His grin broadening, the *mestizo* pulled a knife from his belt and walked to Susan Thorn. He looked her up and down, then reached out and grabbed the shoulder of her coat. He wrenched downward violently, trying to tear the fabric, but it held and Susan stumbled to her knees, feeling in her shock as though her shoulder was broken.

"Take it off," he commanded, then staggered as something hit him. It was Udali. Like a wildcat she pounced on him, clawed fingers going for his eyes, leaving welling scratches on his cheek as they missed. With an oath the man flung out an arm and hit her backhanded, sending her rolling. She didn't make a sound. Susan reached for a knife lying by the fire, but the man was too quick for her. He kicked it away.

The big man watched, grinning now as he enjoyed the show. He set his rifle against a tree and strode forward, then stopped as Udali, off to his side, came to her feet.

"Hey, tough *soldado*." The big man laughed. "I will tend to the white one. That wildcat there wants to fight. You like to fight. You see if you are match for her."

The *mestizo* glared at him, hating him, then turned obediently and went for Udali. She crouched, dodged, tried to claw him again, and again he hit her, knocking her to the ground. He leaned toward her.

The brush above them exploded, and a hurtling figure caromed into the *mestizo,* knocking him back several steps. Before he could recover himself Cooper Willoughby followed him, whipcord arms windmilling, delivering blow after thudding blow to his face, his body, his face again. The *mestizo* backpedaled and Willoughby waded into him, raging fires in his eyes, oblivious to all else. He pummeled the man to his knees, never letting up. Bright blood splattered from the *mestizo*'s face.

Susan screamed a warning, but it came too late. As Willoughby braced himself to swing again, a huge, iron-hard hand clamped on his shoulder and hurled him back. He tripped and sprawled. Moro looked down in disgust at his bleeding companion. "What is the mater, tough *presidario?* You can't fight a beanpole like that? You want me to hold him for you? You want me to kill him for you?"

The tone of it enraged Ruiz. Blood on his face and death in his eyes, he came to his feet and charged at Willoughby. The trader was stunned, trying to get up. Ruiz kicked him in the head and sent him sprawling again. He went after him and kicked again. Somehow, through a fog, Willoughby saw it coming and twisted away. Legs swinging, he caught the *presidario* behind his knee and brought him down.

Both Udali and Susan had started forward. Moro stepped to the tree and picked up his rifle. *"Alto,"* he rumbled, and both of them stopped, frozen. He was pointing his rifle at the huddle of wide-eyed children by the wagon.

Ruiz charged again, and Willoughby sidestepped him, landing a fist in his midsection as he went by. With a fast step Willoughby jumped high and landed with both feet on the man's back, sending him skidding on his face. Willoughby tumbled past and came up against a tree trunk with force that knocked the breath from him. The *mestizo* was tough. Before the gangling trader could recover, he was charged again, and this time a blow to the side of his head made him see bright flashes. He backed off, almost tripped, and circled backward again, trying to clear his head as the enraged *presidario* bored in. He was hit again and again, but he kept moving. Then Ruiz swung and missed, and Wil-

315

loughby grabbed his arm. With all of his strength he pivoted, brought the arm down across his knee and heard the bone snap. While Ruiz was still groping for what had happened Willoughby spun him around, brought a hard knee up into his belly, grabbed his hair as he doubled over, and used the knee again, this time to the face.

He backed off. The *mestizo* was injured, hurt, but even as he fell to his knees his hand found and closed on the knife he had dropped. With a final surge of rage and strength he came off the ground, the knife flashing straight toward Willoughby's open midsection.

There was a roar as of thunder. Ruiz stopped in mid-strike, his eyes widening, battered mouth falling open, then swayed a moment and fell. He did not move.

Through a red mist Willoughby saw little Felipe Ramos over by the wagon, a shotgun in his hands, a double cloud of white smoke spreading around him.

Cooper Willoughby was on his hands and knees, and for all the world he couldn't think how to get up. Come on, ol' son, he told himself desperately, you ain't done yet. But his muscles wouldn't respond. Distantly he heard a scream, and then the ground hit him in the face.

Anton Moro looked for a moment at the skinny trader on hands and knees on the ground, his head hanging down. He glanced at his dead companion, looked at Willoughby again, and shrugged. He looked at the two women. All right. The show was over. He raised his rifle to shoot Willoughby, but the trader sagged forward and fell on his face. Moro lowered the rifle, turned it in his hands, and stepped forward, raising the butt of it to brain the unconscious man. He raised it high, tensed himself, and swung.

His hands slid on the forestock, gouging flesh on the brass ferrules. The rifle remained where it was, upright, refusing to move. Off balance, surprised, Moro half turned and looked around, squarely into the eyes of a huge Indian. The third hand on his rifle was half again the size of his own.

Moro scuttled back a half step, hands coming up, his eyes glazed with sudden terror. "Egg!" he rasped. "No!" But the great right arm wielding the war club had started its arc, and there was no stopping it.

PART FIVE

AN ACT OF LIBERTY

CHAPTER XXVIII

"My sister and I made a little house of sticks.
Inside were stick benches. When the men
marched they stepped on it
and it was gone."
—Madonna Patricia Cruz

Quiet. It hung over the village of Nacogdoches. The Bright Lady rested, waiting, and her silence was deceptive.

It could be just another Sunday morning, Frost Thorn thought as he stood by his front gate watching sunlight settle down upon the cool of morning. A quiet Sunday. No, a silent Sunday. The difference was enormous.

The streets were no more nearly deserted than on any Sunday morning, but what traffic there was, was different. Soldiers. A few scattered foot patrols among the silent, empty houses. Some store fronts were boarded. The few people on their way to Mass were mostly men. There were few women left in Nacogdoches.

Musing on the quiet of the morning, Thorn for a moment expected to hear Luis Ramos's old dairy wagon making its way into town. Then he remembered. Ramos wouldn't be coming anymore. Across the way he saw John Durst tie up in front of the Stone Fort and pause before entering.

"Mistah Frost?" The voice came from behind him, subdued. Jaren stood in the dark doorway, his shotgun in his hand. Since the evacuation, Thorn thought, there were two things Jaren had refused to do—leave the house and turn loose of that damned shotgun. He wondered whether the slave slept with that thing. He decided that he probably did.

"Mistah Frost, I done made some coffee. Do you want some?"

He nodded and walked into the house. It was so . . . so damned empty.

He pulled a chair out onto the porch. "Bring it out here, Jaren. Bring two cups."

"Two, suh?"

"Two. I think we both need some coffee." Partly, he was curious whether Jaren could manage two mugs of coffee without laying down his shotgun. He pulled out another chair, and a foot table.

Jaren managed. He came from the pantry carrying a silver tray with a pitcher, two cups, loaf sugar, spoons, and several cakes piled upon it. He had tied a loop of heavy twine to the gun's trigger guard and hung it around his neck. Thorn shrugged in admiration.

When the service was set Jaren hung back until Thorn told him to sit down. It went against the black's ethic, in a way. He had no reluctance to drink all the coffee he wanted out in the pantry, but he was uncomfortable sitting down with the white folks, like he was one of them. It threatened his status as majordomo of the household.

"Jaren, tell me, why do you carry that gun around all the time?"

Jaren hurried to chew and swallow a bit of cake. "It fo' the chand'liers, suh."

322

"The chandeliers?"

"Yes, suh." He swallowed coffee, took another bite of cake, and looked out across the plaza. A patrol of three soldiers was passing the gate and Jaren frowned at them.

Thorn packed and lit his pipe. Jaren refilled his coffee cup. The morning sun was climbing above the trees to the east, and its weight could be felt. It was going to be a hard, hot day. There was commotion beyond the buildings fronting on the Camino Real, and a moment later a cavalry patrol came in, clattered past the Red House, and went on across the plaza to the Quartel. Captain Renaldo Musquiz was in the lead.

On impulse, Thorn finished his coffee and stood. Maybe there was news. He started down the steps, then turned back. "You can put these things away, Jaren. And what do you mean, 'for the chandeliers'?"

The slave looked at him solemnly. "Why, Miss Susan done told me, 'Take care of Mistah Frost, take care of the house, and don' let no strangers get near them chand'liers.' Musn't nobody fool wit' them, suh. They comes from Paris."

The *Alcalde,* Encarnacion Chireno, came from his own house now, obviously drawn by the sounds from the plaza, and Thorn and the village leader walked together toward the Quartel. Chireno's face was drawn. He had not been sleeping well. Who, for that matter, had? There had been, as yet, no news from the women and children. There should have been a message by now that everyone was all right, safely ensconced somewhere to await the outcome at Nacogdoches.

And what would be the outcome? Outcome of what? Everyone knew now that there would be a fight. But no one had yet given any orders, no one had yet started anything. Part of the starting would be up to the *Alcalde,* and Chireno had not yet issued any orders to Vicente Cordova and the militia.

Thorn did not press the man. Chireno had much to consider. When the time was right, he would do what he would do.

"There have been more reports of Indians," Chireno said. "Did you know? Yesterday a man came from Carrizo Creek. The Cherokee have been seen there in large number. They do nothing, though. They just keep their distance, wait, and watch."

"Have you any news of the trader, Willoughby?"

"None. In fact, the man yesterday was the only messenger I have seen. No one has come from anywhere these past two days."

At the Quartel they waited, knowing Musquiz would come out, and eventually he did. The captain had changed his uniform, cleaned himself, and was on his way to the Red House. When he saw them he turned in their direction.

"Any news, Renaldo? Anything you can tell us?" Thorn asked.

"Little enough," Musquiz told them. He seemed distracted, thoughtful. "You may have heard ... I suspect you know more than I about it ... that the men of the Ayish settlement have declared for Santa Anna."

"Yes."

"And that many of the troops are leaving, many have left Texas to go to war inland."

"That too."

"Then I don't suppose there is anything I can add. Except ..." He broke off, again seeming puzzled, concerned. They waited.

"I have seen a strange thing this morning. A scout came in during the night with news of an Indian gathering northeast of here, about twelve miles. I took a cavalry unit and went to see. We found them, *señores,* and we watched. There were many, perhaps nearly a hundred, all warriors, all Cherokee as best I could determine."

"Are they preparing to make war?" Chireno asked.

Musquiz shook his head. "I don't know. They were all mounted, all with war clubs. There is a recent burnoff there. The land is clear on a hillside except for some new brush and the standing trunks of a few dead trees. We watched from a ridge, some distance away.

"They were grouped at one side of the clearing, and one by one they rode out across the clearing, making a long line, walking their horses. There was one tall burned stump, a little taller than a man on horseback, with something on it, and they rode past this, and each one stopped there to look, then rode on, circling back to where they began. When all had ridden past the stump, they regrouped and turned into the woods. We lost sight of them from there.

"When we were sure they were gone we rode down there to see for ourselves. It was the body of a man, *señores,* hung up on that stump like . . . like a rag doll thrown over a fence post. He had been dead two or three days and the birds had been at him, but I think it was Anton Moro. I am sure of it."

Thorn and Chireno looked at each other, puzzled, then back at Musquiz.

"Exactly. I too am at a loss for an explanation. And there was one thing more. A rifle—American style, large bore—lay by the stump. Really, what was left of a rifle. The stock was shattered, and the barrel . . . *señores,* upon my honor, that barrel was bent, curved almost in a bow. I have never seen such a thing."

They thought about it. Then Thorn asked, "Did you bring him back?"

Musquiz shook his head. "The way those Cherokees behaved, I thought it best not to do more than look. We scouted a little way into the forest. The Indians went east from there. Then we came back."

Through the day the men of Nacogdoches worked and waited. The soldiers kept their distance on the streets, and there was no sign of Colonel Piedras until shortly before noon, when bugles sounded and the garrison was mustered in the plaza for inspection.

Through the previous day and during this morning the merchants of the town had been assembling and packing their wares, cutting lumber to board up stores. With the military assembled in the plaza and the side streets cleared, wagons and carts appeared from everywhere.

By the time Piedras had finished his inspection, most of the remaining goods, merchandise, and stores of Nacogdoches, virtually all the portable wealth of the town, was on its way to Carrizo Creek, and the business places were closed for the duration.

Riders still came and went, in and out of town, but they were furtive now, using the back trails. Early in the afternoon Will Goyens rode in from the west, mounted on one of his best saddle horses. He looked around, and found Thorn and Chireno at Chireno's house.

"I came to tell you the women and children are safe," he said. "Some of them are at my place, and we'll tend them for you. Most of them went on to Bean's old place, and there are men there looking after them."

The two men breathed a sigh of relief. They had been worried more than they wanted to show.

Goyens grinned. "Yeah, I can imagine how you feel. But I didn't want to report in until I knew they were all safe. There was a slight delay in the proceedings. One of the women took a wrong turn and got lost."

"Got lost?" Chireno frowned. "How can anyone get lost on the Camino Real?"

Thorn snorted. "Women! I swear to God! I told Susan she'd have trouble keeping that bunch out of trouble. Who was it that got lost, Will?"

Goyens's grin widened. "I almost hate to tell you, Frost. It was Susan." At Thorn's stunned look he hastened to add, "Don't get on her about it, Frost. She feels bad enough about it already. The thing is, they all got back safe and sound and no harm done. Just slowed things up a bit."

Thorn swore. The idea of Susan and that wagon load of babies—lost. Out in the woods. Alone.

He shook his head. "God watches over children and fools . . . and women."

"More than God, sometimes," Goyens said, his expression suddenly very sober. But he refused to elaborate on the cryptic remark. "Oh, if you see Alexander Horton, tell him I have his deputy at my place too. He's banged up a bit, but he'll be all right. That girl of his is taking care of him."

"What happened to him?" Thorn and Chireno glanced at each other, both remembering the strange thing Captain Musquiz had told them about.

"I don't know." Goyens shrugged. "He won't talk about it. Just says he had a scrape, that's all. And you know, in a way it was a good thing your wife got lost out there. It was her that found him and brought him in."

Thorn and Chireno looked at each other again.

"Will," Thorn asked quietly, "you know where there

327

is a burnoff out in the woods, northeast of here, about twelve miles?"

Goyens thought about it. "Yeah, I think so. A hillside burned over. Happened last year or so. Why?"

"How many miles would you say that is from where Susan found Willoughby?"

Now it was Goyens's turn to be puzzled. "Oh, twenty-thirty miles, I suppose. Why?"

"Nothing. Just wondering."

John Durst was the last to get his goods moved out of Nacogdoches, because his were the hardest to get. Durst owned the Stone House, and though he allowed the army to use a portion of the building as storage, most of it was a storehouse for Durst's considerable inventory of trade goods.

There was no way to secret his merchandise away from the place, so while he waited there, seemingly making a routine inspection, the other merchants hauled their loads and brought back enough wagons, carts, and mules to clean him out.

Early in the afternoon they descended upon the Stone House, twenty or more men with hauling equipment, walked in past the single, surprised guard and the supply sergeant on duty, went upstairs and into the right-hand room, and with Durst supervising brought out every last item belonging to him, loaded up, and drove away, out of town.

It was gone before the soldiers knew what had happened. The valuables were out of town and gone ten minutes before Colonel Piedras came storming from the Red House, two armed soldiers behind him. At the Stone House he looked around, came back out, and turned full around looking at the town around him as though seeing it for the first time. Several of the citizens were standing idly by, watching, their expressions ranging from innocence to triumph.

Piedras started to approach them, then changed his mind. He glowered at the men, turned, and stalked away toward the Red House. A few minutes later foot patrols issued out in all directions, looking at and into the commercial buildings along the streets. Most of them were boarded up. Those that weren't were quite empty. The patrols reported back to Piedras, who stormed and cursed, then ordered the streets cleared and the town closed.

Only a handful of civilians remained now in Nacogdoches, and these got off the streets. The soldiers had orders to shoot. John Durst watched the flurry of activity impassively. Of all the Anglo settlers in the Nacogdoches district, possibly excepting Peter Ellis Bean, John Durst had the most complete understanding of Iberian ways. He had never been a citizen of the United States. Born in Spanish Arkansas, he had been a subject of Spanish cultures all his life.

When the order came to clear the streets, he stepped down off the porch of the Stone House and stood for a moment looking across at the Red House.

"Piedras," he muttered, "you are an ass. You held the trust of good people, and you abused it. That is unforgivable."

He untied his horse, mounted, and headed out toward where he and his Harriet had built their new house on a hill overlooking the Angelina River. He had made up his mind. Tonight he would pack and prepare. Tomorrow he would head for Carrizo Creek, where Vicente Cordova waited with the militia. He had had more than enough of Jose de las Piedras.

Most of the soldiers in Piedras's command had never actually had orders to shoot, except in battle. There was no battle here, just a silent little town with most of the people gone. And most of them knew most of those who were left. They had nodded to them on the street, chatted with them in Sim's Tavern, bought or pilfered things in their stores. Most of the soldiers had no intention of shooting an unarmed civilian just because he was walking in the street.

Most of them thought this way. A few did not. When Charles Stanfield Taylor unbolted the door of his empty shop and stepped out for a breath of air, there were soldiers patrolling across the street. He waved at them. A couple of them waved back, and the corporal with them motioned him to go back inside. He misunderstood the signal, smiled, and stepped further into the street. Suddenly, in the group, a musket came up, leveled at him.

Startled, he ducked, turned, and ran back into his store. As he slammed the door a musket ball burst through the wood, pelting him with splinters. He ran into the back room, bolted that door, grabbed a rifle off the rack, and sank back into the corner, white with shock, laboring for breath, his hands shaking uncontrollably. There were no more shots.

In the dark of evening men slipped through the shadows and made their way to the house of Encarnacion Chireno, the *Alcalde* of Nacogdoches. A little later they departed, and in the dark of evening hoofbeats sounded outside the town, going away.

The *Alcalde* had made his decision. The call went out to the militias of Ayish Bayou, Tenaha, Sabine,

White River, and Bevil's Diggings. Nacogdoches must be relieved of Colonel Piedras. God and Liberty. Gather the militias and assemble on the banks of Carrizo Creek. Vicente Cordova was waiting.

CHAPTER XXIX

*"The powder and shot requisitioned on the 12th
of June have not arrived. Lamp oil is nearly
depleted. No provisions are arriving from
outside and our supply of corn is very low. We do,
however, have plenty of coffee."*
—Supply Sergeant Isidro Cos

During the past few days Alexander Horton had
made a trip into the Neutral Strip, one to Bevil's Diggings, and one clear over into Louisiana. As a result,
two large and boisterous drunks were stockaded at
Bevil's Diggings awaiting the sober honor of rebuilding
a barn under armed guard, some positions were open
among certain outlaw organizations in the Strip, and a
sheriff at Natchitoches owed his Texian counterpart a
favor.

But the time involved had left Horton anxious and
edgy. For various reasons he was trying to stick close
to Ayish Bayou. Things were getting ready to pop at
Nacogdoches and he didn't want to miss it. Also, he
had a missing deputy again. He swore if Willoughby
hadn't quit every time he'd opened his mouth this past
month, he'd fire him. As it was, he had to keep him

on, because you don't accept a resignation from a prisoner.

Also, the Cherokee were stirring like hornets around a shook nest, and things were on the verge of getting serious.

He had worn out three horses, lost about five pounds, and kept his irritation active by reminding himself that his original plan this summer had been to court little Patsy Mullen. Or maybe Rosemary Gaines, or Becky Tice—or all of them, time permitting.

So far the summer was half over, cropping time was coming on, and he hadn't so much as how-de-do'd a one of them. And now there was a war brewing up and he couldn't miss that.

Benjamin Lindsay walked out to the road as the sheriff rode up. "You heard, huh?"

"Heard there was a call for militia assembly. Not where."

"Rider from Nacogdoches. Said Chireno wants all the militias at Carrizo Creek. Cordova is already there. I'm fixin' to leave as soon as I get packed. Some of 'em have gone on ahead. Those on duty now will assemble at Huston's in the morning and go as a group. Your brother-in-law will be leadin'."

"You heard anything from my deputy?"

"Well, I don't really know. The fellow from Nacogdoches said he heard maybe Moro had been took out, but he didn't know anything more than that about it."

"You mean he got him?" Horton's eyes widened. "Then he musta got him in a corner and called in plenty of help. I told you Coop Willoughby was smart."

"You goin' on to Carrizo Creek then?"

"Yeah. First I'll stop to see James and Sis. Maybe

I'll go ahead on with the militia. You take care now, Ben. See you at Carrizo."

Captain Stephen Prather, late of the United States Army and more recently of the demise of Fredonia, called up his militia at Bevil's Diggings and rode for Nacogdoches. Not all of them could come as a group that day, but they would be along. "God and Liberty," the message said, and his nostrils flared and his eyes glowed as he led men to respond.

John Bradley, duly elected Captain of Militia at Tenaha, led his men south by southwest through rolling, pined wilderness bordering the Indian lands. At Tenaha Creek crossing they were joined by another small company led by the Bailey Andersons, senior and junior. They veered southwest and put the miles behind them, homing on Carrizo Creek east of Nacogdoches. At his settlement on the Sabine River James Bradshaw gathered his men, many of whom already had several miles behind them, pointed his pony's nose due west, and set off at a canter. To the south of them the Reverend James B. McMahan, of the Methodist persuasion, flanked by his son Samuel, led another group. He carried his Bible in his coattail pocket, his primed rifle in his hand.

At the Snow River settlement Samuel Looney surveyed the large party of woodsmen and farmers he had assembled, spat, and grinned. "If you ain't a sorry-lookin' bunch!" Then, turning his mount, he yelled, "Let the Neches be heard from!" The first quarter mile of their journey was a ragged cavalry charge.

Simal P. Hopkins tied a bedroll behind his saddle, kissed his wife, and mounted the recycled plowhorse to look around for a moment at the tiny cluster of shacks and sheds that was the settlement of Ayes Bawe. Of the twenty-eight human beings in this struggling, remote little place, only two at the moment were able-bodied men. Hopkins and Chester Corey had flipped a coin to see which of them would be the Ayes Bawe militia. Hopkins won. With a last look around, Hopkins headed in the general direction of Carrizo Creek.

By the evening of Monday, the 30th of July, 1832, the lawfully organized civilian militias of East Texas had begun to assemble on the banks of Carrizo Creek. Many had not yet arrived, but they were coming. Camps sprawled up and down a section of creek on both sides of the camp of Vicente Cordova's Nacogdoches company. Fresh-dug holes dotted the creek bank below where the stores from Nacogdoches were baled, stacked, and covered. From these holes had been extracted hidden powder and shot placed there in the past by Cordova and his men. The holes were left open. They made convenient latrines.

Antonio Menchaca prowled the camps as they were set up, astonished and enthralled at the variety of battle dress chosen by the assembling army. Most of the men present so far were of Spanish origin, and many wore wide *sombreros* with pointed crowns, shading cotton shirts, baggy cotton pants, and rawhide sandals. Most of these carried muskets of varying lengths and long-bladed machetes or corn knives.

Anglos fresh out of the United States tended to favor buckskins and woolsey fabric, with slouch hats or fur caps, and most wore either mule-hide boots or various kinds of moccasins. Their knives were of several varieties. Some favored the wide-bladed fighting knife, others the slim Arkansas toothpick, and many the Green River knife from Sheffield, England. Few of them carried muskets. Some had fowlers, but most favored rifles — ornate Kentuckys, sleek Ohio designs, here and there a few Hawkens fresh from St. Louis.

These classes made up the bulk of the men on Carrizo Creek. But among them were colorful exceptions. Donald McDonald, Canadian-born descendant of the McDonald clan by direct lineage from the Third McDonald, showed up with his tam-o'-shanter cocked upon his head, feather plume and crest of the Highland Regiment aloft and sparkling in the sun. Carefully packed in his saddlebag was a full-dress Highlander uniform of bright McDonald dress tartan, complete to the kilt and *sghean-dhub*. He would wear it to battle.

Adolphus Sterne wore Prussian military boots from Cologne. Charles Stanfield Taylor preferred to go to war in a suit of clothing which would have passed as proper in the best London quarters. John Durst could have attracted admiring glances in Mexico City, and Isaac Watts Burton sported the field cap he had brought from West Point nine years earlier.

Menchaca made notes. If he ever got back to his tailor shop he would open some eyes.

It was a motley scene, and as the evening dimmed and fires were lit, a whiskey keg was broached here and there in the Anglo camps, and it became more colorful still. There was almost nothing upon which any majority of the crowd would agree — except one thing. They had gotten their fill of military rule by a royalist Mexican government. Most of those who were loyal to anything were loyal to Mexico. Most of them were citizens and proud of it. Out here on the frontier they had mostly shaken their heads and looked the other way when oppression became tyranny in the interior states. It was a long way from East Texas to the rest of Mexico. But of late, President Bustamente's regime had slopped over into Texas—a seeming stream of petty tyrants with federal credentials. The ex-Yankee Colonel Juan Davis Bradburn at Anahuac. The ex-Serbian George Fisher. And Colonel Jose de las Piedras at Nacogdoches. It was enough. God and Liberty.

As the spirits flowed it was all the leaders, particularly in the Anglo camps, could do to avert an immediate attack by some of their men. "Hell, Mac," a self-chosen spokesman argued, "we can get it done and over with and all go home. There ain't nobody in the damn garrison can stop us."

"Ye're thinkin' o' Piedras hi'self," McDonald pointed out. "Best think also o' Musquiz. Aye, and Medina as well. 'Tis them that'll lead the troops, lad."

It set them back. Two hundred professional soldiers in a fortified town, with Musquiz and Medina directing them, would be no easy target. To put a cap on it McDonald said, "Think hard on it. Do ye think the Twelfth Battalion couldna' turn an attack? And once turned, 'twould be no scabby *presidarios* ridin' out ta bid ye good day. 'Twould be the Company of Monclova."

They went back to their kegs and their waiting.

The great stockpile of valuables from the stores of Nacogdoches was a temptation, and though the merchant-militiamen kept an eye on it, there had been some pilferage and looked likely to be more. The shed and tarpaulin lean-tos where the goods were stored were adjacent to the Nacogdoches campsite. The other sites were spread around it on both sides, with some distance separating its upstream side from the next camp. What worried Taylor and Edwards, and the rest, was what might happen to the goods when the militias

337

marched. Who then would defend the merchandise?

Frost Thorn and Will Goyens rode out to the site after dark, slipping away from the shuttered town to find out what was going on at the creek. They found a little sub-camp at the cache, defending it against nimble-fingered friends from other settlements. It was here several of the leaders came together to discuss the mobilization of forces, and it was here John Bowles came to call.

There were perimeter sentries at intervals all around the amassed campsites, but it appealed to the Cherokee's sense of humor to simply slip past them and go right on into camp unannounced. This he did, with fifteen warriors. The sentries never saw the dark forms that passed them by in the night.

Bowles and his party were dressed for the trail, Cherokee-style, and were, as one woodsman would later comment, "as savage a lookin' bunch as ye might ever wanta see."

At the cache fireside Samuel Looney was holding forth on his views of the proper way to drive Mexican colonels when he stopped in mid-sentence, dropped his coffee cup, and said, "Hot damn," scrabbling to reach the rifle propped behind him. The others looked around. There in the firelight were sixteen dark warriors, naked chests gleaming in the flickering glow. They had materialized like ghosts.

John Bowles, Standing Bowl, son of Diwali, the Bowl, war chief of the Texas Cherokee nation, raised a hand and addressed himself directly to Frost Thorn. "Friend of my people, once again your word is good. You have promised a thing would be done, and it was done."

Amid the stares of his companions, Frost Thorn got to his feet, at a loss as to what the Indian was talking

338

about. He raised his hand. *"Osiyo,* John Bowles. We did not know you were coming."

"Of course not," Bowles said in Spanish, and grinned. Switching back to his own language he swept a hand to indicate those with him. "I have brought some who owe a service. Frost Thorn said that the trader Willoughby would do what he said. Gu'nasoquo doubted, and Gu'nasoquo has been proven wrong. It is his wish to make amends."

The scar-faced warrior stepped forward and held out a hand to Thorn. *"Osiyo,* Frost Thorn. It is as Diwali Gadoga says. Your friend Willoughby promised to bring us the one who killed our brother Utsada. You vouched for him. It has been done. The one who killed Utsada has paid. What may we, as clansmen of Utsada, do for you?"

Frost Thorn was thoughtful for a moment, then the corners of his eyes crinkled. He glanced at Taylor, then at Goyens, and nodded.

There would be no more pilfering of the Nacogdoches trade goods stored at Carrizo Creek. Of all the tough men encamped there, of all the ready fighters in the militias arriving, no one or several were about to get past the fifteen Cherokee warriors camped on the cache itself. Some of them raised cain about the Indians being there, but there was little they could do.

Encarnacion Chireno arrived at the camp on Carrizo Creek, accompanied by the Moras, Adolphus Sterne, and Augustus Hotchkiss, recently elected to the *Ayuntamiento* of Nacogdoches. Two other members, Antonio Menchaca and Charles Taylor, already were there. Vicente Cordova and Nathaniel Norris escorted them.

339

After inspecting the Nacogdoches militia, which now was almost fully present, the group sought out the Ayish Bayou camp and Ben Lindsay. Bullock, Bradley, Sandy Horton, and Simal Hopkins joined them there.

"It is no longer possible," Chireno told them, "to tolerate the Commandant of East Texas. We can no longer accept him in Nacogdoches, nor will we recognize his authority in civil matters anywhere in this district. Accordingly, the *Ayuntamiento* of Nacogdoches has declared itself and its town separated from the military command."

"That's fine," Hopkins pointed out, "but now he's still in the town and all you folks are out here."

"He has two hundred soldiers."

"We'll have more militia than that in a day or two," Bullock said. "Then we'll haul him out and send him on his way. Our bunch from Ayish has been ready for a month now to do that."

"My men are ready to head on in there right now." Sam Looney grinned. "Trouble is, what we got here is a mess of different militias. What are we gonna do, have us a foot race to see who gets there first?"

Chireno shook his head. "We propose," he said, "that all our units be combined under a single command. For the present purpose, we need a district militia."

"Keep us from stumblin' over each other, all right," Bullock agreed. "Our boys'd have to have a vote on it, though. The Ayish militia is duly constituted as a unit, and we can't change that without a vote."

"Snow River militia's easier'n that," Looney said. "I just knock some heads, is all."

Simal Hopkins said, earnestly, "I can speak for the Ayes Bawe militia, I guess. I'm the captain. Matter of fact," he added, "I'm all the militia Ayes Bawe has

340

got."

"You take the right flank," Looney said, chuckling, "an' the rest of us'll take what's left."

Chireno ignored the banter. "We are willing to submit our proposal to election," he said.

"It's your town," Bullock said bluntly. "Why don't we all just form up as support to your militia. I'd follow Vicente Cordova. I reckon all of us would."

"Speak for yourself, James," Looney rasped. "I ain't decided that yet." Cordova, seated nearby, glanced quickly at Looney and the two, the Spaniard and the Anglo, held each other's stares for a long moment. There might be a common purpose for these two, but there would never be a meeting of minds.

Chireno raised a hand. "No, I think we must be one unit. We must never let ourselves be classed as revolutionaries, or as insurrectionists. We are not out to overthrow a government. We are out to protect a government, by enforcing civilian authority over a military despot. It must be done properly."

Ben Lindsay nodded. "He's right. If we don't do this proper we'll wind up wishing we'd never done it at all. This isn't Fredonia. This is East Texas, United States of Mexico."

Looney started to make a harsh comment, then decided not to.

"When do we vote?" Bullock asked. "Most everybody ought to be here by tomorrow."

"Tomorrow then."

"In the meantime we got a militia to drill," Bullock said.

The drills, staged in a clearing back from the creek, provided a lively afternoon's entertainment. The units drilled separately, each after its own fashion, as some of the old soldiers among them looked on in utter disbelief. Most of the Anglo men had little use for close-order drill and even less use for command. Each considered himself a law unto himself, and was a stranger to discipline. Most of these men could bark a squirrel at a hundred yards or whip their weight in aborigines, but their attempts at marching in a column were disastrous.

In contrast, the Nacogdoches militia was a well-ordered and well-trained unit. Civilian soldiers, they were nonetheless predominantly Spanish and had two things going for them—the demanding leadership of Vicente Cordova and their natural Iberian love of organized display. Most of them couldn't hit a barn at twenty yards, but they marched, wheeled, and maneuvered with zeal.

"Look at them Meskins," a woodsman growled in disgust. "Gawddam! That there sergeant whistles an' they come runnin' jes' like they was real soldiers an' he was a real sergeant. Don't that beat all?"

"It's 'cause they're a igner'nt people, George," his companion explained. "They cain't help it. They allus picks the smartest one in the crowd to lead all the rest around. It's how the Good Lord patched 'em together."

A third shook his head in sympathy. "Must be pure hell bein' organized."

Across the field several Spanish settlers watched the Anglo maneuvers in amazement. "It is hard to believe that such as these won a war against the British . . . not once, but twice. Look! Their sergeants, their officers, can barely control them. When they do not feel like following an order, they simply ignore it."

"Have pity for them, Luis," a companion said. "They are a primitive people. They probably are doing their best."

It was at Carrizo Creek that a phrase was coined

which would remain long in common usage: *"soldado goddamns."*

While the men of the two factions marveled at each other's inadequacies a small, forgotten third group, watching from the shade near the merchants' cache, was thoroughly enjoying the spectacle. To Gu'nasoquo and his warriors the entire proceeding was the funniest thing they had ever witnessed.

CHAPTER XXX

"Even the fondest toradero does not invite even his best bull into his house."
—Captain Francisco Medina

Piedras fumed at the desertion of Nacogdoches, and raged at the evacuation of all the stores. In his plans he had counted on the supplies in those stores to help him hold off a siege. He got little sympathy from his two senior officers. Medina assured him coldly that there would be no siege at Nacogdoches. Any attacking force would either be driven away immediately or would come right on in almost immediately. There was nothing to keep them out. Musquiz said little, but his very silence angered the colonel. He could sense the contempt beneath it.

The town now was almost deserted except for the garrison. Those few civilians who remained stayed in their houses or went about quietly by the back ways, avoiding the streets. And traffic between Nacogdoches and Carrizo Creek, while covert, was constant. At one point Piedras ordered the town closed and all traffic stopped. The civilians ignored the order and the soldiers had no way to enforce it.

A new copy of the colonel's mandates to the citizens

of Nacogdoches was posted on the *signatorio*. New orders were appended to it. The citizens of Nacogdoches were to return to their homes, the stores were to be returned, and the civil militia was to assemble itself and report to the Commandant for attachment to the military garrison. There was almost no one left to read the orders. Those who did, ignored them.

Padre Jose Antonio Dias de Leon and Doctor Augustin Martinez de Lejarza were brought before the Commandant. "So," Piedras spat out, "you gentlemen are still in town and have not taken to the woods."

Neither commented. They had no wish to set the colonel off on another tirade.

"My patrols tell me the traitors are assembling on Carrizo Creek. I want both of you to remain within the limits of the town. I will not have you going off to join that rabble following the traitor Chireno. Do you understand me?"

"But Colonel," the priest argued, "I cannot remain always in town. I have duties. My interest is men's souls, not their politics."

"Bah! Since when is a priest not involved in politics? Between the Church of Rome and Freemasonry, Mexico has become a den of political intrigue. Your stupid scheming"—he pointed a finger at the padre—"has brought us to the state we are in now—with traitors running loose all around us, treachery even here in our own command, scoundrels everywhere plotting the overthrow of the supreme government. You! As much as anyone I hold you responsible!"

The priest was shocked at the outburst. He dropped his eyes.

"I repeat, you are to remain in your church, doing Church business, and that is all."

"My son . . ."

"And don't call me your son!" Piedras thundered.

345

"Get out!"

Two privates in the outer office cast worried glances at each other. It was a bad day to go before the Commandant for punishment. The sergeant major with them showed no expression. The old priest, eyes downcast, walked through the outer office.

"And if you are not here when I want you, Padre," the colonel roared after him, "I will come after you!"

"And you, Doctor." Piedras brought his attention back to the embarrassed Lejarza. "You have contracted to be the army's surgeon in case of hostilities. I am invoking your contract. You are to remain here and on call at all times."

"I know of no hostilities, Colonel," Lejarza said quietly.

"Then you also are a fool! Nevertheless I have declared, weeks ago, that this entire district is under martial law. You are now in my command. Is that understood?"

"Yes."

"With respect, Doctor! You are in the Army of Mexico now. You will behave as a subordinate!"

"Yes, *mi coronel*."

"Further, you will cease the service of civilians as of now. Unless I give you permission, you will treat no one but the members of this garrison."

Later, Piedras sent for his captains. Francisco Medina, commander of the 12th Battalion, and Renaldo Musquiz, commander of the Company of Monclova, were in full battle dress. The colonel had so ordered it earlier in the day.

"What intelligence have you?"

"Militia companies continue to gather at the creek," Musquiz recited. "Their numbers are not known at this time."

Medina added, "The *Alcalde* has ordered the town

346

emptied. There is a ten-dollar fine on those who remain. A few remain, but effectively the town is empty."

"I know all that. What can you tell me that is new?"

"One of the militia companies at Carrizo Creek," Musquiz said, "is the civil militia of Nacogdoches. Our own citizens." The last was unnecessary, but it was a pleasure to deliver such a report to such a commander.

"So, the militia again has refused to assemble for me."

"They *are* assembling, *mi coronel*. But at Carrizo Creek."

Piedras shot him a murderous look. "You said, Captain, that you do not know the numbers assembled there. I happen to know Ayish Bayou alone has promised one thousand men to support the militia of Cordova."

"That is impossible. There are not that many guns in the entire Ayish Bayou district. I believe your spies are confused."

"What could you know about it?" Piedras asked, silkily. "At least my spies keep me informed. Your patrol tells me nothing. How do you know thousands of Anglo mercenaries are not at this moment crossing into Texas to join this gathering on Carrizo Creek?"

Musquiz's eyes blazed but he held his temper. "I said we do not know precisely how many are on the creek. We do know there are *approximately* three to four hundred."

"Three to four hundred! How can there be three to four hundred when Ayish Bayou alone has sent more than a thousand? How are we to withstand thousands of men in a concerted attack, my captains? I had counted on our militia to defend us, but they have turned on us. I had counted on the Indians to defend us, but something has happened and they will not. They declare themselves neutral. Ah . . ." He pressed his hands to his temples. "You are dismissed."

Outside, Medina said to Musquiz, "His war is not going his way, I am afraid."

Musquiz growled, "Si. A pity he could not keep his war inside his head where it started."

Alone again, Piedras set to work to write another dispatch to the military commander of Coahuila and Texas. During the past weeks he had kept a flood of dispatches going west. Almost nothing had come back. At the moment he did not even know who the military commander was . . . or exactly where. With the troubles in Mexico, little attention was being paid to this tiny outpost garrison alone in the wilderness.

Carefully he detailed—as he saw them—the circumstances of the past week. Much of it he had said before. He repeated the *Ayuntamiento*'s failure to cooperate with him, the failure of the militia to respond to his orders, his own courtesy and civility in dealing with them, and their evasions and disobedience in response. He reported that a thousand colonists had been offered by Ayish Bayou, and the assembly of the men of the east districts. He reported the evacuation of the town, the closing of the stores.

"They are gathering from every direction," he wrote. "I do not know how soon they will begin hostilities. I depend entirely upon my own men, and they are willing to join anybody's cause."

With sudden inspiration he asked the Commandant, with the political leadership of Texas, to come personally to Nacogdoches to intervene. That, he felt, might resolve the problem.

The message was dated and signed: "God and Liberty. Nacogdoches, July 31, 1832. Jose de las Piedras."

When it was completed and on its way, he walked to his window and looked out at the nearly deserted Plaza Principal. One thousand men, from Ayish alone. One thousand Anglo invaders . . . and who knew how many more. He knew what no one else seemed to know. The Anglos were organized. This was part of their plan, to take Texas from Mexico. Why would no one see it? His head ached again, and it brought fury to his eyes.

"You will pay for it!" he screamed. "I'll make you pay!"

The guards outside the Red House didn't even bother to look up.

Colonel Peter Ellis Bean rode into Tenoxtitlan on the Brazos River, followed by his youngest son, Isaac. The boy took both tired mounts and ambled off toward the river to do whatever eleven-year-old boys do while waiting for their fathers.

Tenoxtitlan, twelve miles north of the Camino Real, was one of Mexico's new expansion posts and served as a western trading post for the Indians of East Texas and an eastern trading post for such of the plains tribes as were friendly at any given moment. At the moment there were two short, burly Comanches there under trader's truce, among the several Indians of other tribes. The Comanches were the only ones Bean did not know by name, and when he paused to look them over they gave him the respect sign signifying a man of authority. Though he wore no uniform or emblem, they recognized him as that.

The post was no more than a jumble of log buildings and sheds surrounded by the camps of the various Indians there to trade. The largest trader located at Tenoxtitlan was the John Durst Company out of Nacogdoches.

Lieutenant Colonel Francisco Ruiz appeared at his door and waved to Bean. "Come in out of the heat and have a glass of wine." Bean complied.

"River's up," he said in English as he stretched his legs in the colonel's shaded windway.

"It is a bad time for those downriver," Ruiz said. "There has been flooding and there may be more. The Comanche say the heavens have opened this summer in the Llano Estacado. You see how red the water is? They say the land is bleeding."

"More like the top half of north Texas is on its way to Brazoria," Bean allowed. "Are you well?"

"*Si,* my great belly is well, my spirits are high, everything with me is fine. I wish I could say the same for our country. You know, I suppose, that full revolution is going on in Mexico now."

"Yes." Bean nodded and sat in one of the wide hide-back chairs in the windway. The shade, the breeze were comfortable. "Just what we need. Another revolution. You know why I am here, Francisco. I am riding circuit, looking for volunteers to help the Nacogdoches militia."

"*Si,* I assumed. I have seen it coming. First Bradburn at Anahuac a month ago, now Piedras. It is no surprise."

"And your position?"

Ruiz shrugged. "Colonel Piedras has not asked me for assistance. I do not think he will, because I might refuse. Too many times I have tried to tell him he was wrong in his dealings with Nacogdoches. People will not stand for such abuses, particularly not the people Piedras must deal with where he is. He has not listened. It is his concern, not mine. Soon I will close this post and go south. When I reach Bexar I will put myself at the service of General Santa Anna." Midway along, Ruiz had lapsed into Spanish. It made no difference to Bean.

"You are a *Santanista* then. I thought so."

"I am a Mexican," Ruiz corrected. "I do not know if

350

this Santa Anna will be good for Mexico. I do know that Bustamente is not."

"I wish you would remain in Texas," Bean said. "If Piedras is driven out, that leaves only you. Between the Anglos east of us and the Plains Indians west, we need a military presence."

"This little post?" Ruiz chuckled. "It would be nothing. It would be worse than nothing, because people would see it here and depend on it to do what it cannot do. Better they know they are alone, and depend upon themselves. You saw the Comanches out there, trading? You think they do not know exactly our strength here? No, alone in Texas my men and I are wasted. At least in Mexico we can count for something."

Bean nodded and sipped his wine. Ruiz regarded him shrewdly.

"Peter Bean, I think you are out this way for more than to deliver a 'God and Liberty' call."

Bean smiled. "Of course I am. There will be a fight at Nacogdoches, and the Indians know it as well as anyone. I don't want my Indians involved in it."

"You think they will get involved?"

"Mostly, no. I was worried about the Cherokee, but their position now is clear. They are neutral. The Shawnee will stand with them, I think, and most of the others. Oh, there will be some young bucks hanging on the sidelines, wanting some action, but I don't worry about them. No, I am concerned about the Kickapoo. I went to their grounds, but they were gone. They still could be trouble."

Ruiz nodded. With the Kickapoo's tribal hatred of white people, they were an uncertainty. If a fight broke out, it was entirely possible the Kickapoos might jump into the middle of it, fighting both sides, just to kill as many whites as possible. Even the lordly Cherokees had

351

not been able to exercise much discipline over the Kickapoos.

"I know where some of them are," Ruiz said. "I can set you on the trail if you like. They have been here, and have gone back east."

Night was approaching on July 31st as Pete Bean and Isaac approached the Trinity River. They slowed their horses to a cautious walk and Bean sniffed at the air. The wind was from the east, and someone was camped at the crossing ahead. Motioning Isaac forward, Bean leaned toward the boy, pointed down toward the river, and said, "Who?"

Silently Isaac slipped from his horse and crept forward, disappearing in the dusk. A few minutes later he was back. "Indians."

"What kind?"

"Kickapoo."

His father nodded. The boy was learning well. "How do you know?"

"Indians because the camp don't smell as bad as a white man's camp," Isaac said, keeping his voice down, reciting. "Kickapoos because that's who we're looking for, and because they're downstream from the crossing. Cherokee or Shawnee would be upstream."

There were four Indians in camp. Bean and his son scuffed their boots, rattled harness, and made as much noise as was seemly coming in. They didn't want to surprise the Indians. At the edge of the cleared wash where the fire burned Bean called, "I am Pete Indian Agent."

A large man by the fire raised his hand. "Come in, Pete Indian Agent. Eat with us."

Bean was about as safe among the Kickapoo as any white man was likely to be. Like all the tribes, they

352

respected the Indian law of traders and diplomats, and they saw Bean as both. Therefore he could come and go as he pleased . . . usually. Close cousins of the Sauk and Fox tribes, the fierce Kickapoo were in no way tamed, simply reduced by the advance of the whites across their receding lands. With this reduction had grown a hatred for white people that few tribes, not even the most recalcitrant Shawnee, could match. They were warlike, arrogant, and bitter, and more aware than anyone else that they had been reduced to stealing and occasional stealthy pillage and murder.

Bean had difficulty with their Algonquian tongue, similar in its syllables to the Shawnee but far removed in its usages. But one of the Kickapoo, Skunk Man, spoke some English and a little Spanish.

"You far from home, Pete Indian Agent," this one said. "You come as friend or Indian agent?"

"As always," Bean said, "I come as whichever is needed at the time."

"Then be tonight as friend," Skunk Man said.

Bean and Isaac got their horses unsaddled and tied. It was all right now. For this night at least they were accepted. There was food and they shared it.

"You come from Tenoxtitlan," Bean said, indicating the pile of trade goods and the seven pack animals tied with the Indians' four saddle horses.

"Sure," Skunk Man told him. "Indian can't trade at Nacogdoches now. Must wait. We don't wait for anybody. We go Tenoxtitlan. Nacogdoches traders all closed up. Hell with them."

Bean had been gone. It was the first he had heard of it. "All? John Durst? Frost Thorn?"

"All closed up. Goods all gone from town. Damn stuff all gone."

"Your people have moved from their grounds."

"Sure. Too close to damn Cherokee. Damn Cherokee

353

do wrong, say Kickapoo give back damn stuff from white man, say Kickapoo stay out of white man's war, say Kickapoo do this, don't do that damn thing."

Ah, Pete considered. Diwali was enforcing his position.

"Damn Cherokee always doin' that," Skunk Man went on. "Damn Cherokee come say we give up what we got from white trader Will Be. Damn Cherokee send man to take away. Hell. Damn. Kickapoo move out. Too damn close to damn Cherokee."

"One man?" Bean asked.

"Damn right one man. Man was Egg. You know Egg, Pete Indian Agent?"

Bean nodded. That explained it.

"Will your people stay out of the white men's war?"

"Hell yes. Damn Cherokee say stay out, not enough of us tell damn Cherokee go to hell. But we watch, you damn right. Do this man Skunk Man good to see white men kill each other. Be plenty good, damn right."

The hard eyes directed across the campfire glowed cruel with its light and Bean shook his head. There would be no arguing with Skunk Man. At any rate, he knew what he needed to know.

CHAPTER XXXI

*"Sure we need an army. We got one. We're it.
What we don't need is that other one."*
—Samuel Looney

Tuesday, the 31st day of July, 1832, dawned clear at Carrizo Creek. The National Militia, made up of militia units from Nacogdoches, Ayish Bayou, Tenehaw, Sabine, Bevil's Diggings, and Snow River, along with Simal Hopkins from Ayes Bawe, gathered to elect its officers.

The gathering place was a modest rise at a clearing on the bank of Carrizo Creek, a place called Pine Hill. Two hundred and fifteen men gathered there, about half of them from Nacogdoches.

On the rise, *Alcalde* Encarnacion Chireno raised his hands for quiet. Considering the impatient nature of most of his audience, he came straight to the point. "Men of the District of East Texas, the United States of Mexico! On this day we elect the leaders of this National Militia. Since yesterday, men have gone among you, advising of the qualifications of those considered candidates. You have had all night to consider your choices. Are there nominations now for the chief officer, who shall be commissioned colonel?"

A voice in the ranks called out, "Most ever'body I've talked to favors ol' Jim Bullock. He's got experience with Andy Jackson."

"I say Jim Bullock!" another shouted.

"Jim Bullock for colonel!" It was a planned campaign. A number of the Anglos didn't want to chance having a Spanish chief officer.

"I still like Stephen Prather," an Anglo protested from the sidelines. "He's the fightin'est damn volunteer we got here."

Someone near the center of the group called back. "That ain't no good, George. He's a fighter, but he ain't no way political!"

"So?"

"You got to be political to run two herds together."

"Let's all speak Spanish!" someone shouted.

"Hell, learn English!"

Bullock, standing near Vicente Cordova, glanced at him. Cordova spread his hands and shrugged. Chireno was trying to get some semblance or order into the proceedings, but was rapidly losing ground. Most of the hubbub was from the Anglos, but their Spanish counterparts were at a loss how to react. Alexander Horton stalked up the hill to stand beside Chireno. Without hesitation he raised his rifle and fired, just over the heads of one of the more boisterous clusters.

"Shut your mouth, damn it!" he ordered into the following silence. Then, sticking a piece of patch cloth into his mouth to moisten it, he poured powder from his horn and began reloading.

"I have the name of James Bullock in nomination for the position of colonel," Chireno said gravely. "Are there any further nominations?"

A Spanish man near the front asked, *"Señor* Cordova, would you like to be colonel?"

"Not particularly, Jose, thank you," Cordova said.

"Do I hear further nominations?" Chireno asked again.

"No!"

"He'll do. Get on with it!"

"Bullock for colonel!"

Alexander Horton frowned as he cut his patch, set a ball, and rammed it home. The noise was building again. But Chireno quelled it with raised arms. "Then all in favor of James Bullock for colonel say 'Aye'!"

"Aye!" It was a roar.

"All opposed, say 'No'!"

"No!" This also was a roar.

"I think we better get a show of hands," Ben Lindsay told Chireno.

Running unopposed, James Bullock was elected colonel by a vote of seventy-two to sixty-five. Seventy-eight abstained, unsure how to resolve the issue or—in most cases—what the issue was.

Chireno bowed and stepped aside. "The assembly is yours, Colonel Bullock."

Bullock stepped up. "Thank you, *Alcalde*." Then to the men, "I have met with other unit captains. We all agree on organization. The National Militia should have five captains, a lieutenant, and six ensigns. Nominations are in order."

It took the better part of an hour and three more reloadings by Alexander Horton, but they got a contingent of officers elected. Vicente Cordova and four men of English or Scotch-Irish descent were captains. All of the ensigns were Spanish, except for Adolphus Sterne, who would be sent home when the shooting started.

The structure of officers lasted three hours. Following a separate meeting of the Anglo militia units, fourteen more officers were named—three lieutenant colonels, two majors, five captains, four more lieutenants, and another ensign to take Sterne's place when he went home. Every additional officer was Anglo.

"We needed to keep control of this shootin' match," Looney said as he presented the amended list to Bullock. "Can't be sure them Spaniards would actual fight against Spaniards."

Haden Edwards was aghast. "Mister Looney, have you read any history at all? My God, sir, the Spanish *always* fight the Spanish. At every opportunity."

"Look at this list," Bullock complained. "Twenty-seven for God's sake officers! Even if you don't count Wyatt Hanks twice, which you did. Hell, one more meeting and there won't be anybody left for anybody to give orders to."

"Then let's stop meetin' and go beat hell out of Piedras," Looney said.

Bullock shook his head. "Not yet. It wouldn't be legal. The *Alcaldes* say somebody has to call on Piedras first, and give him a chance to back out."

"Who's gonna do that?"

"A committee, of course. Who else?"

To keep them occupied, Bullock assembled his officers at a point midway between the Nacogdoches militia and the east settlements and Neches camps . . . halfway between a hundred frolicking Anglos and a hundred glowering Spanish Mexicans. They would stay there until the order came to move. They would keep the allied militias from killing one another.

Late in the evening—July 31, 1832—three riders left the encampment heading for Nacogdoches. Isaac Burton, Phillip Sublett, and Henry Augustine were the committee selected to call upon Colonel Piedras.

It was fully dark when Burton, Sublette, and Augustine arrived at the near-silent town. What they had to do was give Jose de las Piedras an honorable chance to stop sucking eggs. What they also intended to do was get out of town afterward, with their skins. They had developed a plan on the way in.

They scouted the place carefully, marking where the guards, the patrols, the watchers might be. Then leaving their mounts behind Will Goyens's dark shop, they made their way to the Red House. A lamp burned in Piedras's office. A lone sentry stood by the outside door.

"Do you suppose there's more than him inside?" Sublette whispered. No one answered. Who could tell?

The first inkling the sentry had of trouble was when something prodded him in the back, a hand reached past and relieved him of his musket, and a quiet voice said, "Don't you move, sonny."

There was no one in the outer office.

Colonel Piedras, in full uniform, was at his desk, papers piled high around him. He looked up and froze. Two men stood before him, both Anglos, both armed. "What do you want?"

"Keep your voice down, please, Colonel," Isaac Burton asked respectfully. "We are representatives of the National Militia, duly appointed as envoys. We have two questions. First, will you agree to support General Santa Anna?"

Piedras's eyes widened and his face paled. The corners of his mouth grew white. With visible constraint he held himself in check. "You are envoys of nothing. A bunch of traitors and adventurers. I will remember your faces."

Patiently Burton repeated the question. "Will you agree to support General Santa Anna?"

"I will not!"

Burton nodded. "And secondly, will you agree to receive appropriate delegations from the National Militia under a flag of truce, honorably, according to the articles of war?"

Piedras seethed, but the rifle in Augustine's hands was unwavering. "I see no honorable delegation."

"We are calling in advance, Colonel. We need your word. Will you agree?"

Piedras half rose behind his desk, then dropped into his chair again. He had no choice. "You have my word of honor," he gritted. "But only applying to credentialed delegations. This does not apply to the two of you."

"Three," Augustine corrected him. "That's all right. We'll look out for ourselves. Write it."

His hands shaking with fury, Piedras wrote and signed a safe-passage permit for qualified representatives of "the subjects this day gathered at Carrizo Creek." He refused to name the National Militia. Burton accepted the paper and nodded. By the time Piedras, the rifle no longer pointing at him, could reach his sword and scream for his guards, they were gone.

CHAPTER XXXII

*"Summer storms . . . they can get fierce
in Texas."*

The options now were clear. Colonel Piedras would surrender his garrison at Nacogdoches to the National Militia, and nominally to the cause of General Santa Anna, or Colonel Piedras would be attacked.

On the evening of August 1st Encarnacion Chireno stood before the motley army assembled on Carrizo Creek. Isaac Burton's report and the pass he had brought back cleared the way for the final formality.

"There is no further toleration of Colonel Piedras," Chireno told them. "He has one choice. He can declare for Santa Anna and surrender his force to an officer of choice, or we will take his force and he will not choose at all. Either way, the garrison at Nacogdoches will either fly the flag of Santa Anna or leave. Either way, Colonel Piedras will leave. We have had enough of him."

There was applause from the mostly Spanish end of the audience, ragged cheering from the mostly Anglo end of it. "Agreed!" "Talk on!" "Bravo!" "Thet Spaniard gits right down to it, don't he?"

"I think it's time we stopped drinkin' and started fightin'," someone shouted, in English.

"Sure, we kin drink after the fight!"

"I'll drink to that!"

"What are the Anglos yelling about?"

"*¿Quien sabe?* They are very emotional people. Always they are yelling or goddamning."

The civil leaders, Chireno and Lindsay directing them, had prepared a document, a statement of intent. In Mexico, the difference between spontaneous rebellion and a noble cause was proper documentation. The statement read:

"At a large meeting of the inhabitants of the districts of Ayzes, Tenaha, Sabine, Bevil Settlement, and Nacogdoches, assembled pursuant to an invitation of the municipality of Nacogdoches, on Carrizo Creek, on the 2nd day of August, 1832 . . ."

"This ain't the second, it's the first. Has been all day."

"Tomorrow will be the second, *señor,* and tomorrow this will be delivered."

"Early?"

"Early."

"Fine . . . get on with it."

" . . . for the purpose of defending the civil authorities of the State and the invaluable rights of their fellow citizens against military usurpation. A committee was appointed to draw and report such resolutions as may seem appropriate and suitable. The said committee reported the following resolutions which were unanimously adopted, to wit:

"Taking into consideration the repeated violations of the Constitution and laws of our country by military despots, and sympathizing with the noble and patriotic efforts in favor of the republic of one of our most illustrious and virtuous officers and fellow citizens . . ."

"Who's that you're talkin' about?"

"General Santa Anna."

."He ain't illustrious and virtuous. He's a Mexican general."

"Shut up, George! Read on, there, feller."

". . . and fellow citizens, we pledge ourselves to make common cause to him; believing this course to be due to our families and the posterity; and therefore be it resolved:

"First. That we pledge our country and each and every one of us, in presence of Almighty God to use every justifiable means in our power to defend under the flag of Santa Anna the Constitution and the republican federal rights of the State against military usurpation, to reestablish the civil authorities, and to protect them against the interference and the harshness of an arbitrary power.

"Second. That whereas Colonel Piedras, commander of the garrison of Nacogdoches, has declined to embrace the cause of the meritorious Santa Anna . . ."

"The what kind of Santa Anna?"

"Meritorious."

"Bullshit."

"Shut up."

". . . and furthermore is making every effort to oppose it, by means of an appeal to the Indians who murder indiscriminately every age and sex . . ."

"Amen!"

"Hell they do. They don't do that!"

"Some 'em do."

"Which ones?"

"Shut up, all of you! Read on, *señor.*"

". . . every, ah . . . ah, yes . . . sex. Every age and sex . . . we consider him as an enemy to the constitutional principles, as advocated by *Señor* Santa Anna:

therefore, be he removed from his command.

"Third. That a commission of two officers be appointed to demand Colonel Piedras to surrender the command of his battalion to some officer who shall receive it and the flag of Santa Anna; and in case the said *Señor* Piedras should decline to do so, we shall unite our endeavors to compel him, by the force of arms."

"If we wasn't already figurin' on that, what'n hell we been doin' here for three days?"

"I been here five."

"That makes it sound like we just now got around to thinkin' on this, though!"

"What are the Anglos yelling about now, do you suppose?"

"*¿Quien sabe?*"

"Shut up, all of you!"

"Yeah, but he ain't tellin' it like it is. Does that say . . ."

"Sandy . . ."

Ka-blam!

"Thank you, Sandy. Go ahead, *Señor.*"

"Gracias. Fourth. That a copy of the foregoing resolutions be furnished to the Supreme Authorities of the State, trusting that they will approve our principles and motives, and our readiness in sacrificing our lives for the cause of our country, its Constitution, and laws.

"It is signed by James Gaines, Mican Charima, Benjamin Lindsay, Adolphus Sterne, and Antonio Menchaca, countersigned by Jose M. Mora."

"Is that all of it?"

"*Si, señor.*"

"Move we approve."

"Second."

"Yeah, but he still makes it sound like we . . . "

"Sandy . . ."

364

"Never mind. Aye."

"Aye."

It was called "An Act of Liberty."

Very early on August 2nd, Samuel S. Davis and Henry William Augustine rode up to the barricades, their white flag of truce hanging limp in the moist dawn. A sergeant ordered them to dismount and conducted them to Sub-lieutenant Silvestre Leal, Officer of the Day.

"You come to see Colonel Piedras?"

"We didn't come to see no *teniente segundo!*" Davis exploded. Then he shook his head and grinned. "I'm a little nervous."

Leal led the Anglos into town and turned them over to Captain Francisco Medina outside the Red House. Medina nodded. "Sam. Henry. Are you messengers of war?"

"That's up to your colonel, Captain." Augustine handed Medina a folded piece of paper. "I expect this to be honored."

"A safe conduct from the colonel? How in the world did you . . . never mind. Of course it will be honored. Come in."

The colonel was eating breakfast. After a single, peremptory glance he ignored the men, keeping them standing until he was finished. Then he looked at them again, with contempt. "More Anglo traitors from the National Militia. What does your mighty army demand this time?"

Davis, angry from the waiting, was just as blunt. "The legal civil authorities of these districts demand your resignation. You are allowed four hours in which time you may turn your command over to another officer. The time is now seven o'clock . . . or was when we came in. Your response will be taken before eleven."

Piedras singled out Augustine. "I have seen you in this office before. I could arrest you here and now. I could arrest both of you. I could have you executed and buried before eleven o'clock."

"We carry a flag of truce, Colonel," Augustine said levelly, "as well as your own safe conduct. Even barbarians honor the flag of truce."

"Out!" Piedras exploded. "Get out of my office!" As they turned to leave, their duty done, Piedras stood. "Wait! I will tell you now. I do not need four hours to know my duty." Fumbling around for paper he dipped a quill and wrote furiously. When it was done he handed the paper to Captain Medina, who in turn handed it to Davis.

"Now, out!" the colonel rasped at them. "I will not surrender my command—not to foreigners, not to invaders, not to traitors . . . not to anyone!"

Medina saw them safely back to the barricades and their horses. "I have many friends out there." He waved eastward, toward Carrizo. "I will not enjoy seeing them die."

When Sam Davis and Henry Augustine rejoined the National Militia they ignored Chireno, Lindsay, and the other civil authorities there. From now on, this was a military operation. They went straight to James Bullock, who called John Durst to help translate the response from Piedras. Piedras had written, "My officers and men are determined to support the Government, the Constitution, and laws, as they have sworn to do. They will admit no *pronunciamento* whatever. The four-hour delay will expire at 11 A.M.

"God and Liberty: Nacogdoches, August 1st, 1832. Jose de las Piedras."

"He thinks this is the first day of August." Bullock mused. "it's the second, isn't it?"

366

Durst glanced at him. "Yes, It's the second. Does it matter?"

Shortly before eleven o'clock Colonel Piedras came forth from the Red House in full battle dress. Calmly, followed by his orderly and two escorts, he inspected the preparations, the fortifications on the east road, the readiness of his cavalry, the placement of his infantry. He called his officers to him and requested comment.

"I strongly suggest, *mi coronel,*" Musquiz told him, "that we take the initiative."

"In what manner, *Capitán?*" For the first time in months — maybe in years — they saw the Piedras who had once been a first-rate officer of Mexico. The issue now was resolved. All else was put aside and the commandant was, in a way, himself again.

"Captain Medina and I have discussed this," Musquiz said. "We believe there are no more than three hundred or so men out there. If they approach from the east, they must converge at a point just beyond the barricades. I could take the Company of Monclova at full charge and split their ranks at that point, then wheel to come back through them. We could devastate them, *mi coronel.*"

"And at that point," Medina added, "I could attack with two companies of infantry, one frontal and one from the right, where the dry wash intersects. I believe we could end this affair quickly, sir, and without unnecessary bloodshed."

Piedras nodded. "Your tactics are faultless, my captains. But, as before, you have misjudged our enemy. That is not three hundred men out there, nor is it a gaggle of angry peasants as I believe you suppose. They have been careful to have you think that. No, gentlemen, this is to be a full assault. There are several thousand American mercenaries behind that pathetic militia. They are waiting to trap us. No. Thank you for your comments. But in my judgment this militia action is only a feint, to draw us out. Texas is being invaded from the United States of the North. There may be— probably are—regular troops behind those mercenaries. We are completely outnumbered.

"We will defend."

He turned away. Medina and Musquiz glanced at each other, sadly. Mercenaries? Regular troops? They knew what was out there. A few hundred irate civilians organized as the National Militia. Nothing more. For a moment it had seemed the old Piedras was among them again. But it was only the usual Piedras in battle dress.

Shortly after eleven, Will Irwin led a handful of Red-landers through the woods along a shallow wash and directly into Nacogdoches. As they passed Adolphus Sterne's house the German came out onto his porch. With his men deployed to watch for troops, Irwin rode up to speak to him.

"Tell them do not come from the east, Will," Sterne told him. "Those barricades on the eastern entrances are the strongest point. Come around north to Bonita Creek, and in that way. You will be behind the main body."

Irwin nodded, beckoned to his men, and they rode a short way and then disappeared into brush. Sterne watched them go, then went back into his silent house. He had only given advice. He had not fired on the flag of Mexico.

The National Militia in a body left Pine Hill and moved west to near the edge of town, arriving about two o'clock. Vicente Cordova objected to moving in directly from the east. He knew how the defenses were organized, and Will Irwin's report had confirmed it. Cordova was an experienced Indian fighter. He urged

368

circling to the weakest point, then attacking from there. John Durst agreed with him. So did Stephen Prather. Bullock was the colonel. His orders stood.

When the militia reached the edge of town, its forward companies broke and tried to rush the barricades. Soldiers of the 12th Battalion opened fire, driving them back. As they tried to regroup and withdraw, the barricades were drawn inside and a unit of the Company of Monclova charged through, almost among them, then wheeled and disappeared back between barricades. It was the first clash.

One of the Nacogdoches men was down and several had injuries. Bullock changed his mind about attacking from the east.

Leaving Samuel Lewis in charge of about a hundred men outside the barricades, Bullock took the remaining one hundred and seventy, withdrew quietly to the rear, then swung around to the north.

At the east barricades Lewis's men spread across the road and up both shoulders, pushing forward, firing as they moved. The soldiers' musketry had far greater firepower than the slow-loading long rifles of the militia, but when the rifles spoke they were deadly. Here and there a soldier dropped behind the barricades.

Captain Medina sent a runner back the fifty yards to where Captain Musquiz was regrouping his Company of Monclova. There were not enough men out there. The militia had split itself. Musquiz received the message and nodded. Dividing the Company of Monclova into three squads, he began a prowl of the town. A few infantry followed.

From the north screen of the forest, Bullock led his men along North Street, the Camino Norte, to the intersection of the shallow ravine where brush would give some concealment. On foot now, they turned and penetrated to the corner of the church plaza, where Will

Irwin and his seven men joined them. As a body, they passed the church, then spread. Vicente Cordova led a large party along the ravine toward the old Stone House. Sandy Horton stopped suddenly.

"I hear a French horn."

Before any could respond, a cavalry charge pounded down upon them. Captain Renaldo Musquiz was in the lead. The militiamen threw themselves against the walls of the ravine, their panicked shots going wild. From the left a squad of eight foot soldiers fired a volley from behind a picket fence, then retreated to reload. The man behind Horton in the ravine cursed and passed out, blood flowing from his right arm.

Musquiz's cavalry unit charged to within feet of the embedded militiamen. The charge broke there and someone shouted, "He's down! Their captain is down!" Four rifle balls had taken Renaldo Musquiz, almost simultaneously, hurling him from his horse. Another cavalryman was down near him, but was dragging himself away. Musquiz lay still.

Coming out of the ravine the militiamen, those with loads in their guns, fired at the retreating soldiers. Fire and load, fire and load, hold the ravine and advance. Patchcloth dangling from dry lips, ramrods dancing, sweat pouring, and blood seeping, they moved forward a step at a time.

At the barricades Lewis's forces, with long-rifle fire from the flanking brush, drove the infantry back. One moment they were outside, the next they were in, and the soldiers withdrew before them in a frenzy Captain Medina and his officers could not control. Now the mettle of the 12th Battalion showed itself, and failed. Too few were true soldiers. Too many were *presidarios*. Under fire, they did not hold. Some broke and ran.

One private, fresh from a Mexican jail, ran only a few steps before he found himself at the point of a sword held by Colonel Piedras. Terrified, the soldier tried to defend himself with his useless musket. Piedras's sword danced and a bright scar appeared on the soldier's face. "Turn and fight!" Piedras roared. The soldier turned, saw the militia streaming through barricades behind him, and went to his knees. Piedras turned away, sickened.

Bullock and Cordova held at the Stone Fort and Bullock sent runners to the other units. Hold and regroup. Hold. It was moving too fast.

As the summer sun slanted to the west the firing diminished. The National Militia held nearly half the town, a wedge from the Plaza Principal to the east edges of Nacogdoches. Militia occupied the Stone Fort, Thorn's store, Sim's tavern, Robert's store and a number of houses. They had been stopped at the Quartel, the clustered military centrality extending to the barracks, some houses, and the Red House. The houses beyond were blank, closed and in some cases boarded.

In weeds at the edge of the Camino Real, waiting to be found, lay a body torn by musket balls. The *Alcalde* of Nacogdoches, Encarnacion Chireno, would not see his peaceful town again. For him it was all over.

The Bright Lady had claimed others as well. Will Hathaway had died at the barricades, a wounded soldier's bayonet through his throat. The tiny settlement of Ayes Bawe would not see its one-man militia again. Simal P. Hopkins lay broken on the bank of the dry ravine, a load in his old rifle that had refused to fire.

There was no chance to make a thorough count just yet. There still was much to do.

Smoke hung in the evening air. Shots echoed in the fading light.

Through the night Cordova's Nacogdoches militia tallied the score, piecing together reports. Twenty-five or more soldiers were dead, they believed, and three — possibly four of the National Militia. There was no accounting the number of wounded soldiers, but the militia had five seriously wounded, including at least one who might not see the morning.

Cordova told those around him, "Renaldo Musquiz had already decided to declare for Santa Anna. He was going to see his company to Bexar, then declare."

"Why didn't he do it right here then?" Sam Looney growled.

Cordova said quietly, "Because he was an honorable man."

"Crazy as hell, if you ask me," Looney blurted out. Cordova's eyes flashed, but then he turned and walked away.

"Ease up on these Spanish, Sam," Bullock advised.

"Hell, we might need 'em right now, but not for long. I feel it. After this, us Anglos will have East Texas, an' I reckon we can keep it."

"Sam, we got nothin' but what we always had. We are settlers here, not invaders. How many of our boys you think would give up bein' Mexican citizens?"

"Not many, I reckon," Looney conceded. "We got nothin' ag'in Mexico, or ag'in bein' in Texas, but we ought to be running it, that's all."

"Sam, how about checking it out out there."

"Don't need to. I can hear it."

"Yeah, well spread the word to cut that out. It's too dark to see anything. They're just wastin' powder."

The Plaza Principal was dark and deserted, a shadowed no-man's-land. The militia held the east perimeter, the troops held the rest. They sat the night out that way, satisfied. Neither side sent out patrols. Several times during the night Vicente Cordova went to a darkened window and peered out, puzzled. But when someone asked what was bothering him, he just shook his head.

372

With first light, Captain Wyatt Hanks stepped out of the back door of Thorn's store. Some of the men already had a small fire going and were boiling coffee. It was going to be a hot day.

"I ain't heard no shootin' yet this mornin'," Hanks allowed. "Sure is quiet out there." He beckoned to John Thompson. "John, how about you take some men and swing around there on the north. Don't show yourselves."

"Sure thing." Thompson gulped his coffee. "What we lookin' for?"

"Soldiers."

"Soldiers?"

"Any kind. Bring us some, if you can lay hands on 'em. One or two be enough."

"You got 'em. Almazon, Dan, you get to come with me." He turned to John Roberts. "This here's your town, John. You want to be scout?"

Using buildings for cover, the four of them, Johnson and Roberts, Almazon Huston and Daniel Vancel, moved out. Their passing marred the silver dew of morning.

They went along a side street, wary in the stillness. Motion at the corner of the Plaza startled them, but it was only Padre de Leon, coming their way. "Padre," Roberts demanded, "what are you doing out on the street?"

The old priest shrugged. "During the night, Colonel Piedras moved his soldiers out. They have gone. But they left behind their dead and wounded. I have come to find Doctor Hendrick. Where is he, please?"

"Over at the Stone House. You saying the soldiers have gone, all of them?"

"All who could travel. The rest are dead or need help." Turning away, the priest walked on toward the Stone House. Thompson sent Dan Vancel to report to

373

Hanks, while he and the others continued their reconnoiter. The military corrals were empty. There was no sound from the Quartel area. Thompson sent Huston to report to Hanks, and then he and Roberts sat down to wait. They weren't about to enter any of those buildings alone.

They both jumped when a door opened down the street. A woman came out, and walked toward them. Graying hair glinted under her *mantilla*. She came up to where they stood.

"*Señor* Roberts, good morning. Do you happen to know the width of the street there where it enters the Plaza?"

"*Buenas dias, Señora* Ybarbo," Roberts stuttered, sure he had misunderstood her Spanish. "The street?"

"*Si*. There where it enters the Plaza. How wide is it?"

He shrugged. "Maybe it is thirty feet, maybe a little more."

She considered. "Yes, that will do. Thank you, *señor*." She turned away, back toward her house.

CHAPTER XXXIII

"Sometimes it is best to be overestimated."
— Vicente Cordova

When the National Militia advanced on those buildings held by wounded soldiers, an army sergeant waved a white flag from the door of the barracks. When it drew no fire he stepped out and leaned against the wall for support.

Men ran to the Red House and kicked in the door. Piedras was gone. The army was gone, leaving behind it one dead captain, two dead sergeants, twenty-three dead privates, and a number of wounded.

Bullock called for Sam Looney. "Sam, take some men and follow them soldiers. Don't bother 'em, just help 'em on their way. I'm sure all he's trying to do is get to Bexar."

"Right." Looney grinned.

"And I mean it, Sam. Don't try to tackle them."

"We're on our way." Looney grinned again.

Alexander Horton stepped forward. "I'm one of 'em."

"Fair enough," Looney said. Stepping out into the Plaza he roared, "Henry Augustine! George Jones! John Noilin! John Roberts! Horatio Hanks! James

375

Bradshaw! George Lewis! Jack Thompson! To me!" Looking around he added, "You too, Isaac Burton! And Bill Lloyd! You boys get your mounts. We're gonna follow the soldiers."

Hiram Brown came running as well. "Not without me, you ain't."

"Sure thing, Hiram. Saddle up an' let's git."

Alexander Horton was in the saddle and moving before the bulk of them got started. Horatio Hanks was right behind him. Sweeping around the plaza, they found where the soldiers had pulled out, south from the town and then angling west.

"Horatio," Horton called. "Get back there and tell Looney they're on the John Durst Road."

Hanks ignored him, coming forward to see for himself. The tracks were clear. "All right," the phlegmatic younger Hanks conceded. "I'll tell 'em. But this ain't the John Durst Road."

Horton's head came up sharply. He looked around. "The hell it ain't. This is the John Durst Road sure as shootin'."

"Well. I don't call it that."

"Then what do you call it?"

"I don't call it anything. I never paid no mind to it before."

"Horatio." Horton glowered. "You could aggravate the ears off a ostrich."

"Ostriches is like big turkeys," Hanks said levelly. "They ain't got any ears."

"Go!"

Hanks went.

With Horton riding scout, Roberts moving up at times to join him, the militiamen rode hard. Looney had no intention of letting Piedras get away. Bullock wanted it ended without further bloodshed, but Looney and most of his group had the smell of gunpowder in their nostrils and they weren't through yet.

Crossing Loco Creek at a run, the remaining men hard on their heels, Horton and Roberts suddenly hard-reined their mounts. They had run right up on the heels of the retreating Mexican army. Their companions slid and skidded in among them, and two or three raised rifles and opened fire. They were fourteen men against an army of regulars but, as a matter of fact, at that moment none of them thought about that.

At the firing, the rear troops scattered and ran. Colonel Piedras, at the head of his retreating column, swung around in his saddle and barked immediate orders. Squads about, form and fire, field defense perimeter. Some of the muskets thudded, but the militiamen had backed off out of sight to reload and rethink.

Captain Medina said, "Colonel, break off. We do not know the size of the forces behind them."

"We will stand," ordered Piedras. "They are a handful."

"Impossible, Colonel, even if they are a few. We are in the clear and they are mobile. With those long rifles they can stand off and butcher us."

Piedras nodded. "Withdraw!" he ordered. At times bravery was not enough.

The Anglos watched the army retreat down the road. Looney called to Roberts, "John, how far from here to Durst's Ferry on the Angelina?"

"About seven miles, I reckon."

"Then let's get to movin'. We'll circle, and be at the ferry waitin' for them to cross. Sandy, you an' John lead out again."

Keeping to the forest, staying off the road, the fourteen men pushed their mounts steadily, covering the miles. When they reached the Angelina River they swam across, and circled back downstream to where they had a view of Durst's ferry. It was untended. John Durst

377

had ordered it closed several days ago. That would make no difference to the approaching soldiers. They would man it themselves.

Belly-down on the ridge above the west bank, they concealed themselves and waited.

"I don't think Bullock wants us doin' this, exactly," Horton commented to Roberts.

"Bullock's still back in town. Looney's in charge out here."

Horton held up a hand to those behind him. He was concealed from view from the east bank. "I see three soldiers. One of 'em is a sergeant. Pass the word."

Looney nodded when he got the report. He sent word back that no one was to fire. He didn't want three men. He wanted the whole hundred and fifty or more that Piedras had with him.

The three Mexican soldiers rode slowly up to the silent ferry crossing. Sergeant Marcos Sanchez led. All was quiet. Satisfied, he and the other two dismounted and led their horses to the river's edge to drink. No one knew which of the militia fired first, but in a roar of rifle fire all three soldiers were dropped where they stood. Horton jumped to his feet, raging. "Gawddamned bloodthirsty bastards! Just can't wait to shoot somebody, can you?"

"Sandy, dammit, git down!" Looney yelled at him. "There'll be more comin' around that bend any minute!"

Beyond the bend, Piedras heard the firing and knew that his scouts had run into trouble. He had no idea of the force against him or where they were. But he knew he had to get his command across the river. "Form platoons!" he yelled at Medina. "Prepare to attack by platoons!"

Medina wheeled his mount toward his colonel, followed by Lieutenant Juan Gallardo, who now commanded the Company of Monclova.

"We had better reconnoiter first, Colonel," Medina said. "We do not know how many they are. We do not know their positions."

"No, but we know who they are," Piedras spat at him. "Those are renegade American Anglos, and they stand between us and Bexar. Captain, I am getting tired of you questioning my orders, hindering my command. Had I time to think of it I might question your courage!"

Medina stared at him. "I would not question my courage, Colonel. Not ever." God, he thought. We fight among ourselves.

Piedras looked past him. "Lieutenant Leal, take your platoon forward and attack! Immediately!"

Leal glanced quickly at Medina. Medina nodded. The sub-lieutenant saluted Piedras. *"¡Si, mi coronel!"*

Around the bend Leal led his men to the tree line above the river. Breaking into the clear, he formed them into a line for attack. Before they could move forward, a withering rifle fire broke from the far bank. A private pitched from his horse. Another horse went down, rolling on its rider. Leal felt a searing hammer blow to his shoulder, and his vision blurred. A private on foot grabbed his reins and turned his horse back. A sergeant ordered retreat. The long rifles were deadly. The long rifles spoke and did not miss, it seemed.

Piedras ordered three more attacks. Each was repulsed before reaching the river's edge. Each cost casualties. At Medina's insistence, Piedras withdrew around the bend and ceased the attacks. No one knew what to do.

The Anglos were in fine shape. Not a one had a mark on him. In a way, Looney felt admiration for the Mexican soldiers over there. They had charged down to the river bravely, armed with their muskets, but what

379

could they do against a concealed enemy with rifles?

"Damn Mescan mentality," Looney growled. "Cheaper to use soldiers for cannon fodder than it would be to give 'em somethin' decent to shoot."

"Sam," Horatio Hanks offered. "They's fourteen of us here, countin' the high sheriff there. Why don' we surround them soldiers an' attack?"

Looney growled at him and Horton suggested, "Shut your damn mouth, Horatio."

"Hey," Noilin said, "it's gettin' dark."

They looked around them in surprise. "Lordy!" Isaac Burton commented. "Warrin' sure makes the time fly, don't it?"

Looney said, "Sandy, you and Roberts see if you can get over there an' scout 'em out. See what they're doin' now."

In the gathering dark across the river the command formed a circle, men outside and horses in the middle. They waited, ready and anxious. Who could tell when the crazy Anglos would attack, shooting at them from a mile away?

Captain Medina joined Colonel Piedras, Lieutenant Juan Gallardo, and the contract doctor, Surgeon Lejarza. "Colonel, soon it will be dark. Do we leave our wounded and try to get past those militia? Or do we stand and fight?"

"Neither," Piedras said. "There is a light up there, on the hill. Is that the home of John Durst?"

"Yes, Colonel," Gallardo said. "It is called Rancho Angelina."

"Good. We go there. Get the command ready, Captain."

"Si, *mi coronel*." Medina shrugged. They were giving up their best chance of either winning or getting away. And they were going the wrong direction. "Sergeant! Get the men ready to move out!"

Piedras walked away, hands behind his back, surveying his command.

Gallardo stepped closer to Medina. "I tell you, Francisco, we need to put a stop to all this. It is crazy. We lose men, for nothing."

"He is right, Captain," the surgeon said. "You are second in command. You must do something."

"We cannot win this fight," Gallardo persisted. "This is not field combat. We have no chance against those rifles. You have seen their distance, their accuracy. Ah, to have a hundred of those!"

"The National Militia is no foreign army," Lejarza said. "Those people are not enemies, they are our citizens, our friends. We all know there are no invaders out there."

Medina was deep in thought. "Get mounted," he told them. "Tonight we will discuss it. Pass word to the other officers. Now, get the men moving, as ordered."

Harriet Durst conducted herself as the lady she was. She served the officers at her table while servants carried food out to the rest of the men. She disliked the strutting, erratic Colonel Piedras—had always disliked him. But he was in her house, and she would be gracious. Besides, she had no choice in the matter. Piedras had an army with him. She had only a flock of servants and children. Seven of the children were hers.

There was light, if strained, conversation through dinner, then Captain Medina got to his feet. "Mrs. Durst, may we use your dining room for a short while, privately?"

"Yes, of course," she said, gathered her two table servants, and left the room.

Piedras said, "What is it?"

"Colonel, your officers are about to have a meeting,"

381

Medina said mildly. "We are going to decide what we should do."

"I forbid this!" Piedras jumped up. "I am in command here!"

"That is one of the things we must decide."

"This is treason!" Piedras shouted.

Lieutenant Gallardo, slim and somber, was thinking of the death of Captain Renaldo Musquiz. A useless, senseless death. He had seen his captain fall. In a mild, cold tone he said, "Colonel, if you interfere, a charge of murder may be added to our crimes."

Piedras looked around him, the blood draining from his face. Some of the other officers also had risen to their feet. Lieutenant of Cavalry Jose Martinez, the bold one, smiled at him. "He is correct, *mi coronel.*"

Quietly, from his corner of the table, Sub-lieutenant Silvestre Leal, a heavy bandage on his shoulder and his face showing pain, said, "We stand together."

"For the Constitution of 1824, for His Excellency General Santa Anna, for an end to this business here," Gallardo put in.

Slowly, Piedras sank back into his chair. There was nothing he could say.

Captain Francisco Medina looked around him. There was no dissension there, no disagreement. He knew his sergeants too would go along with them. They were tired of senselessness, tired of fighting their friends. There was no point in considering how the enlisted men might feel. Enlisted men go where they are ordered.

"I hereby assume temporary command of the District of East Texas," Medina said. "And we, the officers and men of the Twelfth Battalion and the Company of Monclova, do pronounce in favor of General Santa Anna and the Plan of Vera Cruz. We will surrender ourselves to the National Militia of East Texas, and request that those gentlemen allow us to return to the interior of Mexico, where we may assist in the revolution of General Santa Anna."

With a final glance at the shaking Piedras, he said, "Lieutenant Gallardo, please go out and inform the men that we will be going home."

There was silence in the room for several minutes. Outside they could hear the lieutenant's voice. Then there was cheering. It rattled the dishes in Mrs. Durst's pantry.

"Doctor," Medina said, "please ask Mrs. Durst if I might send her nephew to contact the militia. I do not think a soldier should go abroad down there tonight."

James H. Durst walked proudly through the darkness to the edge of the river, a slave carrying a torch ahead of him. He was only twelve years old, but he was sure of himself and bold as he strode down the incline to the water's edge.

"Are any of my uncle's men over there?" he called.

"Right here, son," Sam Looney answered from the darkness of the far bank.

"Captain Medina told me to say the army wants to surrender. Captain Medina said to tell you he is in command now. He said you should come to Durst house tomorrow."

There was a pause. Then, "Go back and tell the captain we'll be there at sunrise."

"Yes, sir, I'll tell him."

From the far bank they watched him ascend the ferry ramp, then go on up the hill until the torch light faded.

"Anybody bring a jug along?" Roberts asked in the darkness.

"I got one, sure enough," someone said.

"Feel the need of a nip, do you?" Burton asked.

"I just been thinkin'," Roberts said. "That's the whole damn East Texas army up there an' they ain't but four-

383

teen of us over here. We could have got right busy if they hadn't surrendered first."

PART SIX

EAST WIND
OVER TEXAS

CHAPTER XXXIV

*"No man can walk both sides of a road
at once."*
— James Bullock

My Dearest Meg,

One can never know how a situation or an event might color one's thinking, until it occurs. There is a thought in my mind at this moment that I never would have considered until my recent adventures in Texas. And no more than I could have anticipated the thought can I predict whether it will persist after my happy return to you. So I may, if I can choose the words, share it with you now.

But first, a report. The hostilities in Nacogdoches are at an end. The war the Colonel Piedras precipitated is over, and he is no longer in command in East Texas. The details are not pleasant, but I will share them with you in time.

The actual Battle of Nacogdoches took place the afternoon and evening of Thursday, the second of August. There were a number of casualties among the militia, a score and more among the soldiers. They fought in the streets of the town. Among those who died was the *Alcalde* of Nacogdoches, a fine gentleman named

387

Encarnacion Chireno. He was a good and decent man. Another good and decent man was one of the officers of the garrison, a Captain Renaldo Musquiz. And others . . . so many others.

Quite a lot of Indians watched the battle from hill-sides, but none participated. I understand that an act of heroism by one of the settlers caused them to remain aloof. On the morning of Friday, the third, it was found that Colonel Piedras and his command had left the town. Some of the militia went after them to hurry—or harry—them along their way, but at this time nothing has been heard back from them.

Immediately upon departure of the military, the town began returning itself to normal. Some of the men here, led by Adolphus Sterne, took it upon themselves to collect and bury the dead from both sides. There were Masonic funerals this morning at the graveyard. Very moving indeed.

Most of the newly combined National Militia is still in town on this Saturday, but it has split into two parts. The Nacogdoches men have disbanded and are going about getting their town in operation. The remaining militia, acting as an interim guard, consists of the hundred or so men from surrounding communities under the command of Colonel Bullock. Only a small contingent under Captain Vicente Cordova remains among them to coordinate affairs with the town—and, I suspect, to keep the visitors in line.

With the eastern militias assembled here and the military absent, the town has a different flavor. It is like an American community. English is spoken freely now, almost predominating over the Spanish that was general before, although the older settlers here in the town, of both (or all) races, persist in Spanish—which is, of course, the law.

A strange and whimsical footnote to the activities here, developing as the evacuated women and children begin returning from their places of shelter. There is to be a fiesta. Some of the women had been planning it, and apparently went right ahead with their arrangements even in the midst of hostilities. It may not be much of a fiesta, but it will be held. It will be tomorrow. One of the Spanish ladies here has drafted a crew of Anglo militiamen to replace hitch-rails on a street leading into the Plaza, to widen the avenue for a procession to open the festivities. I can hardly wait for the party. Was there ever such a case of civility prevailing over hostility?

Wagons, carts, pack animals, and foot traffic are flooding into the town from all sides. Two of the stores already have reopened today, and more will before the day is over.

I will close this message, as I understand there is a party eastbound for Gaines' Ferry soon, and they can post it for me. I will tell you more as soon as I return, which, God willing, will be very soon now.

But in the meantime, I want this letter to arrive ahead of me so that you can be considering the question I mentioned earlier—that I might or might not ask when I return. Should I decide to ask it, I want you to have had time to consider.

The question is this:

Do you think, my dearest Meg, after I complete my obligation to Mr. Whitmire that you might consider emigrating to Texas? The way is open now, and people will again be coming in. They will come like a wind too long withheld, and this east wind will blow across Texas, I believe, as long as it takes for questing people to fill the lonely places in this beautiful land. I cannot help but dream of being one of them.

Think about it, Meg, and keep yourself well for me. I will return to you soon.
Your husband,
John Sanford Smith

It was Samuel Looney's privilege to accept the surrender of Colonel Jose de las Piedras, and he did so in characteristic style. He took the colonel's sword, walked out on the hillside, and threw it into the river. Then he sent riders to Nacogdoches to report that he had the Mexican army in custody.

It was Saturday morning, August 4, 1832.

Near noon, the militiamen on guard at Durst's Ferry heard a shout from across the river. "Hey, over there! Ain't there anybody runnin' that barge?"

Isaac Burton shaded his eyes. "Who is that?" he called back.

"Isaac, have you gone blind? It's me, Jim Bowie, come to the rescue!"

"Jim Bowie? Just hang on there, we'll get this thing started across!"

With the ferry in operation, Bowie and fourteen other men crossed from the west bank. All fifteen of them had come from San Antonio de Bexar.

" 'Fraid you're a little late, Jim," Burton apologized. "We got this business all finished here. We got the whole East Texas army up there at Durst's house waitin' for word from Nacogdoches about what to do with 'em."

Bowie and his contingent rode on up to Durst's. Sam Looney welcomed them. "We can use some extra guards up here," he said. "It ain't proper to leave your captives unguarded even if they're friendly. But there's nearly a hundred and seventy of them, and just twelve of us."

Bowie goggled at this. "Twelve of you captured a hundred and seventy soldiers?"

"No," Looney admitted honestly. "There was fourteen of us at the time." Captain Francisco Medina, standing nearby, smiled but kept his own counsel.

Sandy Horton and Roberts returned that afternoon with John Durst. Bullock and a commission would be out in a couple of days. They were busy in town. In the meantime, the soldiers were to be held at the ranch.

"What are they busy doin'?" Looney asked.

"You wouldn't believe it," Roberts said. "They're goin' to have a fiesta there tomorrow."

"How'd they get a fiesta put up this quick?"

"Some of the women been plannin' it for a month. Sure got to hand it to 'em, knowin' what day the war would be over before we even knew when it was gonna start."

John Durst, who knew the event was an annual ritual for the town, said nothing. It pleased him that something could take his Anglo counterparts so off guard.

All day Sunday, in Nacogdoches, the ceremonial processions commemorating the return of the Gil Ybarbo clan would be followed by real processions as wives and families returned to their homes from where they had taken shelter. Some were returning to wounded husbands and fathers in Nacogdoches. A few, like Candida Chireno and her brood, would return to an empty house.

Through the fourth, fifth, and sixth days of August the process of treaty-making took place. First the officers of the 12th Battalion and the Company of Monclova drafted and approved articles committing the entire command to support General Santa Anna and to proceed from East Texas to some place where that support might be worthwhile. As an amendment there was

391

an article, jointly approved with a committee of the militia, granting Colonel Piedras safe conduct and accompaniment to the custody of Colonel Antonio Mexia, who was then on his way back from Anahuac to Matamoros.

Each article of agreement had to be deliberated, debated, adopted, and then duly signed by various representatives of both sides.

The final document was dated the sixth of August:

"At a meeting of the Corporation and the officers of the National Militia, under the command of General Bullock, commanding the united forces of Nacogdoches, it was unanimously resolved that the foregoing treaty entered upon by the command of Adjutant Looney on the Angelina with the officers of the 12th Battalion was ratified in all its parts. It was signed by Antonio Menchaca, Adolphus Sterne, Juan Mora, Jose Mora, Ensign Malldred D. Doya, Lieutenant Nathaniel Norris, Captains Bailey Anderson, Vicente Cordova, and Fredrick Moz, Adjutants Isaac Burton and Wyatt Hanks, and Colonel Samuel Looney. General Bullock approved."

Some of the Mexicans noted the rising ranks of the Anglos. Soon, it was said, the militia would have an emperor, ten generals, and all the rest colonels.

Final casualty reports for the conflict also were tallied.

The militia had three dead—another died a few days later—and seven others were wounded but would survive.

Among the military, thirty-three were dead, seventeen wounded.

Throughout, the Anglos were nervous. Parties of Indians were seen on the ridges, watching. Always watching.

All in good time, Colonel Piedras was turned over to Asa M. Edwards for escort to Velasco, and from there by ship to Mexico. James Bowie and his fourteen Bexar men escorted the rest of the army back to Bexar.

Udali had gone. With the first trading group from the Cherokee to the reopened stores of Nacogdoches had come her father Dita-staye-sgi, her brother Atasi, and Atasi's friend Tenuto, and they had taken Mistletoe home with them.

Willoughby felt empty. Frost Thorn's big house, so full of life again now that the trouble was past, was suddenly lonely without Udali, speaking in her marginal English, wearing high-fashion clothing, and learning the ways of ladies of style. For Willoughby, staying at Goyens' Inn and spending as much time at Thorn's as Susan and propriety would allow, it had been an idyll. But now it was over.

He resented the way old Cutter, Dita-staye-sgi, had looked at him when he mentioned visiting Udali in the Cherokee village. Cutter had just looked, said nothing, and turned away. Atasi and Tenuto likewise were cool and noncommittal. He couldn't get a word out of any of them. So off they had gone, taking Udali, and now he was alone.

Oddly enough, even the Thorns didn't seem particularly sympathetic. Oh, there were kind words, but Frost and Susan seemed to pass it off as though his loss really amounted to nothing. And when he went to Sandy Horton for what he was owed for those days as a deputy, Horton paid him, shrugged him off, and turned away.

"What I have to do," he explained to Haden Edwards that evening on Frost Thorn's front porch, "is to start over again from scratch. If I can get back on my feet again, I can go back to Udali's mother and maybe this time I can . . ." He rambled on. He was talking to Edwards because Edwards was the only one polite enough to listen. The rest were there, but paying no attention to him at all.

Edwards listened for a time, then shrugged. "If that's what you need to do, feller, then you better get on with it."

That was enough. He slept fitfully that night, and with early morning packed his worldly possessions, saddled his horse, and headed east out of Nacogdoches, oblivious to the open window behind him at the Thorn house, where eyes watched him depart.

"Honestly, Frost," Susan chided her husband, "you didn't have to carry it so far. Look at him. The poor man."

"Hush, sweets, I know what I'm doing. Just watch."

At the edge of town, entering the Camino Real, Willoughby was suddenly brought up short as first one, then another half-naked mounted form pulled into the road in front of him. Warily he lifted a hand. " 'Siyo, Gu'nasoquo. 'Siyo, Nunnehidihi. 'Siyo, Tenuto. 'Siyo . . ." His tongue knotted as the fourth great form appeared. It was Egg.

Without a word Gu'nasoquo gestured him back, then pulled in beside him, forcing his mount to turn north. Nunnehidihi flanked him on the other side. Tenuto on his racing pony pranced out ahead, and Egg brought up the rear. In this manner, with Willoughby neatly boxed, they crossed the wooden bridge and rounded the bend out of sight.

"Ah," Susan said.

"Ah, yourself," her husband said. "It's early. Come here."

In the woods to the north the procession had gone almost halfway to the Cherokee villages before Willoughby managed to get a word out of any of his stolid companions. And when he did it was only, "You have business with the Aniyunwiya, Willoughby."

They traveled on.

They camped for the night and he tried again, but they would not talk to him. He noticed that they put Tenuto, the youngest and most voluble of the four, out on guard.

They seemed friendly enough. It was just that they wouldn't talk to him. Something like desperation kept welling up in him. Then he would look at the stolid faces around him and see no ill will there, only purposefulness. He had his rifle, but what was he going to do? Shoot one of them? For what? For inconveniencing him? For playing some stupid Indian game at his expense? With morning, they moved on.

It was almost noon when they arrived at the creek at the base of Diwali's village and started across. There was a lot of activity.

Willoughby turned in his saddle. Where there had been four warriors flanking him, now there were a dozen. In the past mile or so others had joined them, making a procession as they crossed the stream. Below Diwali's lodge they drew rein and dismounted. Tenuto took Willoughby's horse.

Diwali and John Bowles came out of the chief's lodge. Soberly Diwali raised a hand. " 'Siyo, Willoughby. *Tsi-ta Aniyunwiya.*"

Willoughby copied the salute. " 'Siyo, Diwali." But when he started to question the old man, Diwali turned away. With Egg's hand on his shoulder, Willoughby marched smartly on past and back into the village, through no particular choice of his own. Twenty or more warriors now trailed along after him. At the area of the *aniwaya* they stopped. While the others surrounded him stolidly, Egg wandered off toward Atasi's lodge and returned eventually, clutching a package. With enormous dignity he bowed, and handed the package to Willoughby."

Mystified, the smuggler opened it, and for a moment dizziness overcame him. Fine white linen lay there, yard upon yard of it, folded and tied. Egg laughed, and one by one the others joined him. Tenuto prodded Willoughby's shoulder and pointed off toward a shed where there were mules—and packs hanging on poles. His own mules. His lost-to-the-Kickapoo-damn-own mules! And the packs bulged with the substance of trade goods.

He looked around him, dazzled, at half a hundred coppery faces grinning at him. When he turned back, Dita-staye-sgi stood glowering before him.

Past the Cutter, the braves and some women were beginning to form themselves into two long lines, a gauntlet of happy, savage faces, and the gauntlet led to the doorway of Nanitsa. Udali and her mother stood there, waiting for him.

Dita-staye-sgi frowned and took Willoughby by the arm. "You move too slow," he growled. "My wife Nanitsa awaits her gift. It is not a good idea to keep my wife Nanitsa waiting.

SADDLE UP FOR ADVENTURE
WITH G. CLIFTON WISLER'S
TEXAS BRAZOS!
A SAGA AS BIG AND BOLD AS TEXAS ITSELF,
FROM THE NUMBER-ONE PUBLISHER
OF WESTERN EXCITEMENT

#1: TEXAS BRAZOS   (1969, $3.95)
In the Spring of 1870, Charlie Justiss and his family follow their dreams into an untamed and glorious new land — battling the worst of man and nature to forge the raw beginnings of what is destined to become the largest cattle operation in West Texas.

#2: FORTUNE BEND   (2069, $3.95)
The epic adventure continues! Progress comes to the raw West Texas outpost of Palo Pinto, threatening the Justiss family's blossoming cattle empire. But Charlie Justiss is willing to fight to the death to defend his dreams in the wide open terrain of America's frontier!

#3: PALO PINTO   (2164, $3.95)
The small Texas town of Palo Pinto has grown by leaps and bounds since the Justiss family first settled there a decade earlier. For beautiful women like Emiline Justiss, the advent of civilization promises fancy new houses and proper courting. But for strong men like Bret Pruett, it means new laws to be upheld — with a shotgun if necessary!

#4: CADDO CREEK
During the worst drought in memory, a bitter range war erupts between the farmers and cattlemen of Palo Pinto for the Brazos River's dwindling water supply. Peace must come again to the territory, or everything the settlers had fought and died for would be lost forever!

POWELL'S ARMY
BY TERENCE DUNCAN

#1: UNCHAINED LIGHTNING (1994, $2.50)

Thundering out of the past, a trio of deadly enforcers dispenses its own brand of frontier justice throughout the untamed American West! Two men and one woman, they are the U.S. Army's most lethal secret weapon—they are POWELL'S ARMY!

#2: APACHE RAIDERS (2073, $2.50)

The disappearance of seventeen Apache maidens brings tribal unrest to the violent breaking point. To prevent an explosion of bloodshed, Powell's Army races through a nightmare world south of the border—and into the deadly clutches of a vicious band of Mexican flesh merchants!

#3: MUSTANG WARRIORS (2171, $2.50)

Someone is selling cavalry guns and horses to the Comanche—and that spells trouble for the bluecoats' campaign against Chief Quanah Parker's bloodthirsty Kwahadi warriors. But Powell's Army are no strangers to trouble. When the showdown comes, they'll be ready—and someone is going to die!

#4: ROBBERS ROOST (2285, $2.50)

After hijacking an army payroll wagon and killing the troopers riding guard, Three-Fingered Jack and his gang high-tail it into Virginia City to spend their ill-gotten gains. But Powell's Army plans to apprehend the murderous hardcases before the local vigilantes do—to make sure that Jack and his slimy band stretch hemp the legal way!

Available wherever paperbacks are sold, or order direct from the Publisher. Send cover price plus 50¢ per copy for mailing and handling to Zebra Books, Dept. 2456, 475 Park Avenue South, New York, N.Y. 10016. Residents of New York, New Jersey and Pennsylvania must include sales tax. DO NOT SEND CASH.

SWEET MEDICINE'S PROPHECY
by Karen A. Bale

#1: SUNDANCER'S PASSION   (1778, $3.95)

Stalking Horse was the strongest and most desirable of the tribe, and Sun Dancer surrounded him with her spell-binding radiance. But the innocence of their love gave way to passion — and passion, to betrayal. Would their relationship ever survive the ultimate sin?

#2: LITTLE FLOWER'S DESIRE   (1779, $3.95)

Taken captive by savage Crows, Little Flower fell in love with the enemy, handsome brave Young Eagle. Though their hearts spoke what they could not say, they could only dream of what could never be. . . .

#4: SAVAGE FURY   (1768, $3.95)

Aeneva's rage knew no bounds when her handsome mate Trent commanded her to tend their tepee as he rode into danger. But under cover of night, she stole away to be with Trent and share whatever perils fate dealt them.

#5: SUN DANCER'S LEGACY   (1878, $3.95)

Aeneva's and Trenton's adopted daughter Anna becomes the light of their lives. As she grows into womanhood, she falls in love with blond Steven Randall. Together they discover the secrets of their passion, the bitterness of betrayal — and fight to fulfill the prophecy that is Anna's birthright.